ORIGINAL SIN

TOR BOOKS BY LISA DESROCHERS

Personal Demons
Original Sin

Lisa Desrochers

ORIGINAL SIN

TOR®

A TOM DOHERTY ASSOCIATES BOOK

NEW YORK

ORIGINAL SIN

Copyright © 2011 by Lisa Desrochers

A Tor Teen Book
Published by Tom Doherty Associates, LLC
175 Fifth Avenue
New York, NY 10010

www.tor-forge.com

Tor® is a registered trademark of Tom Doherty Associates, LLC.

ISBN 978-0-7653-2809-0

First Edition: July 2011

Printed in the United States of America

0 9 8 7 6 5 4 3 2 1

To Steven, for understanding
without having to ask

Because thou fixest still thy mind entirely upon earthly things, thou pluckest darkness from the very light.

—Dante Alighieri, *Purgatorio*

ORIGINAL SIN

1

✠

You Can Take the Demon out of Hell . . .

LUC

Not that I'm complaining, but one serious downside of being a demon-turned-human is that I'm no longer indestructible. I stare at my bleeding face in the mirror and rinse the razor in the sink. As I examine the multitude of seeping wounds, I wonder how much blood a mortal can afford to lose.

Which brings me to another downside of being human: personal hygiene. Why the Almighty would design humans to require so much maintenance is beyond me. And all these millennia, I thought we demons were the ones who got off on torture.

I'm still having trouble wrapping my mind around all this—my new life. Frannie. I woke up in my car this morning and my heart ached because, for an instant, I was sure it had all been a dream. But it was my aching heart—and the fact that I was asleep in the first place—that convinced me otherwise. Brimstone doesn't ache.

Which brings me to yet another downside: sleep. Now that I have to sleep, I can't protect Frannie like I want to. With some assistance from Starbucks, until last night I was able to hang on. But four o'clock this morning found me sound asleep in my car in front of her house, leaning over the steering wheel and drooling on my sleeve. I'm going to have to discuss shifts with Matt.

Frannie insists she doesn't need a guardian angel, but I'm glad for the help. Of course, I haven't been quite honest with her. She doesn't know that I'm still watching every night. She'd probably beat the crap out of me if she did. It's a little embarrassing to think that my five-two, hundred-pound girlfriend could kick my ass, but unfortunately, it's true.

"Frannie's on her way over."

Even though the voice sounds smooth and musical, it still scares the hell out of me. It's a good thing the razor is in the sink, because if it'd been on my face, it would have left another gash.

I spin and survey my studio apartment for the source of the proclamation. Matt leans against the wall next to the unfinished edge of my wall mural, thumbs hooked into the front pockets of his torn jeans.

"Didn't your mother ever tell you it's rude not to knock?" I say. But seeing an angel standing there, next to a floor-to-ceiling painting of Hell, is more than I can take, and I burst out laughing.

Matt's sandy blond curls are almost to his shoulders, and his tanned face is positively angelic—except for the fact that he's glaring death at me. If I didn't know better, I'd swear he was an avenging angel, not a guardian. But, as I get myself back together, a hint of a smile creeps into those baby blues.

"She might have mentioned something about that."

I hate that Frannie needs a guardian. I hate that I can't protect her anymore. But my power has completely dried up. There's no spark in the plugs. I *do* miss being able to shoot Hellfire out of my fists and blast things into oblivion.

But would I go back to what I was?

Never.

I raise an eyebrow at him. "So, if Frannie's on her way over, why aren't you watching her? Falling down on the job so soon? What the Hell kind of guardian angel are you?"

A grin spreads across Matt's face as he shrugs away from the wall. "She drives so fast not even the Hounds of Hell could catch her between there and here."

I smile thinking about her driving that midnight blue '65 Mustang convertible, top down, music cranked. She does drive dangerously fast, but it's kind of sexy.

"Thanks for the backup last night, by the way," I say as Matt glides over to my bookshelf and scans the titles. "I was hoping this whole sleep thing was overrated. Guess I was wrong."

Pulling my original run Dante's *Purgatorio* from the volumes, he scowls. "I knew you were going to be useless. Why Gabriel thought you'd be any help at all, I'll never understand." He fans the pages and then turns his glare back on me. "You're going to slip back into your old ways. I just know it. Demons don't change."

"But I'm not a demon anymore. There *are* no 'old ways.' Clean slate and all."

"You'll slip." He flips me a self-satisfied smirk, then slides Dante back onto the shelf. "And when you do, I hope it's a good one. I've been dying to smite someone. Nothing would make me happier than if it was you."

"I thought only the hand of God could smite."

An enigmatic smile turns the corners of his mouth. "Don't believe everything you hear."

I walk back into the bathroom, shaking my head, and wipe the last traces of shaving cream from my face with a towel. "When will she get here?" I say, reexamining my wounds in the mirror and tugging at the dark circles under my eyes.

My finger courses along the bloodred scar twisting down the right side of my face—Beherit's parting gift—as Matt peers over my shoulder into the mirror and says, "Now."

I push him aside and cross my studio to the window, throwing up the sash, just in time to see her pull in next to my black '68 Shelby Cobra and climb out of her car. Her face beams as she waves up at me and makes her way toward the door of my building. I sprint down the hall and meet her on the stairs.

She rushes up, smiling. "Hey. Missed you."

Frannie's long, sandy blond waves are windblown and unruly. And I can't help but admire how that white tank top and those well-worn jeans hug every contour of her body without being tight. A large tear in those jeans teases me with a hint of skin, and I shudder.

"Hey," I say. I loop my arms around her shoulders and run my hands through her hair, tying it in a knot at the base of her neck. "I missed you too."

She pushes up onto her tiptoes, stretching her petite frame

as far as it will go, but I still need to lean down and meet her halfway for our kiss. I guide her up the rest of the stairs and into my apartment.

She bounds through the door, and when she sees Matt, her eyes light up. Just watching them together, how happy she is to have him back, I have no doubt that it was her Sway that influenced Gabriel to choose Matt as Frannie's guardian. And, the best part: she looks at him with a light heart and clear eyes now. The guilt is gone. She had to forgive herself for Matt's death in order for Gabriel to tag her soul for Heaven, so I knew she had, but something lightens in my core to see it so clearly on her face.

"Hey, Matt. Long time no see," she says.

Matt's expression is warm and genuine as he regards his sister. "Thought you were going to break the sound barrier on the way over. I was pretty sure you'd beat me here." He hooks an arm over her shoulder. "If you won't drive more carefully, I'm going to have to wrap that Mustang in celestial Bubble Wrap." He rolls his eyes toward the ceiling, contemplating. "And maybe rig the accelerator."

"Touch my car and you're dead, little brother." As soon as the words leave her lips, her eyes widen. "I mean . . ."

Matt chuckles and pulls her back to his side. "Yeah, good luck with that. And I'm not your 'little brother.'"

She swallows hard and offers a wily smile. "Yes, you are. By eight and a half minutes, according to Mom." She shoves away from him and heads to the small wooden kitchen table, where she drops her bag onto a chair.

Up until a few weeks ago, I didn't need to eat, so the only furniture in my apartment was a big, black, king-sized bed—for recreational purposes. The addition of the table and two chairs became necessary when I kept finding food in my bed. And now that laundry is also a necessity—downsides of being human are racking up fast—we eat at the table.

I twine my fingers into hers. "Did you eat? I was going to make omelets."

She gazes up at me, tracing a finger along the scar on my face, and I get completely lost in her eyes.

"Sounds good," she says.

"What?"

A devilish smile breaks across her face. "Omelets?"

"Oh, yeah . . ."

MATT

"Not hungry, thanks," I say.

They both look at me and Frannie cracks a smile. "That's 'cause you've never had one of Luc's omelets. He got the recipe off Rachael Ray's Web site. They're to die for," she says, then cringes.

"I got it, sis. They're good. So, what's the plan for the day?"

Frannie shrugs. "Well, lunch, I guess. Then . . ." She looks at the demon, and an impish grin pulls at her lips. "Are you thinking what I'm thinking . . . ?"

I roll my eyes and glower at Luc.

He leans back into the table and smirks at me as Frannie heads for the fridge. "Get your mind out of the gutter, cherub. The Mustang needs an oil change."

Luc pushes off the table and moves to the kitchen, bringing a pan and bowl out from the cabinet below the stove. Frannie retrieves the eggs, milk, and a few bags of veggies from the fridge. As they move around the kitchen, they don't speak, but as they work, they seem completely unaware that they are always touching—connected. And perfectly in sync.

Suddenly, it feels too intimate. How can cooking lunch be intimate? I clench my teeth to keep from groaning. I can't stand this. I have to get out of here.

"So, if you guys don't need me, I guess I'll go."

Frannie turns back to me and smiles. "Sure you don't want an omelet?" she says, holding up a tomato.

I can't help smiling back. "Got to watch my girlish figure."

She cracks up as I push through the wall into the hall, where I stand guard.

Alone.

As usual.

I slide down to sit on the floor, my back against the wall. When Gabriel pulled me out of training to work with me himself, he said he had a special job for me. A job no one was better suited for. When he told me I was going to be Frannie's guardian, I couldn't believe it. I wasn't proud of how I'd treated her in life, and being seven was no excuse. This was perfect. How many people get the chance to make amends with their twin sister from the other side?

What he failed to mention is that my sister is in love with a freakin' demon. How did he let that happen?

So here I sit, banging my head against the wall helplessly while my sister is in there—in danger. Gabriel was clear. I can't interfere. He says it's her life. Her choice. He says things will work out.

I don't believe him.

And it's only a matter of time before the demon does something to prove me right.

FRANNIE

"Gabe has me experimenting with this Sway thing," I say after lunch, handing Luc the cast iron skillet to wipe down.

His eyes tighten and he doesn't even try to hide the jealous edge to his voice. "Let me guess: late at night, all alone in your room."

I can't help the flutter in my stomach or my blush, and I hate that I feel guilty. But I do. I still don't have a grasp on what I feel for Gabe. All I know is that I need him. When he's around, I can almost believe that things are gonna be okay, and when he touches me, all my panic seems to melt away.

I plunge my hands into the soapy dishwater and start scrubbing dishes madly. "Sometimes. But if the only person I can Sway is Gabe, that's not gonna accomplish much."

He slams the pan down onto the counter with a crash that shakes the floor and stares at his hands, splayed on either side of it. "I sincerely doubt there's much you couldn't get Gabriel to do for you just by asking."

I start, because it's Gabe who can read my mind, not Luc. But the way he's looking at me makes me wonder.

I sigh deeply and take a second to get myself back together.

"Anyway . . . we've been hanging at the park, mostly." I feel my chest tighten as I push back the frustration that threatens to take charge of me every time I think about this whole stupid thing. "He thinks kids should be easier to influence. But I seem to be better at instigating stuff than stopping it."

He yanks the pan off the counter by the handle. "Well, that bodes well for world peace."

I drop my face into my soapy hands and groan. "I suck at this. I don't know what he thinks I'm supposed to be able to do, but I can't even break up a sandbox scuffle over a pail and shovel." I hate the tears seeping from my eyes into my hands. I hate everything right now. "I can't do it. It doesn't work."

I don't look at him as he turns me and presses me against the counter, his body hot against mine, his voice suddenly soft. "I'm sorry, Frannie. You know how hard this is for me . . . sorting all these *feelings*. Everything is going to work out." He lifts my chin with his finger and wipes the suds off of my forehead with his hand. "It'll all come together." He quirks an eyebrow. "I'll let you practice on me."

I sniffle and wipe my nose on the back of my arm. "I did already."

He grins and looks down at himself to be sure he's still intact. "Should I be worried?"

I sorta smile back. "No. I already did my thing on you without even knowing it. You were like my lab rat or something. My first victim."

Before I even knew what Sway was, or that I had it, I was

using it on Luc. 'Course, at the time, I also didn't know Luc was a demon. But I wanted him. A lot. And I got him by sorta accidentally turning him mortal with my Sway.

He pins me tighter against the counter, and I can't ignore how his body against mine makes me feel—like Jell-O. The look in his smoldering black eyes sends my heart racing. "And how did that experiment work out?"

I feel myself getting hot all over despite the cool dish suds running down my arms. I loop my soapy hands around his neck and watch him grimace as the cold water drips down his back.

"I don't think I'm done finding out. It's an ongoing investigation. You know, like . . ." I press myself harder into him, "What happens if I do this."

I feel his body react, muscles tensing, his breathing becoming faster. I smile.

"Or this," I say, reaching up onto my tiptoes to kiss his Adam's apple.

"Interesting reaction," I say when he tips his head back and shudders. "I'll have to log that in my journal."

"So, it sounds like when you do what comes naturally, your Sway works just fine. Maybe you're just trying too hard." He drops his head and looks at me, those fathomless black eyes still on fire. But then he pushes away. "If only I could finish what I've started."

I tug him back to me by the waist of his jeans. "Why can't you?"

"Because the woman from the library told me to call her at one." He nods to the clock on the microwave, which reads 12:58.

I shove him away and turn back to the soapy sink full of

dishes. "You're such a tease." I shake my head, frustrated. "See how well my Sway works? I couldn't even entice you to blow off a phone call."

His hands slide down the curve of my hips and I look over my shoulder at him. "Oh, you enticed me just fine," he says with a beautifully wicked grin. "The only reason I can resist right now is because I'm fairly certain we can pick up where we left off when I'm done."

"Don't be so sure," I say, knowing he's right. "You snooze, you lose."

He looks genuinely concerned for a heartbeat; then his face clears. "We'll see about that." His smile is back, and all kinds of wicked ideas flash behind his eyes. He sits in one of the kitchen chairs and pushes back, balancing on its back two legs as he dials.

He hangs up ten minutes later while I'm stacking the last of the dishes, an old set of my mom's, back into the cupboard. Lowering all four legs of his chair back to the ground, he says, "I start Saturday."

"I don't know why you think you need a job. You should be able to live forever. . . ." I catch myself as he grins. "I mean, for the rest of your life, anyway, on your insane bank accounts."

His gaze settles into mine. "And so could you."

I turn back to the counter and ignore the thrill that races through me with everything he's implying. "I'm not taking your money, Luc." We've done this already.

"Fine. So, you'll be working, and I could spend all day hanging around that pizza place, or I can attempt to become a productive member of society."

"I guess it's best," I admit.

Luc tended to distract me when he was around. My first week at my new job was pretty rough, culminating with the pizza Ricco made me pay for after it slid off the tray and onto the floor on my way to a table.

I hang the dishcloth over the faucet and turn back to face Luc. "Ricco would probably have you arrested for stalking me and scaring away all the customers if you hung at his place all day. You still have that *dark* thing happening, you know. They'd lock you up and throw away the key."

"Speaking of keys . . ." He slides his hand into his pocket and pulls out a shiny silver key, holding it up so it glimmers in the dim lighting. "It's to the apartment. I know it's only for another couple of months, but I want you to be able to come and go as you please."

I settle into his lap. "I thought that's what I was doing."

"You shouldn't have to knock." His arms circle me and pull me closer.

"You're not afraid I'll walk in on you doing something you're not supposed to be?"

"The only person I'd be doing that with would be you." His expression takes on a suggestive edge as he slides his hand under my shirt. "And you'll already be here."

When I press my lips to his, my heart rate doubles. He starts to pull my shirt over my head.

"Don't mind me. . . ." Gabe's voice comes from the door and scares the snot out of me.

I turn and there he is, leaning against the doorframe looking all angelic: glowing smile, platinum waves, and insanely beautiful blue eyes shining out of a strong, tanned face. Nobody should be allowed to look that good.

Luc blows out a frustrated sigh and eases my shirt back down. "For the love of all things unholy, what is it with you celestials? Will you please learn how to knock?"

"And miss the show?" he says, smiling at me as I yank at my shirt.

I extricate myself from Luc and stand.

"For an angel, you're quite the pervert," Luc says.

Gabe relaxes back into the wall and tucks his hands into the pocket of his jeans. "Some things are worth losing your wings for." His smile is gone and his blue eyes pierce mine. "Anyway, I really just came to say good-bye."

"Good-bye?" The panic that lives constantly in my gut creeps into my voice. As guilty as it makes me feel, there's nothing I can do to stop my heart from fluttering when he looks at me like that—like he's seeing my soul.

Luc notices my awkward stare and the color in my cheeks. He pulls himself out of the chair and glares at Gabe. "Don't let the door hit your ass on the way out."

"Won't be using the door, dude." He saunters over to Luc's wall mural. "You know you're playing for the other team now. You've really got to do something about this," he says, running a finger over the roiling orange and gold molten surface of the Lake of Fire.

"Hey, you can take the demon out of Hell, but you can't take Hell out of the demon." Luc's grin makes my heart go from fluttering to sputtering.

Gabe's eyes slide back to mine. "You're going to be fine,

Frannie," he says. And a part of me hates that he's in my head—reading my mind. That he knows how I feel about him, even if I don't.

But then I register what he's saying. My sputtering heart speeds up as an overwhelming sense of alarm takes over at the thought of Gabe leaving. "You can't go." It's all I can say without sounding totally hysterical or giving away the shake in my voice.

He steps forward and brushes the hair out of my face with a sweep of his hand. "It's better this way. For everyone," he adds, glancing toward Luc.

"But—"

"You'll be in good hands, Frannie. Matt will be here if you need him, and Luc . . ." His jaw tightens and his eyes narrow almost imperceptibly. "Luc won't let anything happen to you."

Luc, perceiving the challenge in Gabe's words, steps forward and loops his arms around me. "You're right, I won't."

I pull out of Luc's grasp and step toward Gabe. "Why?"

He lifts a hand and brushes his cool fingertips along the line of my jaw. I breathe in his cool winter sunshine and feel calmer just standing here next to him. When he answers, his voice is soft and low—meant only for me. "It's really not wise for me to spend too much time around you, Frannie."

"But—"

"You're both tagged for Heaven, and if you need to leave, your celestial Shields will keep both of you hidden. With Matt watching, you'll be fine. But I can't stay here." His gaze drops to the floor.

I swallow thickly past the lump in my throat. "Okay," I say, knowing he's right, because there's a reason that I'm dreading turning around and looking at Luc. I can't deny that, as much as I love Luc, I have some deep connection to Gabe. Luc is my heart and my soul, but Gabe is my anchor. I hug him and pull away as I feel tears sting my eyes. I step back and Luc's arm eases around my waist, feeling much less possessive. I look at him, sure of what I'll see, but his eyes are soft and full of compassion. He gives me a gentle squeeze and a reassuring smile.

I turn back to Gabe and stare into his blue eyes, endless as the sky. "So, when will I see you?"

"I'll be back here and there to check on you."

"You promise?" I know how desperate it sounds, but I don't care.

He lifts his eyes, but not his head, gazing at me out from under his long white lashes. "Promise." He continues to stare at me, and even though his lips don't move, I swear I hear him add, "I'll always be here for you."

I nod again and choke back the threat of tears. I open my mouth, but there aren't words, so I close it again. But my eyes say what my mouth couldn't. And I know he sees it, because his eyes mist and he swallows hard as he disappears.

"Sorry, Frannie," Luc says, pulling me to him. "I try not to be jealous, to understand your connection. . . ."

"It's not your fault." I hold him tighter. How can I expect him to understand it when even I can't figure it out?

His hand drifts to my face and he pulls me into a kiss, his lips gentle on mine, as if he's afraid of breaking me. I wind my fist into his hair and pull him closer, but it lasts only a second before I draw back, ashamed. I'm looking for something in his kiss that isn't there. Something that I've felt in only one other kiss. I'll need to find a different way to calm my nerves.

I ignore the question swirling in Luc's eyes as he gazes down at me, his brow creased.

"Help me change that oil before work?"

I can tell by his resigned sigh that he knows I was thinking of Gabe, and I hate that I'm so crappy at hiding it.

"Your wish, my command," he says. "What time do you have to be there?"

"Three."

He glances at the clock in the kitchen. "We better get on it. You have everything?"

"In the trunk." I pull my keys from my pocket, jingling the two keys that now dangle from my rabbit's foot key chain with a tentative smile.

He smiles back and takes my hand, leading me to the door. "I forgot to test your key," he says. "Try it."

I jingle my keys again as we step into the hall and use the shiny new one to lock the door behind us. I pull the key from the lock and feel him press into me from behind, his hands gliding gently around my waist to my stomach. His lips trace a line across my cheek to my ear, where he whispers, "We're in this together, Frannie. Everything's going to be fine."

I spin in his arms and kiss him again, this time wanting only him. Warmth from his kiss spreads through me till I'm burning with it.

Twisting my finger down the scar Beherit left on his cheek, I shudder and think about how close I came to losing him. I want to tell him how much I trust him and that I know he'd do anything for me. He proved that when he risked his own life to save me from Beherit. I want to tell him I'd do anything for him too. But I can't manage words past the lump in my throat. Instead, I turn back to the door, blinking away tears, unlock the deadbolts, and pull him into the apartment.

I lead him to the bed, then pull him into another kiss. We sink into the sheets, and I just want to lose myself in him—not to have to think about anything for a little while. But when I reach for the button of his jeans, he twines his fingers in mine and brings my hand up to his face, where he kisses the back of my fingers.

"Not like this, Frannie. Our first time isn't going to be because of him."

"It's not 'cause of him. I just want us to be closer." But even as I say it, I'm really not 100 percent sure it's true, because those blue eyes and that glowing smile are there in my head. I feel the hole in my heart where he's supposed to be. I miss Gabe already.

"Soon," Luc says, and kisses me. "But not now."

MATT

Gabriel filled me in before he pushed through the wall into Luc's apartment. I'm on my own. When I started to follow him through, he motioned for me to wait in the hall. He said he needed a private moment with Frannie. How he planned to accomplish that with the demon in the room is anybody's guess.

Frannie and the demon came out a little while later, and she looked seriously shaken. But he whispered something to her and they disappeared back through the door.

And I've been sitting here ever since, thinking about what their deal is—the three of them.

Gabriel is a Dominion. One of Heaven's most powerful. Third in line to God Himself. But when I watch him with Frannie, everything about him changes—softens. He'd do anything for her. And the look in his eyes when he told me he was leaving . . . Agony. If I didn't know better, I'd swear he was in love with her.

Could he love her? Angels love everyone. It's what we do. But, I mean . . . is it more than that? Does he seriously *love* her?

I'm still pondering that when Frannie and the demon step out into the hall again. I follow them toward the stairs as they lock step, arm in arm. Just as we reach the bottom of the stairs, the door from the parking lot swings open. Frannie holds it as a stack of boxes with legs walks through. The stack of boxes bumps into her, and the top one slips, revealing the face of a girl. She's about our age but taller than Frannie, with stringy, chocolate brown hair hanging across her green eyes.

"Shit. Sorry," she says just as the top box slips off the stack. The demon grabs it before it hits the floor.

"Got it," he says. "Where you headed?"

"Two eighteen," she says.

He glances at Frannie. "We'll give you a hand?"

"Sure," Frannie says, grabbing a box off the stack. "Are you moving in?"

"Yeah," she says, diverting her gaze. "Thanks, but you guys don't need to help. Looks like you're headed somewhere."

"No biggie. The oil can wait," Frannie says, and turns for the stairs.

Apartment 218 is next door to Luc's. I watch as the three of them haul boxes from the bed of the girl's beat-up hunter orange Ford pickup up the stairs and into her apartment. In three trips, they have everything. The girl wipes beads of sweat from her forehead with the sleeve of her gray sweatshirt.

"I need to get to work," Frannie says. "You got it from here?"

The girl stares at the floor, not meeting Frannie's eyes as she speaks. "I'm good. . . . I don't have that much."

I look at the small stack of boxes in the middle of the room. If that's all her stuff, she's right.

I watch her scan the room. Other than the cabinets in the kitchen, which are painted a cheerful tangerine color, the place looks pretty bleak. Just an open space with peeling grayish walls. Like in Luc's apartment, there's a large window that overlooks the parking lot. The upper windowpane is cracked in an intricate spiderweb pattern that looks sure to explode into hundreds of shards at the least contact. Along the wall to the right of the window is a worn green sofa with a large tear in the middle cushion, which has belched a pile of crumbling foam stuffing onto the floor. Looking around, it's hard to understand the excited glint in the new girl's eyes. To me it's just depressing, which is saying something, since angels don't get depressed.

Frannie holds out her hand. "So, I'm Frannie and this is Luc."

The girl takes Frannie's hand tentatively and shakes it. "Lili." She ducks her head like it embarrasses her to be the center of attention.

"So, where'd you come from?" Frannie asks.

"Oh . . . um . . . nowhere really. I just moved here because I'm going to State in the fall. This was the closest I could afford to the city."

"Well, I'm next door, so if you need anything . . . ," Luc says as he and Frannie move toward the door.

"Thanks," she says, and runs a hand through her hair, pulling the damp strands off her sweaty forehead and giving me a brief glance at her face.

It's a good thing I'm invisible, because as the demon and Frannie disappear down the hall and onto the stairs, I find myself rooted to this spot. I can't stop staring at her. She's unlike anyone I've ever seen before. Or felt. There's something completely foreign about her soul. I can't read her very well; I get only snippets—fleeting sensations. There's a dark side to her, and her soul is already tagged for Hell, but there's also a wounded side, begging for help. And something in those green eyes makes me want to be the one to help her.

I'm so mesmerized by her that I forget myself and don't get out of the way in time as she moves to the door to lock it. As she passes through me, I feel a rush of . . . something.

Desire?

I think so. I shiver as an electric tingle shoots through me, then spin and watch her shut the door and twist the deadbolts.

It suddenly occurs to me that I'm on the wrong side of the door. Those locks are meant to keep others *out*. I back off, but hesitate before pushing through the wall out into the hall. Those eyes. There's something in those eyes.

I step closer and reach out for her face, feeling like a moth drawn inexplicably to a flame. I *need* to touch her. But just before my hand makes contact, she spins away and moves toward the stack of boxes.

Sweet Heaven above. What am I doing?

I shake my head, then push through the wall and just stand in the hall for a long minute, trying to get myself together. *What was that?* I've never felt need like that before—raw desire, stirring something feral inside me. Breathing deep, I jump up and down a few times to shake the tension out, but I'm still not quite myself when I phase into Frannie's backseat. I stay invisible as she pulls out of the parking lot, and it's not until we're halfway down the street, me in the back of the convertible, the wind clearing the fog from my head, that I fade in and allow Frannie and the demon to see me.

"Nice of you to join us," he says as I reach for my seat belt and fasten it around me.

I slouch back into the seat, still feeling a little shaky from whatever just happened with Lili. "So . . . what do you think of that girl?"

The demon shoots me a sidelong glance. "Well, I think she's a girl."

I scowl. "Ha, ha. I mean did she seem, I don't know . . . like she needed help or something?"

Frannie glances into the rearview mirror at me. "Maybe. She seemed really shy and sorta scared. I'll keep my eye on her."

So will I.

2

†

Hell's Kitchen

FRANNIE

By the time I get home and change into my ultratight Ricco's T-shirt, I'm late for work. And Ricco isn't gonna let me forget it.

My sister Maggie's best friend, Delanie—busgirl extraordinaire—stands next to Ricco at the register, her long black hair pulled back in a tight ponytail and a sparkle in her smoky gray eyes. "Hey, Frannie," she says, then glances sideways at Ricco and gives a small cringe before heading to the soda tap.

Ricco scowls at me, his Italian features drawn and dour. I don't take it personally, though. I've figured out that Ricco hates all his employees. He's convinced we're stealing him blind. "You get the three thirty birthday party," he says.

Great. Kids from hell and no tip.

He looks over my shoulder, and a grin explodes across his face—a mouthful of crooked, coffee-stained teeth. He holds his fist in the air, exposing large yellow stains in the pits of his white chef tunic. *"Un toro!"* he says to Luc, waiting for a knuckle bump.

Guess he doesn't mind Luc hanging around after all.

"Un toro?" I say.

A cynical smile quirks Luc's lips and he shakes his head.

I look back at Ricco, and he's still grinning at Luc, but he doesn't answer me. It's probably something to do with chicks diggin' on him. Which they are. As I watch Luc make his way to his regular booth in the back, I see the only other people in the place—a group of four junior high girls in the arcade at the back corner—make a beeline toward the booth next to him.

I realize I'm staring at Luc and smiling dopily when Ricco's voice interrupts my musing.

"You look happy about that party. Maybe I'll give you all of them."

"Whatever," I say, and head to the counter, where Dana, the only other waitress Ricco hasn't driven out of here, shuffles past with a pitcher of soda.

I take a deep breath and try to clear my head. "No pizzas on the floor today," I say out loud, making a pact with myself. I have to stay focused. But I already know it's useless. My heart is aching and it's almost impossible to get Gabe out of my head. I can't believe he's really gone . . . but I know it's true. I can't *feel* him. I didn't realize what a big piece of me he'd become till that piece was missing. I take another deep breath and blow out a long sigh, turning to where Luc sits. I immediately feel guilty again.

"You're smart to keep an eye on him."

I tie my short black apron on and turn to face Delanie where she stands behind me. There's a mischievous grin on her face as she inclines her head toward the booth next to Luc's. Dana drops the pitcher of soda on the table as the junior high girls argue over who has to sit with their back to Luc. Three of them cram into one side, leaving a pouting blonde with acne and braces to slide into the seat backing up to Luc's booth.

Delanie shrugs and heads over to wipe Luc's booth down with a rag.

LUC

I haven't decided whether to tell Frannie she's working for an Imp. I've been watching him carefully, and so far he seems harmless. I'm not sure he even knows what he is. Like their angelic counterparts, the Nephilim, Imps are mortal, so if they don't inherit any noticeable power from their demon parent, they may never know. But there are some telltale signs.

Imps always smell subtly of sulfur. Not really noticeable to the human nose, but mine still picks it up.

Hanging around Matt, I've discovered Imps aren't the only ones with telltales. Angels don't cast a sharply delineated shadow. Their shadows are always a little fuzzy around the edges. So, unless it's pitch dark, they're easy to pick out. Demons are even easier. They can never completely hide the glow of their eyes. There's always a hint of it that's easy to spot with practice—which I've had.

I slide into the corner of the back booth, my back against

the wall, and kick a leg up onto the seat. Delanie comes over and wipes my table with a dirty rag, leaving it worse than it started.

"Hey, Luc. You guys coming to Gallaghers' to hear us play tomorrow?" she asks, sliding in across from me.

"Wouldn't miss it."

"Good. There's supposed to be a scout there. If anyone asks, tell them you're there to hear us."

"You guys going big-time? Will you remember all your old fans when you're playing for packed stadiums?"

A sarcastic smile lifts one side of her mouth. "I wish."

Frannie saunters over with her pad and pen in hand. "What can I get for you, sir?" she purrs.

Delanie grins up at Frannie and slides out of the booth. "See ya."

"What I want—" I rub my foot along the outside of Frannie's thigh. "—isn't on the menu."

She scowls but doesn't pull away. "Where was this an hour ago?"

"I was thinking of a cheeseburger," I say, and fight to contain the chuckle when she rolls her eyes.

"One slice of cardboard cheese pizza, coming right up," she says, scribbling on her pad with a flourish.

I can't stop the smile that pulls at my lips as I watch Frannie walk back to the counter. I breathe deep, force my eyes away from her, and scan the restaurant.

From this vantage, I can see the entire place clearly— including the Imp behind the counter. I take the opportunity to study him while Frannie clips my order up in the window to the kitchen. He's busy messing with the cash drawer, the unchecked avarice clear in his eyes and all over his face. He pushes the drawer closed just as the door opens. He looks up expectantly—but then his face turns to a mask of fear.

The hair on the back of my neck stands on end. A second later, I know why.

Rhenorian.

Maybe a thread of my sixth sense followed me into humanity after all.

Even to an ex-demon, he's intimidating. Seven feet tall and a mountain of muscle, he's got to scare the Hell out of most humans. He rakes a hand through his longish dark auburn hair and steps casually through the door. When he sees me, his eyes narrow and a sneer spreads across his large round face. The girls in the booth next to me go suddenly quiet as he strides over and folds his stocky frame into the seat across from me.

"Lucifer. What a pleasant surprise."

I fight the urge to grab Frannie and run. It's too late for that. Security roams in packs. I'm sure Rhenorian has some of his lackeys stationed outside. And I need to know what he knows—why he's here.

"Rhenorian." I nod at him. "I hardly think this was a surprise."

An enormous grin spreads slowly across the big demon's face. "So, how is this going to go?"

"Well, first, you take a look at the menu," I say, sliding one across the table, "and when you've made your decision, the waitress will come take your order." I glance up at Frannie and Dana, who are staring from behind the counter.

All the humor leaves his face, but the grin doesn't. "You've always been quite the comedian, Lucifer, but you can't joke your way out of this."

"Okay, then. You tell me: How is this going to go?"

"Well, it depends. Easy: You get up and walk outside with me, where we phase back to Hell for your trial. Hard: I pick you up and drag you outside, where we phase back to Hell for your trial."

"Hmm. I see only one flaw in your masterfully devised plan."

He leans toward me. "Such as . . . ?"

"What am I thinking?"

His face darkens to a brood. "I don't know. You've got some Hell-forsaken field or something."

"Think bigger, Rhen."

I glance up and see Frannie behind the counter across the room, straining against some unseen force. *Matt.* I breathe easier knowing she's in his field. Even still, her eyes are trained on Rhenorian, her jaw set and muscles tense. I know that look. She's working out how she's going to take him down. I catch her eye and shake my head almost imperceptibly. Rhenorian's focus is on me, and I want to keep it that way. He seems totally unaware Frannie is the bigger target.

Frannie glares at me, and when I turn back to Rhenorian, a frustrated scowl has passed over his features. "I can't read anything. It's almost as if you were human or something."

I tip my head toward him slightly and raise an eyebrow.

He stares at me for a second with a quizzical look; then his eyes widen as he bounds to his feet, knocking the table into me and sending the menus flying. *"What the Hell?"*

I glance at the girls in the booth behind Rhenorian, who've been watching cautiously.

"Down, boy," I say quietly.

He slides tentatively back into the booth, straightening the table. For a long time, he doesn't say anything. He just stares, as if trying to see through me. "How did you do it?" he finally manages.

"I didn't. It was done to me."

"Someone else turned you human? You found a . . . what? A conjurer?"

I realize that I've probably said too much. To bring the conversation back to me, I say, "So, you get that I'm not *phasing* anywhere. You could just kill me and take my soul back to Hell, if it weren't for the other thing."

He tents his fingers on the table in front of him, and his eyes narrow. "What other thing?"

I fix him in a hard stare, and can't stop my lips from curling into a smile when understanding dawns on his face.

"Unholy Hell! You're tagged for Heaven!" he says, leaping from the booth again.

"So, you see, Rhen, if He wants me back in Hell, it's going to take a little more planning and forethought on your part to figure out how to get me there."

"Why the Hell wouldn't He tell me?"

"I don't know. Maybe He thought, with your limited intellectual capacity—"

He shoves the table up against me, then glares and mutters, "Go suck angel face." He spins on his heel and storms out of Ricco's, leaving the faintest hint of rotten eggs in his wake.

I look up as I push the table away from me and see all four of the girls in the next booth scamper away. And when I glance at the counter, Ricco, Dana, and Delanie are gaping, openmouthed.

Ricco seems genuinely shocked and a little scared. I'm sure I detect a shake in his small frame as he hovers protectively over his cash register. But there's no suggestion of recognition or understanding in his dark eyes. I don't even think he knows demons exist. So, apparently, the demon half of his parenting team didn't hang around. Not surprising. Demons aren't big on the whole nurturing concept.

My gaze shifts to Frannie as she runs across the room toward me.

"It's fine, Frannie."

"What did he want?"

"Rhenorian is head of Security. He's been sent to bring me back. But it seems he wasn't filled in on the details of what that would entail." I look her in the eye. "And I don't think he even knows you exist, so we're okay."

She leans closer, panic still clear on her face. "We're *okay*? We are so *not* okay! He can't have you."

"He can't take me as long as I'm tagged for Heaven," I reassure her.

I consider that while Frannie stares at me. It makes sense that King Lucifer would come after His pound of flesh, I suppose. That would explain why Rhenorian came up to *me* and didn't even seem to notice Frannie, but . . .

"Why would Lucifer send Rhenorian after me and not tell him I was human?" I wonder out loud. "Unless . . ."

And then it hits me: He might not know. My boss, Beherit,

39

was the only one who knew what I was. The only one who witnessed my humanity. If he didn't tell for some reason . . .

But He'll know now. Rhenorian will report back. Then what?

The door swings open again, and every head snaps around to see who it is. When Frannie's grandpa steps through, everyone breathes a collective sigh.

Grandpa walks up to our table. Picking up on the tension in the room, his brow knits. "What'd I miss?"

Frannie shoots me a warning glance as her grandpa slides into the booth across from me. He knows what I am . . . or was. We told him because we needed his help. But he doesn't know how immediate the danger to his granddaughter is. The fact that Rhenorian was here for me, not her, would do little to assuage his concern.

She pastes on a big smile that shines like cubic zirconia.

"Nothing, Grandpa," she says, dropping my plate on the table in front of me. "What can I get you? The usual?"

His expression is guarded. "That'll work." When Frannie heads to the kitchen with his order, he glowers at me. "What's goin' on?"

"Nothing, really."

"That demon bullshit might work on Frannie's parents, but I know a load of crap when I see it."

I draw a deep sigh, and my eyes wander to Frannie, at the soda tap. "It seems that Hell's not thrilled about my defection."

His glower becomes a full on glare. "If you're puttin' Frannie in danger by bein' here—"

"Then I would leave," I finish for him.

He glares a moment longer, then pushes deeper into the booth. "Ya said before that it was Frannie that changed ya." I can see the question perched on his lips, the concern in his eyes.

My gaze drops to my hand and I spin my plate on the table. "I don't know how it works," I say in an attempt to preempt his question with a half answer.

"But you said that however she did it, it's why Hell wants her."

I raise my eyes, but not my head. "Yes."

"So, what are we gonna do to keep them from gettin' her?"

"I'm still working on that."

"This Gabriel guy . . ."

God, how much did we tell him that night? "He's an angel, and he's helping out."

"Did he tag her soul like you wanted?"

This time I lift my head and smile. "Yes."

"And you said that'd keep her safe."

"It should."

He seems satisfied for the moment and smiles up at Frannie as she approaches with his pizza and soda.

MATT

This is perfect. The demon's got his own after him. Maybe that big demon will take Luc out for me. Take him off my hands.

I follow Frannie back toward the kitchen as she places Grandpa's order, but stop when I see Grandpa and Luc with their heads together. I move back to their table to eavesdrop. I can't believe how much Grandpa knows. An overwhelming sense of needing him—wanting to show myself to him—almost knocks me to the floor. If he knows about angels and demons, why not? Why shouldn't I tell him? I've got nobody, and Frannie has everyone. Why can't I have Grandpa?

I'm on the verge of fading in when the door opens and a couple with fourteen kids comes whirling in. A birthday party.

And I'm shaken back to my senses.

I can't have Grandpa, because it's against the stupid rules. We are forbidden to appear to our relatives. It causes too much pain and grief for the living. If I revealed myself to Grandpa just because I wanted to, I'd be risking my wings.

This is the reason so few of us are chosen as guardians, and why the training is so long and intensive. The temptations are nearly irresistible. Most guardians train for centuries before they're ready—at least until all their immediate family is gone—but I trained for only a decade.

I look back at Grandpa and step away from the booth. Maybe I'm not ready after all. Maybe I shouldn't have jumped the queue to be Frannie's guardian.

Maybe Gabriel made a huge mistake.

3

✣

The Devil Inside

FRANNIE

That demon at Ricco's yesterday scared the snot out of me. Nightmares about the ground opening up and swallowing Luc in some gruesome demonic earthquake kept me awake all night. I kept getting up and going to the window to be sure the Shelby was still there. When he pulled out this morning, I felt sick. I thought about telling Matt to go with him.

I always expected Hell would keep coming after *me*, but I never thought about Luc—that they'd want him back too. Bile churns in my tight stomach as I drive, too fast, to get to him. Maybe Gabe should come back. I think we both need a guardian angel.

"I've been thinking." Matt slouches in my passenger seat with his eyes closed. The wind from the open convertible causes his hair to dance and shimmer around his face, making him seem even more angelic.

"What about?"

When he opens his eyes to look at me, they're bright with hope. "Maybe I should try being visible."

"You mean at the house? Could you, like, meet Mom and Dad?" My heart nearly leaps out of my chest as I shoot him a glance.

He shakes his head slowly as a forlorn smile settles over his face. "It's forbidden. I'm not allowed to show myself to any of my family—or anyone who would know me, really."

"But could you have a life, sort of? I mean, like . . . I don't know . . . make friends and stuff?" I notice my white knuckles as I clutch the steering wheel and try to relax.

I glance over again as he shifts uncomfortably in his seat. He looks about to say no, but then he turns back to me, a storm in his eyes. The hope is still there, but clouded with doubt—and sadness. "I don't know."

"So, why do you want to be visible?"

"I just think it would be easier for me to protect you. I don't like that there's this crazy demon tailing your boyfriend."

An icy finger races up my spine as the image from my nightmare creeps back into my consciousness. I breathe a heavy sigh and shake it off. "Well, it'd be easier on me if I knew when you were around."

I catch myself fidgeting in my seat and make myself stop. He doesn't need to know how uneasy it makes me to always be watched. He's just doing his job, and I'm so glad to have him back. I don't want him to feel bad about the circumstances.

He shrugs. "I also think I should get to know some of the people in Luc's building." He gestures to it with a tip of his head as we round the corner into the parking lot.

"Like . . . Lili," I say, pointing to where she's just appeared at the door, carrying a large trash bag.

Matt's head spins, as if spring loaded, in the direction of Luc's building. "Um . . . ," he says, just before he vanishes.

I'm still laughing as I pull into a spot near the door and kill the engine.

"Hey, Frannie." Lili walks past my car and flings the trash bag over the lip of the Dumpster.

"Hey."

She steps up to the driver's door. "I saw Luc pull out a while ago."

"Oh." I glance around the lot. "Wonder where he went."

She shrugs. "Didn't ask. But come in," she says with a wave of her hand toward the building. "You can wait for him in my apartment."

"I'm really on my way to work," I say, tugging at my Ricco's T-shirt.

Her long, dark hair spills across her face as she lowers her head. "Oh . . . okay."

I instantly feel bad, realizing that this poor person knows nobody. She's probably lonely. "But I can wait for a little while, I guess," I say as I climb out of the car.

Lili's eyes light up as she pushes strands of hair off her face with the heel of her hand. She reaches up and touches the crucifix that's come out from under my shirt.

"That's a cool piece. Kinda goth. Where'd you get it?"

I pull it up by the chain so she can get a better look. "Luc."

She cracks a smile. "I was thinking your grandmother or something. That's . . . um . . . romantic?"

I laugh. "Not so much. It's kinda a thing for us."

We head up to her apartment together, and I swear it looks like a bomb went off—a combination of being only half-unpacked and the lack of places to put anything. There's a beat-up green couch in the corner with papers and clothing—mostly sweatshirts and warm-up pants in various shades of gray—strewn across it. The only other piece of furniture is a barstool next to the short kitchen counter. No bed. She must sleep on the couch.

"Want something to drink?" she says, opening the ancient white refrigerator in the tiny kitchen. "I've got . . . uh . . ." She closes the fridge and points to the sink, looking a little embarrassed. "Water."

I shake my head as I take a seat on the empty end of the couch. "No thanks. I'm good."

She shuffles over and joins me, shifting the papers to the peeling linoleum floor. She curls up, lifting her knees to her chest and wrapping her arms around them. "Sorry the place is such a dump. I'm kinda living out of boxes."

I look around. It really is a mess. "Do you want some help organizing?"

"Naw . . . thanks. I really don't have that much stuff." She looks more embarrassed, pulling her knees closer and studying her peeling green nail polish. "The truth is, I just don't have anywhere to put it except back in the boxes."

"My mom has an old dresser in the garage, if you want it."

She answers too quickly. "No . . ."

"Really. You should take it. It's just sitting there, collecting dust and taking up space. Mom will be happy to be rid of it."

She tears her eyes away from her fingernails and looks at me. "Well . . . if you're sure you don't need it . . ."

"I'm sure. We can load it in your truck and bring it over." I give her my best reassuring smile.

She ventures a small smile back. "Thanks."

"And since you'll have somewhere to put some clothes . . . ," I say, fingering the gray sweatshirt on the arm of the couch next to me, "maybe you can expand your wardrobe a little?"

"What's wrong with my wardrobe?" she says, and I realize from the pinch of her face and her defensive tone that I've offended her.

"Sorry. Nothing, really. But it's June and it's only gonna get hotter. Aren't you gonna want something more . . . summery?"

She looks self-conscious, her eyes dropping to the floor, and I suddenly realize that money is the issue. "I'm good."

"All the summer stuff's on sale at the mall. It's the best time to get some really great deals." I'd offer for her to come shopping in my closet, but I'm sure that would offend her even more, and unfortunately, she's not really my size. She's at least six inches taller than me, and I can't figure out whether she's a little heavy or totally stacked. Hard to tell through the baggy sweatshirt.

"I pretty much don't give a crap what I wear," she says, tugging at her sweatshirt.

"Just a few tank tops . . . maybe a T-shirt?"

"Maybe . . ." She looks back up at me. "Well . . . yeah . . . okay . . ." A full smile blooms on her face. "Great. When?"

I tick off my work schedule in my head. "Next Thursday afternoon. I'll see if my friends Taylor and Riley want to come. Girls' day out."

Her smile falters. "Oh . . . if you want to go with your friends—"

"You'll love them, don't worry. And it will be good for you to meet some other people. They're both going to State too."

She still looks uncertain, picking at her nail polish. "All right, I guess."

"It'll be great. We can get that dresser then too."

The purr of the Shelby through the open window draws my attention, and I smile.

"Sounds like Luc's back," she says, rising from the couch. I'm surprised she'd recognize the sound of the Shelby so easily.

I pull myself off of the couch and follow her to the window. "You're good." I watch Luc slide out of the car, grabbing a couple of grocery bags off his passenger seat, and make his way to the building.

Her smile is suddenly big and genuine. "No. You are. I knew it was him because of you."

"Oh." I ignore the warmth creeping into my cheeks.

"If you want to go . . . ," she starts.

"Why don't you come over to Luc's? We can hang out."

Her smile is still there. "Yeah, just what you guys need. A spectator."

My cheeks get warmer. "We don't . . . I mean . . ." I trail off, wondering why I care what this stranger thinks about what Luc and I do.

"Go," she says, tipping her head toward the door. "It's okay."

"All right. But I'll come by at noon on Thursday, and we'll go get that dresser."

Her hair falls across her face as she walks with me to the door. "Okay."

MATT

Frannie steps out into the hall just as Luc reaches his door, and I realize I'm still hovering next to Lili, where she stands in her doorway.

"Hey, Luc," she says with a wave. As she steps back to close the door, I'm desperate for her not to. When the door closes, she'll be gone.

Before I realize I've even done it, I'm down the hall, kicking the bottom out of one of the grocery bags dangling from Luc's hand. An instant later, groceries are strewn across the hall, tomatoes and oranges rolling in every direction.

Lili steps back into the hall and scoops an orange and two tomatoes up on her way to where Luc is glaring at nothing in particular.

"Jesus," Frannie says in surprise, stooping to pick up an onion. "Um . . . ," she adds as she lifts a dripping carton of eggs by one corner.

Lili hands Luc the produce she's collected. "Weird. It's like there was a bomb in that bag."

"Thanks." Luc's eyes shift around the hall as he takes it from her.

Lili picks up a bag of lettuce and hands it to Frannie.

"Thanks, Lili. We got it."

"No problem," Lili says, turning back toward her door.

I can't help following her up the hall, and when she closes it, something inside me squeezes into a tight knot. I lift my hands and lay them flat on the door, fighting to keep from pushing through. Finally, when I'm mostly under control, I turn back to Luc's and find the hall empty.

I slide through the wall into the demon's apartment, where Frannie is putting groceries away as Luc tosses the oozing egg carton into the trash.

He turns slowly toward me. "What was that?"

I shrug, hoping I don't look as guilty as I feel. "What?"

"The exploding grocery bag trick."

I hold up my hands in feigned innocence because I can't open my mouth to deny it.

He shakes his head, his mouth pulling into a tight smile as he sorts through the remaining groceries.

"Matt was telling me on the way over that he wants to try being visible when he's here," Frannie says, closing the fridge.

The demon's eyes lift to mine. "Why?"

I ease over to the table and settle into a chair. "I want to get a feel for the people in your building."

"I don't even have a *feel* for the people in my building," the demon says.

"What about that girl? Lili?" Lightning crackles under my skin, and I hope it doesn't show on my face.

"What about her?" There's a sharp edge to his voice.

I look closer, trying to read his eyes. Finally, I shrug. "Nothing, really."

Frannie leans her hip into the table next to me and looks hopefully at Luc.

"I don't know . . . ," he starts, but then he catches Frannie's expression and his face softens. "I suppose it might be easier if you were visible. At least then we'd know for sure when you were around," he says, echoing Frannie.

I smile, relieved, and swing my feet up onto the table. I tip the chair onto its back legs. "I think—"

Frannie's on me in a flash, shoving my feet off the table and sending my chair legs crashing to the floor. "For Christ's sake, Matt! You might not have to eat, but we do. Feet off the table."

"Sorry," I say, straightening in my chair. "So, I think we should start with people here. I can meet them and we'll see how it goes."

The demon's head snaps up, and something flares in his eyes. "Lili?"

"I guess. And anyone else you know," I say, knowing there's no one else.

Frannie sits in the chair across from me and glances at him. "What do you think?"

His eyes narrow. "I suppose."

"Great. So next time Lili's here, we'll just pretend that I'm hanging out. You know . . . to see how it goes."

Frannie beams at me as she pushes off the table. "This is gonna be great!"

I catch myself praying she's right as she gives the demon a peck on the cheek and heads to the door.

"Gotta get to work. You'll pick me up for Gallaghers'?" she says.

Luc smiles as he walks with her. "Like to see you try to stop me."

4

✢

Wrestling with Your Demons

FRANNIE

The early shift at Ricco's is always so much easier. Even so, I stink when I get home and head straight to the shower. I feel almost human again in a tank top and jeans when I come back to my room.

Matt is sprawled across my bed on his stomach with my earbuds in, scanning through the menu on my iPod. He lifts his head and grins at me, then starts thrashing his head up and down, sandy curls flying, to the beat of the music only he can hear. "In my next life, I'm going to be a rock star!" he yells.

I rush over and yank the earphones out of his ears. "Shhh! You want the whole world to hear you?"

His lips purse and his eyes widen. "Oops."

I crack a smile as I realize what he said. "In your next life?"

"Yeah."

"You get another life?" I say, sitting next to him on the bed.

"No. Not in the real sense, anyway. But when I'm done with my gig as guardian, maybe I'll start a rock band."

"There are rock bands in Heaven?" I say, trying to picture it. "That doesn't sound like the 'choirs of angels' that they talk about at church."

He snorts. "No choirs."

"So the Heavenly refrain is more along the lines of 'Highway to Hell'?" I laugh, thinking about how Father O'Donnell would take that news. When I look back at Matt, he's grinning at me. "What?"

"Do you remember when we tried to sell Maggie to the neighbors?" he says.

I laugh at the memory. "'Cause we wanted a puppy, and Mom said to start saving our money."

"And Mom made us go talk to Father Mahoney about it—"

"And he told us we weren't asking enough for her," I finish for him, cracking up.

He rolls onto his back, laughing. Then he props up onto his elbows. His laughter fades, but his smile is bright. "Father Mahoney had the right idea. Heaven isn't nearly as stuffy as people are led to believe."

I flop onto my back next to him and stare at the ceiling, wondering how things would have been now if Matt were still alive. Up till Mary moved out last month, I was the only sister without a roommate, because mine died. Even though I'm sure Matt and I wouldn't be sharing a room anymore, I know he'd still be my best friend.

"I've been thinking about this Sway thing. . . ." I trail off, not sure how to continue.

"Yeah, I saw that fight in the park last week. Nice job, sis." He grins, and I want to punch him.

"You know what? Just forget it."

"Sorry," he says, but he's still grinning. "So what about it?"

I take a deep breath. "If I turned Luc mortal—"

He rolls on his side and shoves my shoulder. "Everyone makes mistakes."

I hear the laugh in his voice, and suddenly I'm furious. I sit up on the bed and glare at him. "Jesus, Matt! I'm trying to be serious here."

His eyes go wide and he draws back from me. "Sorry . . ."

"I want you to be mortal too," I blurt. "I want you back."

His eyes go wider and he sits up. He just stares at me for a long minute and neither of us says anything. Finally, he starts to shake his head. "No, Frannie. It's too late for that. I have a job now." He scoots closer. "An important one. And I couldn't go back to being your brother anyway. If I were mortal, I'd have to start over again somewhere else. This way, at least I get to be with you." Then a smile blooms on his face. "And being an angel has its perks."

My heart sinks, but I know he's right. "So, this is as close to having you back as I'm gonna get."

"It's not so bad. I can still give you wet willies," he says, then licks his finger and sticks it in my ear.

I jump off the bed and grab a tissue from the box on the night-stand. "Aww! That's disgusting," I say, wiping the spit off my ear.

"Angel spit has magical properties. You should keep that." He gestures to the tissue with a grin.

I glare at him, holding the contaminated tissue by the corner at arm's length. "Such as . . . ?"

His face draws wide in surprise. "I think I might have just lied."

"I knew you were no angel," I say, chucking the tissue in the trash just as Mom calls up the stairs that dinner is ready. I shoot a grin over my shoulder, and Matt disappears as I pull the door open and head downstairs.

I get to the kitchen just as the back door screen slams. I look up to see Grandpa.

"Grandpa!" I squeal, and run over to hug him.

"There's my girl," he says as Maggie steps into the room, and I don't miss the disappointment on her face. I've always been Grandpa's favorite, since Matt and I started working on cars with him when we were little—not that we were much help back then. None of my sisters were ever interested in joining us in the garage, so since Matt died ten years ago, it's just been Grandpa and me every Sunday after church. My midnight blue '65 Mustang convertible was our last restoration project.

"Did you get that Shelby?" I ask, dragging him to the table by the hand.

"On its way." He pulls up a chair next to mine and sits.

"Is it a total rebuild?"

"Yep. Pretty much a mess. Don't know what I'm gonna do without ya when you go off to college."

"Well, don't think about pulling that engine without our help."

"*Our* help?"

I cringe. "Luc was gonna meet us at your house after church."

"Luc wants in, huh?" he says, rubbing his balding head.

I reach up and brush his gray fringe back into place. "If that's okay . . . ?"

"Not sure I want to share my best mechanic."

My cringe deepens into a pleading grimace.

He breaks into a deep belly laugh. "I can see it's an all-or-nothin' proposition."

"He's really good. You won't regret it."

His blue eyes sparkle. "We'll see."

Mom steps up behind him, wiping her hands on her apron and leaning down to kiss his cheek before settling in at her end of the table. She brushes a stray lock of sandy blond hair back into place before picking up Grandpa's plate and serving the chicken.

Watching her, I can't help but think about how much she's changed in the last few weeks. She seems so much more alive, like maybe she's finally letting Matt go. There's a little pang in my heart as I glance around the kitchen, knowing he's here and wishing I could share him with her.

She hands Grandpa a heaping plate of food. "Glad you could make it for dinner, Dad. I don't think you're eating as well as you should."

"I'm eatin' just fine," he says, laying his plate on the table and patting his roundish belly.

Dad comes in from the family room as the rest of my sisters—all but Mary—find spots around the table. "Ooh. My favorite. Chicken and dumplings," he says, tucking his napkin into his lap.

Food is passed and everyone eats, but the Cavanaugh table is never a quiet one. Grace and Maggie fight over whose night it is to clean the kitchen while Dad gives Kate a hard time about her lack of a summer job this year. Everyone has something to say—all at the same time. Mom turns to me when there's finally a lull in the conversation.

"So what are you all dressed up for?"

I look down at my black silk tank and jeans. I wonder what it says about me that this is "dressed up."

"Luc and I are going out to the Gallaghers' tonight with Taylor, Riley, and Trev."

"Trev? Riley's still seeing Trevor?"

I can't help cracking a smile. "Yep, hot and heavy."

"And Taylor's okay about Riley with her little brother?"

"Getting there." That's actually a little bit of a lie. Taylor's still pretty pissed. But that's Taylor—not great in the forgiveness category.

Taylor was the first person I met in Haden, and she's been the perfect friend for me. We moved here not long after Matt died. I was pretty messed up at the time, so it took me a while to realize that my mom was messed up too. What I know now is that Dad moved us here so Mom could be closer to her parents.

Anyway, Taylor was just what I needed. Neither of us is big into sharing our feelings or crap like that. Riley came along much later and is kind of our accidental friend. She and all her *feelings* are dangerous. But I can't help being happy for her that she's found "the one." She always knew he was out there. It's just too bad for her that it turned out to be Taylor's brother.

"Chase is picking me up too, Mom," Kate says. I look over

what she's wearing and push away the tinge of jealousy. She's always totally amazing. In a stroke of universal unfairness, Kate got not only the looks in our family, but also the height. She's the only one of us sisters to break five-six.

"Don't his parents get sick of all those parties?" Mom asks.

"No, they're good with it. At least they know where all their kids are," Kate answers.

Kate's boyfriend, Chase, is one of ten Gallagher kids, and every high school party since the dawn of time has been in their backyard.

Maggie bounces in her seat. "I'm going too."

Dad points his fork at her and fixes her in a hard gaze. "I don't think so."

"But Roadkill is playing there tonight. Delanie wants me to come," she whines, turning her pleading eyes on me.

I pick at the remains of my chicken. "Not up to me, Maggs. Sorry."

Dad regards Maggie with his serious hazel eyes. "You'll have plenty of time for that when you're older."

She pulls a hand through her dark curls and rolls her eyes. "Dad! I'm not a freshman anymore. It's summer, so I'm a sophomore now."

Dad's gaze becomes even more stern. "Maggie . . ."

Maggie jerks back from the table with a shove that nearly knocks over every water glass. At the same instant, two of the three bulbs in the overhead fixture pop loudly and go dark.

"I hate being the youngest!"

With a stomp of her foot, Maggie storms out of the kitchen as the last bulb pops, leaving us sitting in the dark.

Dad looks warily up at the fixture, then he pushes back from the table. "I'll take care of that."

The light in the laundry room clicks on and I hear him flipping circuit breakers in the fuse box. He's back in a minute with new bulbs and climbs onto his chair to change them. "Must be a short circuit somewhere," he says, stepping off the chair.

Mom sighs as the kitchen illuminates, then turns a concerned eye on me. "Who's driving?"

"Luc and Riley."

I see the relief in her eyes as she dabs the corners of her mouth with her napkin.

"Mom," I say, exasperated. "I'm *not* a bad driver."

"I never said you were, dear."

"Whatever," I growl, pushing my chair back and clearing my place.

I rinse my dishes and finish just as the doorbell rings. I bolt for the door and slide through, smiling up at Luc, who stands on my front porch.

He grins at me. "Where's the fire?"

"In my kitchen." I step back to admire him, and my heart struggles to keep a rhythm. He looks crazy hot in a sapphire blue button-down, one tail untucked and lying over a pair of faded black jeans.

"You look . . ." I can't finish. There's not a word. "Nice shirt."

"It's the color of your eyes," he says, and stops my struggling heart.

I breathe deep, tear my eyes away from him, and skip down the porch stairs. He turns and follows me.

"Did you get to your oil yet? We could do that before we go," he says from behind me.

I turn and smile at him. "Like you're really dressed for an oil change." But when I picture him taking off that shirt to work on my car, heat prickles my cheeks and I glance away. "Grandpa said we'd do it on Sunday."

"I'm there," he says, and I'm trying not to picture how good he's gonna look covered in grease under my car.

"Let's walk to Taylor's. See when they want to go."

"There was this guy, Alexander Graham Bell. He invented this thing called the telephone. You really should get one. They're all the rage." A smirk pulls at his lips, making me want to kiss him even more.

I force my eyes away from him before he completely sucks me in. "Ha, ha," I say, waggling my phone in his face. "Don't tell me—you were his Muse too."

Out of nowhere, Luc lunges and twists my outstretched arm into an armlock. Panic sends my heart racing. He leans in from where he stands behind me. "No. Just Dante," he breathes in my ear.

"Son of a bitch," I say under my breath, trying to pull free. Every tug wrenches my shoulder tighter into the lock, sending a bolt of sharp pain up my arm and into my spine. "Cut the shit, Luc. Let me go," I say, knowing there's not a chance in hell he will.

"Uncle?" he asks with a self-satisfied grin.

I stop struggling and turn my head over my shoulder to look at him. "Very good. Your lessons are paying off," I say just before swinging my leg out and taking him down on the front lawn. He lands hard on his back and I pounce on top of him, pulling him into an armlock and pressing my forearm across his windpipe. "Uncle?"

"Uncle," he croaks, eyes wide.

I loosen my arm on his throat, but maintain the armlock and grin as I look down at him beneath me. "I think I like this—you completely at my mercy."

"Neighbors, Frannie," he warns, but there's a smile in his voice.

I let go of his arm and sit up, straddling him. "You saying you don't like it? Liar."

"I didn't say anything of the sort." He rubs his shoulder and then slides his hands along the curves of my waist, sending a shiver through me. "Just surprised you want to give them a free show."

MATT

I swear to God, I almost struck the demon with lightning when he grabbed Frannie. The judo lessons were her idea. Now that the demon's "vulnerable," she thought he should know how to defend himself. But the "judo" always seems to degenerate into something looking more like wrestling, except with a lot of kissing and giggling.

And *now* they're being totally disgusting. She stops thinking when she's with him.

Still invisible, and trying not to look at the public display, I sidle over to where they're getting frisky on the lawn and nudge Frannie's shoulder with my knee. "Get a room, sis."

She springs off the demon and stands over him in a defensive crouch, eyes darting wildly.

Reflexively, I back off a step. "Get a grip. It's just me."

She scowls and straightens up, then turns to offer Luc a hand where he's still lying in the grass. He takes it and Frannie pulls him to his feet. She spins back as color slides up her cheeks. "Do you have to follow me everywhere?"

"Yes!" The demon says it before I can.

I glare in his direction, even though he can't see me.

"Almost," I amend. "Besides, you can't have sex on the front lawn—for more reasons than I can list."

"Shut up." She scowls in the direction of my voice, almost looking directly at me. "We weren't having sex. I was kicking his ass."

The skanky demon steps up behind her and rests a hand on her shoulder. "Let's walk," he says, pulling her toward the sidewalk with a glance in my direction.

She blows out a long sigh. "Yeah."

I trail behind as they move up the street to the park. It's a golden pink dusk, and I examine the shadows under the willows as Frannie and her demon find a bench and sit. He loops his arm over her shoulders and I circle around behind them, trying to stay out of earshot as they talk in hushed tones.

There are rules to being a guardian angel. Rule number one is that we can't interfere in our charges' lives. They have to be free to make their own decisions. Rule number two is that we can't invade their privacy. Or anyone else's.

Luc is human now, so that rule applies to him too—unfortunately.

Still, I can't help myself, and my sense of duty overrides her need for privacy. I move a little closer and lean against the carved bark of a willow not far from their bench.

"Just pick one and focus," Luc says, his voice low.

I follow their gaze and see a group of junior high boys in the skate park directly in front of them. I watch for a few minutes as they razz each other when they wipe out.

"Focus on what? What am I supposed to get him to do?"

Luc cracks a wide smile and throws a glance over his shoulder. "Well, I'm guessing that Matt would strike me with lightning if I said something like, make him speak in tongues, so how about just making him say something nice to his buddies." He lifts the hand that's not wrapped around my sister and points. "That one in the orange shirt seems particularly nasty. See what you can do with him."

She shifts away from Luc and leans with her elbows on her knees, her brow creasing with concentration.

I watch the one in the orange shirt. He does a loop around the half-pipe, then slides down the rail and does a kick turn in front of a smaller kid who is struggling to stay on his board. Orange Shirt Kid looks for a second like he's going to move out of the way. But the next second, he tears past and shoulders the smaller guy off his board. The kid hits the ground on his butt, and Orange Shirt Kid grins, holding his hand up for a knuckle bump as he passes a third boy.

Frannie leans back with her palm on her forehead and groans. "I suck so bad at this."

Luc moves to loop his arm over her shoulders again, but

Frannie pushes him away. "I think I'm having a moral dilemma," she says, her forehead still in her hand.

He laughs out loud and she shoves him.

"Thanks for the support, Luc."

"Sorry," he says as his laughter dies. "So, tell me about this dilemma."

"I don't think it's right to mess with people's heads."

He looks at her for a long minute without responding. Finally, he blows out a sigh and leans toward her. "When I was a demon," he starts, his voice low and strained, as if it's painful to remember, "I couldn't really make people do anything they didn't want to. I could 'mess with their heads,' as you so eloquently put it, but I couldn't make them do anything out of character. I think your Sway might be a lot like that."

"I still don't think it's right." She leans into the back of the bench. "I'm not gonna use it on my family, or on anyone who's not doing something really wrong . . . or bad . . . or something."

"That's your prerogative, I suppose," Luc says. He rubs his temple. "And probably what Gabriel meant when he said they just want you to do what's right."

This time, when the demon draws her closer, she leans into him. "I . . . ," she starts, but trails off.

"What?"

She pulls herself straight and looks Luc in the eye. "This sounds really stupid, but I've always felt like I was meant for something. When I thought I wanted to be some kind of diplomat, it was 'cause I'd always felt like I could make a difference. But this whole Sway thing . . . I'm afraid that whatever

I'm meant for is bigger than I can handle." She leans back into his side. "I'm scared," she says, her voice suddenly small, vulnerable.

The demon sighs and leans his cheek into her hair.

But after just a minute, she shifts away and pulls her buzzing phone out of her pocket. She looks at the screen. "Taylor and Riley are ready to go."

5

✟

Idle Hands Are the Devil's Tools

FRANNIE

By the time we pull up to the Gallagher house, the party is in full swing. Groups of marauding teenagers stream from the cars parked along the woods at the side of the road toward the music in the backyard, whooping and hollering.

Luc and I cross the street to where Riley is parked. Taylor primps her spiky pink and yellow hair, then slides out of the backseat of Riley's car and elbows me. "We need to branch out—maybe crash a party up in Marblehead. I'm sick of this crowd."

Riley skirts around the car to where we're standing. "You're paying for the gas to get there," she says as Trevor sweeps her long brown locks back and hooks an arm over her shoulders.

"Whatever," Taylor responds. Her fair skin flushes as she presses her tongue into the ring through the corner of her lip. She shoots a glare at her brother and spins, storming up the road toward the party. Riley shrugs and Trevor smiles at her, all tanned dimples, as they follow Taylor across the street.

Luc twines his fingers into mine. "There's a project for your Sway," he says with a tip of his head toward my friends' retreating backs.

I shove him. "Yeah, right. We're talking about Taylor. Do you enjoy watching me fail?"

"I enjoy watching you do just about everything." He grasps my hand again and we follow Taylor into the milling crowd.

Delanie's band, Roadkill, is set up behind the house, next to the porch. The music grows louder as we get closer. I pull Luc through the masses to where Taylor, Riley, and Trevor have stopped near the bonfire.

"I'll get us something to drink," Luc says. He squeezes my hand, then makes his way to the other side of the yard, where ice chests are lined up next to the house. I catch myself staring as he goes. My belly flutters and I feel a slow smile creep across my face. God, he's perfect.

"Reefer's on fire," Trevor says in my ear, pulling me from my musing.

My heart leaps into my throat and my head jerks automatically to look at the bonfire, half-expecting to see a flailing Reefer engulfed in flame.

Trevor rolls his blue eyes and points toward the house. "Over there," he laughs, "with the guitar."

I wince as I turn to where they're set up. Even if my ex-boyfriend is useless everywhere else, behind his guitar, he's a genius. And, I have to admit, they sound pretty good. Delanie jumps up and down, her straight black hair swinging wildly behind her, belting out a perfect Avril Lavigne. She's in torn jeans, a leather vest, and heavy black eyeliner. She looks totally different from when she's sporting her Ricco's T-shirt and ponytail at work. Anybody who didn't know would guess she was closer to twenty-five than fifteen.

"Delanie sounds great," Trevor adds; then his eyes flit to me. "But . . . ," he stammers, "they were much better when you were singing for them."

I roll my eyes. "If you say so."

When the song ends, Reefer pulls his guitar off and slips his arm around Delanie.

"It looks like he's over you," Trevor says, jabbing me with an elbow.

"Good," I say. It seems like another lifetime when we were together, even though it really wasn't that long ago.

I glance back at the band and realize that I don't know them all. The bass player is a tall, built, black-haired kid whom I'm sure I've never seen before. I nudge Trevor. "Who's the bass guy?"

Trevor squints across the yard at the small group. "Don't know," he finally says.

"But I'm gonna find out," Taylor says from behind me. I start to turn, but her hand is already on my arm and she's yanking me toward the band.

When we get to the group, Delanie grins. "Where's Maggie?"

I shrug. "Dad wouldn't let her come."

Taylor shoulders up to her, a lascivious glint in her charcoal eyes. "Who's the hot guy?" she says under her breath.

Delanie throws a glance over her shoulder toward the rest of the band.

Reefer takes the glance as an invitation to join us. He slides in next to Delanie and pushes his golden brown dreads away from his soft brown eyes with the back of his hand. "Hey, Frannie," he says, draping his arm over Delanie's shoulders. I wince at the guilty pang and hope Delanie's with him because she wants to be, not 'cause I sorta threw them together.

"Hey, Reef. How's it going?"

He nuzzles into Delanie's neck. "Great."

I bite back the laugh before it escapes. He's not a bad guy—mostly a geek of the *Guitar Hero* variety, and I sorta almost loved him—but why he'd think I'd be jealous, I'll never understand. I'm the one who broke up with him.

When he's finally done making his point—which is something along the lines of *see what you could have had*—he looks up at me. "So, you miss this?"

I crack a wide smile, not sure if he means the music or him. "No." True on both counts.

He looks wounded for a second before recovering. "Well, you leaving the band was the best thing that coulda happened. Delanie's voice is unique—one of a kind." Implying that mine isn't. Which is true. "We've got a major label asking for a demo."

"Holy shit! That's great!"

Taylor elbows me hard in the ribs, making me catch my breath.

"Jesus, Tay, I'm getting to it." I rub my side and glance past Reefer at the guys. "Who's your bass guy?"

"Marc. He's new." Reefer turns and raises a hand. The new guy lifts his gaze from the guitar he was tuning and looks up at me with the hint of a smile, as if he knew we were talking about him. He straightens up and his eyes slide over me. Then he nods and goes back to tuning his guitar.

Reefer jerks his head in the new guy's direction as he turns back to me. "He's the one who hooked us up with the demo. Says the guy owed him a favor."

Even though I'm sure I've never laid eyes on this guy before, there's something eerily familiar about him. I catch myself staring and drop my gaze when he looks up from his guitar again. He lifts an eyebrow at me, quirking half a smile. I turn back to Reefer and Delanie as heat creeps up my neck.

Delanie's eyes light up. She reaches up and gives my shoulder a gentle jab as a smile breaks across her face. "Hey! You should sing something."

Reefer's jaw drops. "I don't think—"

"Not gonna happen," I say, backing away.

Delanie grabs my hand in both of hers, pulling me past the stacked speakers. "Sure it is. What do you want to do?"

I tug my arm back. "Really, Delanie. You don't want to ruin your rep by having me butcher some song up here. Especially if you've got labels scouting you."

Reefer scans the crowd warily. "She's right."

"Do it, Fee!" Riley hollers. I look to see her standing next to Taylor. Trevor grins at me over her shoulder.

But just at that instant, I feel a surge of static electricity so intense that all my hair stands on end. I can almost feel it crackle over my skin.

Matt.

MATT

I stay invisible and hang back from Frannie's group, skirting the woods and taking in my surroundings. Everywhere I look, couples are draped all over each other in various stages of seduction. All pretty innocent, really—no souls in danger at the moment. But as I scan the crowd, Lili's face pops into my head out of nowhere. It's happened a lot over the last two days, since I first saw her, and every time I think of her, an electric zing shoots through me. The same zing I felt when she passed through me in her apartment. I've seen her only twice. She doesn't even know I exist. But there's something about her that makes her hard to forget.

I settle into the trunk of an old maple tree on the edge of the yard and watch. And every time I see a couple touch each other, or kiss, I can't help wondering what it would be like to be with Lili that way—to touch her like that. I close my eyes and let myself imagine it, how her skin would feel. How she'd smell. Taste. I feel myself shudder and crack the back of my head sharply off the tree.

Focus.

I open my eyes. Frannie's talking to the girl in the band, and Luc's at the keg. He hands a beer to a blonde who's doing her best to corner him against the porch rail. She smiles her glistening red lips at him and digs in her purse, pulling out a slip of pink paper. I watch him slide it into his pocket before he grabs another cup and starts to fill it.

Figures my sister would fall for a demonic chick magnet. Heartbreak waiting to happen. Fine by me. The sooner she sees what he really is, the sooner she'll dump him. Maybe I can arrange for her to find that paper. . . .

I scan the yard again, my eyes slipping past groups of people talking and laughing, and on the outskirts of the yard, bodies pressed together in the shadows of the trees.

And Lili's there again, in my head. I try to push her out, but she won't leave. So I let myself go with the fantasy. I feel her pressing herself into me, driving me to want her in ways I shouldn't. But in my fantasy, I can have her. I fold her into my arms, and when she tips her face up to mine, I kiss her. I run my hands over the curves of her body, my senses prickling at her increasing heat as she devours me with her own hands. I feel the intensity of my need for her roll through me—a dizzying wave of despair.

The buzz in my sixth sense feels like being electrocuted. Instantly, I realize the tingling in my fantasy wasn't just from Lili's hands. The demon buzz had been building for a while.

I lost my focus.

I don't even stop to sense where it's coming from—or admonish myself for my lapse. I'm across the yard in a flash, wrapping Frannie in a field.

She stumbles back from her group with a gasp. "I gotta go," she says to her friends, and turns to look for Luc, who's making his way over with two full beer cups.

"Your boyfriend's crew is here," I whisper in Frannie's ear.

"Where?" she says, her eyes wide and darting.

"I don't know, exactly, but there's more than one. Go." I give her a little shove, but she's already moving.

She catches up to Luc. "Matt says we have to go," she murmurs, her eyes darting around. Luc drops the beer and grabs her hand. We walk quickly back to the car, and just as we reach the road, I see three pairs of red eyes peering out from the darkness of the woods. The immense redheaded demon from Ricco's steps out from the shadows and watches us pass. Though he doesn't make a move to stop us, a sharp, electric current crackles through me.

Frannie's in a defensive crouch, ready to strike out, but Luc grabs her hand and pulls her toward the car at a run.

The demon flashes me a menacing grin. Even though I'm invisible, he knows I'm here—just as I'd have known he was here if I were paying attention. Two others, shorter but just as stocky, step out of the shadows as I back toward Luc's car.

What the Hell is going on? Did he come after Frannie?

I glance to Frannie and Luc as they dive into his car. I stare down the group of demons for a second longer, then phase into the backseat of the Shelby.

Luc looks Hell-bent, knuckles white on the steering wheel, as he weaves around the potholes.

"You're not going to outrun them," I say, sinking into the backseat. My eyes shift to Frannie. "Are you okay?" I ask.

"I'm fine."

"Did they do anything to you?"

"No. Just what you saw."

"It's my fault." Luc's voice is faint, almost a whisper.

"Luc, stop." Frannie lays her hand on his shoulder, her face all concern.

Luc continues to stare straight out the windshield, his face tight, jaw clenched. "I don't think it's safe for you to be around me."

"I'm not going anywhere."

His eyes slide to the top of her head, where she's resting her cheek on his shoulder, and he blows out a sigh before turning his attention back to the road. He still looks determined, both hands tight on the steering wheel, mouth set in a hard line. But in that brief glance, I saw it.

The answer.

I watched his eyes shift from tortured to resolved. Maybe he's not beyond doing the right thing after all. If Luc believed he was putting Frannie in danger, I think he'd leave.

With that realization, I gain a little respect for the demon. As a matter of fact, if he weren't a demon, I might even be able to tolerate him being with my sister.

But he *is* a demon.

So I know what I have to do.

FRANNIE

Luc is parked where he always is: under the ginormous maple tree near the fence across the street. I can just barely make out the front fender of the Shelby, shining through the flutter of the leaves in the moonlight. But I've been staring at it for hours, since Luc dropped me off, imagining being out there with him.

I lift my chin off my arms where they're propped on the windowsill and rub the crimp out of my aching neck. I grab my cell phone from the nightstand, meaning to call Luc, but I stare at it in my hand for a long minute before speed-dialing Gabe instead.

It doesn't even ring before the automated voice picks up, telling me what I already knew. I'm not gonna be able to reach Gabe by phone. It's disconnected.

I think about calling to him with my mind—sending him a message that I need his help. Would he come?

I groan internally and pull myself off the bed. Gabe left for a reason. I could sit here and convince myself we need him to come back, but it's really just me. It's stupid and unfair for me to call him back here just because I miss him.

I sigh and pull jeans on under the baggy T-shirt I sleep in. Cracking open the door, I peek out into the quiet, dark hall. The hinges whine as I push the door slowly open, and I make a mental note to oil them. As I tiptoe down the stairs, I make more mental notes. I knew about the squeaky stair at the bottom, but there are others that protest more quietly under my weight.

My pulse pounds in my ears as I reach for the front door handle. With a final glance up the stairs, I pull it open and step quickly out onto the porch.

Luc climbs out of the car and races across the street when he sees me. He grabs my hand and hurries me toward the Shelby. "What is it? What's wrong?" he asks, his eyes darting wildly around my yard.

"I—"

"Is he here? Damn! How did I miss him?" He pushes me into the passenger seat of his car.

"No. It's not that. I just—"

"What did he do, Frannie?" He crouches next to me and looks me over with panicked eyes.

I taste the coffee on his lips as I lean forward, twist my hand into his hair, and press my lips into his. His wired muscles don't relax, but the tension changes. His attention shifts from out there to right here. To me. Which is where I want it. After a minute, he presses into me and cups the back of my neck with his hand, pulling me deeper into the kiss. Finally, I push back.

"I didn't want to be alone."

Luc pulls me out of the car by my hand and crushes me into the curve of his body. "It's not safe for you to be out here," he says softly into my hair. "You need to stay in the house, behind your dad's field."

I push back from him. "My dad's *what*?"

His lips press into a line as he contemplates how he wants to answer that. "There's something about your father, Frannie. I don't know what it is, but I couldn't read him . . . when I was a demon." His eyes slide over the street then back to me. "I also couldn't phase into your house, which can happen only if there's a celestial field."

I think about Dad: Mr. Apple Pie and Baseball. "You think there's something wrong with my dad?"

He shakes his head, but his brow is creased, still contemplating. "Not *wrong*, but he's connected upstairs. You don't know of any reason—?"

"No. There's nothing weird about my dad . . . well, except that he actually likes brussels sprouts." I feel my face involuntarily scrunch.

Luc's black eyes sparkle in the silver moonlight as he smiles and loops his arm around my waist, guiding me back to the house. "What time is it?"

"I don't know . . . maybe four."

"You should be asleep."

I smile up at him. "So should you. Your first day on the job starts in, what, six hours? Don't want to fall asleep and drool on the books."

He turns concerned eyes on me. "Not after what happened at the Gallaghers' tonight. Rhenorian is lurking. I'm not letting you out of my sight."

We reach my doorstep and he pushes the door slowly open. He pulls me into a kiss and when he tries to pull back, I don't let him. When I smooth my hands over his chest, I can feel the thrum of his heart under my fingers, almost as fast as mine. His lips trace a path from my mouth to my ear and down my neck.

I peel myself away and look into his eyes. "I think that means you have to come upstairs with me," I whisper.

I twine my trembling fingers into his and pull him through the door. He hesitates at the threshold and shakes his head.

Please. Please. Please come in.

He draws a deep breath. A guilty smile curls one side of his lips as he steps through. His eyes question me and I answer by turning and leading him quickly up the stairs to my room, hoping the creaking stairs aren't really as loud as they seem.

I close my door and press into him, listening for any sound in the hall. After a minute, when all stays quiet, I relax and look up at Luc.

In the pale silver light of the moon, his eyes sparkle. An electric tingle whispers over my skin when he leans in and kisses me again, raising goose bumps. I pull him to the bed and slide my jeans off. He lets out a shaky sigh as I climb in and hold an arm out to him.

"Frannie . . . ," he whispers, his hand reaching back for the doorknob.

I hold a finger to my lips, then hold my arm out again.

He shoots a glance to the door, then kicks off his boots and slides into my bed. I burrow into him, nuzzling into his neck.

"This is a really bad idea," he whispers into my hair. But as I glide my hands along his chest, his stomach, lower, I can tell his body likes the idea just fine.

I nibble my way up to his ear. "I think it's the best idea I've ever had." I press into him and kiss him hard. "You have way too many clothes on," I whisper into his lips. He props up on an elbow and I pull his T-shirt over his head, then my own. He just stares at my near nakedness for a minute, and I try not to let him see me shake.

"Frannie . . . ," he whispers again, and I realize I'm not the only one who's shaking.

I twist my fist into his hair and bring his lips back to mine. His mouth slides to my ear. "So much for not using your Sway on people."

I shudder at his hot breath in my ear and smile. "You're the one who told me I need to practice."

When he lies back on the pillow, his expression is strained. "I was hoping you might choose a different target. You already know your Sway works on me." He covers me with the sheet, tucking it around me, and sweeps my tangled hair from my face with a finger.

Rolling onto my back, I blow out a frustrated breath. "You want me to use my Sway to lure someone *else* into my bed? Most guys wouldn't need to be talked into sleeping with their girlfriends."

"I would think by now you would know I'm not 'most guys.'" His finger traces the line of my eyebrow. "I've spent seven millennia doing the *wrong* thing. This is one thing I want to do *right.*"

"But I love you. It's not *wrong* to want to be with you."

His face darkens and his eyes go distant. "I'm fairly certain that everything about you being with me is wrong."

"Don't make me use my Sway on you again," I say, touching his cheek and bringing him back to the room.

When his eyes lock on mine, they're deep. "Frannie . . ." He trails off and shifts onto an elbow above me, still gazing into my eyes. "You don't have to use your Sway on me to make me want you. In all my existence, I've never wanted anything more. But I need this," he gestures between us, "to be about more than sex." He cups my cheek in his palm. "I don't want to mess this up by doing something rash."

I shove him. "Are you implying I have some communicable disease?"

He stifles a laugh and tucks in next to me on the bed, wrapping his arms around me and nuzzling his face into my hair.

I want to be mad, but I feel strangely content as I settle into the crook of his shoulder and lose myself in the silk of his skin.

Until there's a crash in the hall.

In a flash, Luc is over the side of the bed and onto the floor, between the bed and the window. I grab my T-shirt off the floor, but when I pull it over my head, I smell cinnamon. I've got Luc's instead. I yank it on anyway and pull the sheet tight around me.

The light in the hall flips on and I hear doors opening as my whole family empties into the hall. After a minute, there's a knock on my door.

"Huh," I say, trying to appear groggy even though my heart is hammering and I can barely breathe. I'm about as far from sleepy as I can possibly get. I've never been this wired in my life.

The door cracks open and Dad peeks through. He looks around and says, "You okay?"

"Uh-huh. What was that?"

"The mirror in the hall fell off the wall. The nail must have given way."

"'Kay," I say, rolling away from him and pretending to be mostly asleep. After a long moment, the door closes.

I lie perfectly still as the house quiets back down and the light in the hall is turned off. After forever, Luc pokes his head up over the edge of the bed. "I told you this was a bad idea," he whispers with a nervous smirk. "If your parents caught me in here . . ."

He doesn't need to finish the thought. We've just started making some headway with my parents. They don't really *like* Luc, but they don't seem to hate him anymore either.

I sit up in the bed and he notices my T-shirt. "I like the look."

"Sorry," I say, and start to lift it over my head.

He holds up a hand, a hint of panic in his expression. "Don't. I have my button-down in the car."

I smile, liking the way he looks without it. I hold my arm up to him again, but he shakes his head even as a slow smile creeps across his face. "I think we've pressed our luck as far as it will go."

He moves to the window, looks down, and hesitates. "This would be so much easier if I could phase out of here."

I climb out of bed and move to his side. "You're gonna break your neck. You should stay." I take his hand and wrap his arm around me.

Stay with me.

"Frannie, please. It was your Sway that got me up here in the first place, against my better judgment, I might add. But I really have to go."

He kisses me, then looks back out into the tree. With a hammering heart, I watch him pull the screen from the window and climb onto the window frame. He reaches up for a branch and tugs it a few times, then grasps it with both hands and swings away from the house. The branch sags under his weight. I gasp when I hear a crack, but it holds him long enough for his foot to catch a larger branch lower down and closer to the trunk. He reminds me of a lithe black cat as he shifts from one branch to another, sure-footed and steady, and eventually swings himself to the ground. I realize I'm holding my breath and let it out in a slow, shaky puff as he steps back to look up at me. And God, he's beautiful.

The horizon is beginning to turn pink with the start of a new day. He backs away slowly toward his car and my heart aches more with every step.

"What the Hell is wrong with you?" Matt's hiss in my ear scares the hell out of me.

I bite back the yelp, then turn to look at him. He's scowling at me, and when he sees my T-shirt, he rolls his eyes. "*Here?* You were going to do that here? With Mom and Dad just down the hall?"

My face is on fire and I have to fight to keep my voice a whisper. "You were *watching*?"

He backs off a few steps. "I'm an angel, not a voyeur. I wasn't watching. But it doesn't take a rocket scientist to figure out that you aren't dragging your boyfriend into your room in the middle of the night to *talk*."

"For your information, we *were* just talking, because *Luc* stopped."

"Yeah. That's why you're wearing his T-shirt." His smile is sour.

I turn to hide my flaming cheeks. "And anyway, it's none of your business what Luc and I do. Or where."

"It's *exactly* my business. My job is to protect you, even if it *is* from your stupid self. I'm not going to let you do this, Frannie. I'm not going to let you ruin your life."

Rage erupts out of my emotional black pit when it hits me . . . what he did. I stand up and shove him as hard as I can. "You ripped that mirror off the wall. Didn't you?"

He staggers back a few steps, and a grim smile curls his lips.

"Jesus, Matt!" I grab fistfuls of my hair and yank before

groaning and turning toward the window. I look out at the Shelby, still parked outside, and breathe deep, then turn back to Matt. "Can we talk about this later?"

His face softening, he nods and disappears.

I climb into bed and pull the sheet over my head. After a long minute, I lift my head out from under the sheet and scan the room. Still empty.

I trace the path of Luc's lips with my hand, still feeling the tingle of my skin from his touch. Closing my eyes, I bring his T-shirt to my face, breathing my heart back to a normal rhythm.

I'm so glad to have Matt back, but who knew having a guardian angel would turn out to be such an epic buzz kill? He's like my own personal chastity belt. Even though I swore I wouldn't use my Sway on family, maybe I should try it on Matt, just to get him to lighten up a little. I need practice, after all.

I smile, remembering how well it almost worked on Luc. 'Course, I really didn't mean to use it. I finally doze off with the smell of cinnamon in my nose and the tingle of fire under my skin. And in my dream, Matt doesn't interrupt us.

6

✤

A Deal with the Devil

LUC

The Haden branch of the Essex County Library is a gray gran-
ite monstrosity near the high school. It's in what used to be the
town hall, one of the older buildings in town, dating back to
the mid-1700s. And like most buildings in Haden, it looks
every day of it. I pull into the parking lot and jog across the
street to the stone building. Glancing at the clock tower, I see
I'm just on time. I'd meant to be early for my first day, but I
dropped Frannie at Taylor's on my way, and I couldn't leave
until I knew for sure that Matt was there.

I can't help the smile as I peer through the glass panel in the
carved wooden doors, then push them open and step inside.
Even my human nose can appreciate the scents of the library—
dust, old paper, and history. I scan the spines on the bookshelves as I make my way to the counter—a rather limited

selection, but all the classics and some excellent obscure titles as well.

The tiny stick figure of a woman behind the curved counter in the center of the cavernous room is filing books off the cart onto a shelf labeled HOLDING.

I stride over, lean across the counter, and clear my throat. When she turns, I hold out my hand. "Hello. I'm Luc Cain."

She looks me over with appraising pale gray eyes. She can't be a day less than one hundred, despite the jet-black curls framing her creased face. She takes my hand with her thin, bony one and grips it with surprising strength. "I'm Mavis Burnes. Head librarian. We spoke on the phone."

"It's a pleasure to meet you."

"Likewise," she says in a quavering voice, releasing my hand. "I have to say, I was more than a little surprised by your knowledge of books and our system," she says, looking me over again. "You're obviously too young to have done any library work in the past."

"But I've spent a lot of time reading." I turn and scan the stacks again, wondering if there's anything in them I haven't read—that's worth reading, anyway.

Chase Gallagher, who happens to be the way I heard about this job, emerges from the stacks in a way-too-bright tie-dye T-shirt. He walks up and drops a stack of books onto the counter, then smooths his dark hair back into his short ponytail with his palms.

"Hey, Luc. Ready?"

"Absolutely."

Chase orients me to the computer and filing systems while

Mavis eavesdrops and interjects to underscore the importance of particular points. He wraps up my orientation with a tour.

"We're moving the kid section over here next week—" He indicates a larger section of the library near the front that currently holds travel references. "—so we'll need you to stay late at least one night—probably Thursday next week—to help reshelve the books."

"Shouldn't be a problem."

He elbows me. "Then maybe we can head over to the Cavanaughs' for our women."

I almost can't suppress laughter, thinking about what Frannie'd do if she heard him refer to her as "my woman." I picture her flipping Chase, head over heels, onto the ground. A smile breaks across my face. He misreads it and wiggles his eyebrows suggestively.

"Those Cavanaugh girls are something, huh?"

My smile widens. "Something, indeed."

He dips his hand into his pocket and comes out with a key. "Mavis always opens," he says, nodding his head toward the counter. "And we'll switch off closing, so you'll need this."

As I take the key from his hand, I glance over his shoulder and see that girl from my apartment building—Lili—slip past an exiting patron into the room. She pauses just inside the door, then turns and looks like she's going to leave again.

"Excuse me," I say to Chase. I stride over to where she's pulling the door open.

"Did you need something, Lili?"

She jumps a little and turns back to look at me, her eyes wide. When she sees me, she exhales. "Oh, hi, Luc."

I smile reassuringly at her. "Can I help you find something?"

"Um . . . I was hoping there'd be like a job board or something."

"You're looking for a job?"

"I barely scraped together this month's rent. I need to find something fast."

"Hmm . . ." I glance around and the only bulletin board I see has library-related notices for children's story time and an author reading. "Let me ask Mavis."

She jumps again when I touch her arm to guide her to the counter, but she lets out another long breath and ventures a small smile. She walks with me to where Mavis is scanning in books.

"Mavis, do you know of anywhere there may be community job postings?"

Mavis looks from me to Lili and fingers the tiny silver cross hanging from a delicate chain around her neck. "Other than the newspaper . . . there's always the community center on Elm Street. That would be your best bet."

"Thanks," Lili says, dropping her gaze.

"Do you know where that is?" I ask as we head back to the door.

Lili nods. "So, you work here?" She scans the stacks before settling her gaze on me.

"As of today."

Her eyes light up as she smiles for real. "So you're not just a pretty face."

I laugh out loud, and Mavis scowls at me over the top of her glasses.

Lili's eyes flick to Mavis. She cringes and lowers her lashes. "Sorry," she whispers.

"My fault." I give her another reassuring smile. "Don't worry. I'll see you later?"

She nods and slips through the door.

But just as I make it back to the counter, the doors swing open and Rhenorian steps through. He browses the shelves up front, but his eyes aren't on the books. They're on me. He nods almost imperceptibly—a reminder that he's watching me.

Stalking me, more like.

But better me than Frannie. I wouldn't say anything to Frannie, but after that party at Chase's house, I'm not sure Matt is as focused as he should be. It was my fault that Rhenorian and his crew were there, but Matt should have known before they got that close. Gabriel chose Matt because he has a vested interest in Frannie, but I'm not sure that's enough.

Rhenorian smiles with a quick flash of his fangs before turning and pushing back out onto the sidewalk. I walk to the door and watch as he slides into the driver's seat of a silver Lincoln with a black faux ragtop. Part of me hopes he'll leave, but when he doesn't, I decide it's for the best. There's something reassuring about knowing your enemy—or at least his whereabouts.

I think about Frannie partying with her friends at the quarry. I tried to talk her out of it, but she wanted to go, and Matt swore he'd do his job. I ended up giving in because Frannie can't live like a caged animal. She needs to have her life. Which means I need to trust Matt.

But still, it's better to have Rhenorian where I can keep an eye on him.

When I leave the library at five, he's still there. He watches me cross the street to the Shelby. I think about heading back to my apartment—keeping to myself, away from Frannie. But I can't make myself do it. I need to see her—to be sure she's okay. So I drive up to the quarry.

And Rhenorian follows me.

Even though he doesn't seem to pose any immediate threat to Frannie, I still don't like it. As much as I hate to admit it, a piece of me wishes Gabriel hadn't left, because my infernal shadow is going to put a serious crimp in my ability to protect Frannie.

The thought that Frannie might be better off if I left flits through my head as I watch Rhenorian tail me. But even if that's true, despite what I promised her grandpa, I'm not sure I could actually make myself do it.

FRANNIE

When I see Luc standing on a boulder near the path, I can't help my grin. I swim to the rocks and pull myself out of the water, pressing into him and totally soaking the front of his T-shirt and jeans. But he only pulls me closer.

Being in his arms on the rocky edge of the quarry brings memories back. I glance over at the rope swing, remembering the night I brought Luc out here, under the stars. I shudder with the memory. It wasn't our first kiss, but it was definitely the most romantic—and the most romantic night of my life up till that point. Something about the stars, maybe. But more than that,

Luc let down his guard and showed me who he really was that night. I'm pretty sure that's when I fell in love with him, though I never would have admitted it to myself at the time.

At the moment, however, one of my least favorite people has laid claim to the rope swing. Angelique Preston is sitting on the wooden disk at the bottom, blond curls blowing back, dragging her foot along the surface of the water as she swings out over the quarry, and trying to look as sexy as possible in the process. She won't actually go in the water, though. God forbid she should trash her hair and makeup and come out looking like a drowned rat. Her double-Ds are barely contained in her black bikini, and I'm hoping Luc and I will be gone before she's had a few more beers and they make their appearance. To her credit, they're totally real. All of us, boys and girls alike, have been watching their progress since sixth grade with fascinated interest.

Riley and Trevor climb the rocks out of the water and come over to where we are.

"Hey, Luc," Trevor says. "Tore yourself away from those books, huh?"

I elbow him. "Shut up, Trev. Maybe if you knew how to read . . ."

He flashes me a sarcastic grin.

"Where's Tay?" I ask.

Riley points down the quarry to a group of guys showing off on the diving cliff—which isn't really a cliff at all. Just a place where the rocks stick out over the water. It's only about a ten-foot drop, but it makes the guys feel more manly to call it a cliff, I guess.

Sure enough, Taylor's up there, looking killer in a red string bikini. I squint to see who she's talking to.

"Holy shit! Is that Brendan?"

Riley nods. "He's back for the summer."

What the hell is she thinking?

My face twists into a scowl. "So Taylor exists again. How nice of him."

Brendan Nelson is the boy Taylor lost her virginity to, and despite all her big talk, he's the *only* guy she's ever slept with. He's also the only guy to ever break her heart. He left for Penn State last year on a full football scholarship, and as far as Taylor knew, they were still together. When he stopped answering her phone calls and never bothered to tell her he was home for Thanksgiving, it became clear they weren't.

"I know," Riley says. "I can't believe she's over there."

Trevor rolls his eyes. "The guy's a total dick."

I look up at Taylor again just as Brendan slithers a muscle-bound arm around her waist. She wraps her arm around his shoulders, and he leans in for a kiss.

And makes me want to puke.

But the very next second, Brendan Nelson is wheeling through the air, screaming like a little girl. He hits the water and the screaming stops, only to start again when he breaks the surface. From the way he's thrashing around, some of his buddies catch on that he can't swim and dive in after him. They drag him to the rocks, him pulling them under every few feet, with much yelling and swearing.

I crack up as Taylor waves at us, then dives off the "cliff" in a beautiful, arcing swan dive. She swims over and pulls herself out of the water. "What a dick," she says, echoing her brother.

I turn to explain the deal to Luc and see his eyes still locked on the cliff. When I follow his gaze, I notice three guys tucked into the trees at the edge of it, all very inappropriately dressed for swimming, in jeans and black T-shirts. I recognize the one in the middle. He's the crazy-tall red-haired guy from Gallaghers' and Ricco's.

I feel Luc's fingers weave into mine. "I shouldn't have come here," he says low enough that only I hear him.

I turn back to the cliff and they're gone. "It's okay. We can go."

He smooths his fingers over my cheek. "Is Matt here?"

I nod, pretty sure it's true, and then a rock flies through the air and hits Luc in the back of the head. He winces and shoots a look behind him—where, of course, nobody is.

"He's here," he says, disgusted.

I glare into the empty space behind Luc. "Let's go."

He smiles and kisses me softly on the cheek. "You should stay with your friends. I just needed to know you were okay"— he shoots a glance over his shoulder again—"and not alone."

I tug his arm. "Stay."

His eyes dart back to the cliff. "It'd be better if I didn't."

"Fine," I huff. "Be that way."

He laughs and pulls me into his arms. "You have no idea how cute you are when you pout."

I crack a smile, then press harder into him and stick out my bottom lip. "Cute enough to make you stay?"

Still smiling, he glances around. Angelique steps off the

rope swing and strikes a pose. He looks back at me and rolls his eyes. "Have fun and I'll see you later."

He squeezes my hand and heads up the path, and in the shadows of the woods, I catch three dark shapes weaving through the trees behind him. I start to take off up the path after him, but something tugs on my shoulder. Matt.

"He's a big boy, Frannie. He'll be fine," comes his whisper in my ear.

So I watch Luc go, wishing he didn't suck so bad at judo.

MATT

Once I know Frannie's going to stay put, I follow the demons up the path behind Luc. Luc climbs into the Shelby, and when Rhenorian and the Tweedle brothers phase into the Lincoln, so do I.

"So, I've been thinking—"

Before I can finish the thought, three glowing fists are inches from my face.

"Nothing like shooting the messenger," I say, lacing my fingers behind my head and slumping back into the backseat.

Rhenorian's eyes follow Luc's Shelby as he pulls out onto the road and drives by. He lowers his fist and the others follow suit. "What do you want?"

"I was about to ask you the same question."

In a nanosecond, his fist is crackling in my face again. "Don't play games with me, cherub."

I roll my eyes. "We could do this all day," I say, pushing his fist out of my face, "or we can figure out how to help each other."

He's silent for a long second, then says, "First tell me if you did it."

"Did what?"

"Turned him and tagged him."

I snort out a laugh. "I'm assuming you mean the demon."

"Lucifer," he confirms.

"First of all, the fact that he's tagged for Heaven is making me want to hurl—if I had a stomach, that is. And second, I don't have the power to turn a demon mortal."

"Then who does?"

This is tricky. I have a feeling Frannie might be in danger if I tell him the truth, but I can't lie. Even to a demon. "Why do you care? What's it to you that the demon is mortal now?"

His eyes narrow as he sizes me up. "I have orders. I'm supposed to bring him back."

"For trial?" I can't hide the hope in my voice.

He continues to glare at me, but doesn't answer.

I shift in my seat and cross my ankle over my knee. "I think we may be on the same side, strangely enough."

"Meaning . . . ?"

"Meaning, it wouldn't break my heart if the demon disappeared."

A malefic smile curls his lips, turning his face into something significantly more demonic. I've captured his interest.

"He's a demon. Just as stupid as any other demon," I say, gesturing at the moronic pair of bookends.

He growls at me and his eyes flare red, but he doesn't move.

LISA DESROCHERS

"So, how hard can it be to get him to sin? Reverse his tag?" I continue.

The big demon leans against the seat. "I'm listening."

"You need him in demon form to bring him back for trial, right?"

"That'd be preferred." Rhenorian's face pulls into a predatory leer, like a cat eyeing a mouse. "But dragging his mortal soul back to Hell is a close second."

"Fine. So if he could be convinced—" I stop abruptly when I realize I almost gave Frannie's secret away. "I think I know a way to turn him demon again."

Rhenorian's eyes flash red. "How?"

"I'll take care of it. You just be ready. When it's time, you'll need to be quick, before she—" I stop again. "Just be ready. It'll be obvious."

His hand darts out and grabs a fistful of my T-shirt. "I need more than that, cherub. Details."

The Tweedle brother sitting next to me in the backseat tries to grab my arm, and I zap him with a crackle of white lightning. Just enough to back him off.

"No," I say plainly, leaning forward and getting into Rhenorian's face to show him I'm not intimidated.

He cracks a grin, watching Tweedledumb smolder, and when Tweedledumber turns to retaliate with a raised red fist, Rhenorian drops my T-shirt and punches him across the jaw. He turns back to me and grimaces. "So, I'm just supposed to trust you? How stupid do you think I am?"

I can't keep the smirk off my face. "Pretty much as stupid as the rest of your kind."

His fist is hot in my face in a heartbeat. I raise my hands, my face a mask of feigned innocence. "Hey, you asked, and angels can't lie."

His fist glows brighter for a moment; then he lowers it with a scowl.

"Just be ready," I say, then phase back to the quarry with Frannie. All I have to do is convince Luc she's better off without him. He leaves, she gets over him, and voilà, he's either dead or a demon again. Either works for me. And if he turns demon, Rhenorian taking him to Hell will ensure that he doesn't change his mind and come back.

I watch Frannie and Taylor splash each other in the face and almost feel guilty. But the truth is, Luc will inevitably let her down. In his true essence; he's a demon. And who knows how much damage he could do in the meantime.

Better for her it never gets to that point. I'm doing the right thing.

7

✠

Guilty as Sin

LUC

I pull into my parking lot and cut the engine. In my rearview mirror, I watch Rhenorian pull into a parking spot in the corner of the lot. I can't see him through the tinted windows, but as the amber dusk swirls closer to black, I catch the glow of red eyes peering at me from the darkness inside the car.

He's on a mission, just as I was. Failure means dismemberment and the Fiery Pit, because I'm pretty sure no one is going to turn him mortal and tag his soul for Heaven. Which means he isn't going to quit.

I sit, watching him watch me, and wonder how this is going to go. How do I get rid of him? As long as I have this shadow, I need to stay away from Frannie. I was selfish earlier, going to the quarry. I can't put her in danger.

Lili's truck pulls up next to me just as I'm getting out of my car.

"Hey, Luc," Lili says, holding up a flat white box. "I ordered a pizza even though I really can't afford it. I was craving pepperoni. You want to go halves?"

"Sounds good." I hold the door to the stairs for her.

She slips under my arm, and when we get to the second floor, she turns, an embarrassed cringe on her face. "Your apartment okay? Mine's kind of a mess."

"Sure." I take the box from her hand and swing the door wide. I drop the pizza on the kitchen table and head to the cupboard for some plates. "What do you want to drink?"

"Whatever you're having is good."

I slide into my chair with plates and two bottles of water.

"What do I owe you for the pie?" I ask, twisting the top off her water and handing it to her.

She tugs a wedge of pizza out of the box and breaks the trailing strings of cheese with her finger. "Ten. I figured with a large there'd be leftovers, but then I thought maybe, if you hadn't eaten, you might want . . ." She trails off and her eyes flick in my direction. "Some," she finishes.

Her eyes connect with mine, and something raw rolls through me, tugging to my bones. With some effort, I break her gaze and pull a slice from the box. "Thanks."

We eat in silence and I have to fight to keep my focus on the pizza. But despite my best effort, I catch them wandering to Lili, trying to decipher what it was I saw in that glance. Finally, I shake my head. It was nothing. Just my overactive imagination. Rhenorian has me all on edge—that's it.

Bracing myself internally, I allow my eyes to meet hers again. "So, any luck finding a job?"

She shrugs. "Working on it. There were some summer jobs on the board at the community center, but I'm kind of late looking, so most of them are already gone."

"I'm sure something will turn up. I'll keep my ears open." I feel my clenched muscles relax as I answer. It was definitely my imagination. There's nothing out of the ordinary—other than those eerie green eyes.

"So, you're working at the library. What about Frannie? Does she have a job?"

I flick the lid of the pizza box with my finger. "Frannie started at Ricco's right after school got out."

She smirks at me. "Ricco's is a little seedy. You let your girl-friend work there?"

I bark out a laugh and tip my chair onto the back legs. "You don't know Frannie very well. I don't 'let' her do anything. She's the boss."

"Really . . . ? You seem like a take-charge kind of guy." An almost smile barely curves the corners of her mouth.

I tear my eyes away from hers and grab for the table just in time to keep my chair from toppling over backward. Because when she smiled, just for a second, what flashed through my mind . . .

I'm on my feet and across the kitchen in a heartbeat. "So you said ten for the pizza?" My hand trembles as I slide it into my pocket.

"Yeah, thanks."

I breathe deep and turn slowly back to her. "Take the last few pieces back with you," I say. "I already ate my half." I venture a smile, but it feels like guilt is plastered all over my face.

She folds the pizza box closed and lifts it from the table. I head toward the door and open it, handing her the ten as she slips into the hall. She spins back and smiles as she reaches her door. "See ya."

What the hell is wrong with me? I thought I had these human teenage hormones figured out.

I'm still standing in the hall, staring after her, when she disappears into her apartment.

Which is why I don't notice Rhenorian until his voice comes from just over my shoulder. "My, my, Lucifer—all the pretty young things. Philandering is a sin, in case you've forgotten. All this time I've been racking my brain, trying to figure out how to reverse your tag, but you're going to make my job easy."

I turn to find him leaning against the wall next to my door. His smile glints like the edge of a blade.

I breathe deep and clear the last vestiges of fog from my head. "You're just jealous."

He cocks half a smile and pushes away from the wall. "I am, actually." His smile pulls into a grimace. "But at the moment, I have bigger problems."

In a flash, his hand shoots out and grabs the collar of my T-shirt, slamming me against the wall. "Who did it?"

I stare him down. "I don't know."

His eyes flare red heat. He leans in, his nose an inch from mine. "Liar."

"That's what I do. It's in my blood." I twist out of his grasp and back into the door of my apartment. "Why does it matter to you?"

He glares a hot dagger. "Because I need them to undo it so I can bring you back."

"So, then, it probably wouldn't be in my best interest to help you with that."

His roar echoes down the hall as I slam the door in his face.

FRANNIE

The party at the quarry dies, and Riley and Trevor drop Taylor and me off at my house. We run into Maggie and Delanie on the way upstairs to my room.

"Hey, Delanie," Taylor says, catching her elbow. "Do you have Marc's number? That guy from your band?"

She shakes her head. "Reefer might. He does all the organizing."

Taylor plants a fist on her hip and gives Delanie a cynical smirk. "Well, can you get it?"

"Right now?" Delanie asks in a *you've got to be joking* tone.

"C'mon, Delanie." Maggie's hand is on the doorknob and she's staring impatiently up the stairs.

Delanie skirts past Taylor. "I'll tell Ryan to call you." She escapes out the door with Maggie.

I roll my eyes and turn to head up the stairs. "Why don't you just tackle her?"

"I would if it'd get me that damn number," Taylor mutters. She closes the door behind her then picks up my iPod and sticks it onto the speakers. She tosses me a bottle of aloe vera from her bag and sprawls next to me on the bed.

"Put that on my back," she says, pulling her shirt gingerly over her head and exposing glowing red skin. She lies on her stomach and unties her bikini top.

"Jesus, Tay. Did you ever hear of sunscreen?"

She glares up at me. "Are you gonna put that on my back or what?"

I squirt a big glob of it between her shoulder blades and smile when she screeches.

"Shit, that's cold!"

"Sorry," I say, not really meaning it.

"Bitch," she says, totally meaning it.

I rub it around her back, making a point to dig my fingers a little deeper than necessary into the reddest spots. Once I've done sufficient damage, I lean off the bed and wipe my hands on her beach towel, which is in a heap on the floor.

"So, what'd Brendan say, anyway?" I say, pulling myself back onto the bed.

"You should have heard him. Holy shit." She sits up and tosses her shirt onto her towel. She starts to tie her bikini top, but winces and slides it off, throwing it to the floor on top of her shirt. "He's all, like, 'Baby, I missed you so much,' and I'm thinking, Does anybody ever really buy this crap? And then he says, 'You know I love you.' And I couldn't help it, I pushed him off the cliff." Her eyes spark and a grin splits her face. "Did you hear him scream? Oh my god!"

I laugh with the memory. "That *was* pretty pathetic." I grab one of Kate's *Elle* magazines and thumb through it. "Are you up for shopping on Thursday?"

"I'm always up for shopping."

"There's a new girl in Luc's building who's gonna come with us."

She looks at me and winces. "Are you taking in strays again, Fee? Remember what happened with Riley. . . ."

I smile as I cut out a picture of Angelina Jolie's lips—life-sized. No, in the case of her lips, larger than life. "She doesn't know anybody. Oh—and she's going to State too."

"Whatever." Taylor rips the magazine clipping out of my hand and holds it up to her mouth. She gets up and inspects herself in the mirror. "Do you think my lips are too thin?"

I bite mine to keep from laughing and toss the bottle of glue onto the dresser in front of her. "Yeah. Just go ahead and glue those puppies right on."

"Ha, ha. That's a good one." She looks around at my walls, which are covered in magazine clippings we've pasted up over the past year. "You're running out of wall space. You sure you don't want to repaint before you leave?"

"I can't think of anything more depressing than coming home from college and having to start all over."

"I guess. Looks like a few spots up near the ceiling still." She points to the corner over my door.

"Yeah. That'll work."

Her eyes catch mine as I start to pull myself off the bed.

"What was that at Gallaghers' last night? You guys just took off."

"There was a guy that Luc knows from before—where he used to live. It's some kind of feud or something."

Her eyes spark and a smile turns up the corners of her mouth. "Like gangs?"

"Sort of, I guess. But Luc was never really in a gang. Not like *that*, anyway."

Her expression turns wistful, her eyes clouding over a little. "I always knew there was something dangerous about him."

If you only knew. "Taken, Tay."

Her eyes clear and snap back to mine. "Yeah. You bite, you know that?"

"No. Thanks for telling me—again. I missed it the first hundred times you said it."

"You bite."

"Got it."

"So, if that guy is from where Luc used to live, it must not be too far away."

"I guess," I say, not knowing where she's going with this, but sure it's somewhere.

"So, where is it?"

I spread glue on the back of Angelina's lips. "South."

"Like Southie? Really? I thought everyone in South Boston was Irish. No way in hell Luc's Irish."

"No way in hell," I repeat. "I don't think he's from Southie." I pull my chair over to the door and reach up to stick the lips near the ceiling.

Taylor pulls a red Sharpie out of her bag and shoves me off the chair. She climbs up and scribbles *Angelina Blomie* in big loopy letters under the lips, then turns and looks at me with a grin.

I look around at all the clippings on my walls with captions authored by either Riley or Taylor. "Why can't you ever write something that's not about sex?"

She grins at me again as she jumps down from the chair. "What else is there?"

Breaking Benjamin blasts from Taylor's bag on the floor. She pulls her phone from the front pocket and sprawls on the bed. Her eyes glint when she looks at the screen.

"Speaking of sex . . . ," she says with a lascivious grin. She lifts the phone to her ear. "Hey, Reef. You got a number for me?"

8

✠

Heaven on Earth

MATT

It's taken two days to work up the guts to do this. I'm so nervous. And I feel like a total loser. I'd be sure I was going to puke, except I don't have a stomach.

I watch Lili slide out of her truck from the demon's window.

What am I doing?

Frannie nudges my shoulder and shoots me a dubious smile. "So, you ready for your big debut?"

Honestly, I'm *not* sure. But I smile back. "You bet."

Her eyes sparkle as she giggles and pushes me aside. "Hey, Lili! Come on up!" she hollers out the window.

The demon sidles over to the window and looks me up and down. "You're nervous."

"No, I'm not," I say, suddenly sure that, stomach or not, I'm going to puke.

He scowls at me. "You're glowing. Either you're nervous or you swallowed a compact fluorescent. Either way, you need to turn it off."

I realize he's right. My self-awareness isn't what it should be. I tone it down and try to keep a brain cell trained on the glow factor.

I stand by the door, waiting for Lili's knock, determined not to leave here today without officially meeting her.

So, of course, when the knock on the door comes, I totally freak and fade out.

Frannie bursts out laughing. "So much for the debut."

Luc pulls the door open with a smirk, and Lili steps through with a six-pack of beer.

"Hey, Frannie," she says through the stringy brown hair dangling in her face.

"What's the occasion?" Frannie asks, pointing at the beer.

She pulls a beer out of the holder and hands it to Frannie. "Got a job at the KwikMart. Just started today. Pay's not great, but it should be enough for rent and food, which is all I need." A devilish smile turns up the corners of her mouth. "I actually swiped a six-pack of beer." Her smile shifting to a frown, she adds, "Which is highly illegal, considering I'm only eighteen, so I'll probably get fired and then arrested."

She drops the six-pack on the table as if it's suddenly poison. "Should have thought this whole celebration thing through a little better, I guess." She purses her lips thoughtfully as she pulls a beer out and hands it to Luc before opening one for herself. "I don't hear any sirens, so hopefully I'm in the clear.

I'll need to erase the security camera tapes when I get to work tomorrow."

Frannie laughs and I can't stop the smile. This is a side of Lili I wouldn't have expected.

"Sounds like a plan," Luc says.

Lili throws herself into one of Luc's kitchen chairs, tips her head back, and takes a long swig of beer. "Ahh . . . refreshing," she says.

I'm not surprised she needs to be refreshed. She's wearing the same loose warm-up pants and baggy gray sweatshirt she was when she moved in last weekend, even though it's got to be almost ninety degrees outside.

Frannie lowers herself into the other kitchen chair. "So, how're you liking Haden?"

"It's okay, I guess. And it's not too far from the subway, so I won't have to drive into Boston for school."

"The T," Frannie says.

"What?"

Frannie picks at the label of her beer. "The subway. It's called the T here."

"Oh."

"Are you going to keep working after school starts?" Luc asks.

"I have to. I need the money."

"Mmm. That's rough," he says.

She shifts uncomfortably in her chair. "Yeah. And I'm on scholarship, so I have to take a full course load."

Concern creases Frannie's brow. "Isn't there anyone who can help you out?"

"No. I don't have any family," Lili says. A shadow passes over her face.

"None?" Frannie says, surprised.

Lili just shakes her head, and her eyes darken and lower to the floor. Frannie drops her gaze as well.

I can't stand the pain in Lili's eyes. Someone has really hurt her. I ease over to where she slumps in the kitchen chair, face half-hidden behind her hair, and kneel in front of her. I want to touch her so badly. I can't even explain the feeling, except it pulls at something in my core—like some deep aching need. I catch myself before the hand I didn't know I'd raised actually touches her face, and force it back down to my side. Staring into her eyes, I wish that, just this once, I *could* read minds.

Who are you?

Her eyes clear, almost like someone threw a switch, and she turns to Luc. "You know, there was a guy checking out your car in the parking lot when I came in."

Luc springs to the window and looks out into the lot. "Perfect."

"What?" Lili says.

Luc and Frannie exchange a glance.

"Nothing," he says.

Frannie and Lili pull themselves out of the chairs and move to the window.

"I should have told him to get lost. Thought he might be a friend or something," Lili says, peering out.

"Don't have any friends," Luc says.

Frannie elbows him. "Except Matt."

"Matt?" Lili eyes Luc with an inquisitive raise of her eyebrows.

At the sound of my name coming from Lili's lips, I feel a rush of excitement, hot and electric, course through me, but it's mixed with fear. Terror, really. What if she meets me and hates me? I may get only one shot at this.

"Yeah. A friend of Luc's." Frannie cracks a smile, and her eyes scan the room. "He was supposed to show up today. Must have blown us off."

I phase up behind her, fade in a finger, and snap her bra strap. She jumps and kicks her foot in the direction of my shin, finding air.

Luc glares through a smirk and Lili looks uneasy.

"Well, I gotta go. Keep the beer." Her face breaks into a smile, and my breath catches. She's so beautiful.

Frannie picks it up off the table and tries to hand it to her. "Take it."

"I've never seen that beer before in my life, Officer," Lili says, holding up her hands and backing away from the table.

Frannie cracks up. "So, are we still good for shopping tomorrow?"

Lili lowers her lashes. "Yeah."

"Great. Riley and Taylor are in too. I'll stop by your place at noon and we can go get that dresser first."

"Okay," Lili says as Luc follows her to the door.

I make a split second decision. I need to talk to her to get past whatever my obsession is. If I slip into the hall behind her and fade in . . . she'll think I've just shown up.

But when Luc opens the door for Lili and she passes through, her hand reaches up and brushes along his ribs—a caress. She looks up at him with a hint of a smile and bites her lower lip. "So, I'll see you later."

His eyebrows shoot up and he glances back at Frannie, who's putting the beer in the fridge, oblivious. "Yeah, later," he says, and smiles.

Suddenly I'm livid. I can't decide whether to smite him right on the spot, or follow Lili out the door, as planned. I opt for the second, knowing smiting should be done in private, and slide through the door just ahead of her. Completely abandoning my plan, I follow her up the hall to her door and study her face as she twists her key in the locks. That sadness is back in her eyes. She sighs and pushes through her door. I almost follow her, but I stop myself. As much as I want to know what's going on, I can't invade her privacy. It wouldn't be right.

I lean back into the wall, slide to a sitting position on the floor, my head in my hands, and try to get a grip on my whirling emotions.

What's clearly at the forefront is hate. I'm shaking with it. I hate Luc—because of Frannie. She loves him and trusts him. But obviously, that trust is misplaced. Because, just for a second . . . the way Lili looked at him . . .

In a bolt of irony, it strikes me that this is what I've been waiting for. I need Frannie to see the demon for what he is. If he's lusting after every girl in sight, that's a start. But it'd kill Frannie if he messed around with Lili.

And it might kill me too.

Because, as I think of Lili, other emotions swirl to the lead.

Jealousy. And lust. I can't deny it, as much as I'd like to: I want her.

A mirthless chuckle works its way up from my chest. Not sounding too angelic at the moment, am I?

But . . . Lili. *God, Lili.* If I could just talk to her . . . touch her . . .

I need to know what's going on between them.

I stand and pace the hall for a long time, working to get my jumbled emotions under control. Finally, I slip through Luc's wall.

But the first thing that catches my eye—a flash of skin in the tangled sheets—feels like a punch to my gut. I push back into the hall and sit with my head in my hands again, forcing myself not to storm in there and pull him off her. It's too late. I got distracted and forgot where the *real* danger was.

Every time they've gotten too close, I've been able to run interference. But I knew I wouldn't be able to do that forever.

How many more ways can I screw up my job because of my obsession over Lili?

FRANNIE

Most of our clothes are on the floor and we move together on Luc's big black bed to the rhythm of music playing softly from the stereo. A tiny part of me wishes he could still shift his essence into me the way he used to when he was a demon. My head swims at the memory of how it felt to have him that close. There's something surreal about being possessed by the essence of the boy you're crazy in love with—even if he is a demon.

But feeling his skin against mine, being this close—closer than I've ever been to another human being—there's something else I want. Something he couldn't give me when he was a demon, because it would tag me for Hell. But now he's human, and tagged for Heaven. I want him closer, and there's nothing stopping us.

When Taylor flung that condom at me after Luc first showed up, she did it to embarrass me. I'm sure she never thought I'd use it. But now, as I think about that condom in my bag, my stomach flutters.

Luc kisses my ear and whispers, "Are you okay?"

I smile up at him. "Better."

"You looked a million miles away."

"Never. I'm right here." I squeeze him tighter. "I love you."

One corner of his perfect mouth curves up. "I know."

He shifts over me on his elbows and leans in for a kiss when it hits me, and I push him back. "Say it."

"What?"

"You know."

He lifts an eyebrow. "I don't."

"You've never said you love me."

He scowls down at me. "Don't be absurd."

Wrong answer.

I feel heat creep up my neck and into my face as embarrassment and anger vie for control. I pull back harder, pressing into the pillows to make room between us. "Why won't you say it?"

"Frannie, they're just words."

The bottom drops out of my stomach as the truth hits me like a slap across the face. How could I be so stupid? I shove him off me and sit. "You know what? Just forget it," I say, yanking on my jeans.

"Frannie—"

I hold up my hand and he stops. My shirt is on and I'm halfway to the door before he follows me. He tries to slow me with a hand on my shoulder, and I think about flipping him by it, but I need to get out of here before I start crying. I jerk away and jog for the door. One of my flip-flops flies off, but I don't care. I reach the door just ahead of him, but all the goddamn deadbolts take too long and he catches me.

"Frannie, listen to me." His hands are planted on the door, one on either side of my head, and I can feel his hot breath in my ear.

A sob catches in my throat just before it escapes. "I . . . it's okay," I say, fumbling with the locks. "But I gotta get to work."

He presses into me from behind and snakes his arms around my waist. I hate that my heart sputters at the feel of him there. And I hate even more that I can't stop the tears that leak over my lashes.

"I've never said it," he says, his voice low in my ear, "because it's not enough . . . those words."

I flip the last deadbolt and reach for the door handle before I process what he said. I stop and press my forehead into the door, trying to think, to breathe.

He spins me, and his hand cups my face as he gazes down into my eyes. "God, I love you." His eyes glisten. "I love you with everything that I am."

His voice breaks on the last word and he closes his eyes and draws a deep breath. His lips press into a tight line before he turns away from me. He walks to the kitchen table, staggering on the last step, and leans his hands on the table for support. My heart pounds, trying to escape my chest, as he hangs his head between his shoulders and just stands there.

"I love you so much, it hurts," he finally says, so low, I can barely hear him.

I'm still leaning against the door, totally frozen in place. I try to open my mouth to say something, but nothing wants to function. My brain can't find words, and even if it could, my mouth wouldn't form them.

He pushes off the table, drags the back of his hand across his face, and turns slowly toward me, his features pulled tight as he struggles for control. He tips his head back, closing his eyes, and draws a shaky breath.

"After seven thousand years, I thought I knew all there was to know." He hesitates, then lowers his gaze and stares at me with tortured eyes for several heartbeats. "I didn't know this was possible." He brings a fist to his heart and holds it there. "I never imagined needing anything . . . anyone . . . so thoroughly. I . . ." He trails off and drops his head once more.

Before I know they've done it, my legs have me across the room and in his arms. I lay my cheek on his chest and listen to his heartbeat, as fast as mine, as he folds me into his embrace.

"You're my life, Frannie," he whispers into my hair. "God, you're *everything*." He lifts me off the ground and kisses me, and the next thing I know, my clothes are off and we're back on the bed. He kisses me deeper, and even though I know it's not possible anymore, I can almost feel his soul swirling with mine. And in his soul, I can feel it: love so intense that it makes me cry again.

He pulls back and wipes my tears away with trembling fingers, the question clear in his eyes. I answer with a kiss, sending him all the love I have. We sink into the sheets, into each other, and there's nothing else. Just him and me. Our souls dance and I let Luc take me to Heaven.

9

For Heaven's Sake.

FRANNIE

My face burns and my belly tingles when I think about yesterday. I walk past Luc's door, and it's almost impossible to make myself keep going to Lili's. But the truth is, if I stop at Luc's, I'll never make it to Lili's.

"Hey, Frannie," she says as she opens the door. She's melting in her usual gray sweats, beads of sweat across her upper lip and plastering her dark hair to her forehead.

"You ready to get that dresser?" I ask.

She shrugs. "Guess so." She steps into the hall and locks up.

I throw a rueful glance at Luc's door on my way by.

Lili pulls her truck into my driveway, past the house, to the detached garage out back. I jump out of the truck and walk past the van in the driveway, choking on the plume of dust wafting out the open garage door. I hold my breath and venture in. Dad's in the back corner, sweeping it out.

"Hey, Dad," I say to his back, pulling my T-shirt over my nose and mouth.

He props the broom in the corner and turns. "Frannie. Come to give your old man a hand?" Sweat carves rivulets through the brown film on his face, and when he smiles, his teeth are shockingly white against the mud of his skin.

"Not really," I say, and shrug. "You know that old dresser?"

He turns and looks in the corner, where the sheet-draped dresser is buried under a stack of junk.

"Matt's old dresser? Yeah."

"Can I give it to Lili?"

"Who?"

"Dad, this is Lili. She just moved into Luc's building."

He turns to Lili with a smile as she steps up behind me. "Sure. If you have a need for it." He holds out his hand.

I turn to Lili, who looks even more pale than usual. Her eyes widen for an instant, and she hesitates before taking his hand. "Hi."

When their hands connect, Dad pauses midshake, then holds her hand for a second longer. "There's something familiar about you. Is your family from around here?"

She shakes her head, looking suddenly sad.

"Oh. Where are you from?"

Lili can't hold his gaze, and her eyes drop to her shuffling feet. "Lots of places. I move around a lot."

Dad eyes her for a second longer. "I could swear we've met before. St. Catherine's, maybe?"

She looks at me.

"The Catholic church," I say, and she shakes her head again.

Dad rubs his forehead, grinding brown mud into his eyebrows and leaving a white smudge on the bridge of his nose. "Hmm . . . I'll figure it out." He smiles. "Well, I'll help you girls load up that dresser."

When we get back, the dresser strapped into the back of Lili's truck, I see Luc's Shelby parked in the lot and I can't stop the smile from spreading across my face. My smile pulls into a grin when Matt appears at my window.

MATT

I watch them pull in, and fight to stay visible. When I walk up to Lili's truck and lean in the passenger window, Frannie's eyes widen and her face bursts into a smile.

"Matt! Hi."

"Hey, Frannie. Is Luc around?" I realize I sound like an idiot. Of course she doesn't know if he's here. She just showed up.

And I'm sure I look like an idiot too, because I can't stop my eyes from flicking past Frannie to Lili every few seconds.

Frannie tries to keep a straight face, but she can't hide the laughter in her voice. "Um . . . well . . . his car's here, so, I guess."

"Yeah. Okay." Don't be a dork. Think. "So . . . are you guys bringing this up?" I ask, waving my arm toward my old dresser in the bed of Lili's truck.

"Yep. You feel like helping?" Frannie says.

"Sure."

Lili walks around and drops the tailgate. I hop in, surprised at how stiff I feel, like my whole body is seizing up—every muscle taut.

"So, I'm Matt," I say, shooting a glare at Frannie.

"Hi. Lili." She doesn't look at me as she answers. "So, you're a friend of Luc's?"

"Yep." I untie the ropes from around the dresser and give it a shove toward the tailgate.

And I can't think of anything else to say.

Frannie pulls the top half of the dresser out of the bed. I hop down and get the other end.

"I'm not totally lame," Lili says, venturing a small smile. "You're giving it to me free. At least let me carry the damn thing."

Frannie slides over. "Take the other corner."

We make our way up the walk and through the door, Frannie and Lili shuffling up the walk backward, and work our way slowly up the stairs. But Frannie trips stepping up onto the landing at the top of the stairs and drops her side of the dresser. Lili tries to compensate, but it's too late. The dresser shifts, pushing me, and I fly backward down the flight of stairs. I feel the back of my head crack sharply off the corner of a stair on the way down, and my arm winds up twisted underneath me where I land at the bottom.

Lili drags the dresser onto the landing. "Unholy Hell!"

Frannie shoots a glance at Lili, then picks herself up and runs down the stairs. "Matt, are you okay?"

I lie here at the bottom of the stairs, not sure how to play this. I should be hurt, but, of course, I'm not. "Um . . . yeah, I think so." Maybe something small. A sprained elbow? A bump on the head? I sit up and wince, still not sure what should hurt.

Lili comes down the stairs. "You hit your head really hard. You should lie still."

My head, then. I groan a little for effect and rub the back of my head, pretending to flinch. "No. I think it's okay."

"You're sure? What about your neck?"

I smile up at her. "Neck's fine."

"Can you get up?" Frannie says, holding her hand out to me.

"Yeah." I reach for her hand and use it to pull myself up. "Thanks."

Lili puts her hand on my back to help me up. At her touch, an electric shock blasts through me, making me groan. With their help, I push slowly to my feet.

"No problem," Frannie says, releasing my hand.

Lili turns and heads back up the stairs, and Frannie gives me the eye. I shrug at her.

"We'll get this," Lili says to me when we reach the top of the stairs. I move gingerly down the hall, rubbing the back of my head as they carry the dresser to Lili's apartment.

LUC

Frannie, Lili, and Matt burst through my door, Frannie holding her key up for me to see. "Do you have any ice?"

"Yeah. What's up?"

She's fighting the amused smile that pulls at her lips. "Matt hit his head."

Matt shrugs and cracks a dubious smile when I turn to look at him. I roll my eyes. This kid is just a tragic comedy of errors.

I head to the kitchen and crack an ice tray into a Baggie, then hand it to Matt, who slides into my kitchen chair and can't rip his eyes away from Lili long enough to thank me.

"You're welcome," I mutter.

He reaches around and presses the bag to the back of his head. "Oh, yeah. Thanks."

Lili walks up behind him. "I'll hold that for you."

A distinctly dopey expression crosses Matt's face as he hands her the bag.

"So, what happened?" I scrutinize Matt.

He grins, trying to roll his eyes to the back of his head to see Lili. "Frannie tried to kill me. Death by dresser."

"Sorry," Frannie says, settling into the other chair.

I look back at Matt. Something is definitely off. "But you're okay?"

"Yeah, just a bump on the head."

Lili's free hand drops to Matt's shoulder and rubs. "It's gonna be sore. If your vision gets blurry or you feel dizzy, you need to go to the hospital."

Matt keeps grinning this big, stupid grin and looks a little spacey. Maybe he really does have a concussion.

"Nope, don't need a doctor." He reaches up and lays his hand on top of Lili's on his shoulder. "What you're doing is working."

It hits me like a lightning bolt. Unholy Hell. Matt's lusting on Lili. Why didn't Gabriel believe me when I told him this was a bad idea?

Lili blushes and backs away from Matt. "Are we still going shopping?" she asks Frannie.

"Absolutely!" Frannie says.

Lili moves toward the door. "I'll go get my money and stuff. Give me, like, fifteen minutes?"

"No problem. Take your time," Frannie says as Lili slips through the door.

When she's gone, I yank Matt out of the chair by the front of his shirt. "What the Hell are you doing?"

Frannie jumps out of her chair so fast, it flips over backward. "Luc—"

"You need to cut the crap and focus," I say, my face an inch from Matt's.

"You need to get the Hell out of my face," he spits back.

"What are you thinking? You can't start a relationship with a mortal."

He plants his hand in my chest and shoves. "I'm not starting a relationship with anyone. I was moving a dresser."

"If you can't stay focused on your job, we're better off without you."

"You really *are* as stupid as you look. If it's between you and me, who do you really think will keep Frannie safer?"

I step right back up into his face. "That should be a no-brainer, but with you distracted, I'm not so sure."

MATT

"I'm not distracted."

I can't believe this guy. All his big grandstanding is just jealousy. With me visible, he's got competition for Lili's attention, and he doesn't like it. What makes it worse is that Frannie can't see it for what it is. She thinks he's being all noble—protecting her. All he's protecting is his ego.

Frannie looks between us, concern creasing her brow. "Luc, I don't think Matt would really try to start something with Lili." Her quizzical gaze lands on me and I look away.

"If he's smart. But at the moment, I'd say his IQ is up for debate," Luc says.

Frannie comes up beside me. "Be serious."

"I'm perfectly serious, Frannie. If he can't stay focused, he's useless to you."

As I listen to them argue, I feel frustration and anger build inside me like an electrical storm. I'm at critical mass, about to explode.

I step up and shove him, daring him to strike back. "You're such a hypocrite, not to mention a jerk." I shove him harder and get what I want when he grabs the collar of my T-shirt and shoves me hard into the wall. I feel my power crackle to life, ready to blast him into oblivion, but Frannie pulls Luc off me, unfortunately, and stands between us.

"Cut the shit, you guys!"

I glare at Luc over the top of Frannie's head. "I'm not starting anything with Lili, but if I was, what's it to you? Why is an angel hooking up with a mortal so different from a demon hooking up with a mortal?"

He sweeps Frannie aside like so much trash and leans into me, his nose nearly touching mine, his jaw clenched. "Because your purpose is to protect your sister, and you can't do that without wings."

Sparks crackle over the surface of my skin. I'm going to kill him if I don't get the Hell out of here. "You know what? I'm done here." Before anyone can respond, I phase out into the hall—where I sit with my back against the wall across from Lili's door, invisible, fighting the urge to phase into her apartment.

But the smell of brimstone pulls me from my thoughts. I bound to my feet, still invisible.

"So, I'm waiting, cherub. Question is: What am I waiting for?" Rhenorian stands next to me, a scowl darkening his already dark face.

"I'm working on it," I snap.

"We're working on a timetable here. We don't have the rest of the millennium."

I lean back against the wall. "Things aren't as simple as I'd hoped," I say, thinking about what excuse I'd have to see Lili without Luc around. None. "If you have a better idea, go for it."

He glares at me, making it clear that he's got nothing.

"How hard can this be? Just take him," I say. Then I realize that's it. I push to my feet and look at him. "You should just kidnap him."

I picture Lili and me together, searching for Luc, getting to know each other, bonding. I could comfort her . . . kiss her tears away.

"And then what?" Rhenorian's voice pulls me from the fantasy.

I bang my head hard into the wall, then glare at him. "You're a demon. Don't tell me you can't think of *some* way to reverse his tag."

He glares back and phases in a puff of sulfur just as Lili's door opens and she steps out.

10

Speak No Evil

LUC

The whole deal with Matt and Lili isn't sitting right. Because the truth is, I've had an uneasy feeling about Lili for a while. Not anything I can put a finger on, but there's something not right about her.

Or maybe it's me. Maybe I'm being unfair. Because there have been a few times that I've caught myself fantasizing . . . about her.

I told myself it was these Hell-forsaken teenage hormones. But it felt like more.

I watch Frannie empty Matt's ice bag into the sink and I know there's nothing else I could ever want. But I have to admit, if only to myself, that I felt the cold edge of jealousy cut through me when I realized Matt was lusting on Lili.

Frannie shivers when I step up behind her and kiss the back of her neck while running a finger down her arm.

"You don't think Matt was acting a little . . . strange with Lili?"

She turns her head to look at me. "I don't know. Maybe. But even if he likes her, I don't think he's really going to *do* anything about it."

"I'm not so sure. But even if he's just ogling her, it's still a distraction."

She turns and presses against me, wrapping me in her arms and making me completely lose my train of thought. "That's why I have you."

"Hmm . . . ," I say, trying to remember where I was going with this. "But I've got my own shadow to worry about." Rhenorian is out there, and he's got two choices: Figure out how to get me back to Hell, or burn in the Fiery Pit for all eternity.

Frannie stretches up and kisses my nose. "Would he leave if I used my Sway . . . convinced him he didn't want you?"

I can't stop the grin. "You'd be willing to compromise your moral standards for me?"

She shoves me away as her brow creases and her mouth presses into a tight line. "Shut up or I'll change my mind. Do you want me to try or not?"

I pull her back toward me. "Maybe," I say into her hair, "but I'm hoping to find out from him what's going on. Since he's figured out I'm human, he seems to be hanging back and watching—more curious than anything."

"But you said he can't take you to Hell, right? You're tagged for Heaven."

"For now."

She squeezes me tighter. "Forever."

"That remains to be seen. Point is, he doesn't seem to be *doing* anything. He's made no effort to reverse my tag." My stomach aches with a guilty pang, thinking about what Rhenorian said: *all the pretty young things*. I push his voice out of my head. "It's creepy. He's just watching."

"Maybe I'm wrong, but it seems like *watching* is better than *doing*." She cracks a wicked smile and her hand glides down my stomach and under my T-shirt. "At least as far as Hell is concerned."

I shudder at her touch. "It's just so unlike him. He's a creature of wrath. For him to hold his temper—just watch—it's completely out of character. It's making me nervous."

She loops her arms around my neck, pulling me down to meet her in a kiss. "So, what do I have to do to make you unnervous?" she says, smiling into my lips.

I grin back. "This is good."

But just then, there's a knock at the door.

"That's Lili. Shopping time."

"I'd tell you to take Matt, but if he's drooling over Lili the whole time, I'm not sure you'd be any safer. Maybe I should go with you." My voice is sour. I can't help it. This has me really worried.

She just stares at me.

I arch an eyebrow. "I like shopping."

"Yeah, I can so totally see you and your demon shadow browsing the sale rack at Victoria's Secret."

I think about that for a second and a smile breaks across my face. "So can I."

She shakes her head as she moves to the door, tying her hair back in a knot. "No. Girls only. Except Matt, I guess, 'cause I can't really do anything about him."

She pulls the door open. "Hey, Lili."

"Hey. You ready?" Lili says, glancing from Frannie to me.

"Yeah," Frannie says. "We'll pick up Riley and Taylor on our way to the mall."

Lili lowers her head, and her hair falls in her face. "Okay."

Frannie gives me a kiss on the cheek. "See you in a while."

I smile, imagining what she might find on that sale rack at Victoria's Secret. "I'll be waiting with bated breath."

FRANNIE

We pull into Taylor's driveway and she comes bouncing down the stairs. Riley and Trevor lag behind, hands tucked into each other's back pockets.

Taylor skips up to the passenger door before realizing there's someone already in that seat. "Oh. Hey. You're Lili?"

Lili slides out of the car and pulls the back of the seat forward. She starts to get in back.

"No." I say, "Lili's shotgun."

Taylor shoots me a glare and I glare right back. She pushes past Lili and into the backseat.

Riley and Trevor finally make it to the car. Once they rip their eyes away from each other, I make the intros and Riley slides into the back with Taylor. Trevor stands in the driveway, looking like a lost puppy as I pull out.

LISA DESROCHERS

"So, what's with the sweats?" Taylor sneers from the backseat.

"Taylor!" I say, and glance at Lili.

"It's okay," she says, and shrugs. But she doesn't turn to look at Taylor. "They're three bucks at Walmart."

I can see some semi-vicious comeback perched on Taylor's lips, but Riley smacks her in the arm and does her best Taylor glare.

"Lili," Riley says, touching Lili's shoulder from behind her. "Frannie says you're going to State."

Lili turns in her seat, but doesn't really look at Riley. "Yeah, that's the plan."

"What are you studying? Fashion design?" Taylor smirks.

I turn and glare at her. "You know what, Tay? Shut the hell up."

"Um . . . Frannie," Riley says. "Road . . . driving . . ." She points a shaky finger forward.

Lili grips the seat next to me, staring out the windshield with wide eyes as I weave through traffic. Taylor and Riley chitchat in the backseat, but I hear Riley's anxious voice rise every time I change lanes. And Taylor keeps talking about muumuus and stuff on sale at Walmart. I should have known it was too much to hope that she would behave.

We score a decent parking spot near the food court and stroll into the mall.

"Aeropostale?" I say, 'cause they always have good sales.

"Sounds good." Riley starts off in that direction and we all follow.

We browse the sale rack, and Lili comes away with three

132

printed tees, a couple of tank tops, and a really cute pair of shorts for thirty-four bucks. I'm a little disappointed I didn't get to see her try them on. I'm still curious about what lurks under that baggy sweatshirt.

Next, we head for Victoria's Secret. It's their semiannual bra sale, so I pick up a new red lace one and a few others. My best find is this short, sapphire blue silk nightshirt, on sale for fifteen bucks, that I'm sure Luc will love.

Lili looks through the D bins and finds two cute ones she can afford. So not heavy, stacked.

We swing into Macy's and hit all the perfume counters. Riley and Taylor spray each other with random scents while Lili wanders to the JLo counter and tries a citrus-vanilla one—Glow.

"That's amazing on you," I tell her, 'cause it is. "You should totally get that."

She cringes a little. "How much is it?"

I look at the counter. "Oh . . . like thirty bucks. Ouch."

Her face scrunches. "I can't." She puts it down and starts to walk away, but then turns back, sniffing her wrist again. "It is pretty fabulous, isn't it?"

I smile at her, glad to see her come out of her shell a little. "It is."

She pulls a wad of small bills from her pocket and smiles back. "Who needs to eat this week?"

Ten minutes later, we all walk away from the fragrance counter smelling like a combination fruit bowl and florist.

"Food court?" I say.

"Totally," Taylor says, because that's where the high school guys all hang out during the day.

I laugh when we get there and look over at the tables. Trevor and Jackson Harris are there with the rest of their crew. They already have a mound of french fries and burgers in front of them. I'm convinced teenage boys can never be more than thirty feet from food or they'll shrivel up and die.

Riley and Trevor make eyes at each other, but Riley displays amazing restraint and stays with us as we head to the Panda Express counter. We grab some stuff to share, and Lili looks a little embarrassed when I tell her it's my treat.

"Hey, I owe you for all that beer," I say.

She sorta smiles, but not really, as we head to the tables. And she doesn't eat much.

Finally, when we've picked at the food as much as we're going to, I roll up all the plates and head for the trash. Just as I'm coming back to the table, Taylor's eyes spark.

"Ooh . . . there's one for you, Lili," she says, pointing full on at a guy skulking by with dirty jeans and a stained gray sweatshirt. He looks at us and trips over his own feet. His brown hair is long and in his face, so it almost hides how red he turns. And I hate to say it, but with that sweatshirt and hair, he does kinda look like Lili's male counterpart. He hurries past and disappears into the throng of summer shoppers.

I glare at Taylor.

But just then, over the piped-in Muzak, I hear a titter of laughter from the other side of a short partition between the tables and the water fountain. It makes all the hair on the back of my neck stand on end. Because I know that laugh. I turn to see Angelique Preston and her posse just coming out of the Abercrombie.

Angelique looks up and sees us. Instantly, her nose wrinkles. She walks within earshot of our table. "Do you guys smell that? Eew. Someone forgot to take out the trash." She glares at me for a second; then her gaze shifts to Lili. "So nice of you to feed the homeless, Cavanaugh."

I shift closer to Lili and when I glance over, I'm shocked to see Riley and Taylor both shift closer as well.

Taylor steps in front of Lili and looks daggers at Angelique. "Fuck off."

Angelique smirks and sashays off toward the Hollister, her minions trailing behind.

And for the rest of the day, Taylor and Lili are attached at the hip. Go figure.

MATT

Taylor was living dangerously for a while, but she seems to have come around. I was right on the edge of putting duck sauce down the front of her shirt until Angelique showed up.

But I have to say, staying out of the changing rooms while Lili was trying things on—especially at Victoria's Secret— took all the angelic restraint I could muster.

The girls make their purchases and finally head back to the car. Frannie drops Taylor and Riley off, and when she rolls into the parking lot at Lili's apartment building, top down and hair flying, I just happen to be there.

"Ladies," I say with my biggest smile as they step out of Frannie's car.

"Hey, Matt," Frannie says.

Lili turns to retrieve her shopping bags from the trunk.

"How'd you do?" I say, gesturing to her stuff.

"Pretty good, I guess. Frannie knows where all the good sales are." She ventures a small smile.

"Cool. You guys heading up?" I shrug a shoulder toward the building.

"Yeah," she says.

I reach for her bags. "I can carry those for you."

Frannie rolls her eyes behind Lili, but Lili clutches her bags tighter. "I think I can manage, thanks."

I hold my hands up in the air. No harm, no foul. "Just offering . . ."

I follow Frannie and Lili into the building, and Lili turns to me at the bottom of the stairs. "Watch your step," she says with a smile. Her eyes spark as they connect with mine, and a hot electric zing shoots through me.

I rub the back of my head. "Yeah." It's all I can think to say. I'm such a moron.

Frannie uses her key in Luc's door, and just as she twists the last lock, there's a crash from inside the apartment. The door swings open and Rhenorian's head jerks up from where Tweedledumb and Tweedledumber have Luc pinned against the wall. He lowers his glowing fist, and a wave of panic surges through me as I wonder how much Lili saw.

Lili. *Crap.*

She's going to expect me to do something to help my "friend."

Rhenorian turns and gives Luc a crack across the left cheek

with his fist—the old-fashioned approach. Then the Tweedle brothers pull him off the wall.

"No!" Frannie rushes toward Luc, but I hold her back and glance at Lili. She's just staring at the spectacle. This could be my big chance to impress her.

So now I've got to save the demon.

Crap.

I step into the room. "Let him go."

Rhenorian smirks at me. "Yeah, right." I see his eyes flick to Lili, and a grin splits his face. "You gonna make me?"

In a fair fight in our human forms, I'm pretty much toast. Which means I can't fight fair. I cross the room and catch Luc's eye. He nods.

At the same instant Luc twists out of the Tweedle brothers' grasp and throws Tweedledumb into the wall, I strike out with an electric punch to Rhenorian's jaw. I hope Lili doesn't notice the hint of ozone it leaves behind. Rhenorian reels back from the punch and glares at me. "For the sin of Satan, cherub, figure out which side you're on."

I shoot a glance at Luc, but he's too busy wrestling Tweedledumb to have heard.

Rhenorian grabs Tweedledumber by the scruff of his neck and stalks toward the door. "It was a stupid plan anyway," he grumbles, leering at me as he passes. Luc releases Tweedledumb, and he follows behind, throwing a glare over his shoulder at me.

Lili stands just inside the door, looking shocked and confused. Frannie slams the door behind the demons and runs to Luc.

"Oh my god! Are you okay?" My sister reaches up and touches the purplish bruise rising on Luc's cheek.

"I'm fine."

Lili trembles as she stares at Luc with wide, frightened eyes. "Who was that?"

"Someone I used to do business with," Luc says, knowing how it will sound, I'm sure.

Understanding dawns on Lili's face. "Dealers."

"In a manner of speaking," Luc answers. Then he turns to me. "Thanks."

I look away, hating the guilty pang. "Yeah, whatever."

Frannie wraps herself around Luc, pulling his face down to hers and kissing the welt. "How did they get in?"

"They knocked. I answered." He smiles a cynical smile down at her.

"Oh, God," she says. "I'll get you some ice." She looks at him a moment longer, raising her hand to touch his face again, then goes to the kitchen.

Lili moves to the door. "I should probably go. . . ." She reaches for the door handle, but hesitates.

I walk over and brush her hand away. "Let me check it out." I crack open the door and peer out into the hall. It's empty. I turn back to Lili. "They're gone."

She glances to Frannie and Luc. "So, if you guys are okay, I'll see you later, I guess."

"Let me walk you to your apartment," I say, and realize I sound a little too eager, so I add, "I think they're gone, but . . . just to be sure."

"Okay," she says.

We step through the door into the hall, and a second later, deadbolts are clicking into place behind us.

She turns and walks the few steps to her door, fumbling for her key. "Okay, well . . . I guess I'll see you around . . ."

"Matt," I say, finishing the sentence she started, even though she didn't imply she wanted me to.

She looks up at me. "What?"

"I wasn't sure if you remembered my name. Matt. My name is Matt." Ugh, I'm an idiot.

She turns the locks and pushes through the door. "Okay. So I'll see you later . . . Matt." Her eyes flick to mine, sending a zing down my spine, and an almost-smile curls her lips. "Be careful," she says, glancing down the hall toward the stairs.

She slips through the door. And I'm alone.

Again.

11

✠

What the Hell?

FRANNIE

Luc is moving books at the library tonight, so he made me promise to stay home. The Red Sox are losing so totally to the Yankees that the game's becoming painful to watch, and Dad's expletives are getting more colorful than usual. He pushes down the leg rest of his recliner and leans forward, elbows on knees. He focuses on the TV as if he thinks he can make his team win through sheer force of will. I pull myself off the floor and start heading for the stairs.

"You giving up on the boys?" he says.

"Me? Never!" I reply in mock outrage.

He smiles, but then his face becomes serious. "It's nice to have you home in the evening for a change."

Mom looks up from her crossword. "You should spend more

time at home, honey. This is it. In another few months, we won't have you anymore."

I lean against the wall at the base of the stairs, my arms folded over my chest. "So, does this mean you're ready to stop treating Luc like some—"

Mom drops the newspaper in her lap. "We've never treated him with anything but respect."

"Be serious, Mom. You don't treat him like Chase. He can never come up to my room."

"Well . . . he . . . I'm . . ."

"What she's trying to say," Dad interjects, looking at Mom with a raised eyebrow and an amused smile, "is that, so far, he has demonstrated he's a responsible young man, and we're willing to give him the benefit of the doubt."

I mentally pick myself up off the floor. "Really. So he can, like, hang out in my room?"

Mom glares at Dad. "With the door open."

I feel the ridiculous grin pull at my lips, and it's useless to try to stop it. "Yeah, okay." I start to turn from the family room when something occurs to me. I wait for the pang in my heart to pass before I turn back. "How come I never had to keep the door open when Gabe was here?"

They look at each other and then at me. "Well . . . Gabe's just an angel," Mom says.

I jump a little. I've got no comeback for that. He *is* an angel. *My angel.* And Luc quite definitely isn't. As I turn for the stairs, I feel the empty ache in my heart—the one I've been able to stave off only by keeping my mind on things other than Gabe and how much I miss him. I force myself to think of something else—anything else. I start to tick off my work schedule in my head as I climb the stairs, but I'm only up to Saturday when I reach the top and bump into Grace coming out of the bathroom.

She pulls the towel off her head, letting her wet hair fall around her shoulders and drip down her back. "You're home."

I glare at her. "Not by choice. Luc's at the library."

She just looks at me in her creepy, Grace-like way, like those pale blue eyes can see through me somehow. But as I start to brush past her, she says, "He's different."

I spin back to her, irritated. "Who?"

"Luc. He's changed."

I stare at her for a minute, not sure what to say, and suddenly I wonder just how much Grace really *does* see.

I nod. "He has."

I turn and head up the hall, but just before I reach my room, she says, "How? Did you—? She trails off, her voice tentative.

When I turn back to her, her eyes are intense. There's no way she could know exactly how much Luc has changed, and there's no way she could know that I did it. But there's something in her gaze that makes me wonder. "Guess he's not as evil as you thought."

As I push through my door, I hear her say, "But he was," more to herself than to me.

I pick up my old copy of Stephen King's *The Stand* off my desk and lie on my bed, trying to get excited about it. But I can't stop wondering about Grace. How much does she know? I shake the conversation out of my head, pick up my phone, and text Taylor: COME W/ME 2 THE COVE 2NITE.

A minute later, my phone buzzes. NOT UP 4 THE COVE, her message reads.

Whaaa? Taylor's always up for the Cove. It gets kinda touristy, but the arcade is the nighttime hangout for the guys from school when there's no party at the Gallaghers'. She ogles the boys while I break my own record on the racetrack simulator.

Y NOT? I text back.

I wait.

And wait.

Just when I'm about to hit my speed dial to call her, my phone buzzes. GOING OUT W/ LILI, reads the text on my screen.

The jealous burn surprises me. This is what I wanted—Lili to make friends. I hit the Call button on my phone, and Taylor picks up on the first ring.

"Okay, I'll do that instead. Where are we going?"

"Sorry," she says, and I feel myself getting really irritated. "We're going to a party Marc invited me to. Don't think it's your thing, Fee."

I love parties. "Since when isn't a party my thing?"

"Listen, Fee . . . it's just that, for some unknown reason, you've become this stud magnet. I didn't miss Marc checking you out at Gallaghers' the other night, and I really don't want the competition tonight."

"You're joking, right?"

"Um . . . no."

"You can't be serious. You think I'm gonna steal guys from you?"

"Not on purpose, I guess, but . . . yeah."

"Fine," I say, and slam down the phone before disconnecting.

"Well, that was mature," I say to myself. "What the hell is wrong with me?"

But I know what's wrong with me. I don't really have any close friends, by design. Taylor's the safest person I could find to be friends with. She never asks me to give too much, and in return, I never take too much. So where all this needy clinging is coming from, I don't know. But it hurts a little that Lili is taking away what we've had for nine years. And it also scares me a little that I didn't realize till just now how much I was fooling myself that I didn't "need" anyone.

MATT

I hear her on the stairs as I wait in the hall, and my head starts to spin. I look down at my human form as I lean against the wall and try to look all casual. I should be doing something, not just standing here, looking like a stalker. She reaches the top of the stairs and I panic for a second, trying to figure out what that something should be. I slide down the wall and sit with my back against it. An old copy of Tolstoy's *War and Peace* materializes in my hand, and black-rimmed glasses materialize on my face. Going for the intellectual look. Can't hurt for her to think I'm smart.

I know Gabriel would be all over me for not staying with Frannie, but she's at the house behind Dad's field. She's safe there. No demon can get past that field.

So I'm here. I can't help it. I need to know her.

Lili rounds the corner from the stairwell, thumbing through

her junk mail, and doesn't see me until she trips over my legs. She swears and looks down to see what she's tripped over. When she sees me, she backs away a few steps, eyes wide.

I pull myself to my feet. "Oh, I'm really sorry," I say, shrugging and holding up my book.

Her eyes narrow as she sidles past me, keeping to the far wall. She backs a few steps toward her door. "What are you doing sitting in the hall?"

"Just waiting for Luc." I gesture toward his door. "I'm really sorry. I didn't mean to scare you . . . or try to kill you," I add with a smile.

That smile seems to do it, because she lowers her shoulders, and her defensive stance softens. "So you're waiting for Luc?"

"Yeah. I knocked, but no one answered."

Her brows press together. "He said something about working late, I think."

"Oh. Thanks. I guess I'll wait awhile."

She turns back to her door without responding, but I swear I see the smallest of smiles curl her lips before she slides the key into the lock. My mood sinks when she pushes the door open and disappears through it. I hear a series of latches and deadbolts click into place as I stare after her.

I wait, hoping she'll reemerge, and I'm just about to phase back to the house when I hear the deadbolts and latches being undone again. The door cracks open and her head pokes through.

"So . . . you can wait in here if you want."

"Thanks."

I walk over and she just stares at me for a long, awkward

minute. I'm not sure what I should say. But then she pulls the door wider. "You want a beer or something?"

My feet start through her door, and for just a second, the thought, *What are you doing?* shoots through my head. But I block it out as a giddy tingle courses through me. "Sure."

She closes the door and I look around. The place is a mess. It looks just like Luc's, except there are dirty dishes and . . . junk, I guess, stacked everywhere. I spy the mail that was in her hand a minute ago strewn over a bigger pile of mail on the counter.

"Sorry, it's kind of a mess," she says, stating the obvious. She picks a small stack of dishes up off the couch and dumps them onto a bigger stack in the sink. "Sit."

I do.

She heads to the fridge and ducks into it, coming out with two beers. She comes over and sits on the couch next to me, close but not touching, and hands me one. The beer helps my dry mouth, and for a long time we make idle chitchat. My mind is racing, and I'm barely able to keep track of the conversation, but I'm glad that she doesn't ask anything that I can't answer.

"Another beer?" she asks, shaking her empty bottle and rising from the couch. Without her next to me, even though we weren't touching, it suddenly feels cold.

"I'm good."

"So, I'm going to a party tonight," she says, ducking her head into the fridge. She turns back to me. "I could ask my friend if she'd mind if you came." She looks down and picks at the label on her bottle. "If you want."

An electric buzz works through me. I know what I want to say, but . . .

"I already have . . . I can't. Sorry." How lame. It's times like this that I wish I could lie.

"No problem," she says, twisting the cap off her beer, but she still doesn't look at me.

"I really want to." The gusto with which I say it brings heat to my face and I'm suddenly afraid I'm blushing. I didn't know that was possible with no blood.

She looks up at me then. "But you have a girlfriend."

"No!" *Just shoot me.*

"So why can't you come?"

"I'm supposed to be doing . . . something." The same thing I always do.

"Blow it off."

"Wish I could."

Her gaze drops to her lap, but she smiles. "Story of my life. The good ones always have something better to do."

She thinks I'm a "good one." I feel all achy inside. Can angels have heart attacks? "Okay. I'll go."

Her wide eyes snap to mine. "Really?"

"Sure."

What am I doing?

Breaking the rules.

There's some strange feeling building in my core—like I'm imploding and exploding all at the same time. I shudder with the sensation and feel the smile break across my face. "Sure," I say again.

I feel all jittery inside, wild, out of control. And I like it. This is what it feels like to make my own decisions. To do what I want. It feels amazing—like maybe I can actually have a life.

I wait in the hall while Lili changes, and when she emerges from the apartment, all rational thought leaves me. She's traded her gray sweats for jeans and a loose black top. Her hair is pulled back into a makeshift bun, and she's beautiful. "Wow."

Sweet Heaven above, why can't I keep my mouth shut?

But when she cracks a smile and blushes, I decide maybe I didn't screw up too bad. I can't take my eyes off her as we head for her truck and drive to pick up Taylor. When we pull into her driveway, it's a little weird pretending I've never been here before, after all the time I've spent on this front porch while Frannie was hanging out here. Taylor comes bopping out and pulls open the passenger door of the truck. When she sees me, her eyes widen for a moment before a lascivious smile spreads across her face.

"Ooh . . . good girl, Lili."

"I'm Matt," I say, holding out my hand.

She takes it and uses it to pull herself into the truck. I slide into the middle of the bench seat and she slides in so our legs are touching. "Taylor," she says as her eyes eat me alive.

Lili leans forward and looks around me at Taylor. "Hope it's okay."

"Boys are always okay, Lili. Especially boys this yummy," she says, pressing her shoulder into mine and grinning.

We drive to the north edge of Boston, into a neighborhood of desolate old brownstones. Every so often, there are groups of people hovering on the sidewalks—some teenagers, some homeless. Everything looks gray: the buildings, the cars, the people. The whole place has the feel of desperation and hopelessness.

"Here," Taylor says, pointing to a free parking spot between a sea of Harleys and an old black hearse.

Lili pulls into the spot as Taylor turns off her GPS and slides it into her bag. "How'd you hear about this party?" Lili asks, eyeing the hearse and looking a little unsure.

Taylor's eyes gleam. "This totally hot guy. He plays in a band."

Lili still doesn't look sure, but she opens the door and steps slowly out into the road. I slide out behind her and walk with her around the truck to meet Taylor, where she stands on the sidewalk.

We walk toward a brownstone on the corner, from which a very loud cover of Jimi Hendrix's "Purple Haze" emanates. A group of teenage guys standing on the corner starts the catcalls. No doubt Taylor looks good, and her short black skirt is designed to attract attention.

The door is open and we walk in. Instantly, the sweet smell of pot wafts down the short, dark hallway into our faces. We follow the music and smoke up the hall to a nearly dark room crammed with undulating bodies. In here, the smoke mingles with the rawer scents of sweat and musk, flooding my mind with visions of primal needs being fulfilled. I feel my own desires stir, and pull a deep breath.

I glance at Lili, who looks mesmerized by the scene. A fascinated smile curls her lips as she surveys the leather-clad crowd through the dim light.

Taylor's mouth dangles open and her gaze is locked on the band, set up in the corner of the room on a low platform. She steps into the room and shoulders her way to the stage through the writhing and gyrating bodies.

My sixth sense buzzes—loudly. There are demons here. Lots of them. But they're so intermingled in the mass of humanity, I'm having trouble getting a fix on exactly who they are.

Lili tugs my shirt and points to the corner, where a keg sits in a bucket of ice. She starts working her way in that direction and I follow. She picks a red plastic cup off the top of the stack and hands it to me, then pulls one for herself. I grab the tap and fill the cups.

Someone bumps me from behind, sending the beer in my hand sloshing over the rim. I turn slowly and a tall, skinny guy, maybe twentyish, stares me down, his solid black eyes telling me without a word that he knows exactly what I am.

And I know what he is too.

"Who invited you?"

Before I can answer, his eyes slide past me to Lili, who steps up next to me. "Was it you, my lady?" He holds his hand out to her. She takes his hand and he brings it to his mouth, kissing the backs of her fingers. A lopsided smile blooms on his dark face. "Because, if that's true, I'll forgive the indiscretion."

"I did." I can barely hear Lili's reply over the music.

"I'm Chax. It's my very great pleasure to meet you."

"Lili," she replies.

I step in front of Lili and pull her hand out of his. "And I'm Matt." The urge to carry her out of here is overwhelming. "We were just leaving," I say, trying not to glare.

His eyes don't leave Lili, but his voice turns to ice. "I wasn't talking to you." He turns and looks behind him, where a shorter guy with long black hair pulled back into a ponytail and the same cold, black eyes is just walking out of the kitchen. Chax sticks his arm in the air. "Hey! Andrus!"

His buddy smiles and starts heading toward us. Bodies seem to part, like the Red Sea, at his passage. He reaches us, and a malefic smile splits his face.

Chax's smile pulls into a leer as he drapes his arm over his friend's shoulder. "Andrus, I'd like you to meet Lili," he says, giving Andrus a nudge.

Lili steps closer to me and I wrap my arm around her waist. With her in my grasp, my power surges and I feel suddenly invincible.

Chax's grin turns to pure evil. "Oh, and her friend, Matt," he adds with a wave of his hand.

Just then the band stops, and even with the chatter, shouts, and calls of the crowd, it seems too quiet.

"Hi," Lili says, tugging at her shirt. She looks hard at Andrus, and he nods thoughtfully.

His tongue presses into the ring through his bottom lip. "And may I ask how you heard about our little gathering?"

Lili's eyes flick to Taylor, where she's taking a hit off a joint that a tall, built guy with shaggy black hair just handed her. He's dressed in torn jeans and a ripped black T-shirt, and a black bass guitar hangs on his back.

"I think that guy invited us . . . or our friend, anyway," Lili says.

Andrus elbows Chax. "Marc's found a new toy." He looks back at Lili with a predatory grin.

I've seriously got to get these girls out of here.

My grip on her waist tightens. "So, Lili . . . you ready to go?"

Chax's smile widens and his eyes flare in the dim lighting, never leaving Lili. "You're not leaving yet. The party's just starting." He grasps Lili's hand, tugging her out of my grip, and leads her to a couch in the back of the room, where a spot magically appears. He settles into it and taps his thigh for Lili.

Jealous rage courses through me, and the urge to smite him is almost irresistible. I can picture summoning my power and blasting him into oblivion—or at least back to Hell.

"Um . . . I don't think so," she says.

Good girl.

She looks at me, and just for a second, it feels like she's seeing the real me. Her eyes lock on mine, and her mouth tilts up with the hint of a smile. She reaches for my hand and laces her fingers in mine, and my insides explode in a burst of ecstasy.

12

Facing Down Your Demons

FRANNIE

I'm going seriously stir crazy. I sit in my desk chair and prop my chin on the windowsill, staring mindlessly at the pink and gray swirling dusk and watching for the Shelby.

Where the hell is Luc? How long can moving a bunch of books possibly take?

Less time if I help.

I jump up, slide on my flip-flops, and skip down the stairs. Passing through the family room, I wave at Mom and Dad on the way out. "Going over to the library."

"Gosh darn Jeter!" Dad yells at the TV.

"Daniel!" Mom chides, and then turns to me. "Aren't they closed this late?"

"Luc's working late, moving books. I'm gonna help," I say, edging toward the door.

"Fine, but call us if you're going anywhere else."

I bop out the door, slide into my car, and turn the key . . . and scream when a ginormous auburn-haired demon phases into the seat next to me.

"Hello," he says.

I spring from the car without shutting it down.

My instinct, obviously, is to run. But then I remember Luc saying he wanted information. I root my feet to the ground and grope for the crucifix dangling from the chain around my neck, trying not to look as scared as I feel. I remember the damage my last crucifix did to Belias, and hope I don't have to use this one.

"Who are you?"

"My name is Rhenorian," he says in a soft voice, obviously trying to soothe me. He smiles. "But my friends call me Rhen."

My heart is trying to commit suicide by throwing itself relentlessly against my rib cage. "What do you want?"

He looks at me as though he's trying to peer right into me. "He did it for you, didn't he?"

"Who? Did what?"

"Lucifer. He's human."

"I know."

"How did he do it?"

"I . . . I don't know," I lie.

"He said someone else made him human. Who?"

"I don't know," I repeat.

He turns my key, shutting down the ignition, pulls it, and steps out of the car. He stretches to his full height, towering over me, and an icy smile pulls at his mouth. "You're a terrible liar." He tosses the keys over the car to me. "Take it from a professional."

As panic flutters through me, somewhere in the back of my mind, it's occurring to me that Matt should be here. "I don't know how it works."

He steps slowly around the car. "I think you do."

"Is that why you're following Luc?" Fear closes my throat, strangling the words. What am I doing? He's not gonna tell me anything.

I back away a few steps and focus. *You don't want Luc.*

He hesitates for a second, and his face goes slack. But then he shakes his head and looks back at me with sharp, clear eyes. "I'm going to find out."

"He can't tell you how it works either. He doesn't know."

His eyes lock on mine. "We'll see about that."

I drop into a crouch as he advances toward me, ignoring my pounding heart, and try to stay focused on his mind. *Go away. You don't want Luc. You don't want Luc. You don't want Luc.*

He backs off a step, looking confused.

You don't want Luc, I push again.

The gun of an engine catches Rhenorian's attention and he looks up, his face clearing, just as Luc's Shelby screeches to a stop at the curb.

Luc flies out of the car, eyes wide, and stands beside me. "Leave her alone, Rhen."

Rhenorian flashes a sharp smile at Luc. "When I have answers."

"For the love of all things unholy, Rhen! There's nothing to tell."

I breathe deep and focus on his mind again. *You don't want Luc.*

"Leave," Luc says.

I back off a few steps, never taking my eyes off him. He doesn't make a move toward me, but his eyes are trained on me too, and there's something in his expression that I can't really read.

We turn for the house and I hold my breath as we hurry up the walk, half-expecting him to try to stop us.

Go away. You don't want Luc.

"See you around," he says to our backs.

We slip into the house and close the door behind us. I lean against the wall, shaking, sure I'm gonna throw up. Kate is just coming down the stairs. Her face scrunches when she sees Luc. "Hey, how'd you beat Chase?"

Luc twines his fingers in mine and shoots me a concerned glance before turning to Kate. "He was closing up when I left. I'm sure he's right behind me."

Mom looks up from her crossword. "That was quick."

I push away from the wall. "Yeah, Luc just got here. Saved me the trip." I hope she doesn't notice the shake in my voice. "We're going upstairs."

She just looks at me, the meaning in that stare clear.

We slip past Kate on our way up the stairs. In my room, Luc closes the door. I think about Mom's door rule, but don't open it. "What happened?"

"I'm fine. Thanks for asking," I say.

He pulls me to him and nearly squeezes the life out of me. "Frannie, when I saw you out there with him . . ."

I push away from him again. "I was bored. I thought if I came to the library and helped, you'd get done faster."

His eyes narrow and his lips press into a hard line. "Where the Hell is Matt?"

"Good question."

"This is wrong. *Gabriel* was wrong. Matt can't handle this." His words are quiet, but his eyes aren't. A storm is brewing in those black pools.

"Stop it, Luc. Matt's here. I'm sure he would have done something if I was really in danger."

"Call him," he says, challenging me.

I step closer to him and smile my best sultry smile, which probably isn't all that sultry, but it's the best I got. "I don't want him now." I slide my hands over Luc's T-shirt, trying to distract him. Because, truth is, I'm pretty sure Matt's not here.

Luc loops his fingers around my wrists and brings my hands to his face, where he brushes his lips over the backs of my fingers and looks hard into my eyes. "Call him."

"No," I say, yanking my hands away from him. "You call him."

"If I do it, he won't come out of spite—or if he's distracted. If you call him, he has no choice."

I cross my arms and pull them tight against my chest. "Fine."

MATT

Sitting here with Lili, it'd be easy to forget where we are—in a room full of demons. The band grinds away, its pounding rhythm shaking me to the core.

I glance over at Taylor. Even though the band is playing, the bass player has her pressed up against him, her arms slung over his shoulders, swaying together and locked in a kiss. I know I should go over there and retrieve her, but with Lili this close to me on the couch, her heat making me warm all over . . . I'm not going anywhere. Her hand in mine feels amazing. Electric.

I slide my arm over her shoulders and pull her closer. Even in the dim lighting, there's no mistaking the look she gives me. I twist a finger into her hair as her hand shifts to my thigh, and what I feel is totally foreign. It spreads through me, and my insides stir, along with certain parts of my outsides, until all I can think about is Lili. Everything else falls away as I reach for her face and lean in to kiss her.

And then I feel the mental tug.

Frannie.

Damn!

I spring from the couch. "I have to go, Lili . . . sorry."

"What?"

I grab her hand and pull her off the couch. "I have to go—right now. So do you. You can't stay here."

"Okay, I guess. Let me find Taylor."

"She's over there." I gesture to the stage as I back toward the door, feeling my grasp on my human form start to slip. "Grab her and get out of here."

"You're not waiting?"

"Can't. Sorry," I say, backing down the hallway toward the door. "Get Taylor and go. Now."

"How will you get home?"

"Don't worry about me. Just grab Taylor and go." I hold her shocked gaze for a second longer, then I turn and run from the room before I'm forced to phase right in front of everyone. This is the risk of being visible. As a guardian, when my charge calls, I have to find her immediately, no matter what I'm in the middle of.

Once outside, I swear under my breath as I phase into Frannie's room. When I look up, Frannie's sitting on the bed and Luc stands near the door. And they're both glowering at me.

"What?"

"You're joking, right?" Luc says. The calm in his voice is betrayed by his fists, clenching and unclenching slowly at his sides.

My eyes shoot to Frannie and I step toward the bed. "Are you okay? Did something happen?"

She just stares at me with questioning eyes.

"Where the Hell were you?" Luc growls.

"I was . . . I didn't feel anything." I drop my eyes from hers, and an involuntary grimace pulls at my face.

"I don't care what you 'felt.'" Luc's voice is acid. I look up as his jaw tightens and his eyes narrow. "Frannie was in trouble and you, the great guardian, were nowhere to be found."

I close my eyes, feeling cold dread fill my insides. "What happened?"

"Rhenorian was here," Frannie says.

I lift my eyes to hers, relieved. "Is that new? I thought he's been following Luc."

"*He* was here, *I* wasn't," Luc says, and I feel the sharp edge of his glare.

His words are like a punch to the gut. This wasn't my deal with Rhenorian.

I work to keep my voice steady, and my eyes don't leave Frannie. "He came for *you?*"

"Sort of. He wanted to know how Luc turned."

Luc's eyes snap to her too. "That's what he wanted? He wasn't after you?"

"No. He was asking about you being human. He thought you did it for me, and he wanted to know how."

Luc turns and drops into Frannie's desk chair, elbows on his knees and head in his hands.

I move to the window and look out. Rhenorian stands on the sidewalk near the neighbor's shrubs, his eyes trained on the house. He sees me looking and salutes in my direction. I glare at him and send a warning—a flash of white light. If he's screwing with Frannie, he's no longer an ally. But as much as I hate to admit it, he's still my best hope to get Luc away from my sister.

I turn my glare on Luc. "So, it seems to me that you're the one putting Frannie in danger."

Luc lifts his head from his hands. His face is tormented, as if he's figured this out on his own. He looks with agonized eyes at Frannie. "He's right. Rhenorian wants *me*. If we were apart, he'd have no reason to approach you."

Yes . . . just go with it, Frannie.

But the panic that flashes in Frannie's eyes tells me she's not going to.

"You're not going anywhere," she says. She hauls herself off the bed and moves toward Luc.

"Frannie, be reasonable—" he says, grasping her hand as she reaches him.

"You should let him go, Frannie. He's putting you in danger. Even he sees that," I say in one last-ditch effort, but I can see it's useless. Frannie slides into his lap and wraps her arms around his neck.

"Nope. If you leave, you're gonna have to take me with you," she says.

Stubborn, as always.

Hope lights Luc's face. "Maybe that's what we need to do— just leave. With our Shield, they shouldn't be able to find us. We'd just have to shake them. What if we go to L.A.? We could leave early."

"And tell my parents what?"

"They'd buy it if you said we decided to go early. Use your Sway."

She looks hard at Luc. "I'm not gonna use my Sway on my parents, Luc. And anyway, I'm not ready to go yet."

"So, if you're staying, and so is he—" I glare at Luc. "—we need to figure out a way to keep Rhenorian away from you."

Luc glares right back at me. "You staying put would help. You have one job, Matt."

He's right. And I have to start doing it. I was an idiot to think, even for just a second, that I could have a "life." This obsession with Lili has to stop. Getting to know her was a huge mistake. It hasn't changed anything, except maybe to make things worse. I let her talk me into abandoning Frannie. It won't happen again.

I didn't know it was possible for angels to get headaches, but as thoughts whir through my head in a dizzying blur, I'm pretty sure that's what's happening. I ease onto the edge of Frannie's bed, lean my elbows onto my knees, and pinch my forehead. "I'll worry about Frannie. You figure out what to do with Rhenorian."

13

✦

Hell's Belles

LUC

Matt seems to be taking his assignment more seriously in the last three days. I've had Frannie test him, calling for him at random moments, and he's always been there. This morning I'm less worried. Frannie's with her family at church, and the chance that Rhenorian—or any other demon—is going to follow her in there is pretty slim. Not that the whole religion thing is going to scare us off. It's just too hard not to laugh out loud. Not a wise tactic when you're trying to blend.

There's a knock on my door, and I'm hoping maybe Frannie blew off church. But when I open it, Lili stands in the hall with a white cereal bowl. "Hey. I ran out of milk, and my Froot Loops aren't happy about it. Can I borrow some?"

"No problem," I say, swinging the door wide. She slides in under my arm and I push it closed.

"Thanks. I'm starving and the only thing I've got is Froot Loops. Pretty pathetic, huh?"

I open my refrigerator and show her the contents: a nearly empty half gallon of milk, half a stick of butter, a mostly empty carton of eggs, a lonely slice of leftover pepperoni pizza wrapped carelessly in cellophane, and a paper box from Ming's Bamboo House containing God only knows what. "Not so pathetic," I say with a smile.

She smiles back, and for the first time, I notice that she's actually rather attractive. She's pulled her hair back this morning so I can get a good look at her face. Even with no makeup, she's a classic beauty.

"Grab a bowl and a couple spoons. I've got plenty of Froot Loops to go around." She puts her bowl on the table and runs out into the hall, leaving the door open. She's back in a minute with a store-brand box of Fruity Ohs. I toss a bowl onto the table and she fills it, then divvies up the last of the milk between the two bowls.

She sits in the chair across from me and peels off her extra large gray sweatshirt. Under, she's wearing a pair of faded denim shorts with a low-cut, nearly transparent white tank top, and a black bra underneath.

So, *wow*.

"Is that new?" I say, gesturing to her outfit.

She smiles shyly. "Yeah. Frannie helped me find some good deals."

I never would have guessed *that* body lurked under all her usual frump. She rests an elbow on the table and cradles her cheek in her hand. I catch myself staring at her cleavage, which is enhanced by the gesture, and force my eyes to the orange, green, and yellow loops floating in the bowl in front of me. I'm totally flustered, my thoughts a tangled mess.

"So, is she around?"

"Who?"

"Frannie." I hear the smile in her voice, but I still don't look up.

"Church. She's at church." I clear my throat. "So, when do classes start?" I ask, watching the tip of my spoon bob the floating loops one by one.

"Six weeks. Hopefully I'll have enough money socked away from my job at the KwikMart by then to pay for books."

"Good luck. That's about when Frannie's classes start too. We'll be leaving for L.A. in a month."

"That's a big move. You excited?"

I look up and work to glue my eyes to Lili's face. "It will be good for us to start fresh somewhere away from here."

My eyes follow her fingers as they move from her cheek to the strap of her bra, peeking out from under the tank top. "We all need a fresh start sometimes," she says, her voice soft and low.

"Mmm," I agree, focusing back on my bowl and scooping a spoonful of cereal into my mouth.

"What are you going to do in L.A.?"

"Not sure yet," I say between mouthfuls. "Maybe look for a job."

"Doing . . . ?"

"Good question."

"You should look into modeling. The big shops are in New York, but L.A. has some good agencies too."

I look up at her and laugh.

"You think I'm joking?" she says with raised eyebrows.

I pull my eyes away from her. "Yes."

"Well, I'm not. You've got a look the ladies drool over—dark and dangerous."

I lift my eyes back to hers. Her look isn't so bad either. And as she locks her gaze on mine, something primal stirs in me. I'm seeing something in her gaze that I shouldn't be.

"We'll see," I say, lifting my bowl from the table. I stand and walk over to the sink, focusing on rinsing my bowl. I clear my mind of everything but Frannie's face. When I'm back under control, I push away from the counter and turn toward her. "I've got to get to the library."

She pulls herself out of the chair. "Thanks for the milk." She goes to pick up her bowl, but ends up knocking it to the floor, where milk and Fruity Ohs splash and scatter. "Shit!" She stoops down and starts scooping the Fruity Ohs back into the bowl.

I grab a wad of paper towels and crouch down beside her to sop up the milk. When her hand brushes mine, a shudder races through me. I pull my hand away and pretend I didn't just feel the most carnal desire I've ever experienced.

"Sorry," she purrs.

"No problem. I've got it." I wave her off, but I can't look at her.

She stands and pauses at the door. "If you're looking for something to do after work, I'll be around."

She closes the door behind her and I drop back onto my butt on the floor. I sit here forever, trying to breathe and figure out what the Hell just happened.

FRANNIE

"This guy is to die for," Taylor says into the mirror as she touches up the lip gloss on her swollen lips. She swoons slightly. Now that's something I've never seen her do before.

"We've been together every night since Thursday," she continues, "and last night, in the back of his hearse, he went d—"

"Too much information, Tay," I say, holding up my hand. "Don't you think maybe things are moving a little fast?"

She gives me the patented Taylor glare in the mirror.

"I mean, you just met him."

She tucks her lip gloss into her bag and spins, hands fisted on her hips. "You're one to talk. It wasn't that long ago that you were making out with not one, but two hot guys."

My heart spasms at the thought of Gabe, and I drop my eyes. "That was different."

"Only because there were two of them—which makes you twice as bad as me."

I lift my eyes back to hers. "And, it was just kissing."

A lascivious smile pulls at her lips and she raises her eyebrows at me. "But not anymore . . ."

Heat creeps up my neck.

"I knew it!" she bellows in triumph.

I shake my head and sink into my desk chair. "So how was

that party you and Lili went to?" I sound only half as spiteful as I mean to.

She saunters over to my bed, where she flings herself onto my pillows. "Amazing." But then her grin pulls into a scowl. "Until Lili dragged me out of there."

"And you said Lili brought a guy?" I say, interested despite myself.

"Yeah. He was pretty hot too. He's got this wavy dark blond hair, kinda like yours but shorter, and these gorgeous blue eyes. I think Lili's diggin' on him."

I smile at the thought of shy Lili diggin' on someone. "What was his name?"

"Matt."

My breath catches in my throat. *Holy shit!* How many Matts who look like me could Lili possibly know? "Really . . . ?"

I try to wrap my mind around that. Luc was right. Matt was out partying with Taylor and Lili while Rhenorian was stalking me in my driveway.

Taylor lifts her head and quirks an eyebrow. "Do you know him?"

"Yeah. He's a friend of Luc's." Not to mention my brother/guardian angel. "That's how Lili met him."

"Well, I would have taken a run at him if it wasn't for Marc, but . . . well . . . you've seen Marc. He's oh-so-tasty." She sits up and wiggles her eyebrows.

"And a good kisser, from the looks of your lips." I smirk at her.

A lascivious smile curls her swollen lips, and her eyes spark. "Uh-huh. He's *very* good with his mouth."

I hold up my hand again, warning her to stop there. "So, are you hooking up again?"

"Tonight, at the Cove."

"Okay if Luc and I come?"

She looks wary for just a second. "Sure. I guess. So, are you heading over to Luc's?"

"No. He's at the library this morning, then he's meeting me at Grandpa's."

She scoots to the edge of the bed. "Can you give me a ride on your way?"

"You want a ride to Luc's?"

"Lili's."

"Oh. What are you guys up to?"

She flops back onto the bed. "Just hanging out."

I wait for my invitation, but it's obviously not coming. "Take the bus," I say, my voice bitter.

She rolls onto her hip and props herself on an elbow. "What's your problem? You're going to your grandpa's. You just said."

"Don't know. I guess I thought we'd hang out before I have to go."

"We are. Then I'm gonna hang out with Lili."

"Fine," I huff. "Don't let the door hit your ass on the way out."

She hauls herself off the bed, glares at me, then pulls the phone from her pocket. I turn, grab a random book from my stack, and pull it open. I stare at it as Taylor storms out of my room. But before the door slams behind her, I hear her say, "Hey, Ry. I need a ride to Lili's."

LUC

The library is always quiet on Sundays. I'm finishing up and getting ready to head to Frannie's grandpa's when I look up from the computer screen and see Taylor and Lili come wandering through the library doors.

Taylor looks up and smiles at the surprised expression on my face. The library's not her typical hangout.

Lili's still in her tank top and shorts, so I glue my eyes to Taylor. I step out from behind the desk as Mavis scowls.

"Ladies."

Taylor sidles up, too close, as usual. "Hey, Luc. What you working on?"

I wave an arm at the computer. "Cataloging the new arrivals." I glance at Lili, then back at Taylor. "Is there something I can help you find?"

Taylor elbows Lili. "No, thanks. Just researching a theory that Lili has."

I look at Lili with a raised eyebrow. "A theory?"

"It's nothing." She loops her arm through Taylor's and starts to pull her toward the computer stations. "We can find what we need on our own."

Taylor cranes her head over her shoulder and grins as Lili pulls her away. "See ya."

They huddle together at a terminal and search the catalog for several minutes, then disappear into the stacks. When they reemerge ten minutes later, they have three large books. Two of them, I recognize and am intimately acquainted with: *Demon Lore* and a modern translation of *The Lesser Key of Solomon*.

The third, a more modern text on black magic, I know only in passing.

They spread the books on a table and hover over them, whispering and giggling. Two or three times, they burst out laughing, and Mavis shuffles over to hush them. Despite the fact that Mavis's tiny frame would probably blow away in a stiff breeze, in her library domain, she's intimidating enough that the girls don't giggle again until she's gone.

Mavis pulls her sweater tight around her and takes a slow sweep through the high stacks, straightening books in her obsessive-compulsive way; then she shuffles back to the desk. She glowers at Taylor and Lili on her way by.

I walk over and see a small notebook on the table between them. Lili jots something into it as I approach, but she closes it before I can get a good look. I slide my hip onto the edge of the table. "Did you find what you were looking for?"

Lili looks up at me, and a smile plays at the corners of her mouth. "We're good, thanks."

"Speak for yourself." Taylor elbows her, and that signature lascivious grin spreads across her face. "I'll always take a little librarian with my books."

"I'll get Mavis, then. She's the little one," I say, peering past Taylor at *The Lesser Key of Solomon*. The page they have it open to involves Earthly demon conjuring and manifestation. A load of crap, really. There's no ritual required, as the book would suggest. We just show up where we want to, when we want to. Not too much a mortal can do about it either way.

"Let me know if there's anything else you need," I say, and push off the table. Both girls watch me walk back to the counter.

"Kids these days," Mavis says when I return, forgetting that, as far as she knows, I am one. "They have no respect for anything." She catches herself, and her scowl shifts to a fleeting smile. "Well, some of them, anyway. You're an old soul, Luc." Her scowl returns as she looks past me at the girls. "Devil worshippers, probably," she says, tugging on the chain around her neck and fingering the cross.

There's nothing I can do about the smile that pulls at my lips. "Why would you say that, Mavis?"

"That book—*Modern Black Magic*. They were copying down the pentacles in it. I don't understand kids' fascination with vampires and demons. The darker, the better. It's all they want to read about. What happened to the classics?"

"There are some dark classics. Bram Stoker, Mary Shelley, Edgar Allan Poe," I say, sticking to authors who aren't older than the building, and making a mental note to ask Frannie to find out what Taylor's up to.

She shakes her head. "The world's going to hell in a handbasket, and this generation—" She sweeps a hand toward the girls. "—is taking us there."

My smile widens. "We'll see."

Just then, the door swings open and Rhenorian strides in. He grins at me and takes a slow circle of the library. When his eyes find Lili and Taylor, his stride slows and he looks momentarily surprised. He flashes me another chilly grin and leaves.

All the pretty young things.

With a quick glance at Lili, I heave a guilty sigh. "You know what, Mavis? You might be right."

Taylor and Lili scrape back their chairs. Lili looks at me out from under her long, dark lashes as she flips her hand through the lore book; then they file out the door behind Rhenorian. I go to their table to reshelve their books and find the lore book open to the story of Adam and Lilith. I read through the story of Adam's first wife—how she left Eden in a huff and, after roaming the Earth for years seducing men, allied with Lucifer.

The first succubus.

Some things, the mortals got right.

"What the Hell are you two up to?" I say to myself as I close the book.

14

✣

For All Eternity

FRANNIE

Grandpa ambles out of the garage as I pull up to his house with the top down. I climb out of the car and he crushes me in a hug.

"We pulling that engine today?" I say, looking over the Shelby Cobra in the workspace.

Grandpa walks over to the car. "Got it set to go. You work the winch," he says, gesturing to the control lever.

"Luc will be here in a minute," I say, looking over the winch chains, bolted to the engine block. "We should wait."

He scowls at me. "I've been doin' this all my life. I don't need some kid doin' it for me."

"I love you, Grandpa, but you're not as young as you used to be. Just let us pull the engine."

"It's a winch, Frannie—hydraulic. Nothin's gonna happen."

I glare at him just as Luc's Shelby rolls into the driveway. He steps out of the car and walks through the open garage door, glancing between us. "So . . ."

"Tell Grandpa to back off."

Luc laughs out loud and his eyes shift to Grandpa. "She thinks you're going to listen to me any better than she does? I can't imagine where she would have gotten such a ridiculous notion."

A smile breaks across Grandpa's face. "You take the engine and I'll work the winch."

Luc raises his eyebrows at me in apology before sliding in next to me, gently brushing me back from the car. "Ready," he says.

Grandpa pumps the winch while Luc guides the engine block and transmission clear of the car.

I grab the engine stand and slide it into place, but Grandpa nudges me out of the way. "Luc, you know how to work the winch?"

Luc steps over to the control. "Yes, sir."

Grandpa quirks a crooked smile, as if sharing a secret. "Call me Ed."

Luc smiles back. "All right, Ed." He steps to the winch and works the release. The engine eases into position on the stand, where Grandpa bolts it in place.

Luc glances at me with a raised eyebrow, clearly proud of himself for gaining Grandpa's trust, and I glare back.

I want to scream. Not only are they leaving me out, but they've even got this whole bonding thing happening. I know that should make me happy, but at the moment, all it does is piss me off.

"Well, I guess you guys don't need me," I say. I spin and storm into the house, slamming the door behind me. I drop onto the couch, hating Grandpa for not realizing he's gonna get hurt if he keeps doing the strenuous stuff, and hating Luc more for going along.

Behind me, I hear the garage door open, and a second later, Luc sits next to me on the couch. He moves to hook an arm over my shoulders, but I shift away.

"Don't even think about it."

He drops his hand, then leans forward, elbows on knees. "I had to choose which one of you to piss off, and I was pretty sure you'd let me make it up to you. Was I wrong?"

"Yes," I huff, pressing back into the couch and folding my arms stiffly across my chest.

"Frannie . . ." He reaches for my hand, but I yank it away.

"He's gonna kill himself out there, and you're gonna help him!"

"He was only working the winch. I wouldn't have let him hurt himself."

We both jump with the crash and yell from behind us. When we explode through the door into the garage, Grandpa's on the cement floor with his leg pinned under the transmission. He looks up at us and winces. "Goddamn bolt broke."

We run to him and I kneel down. "Oh my god, Grandpa! Are you okay?"

"Fine," he says. "Just stuck. Can ya pull this thing offa me?"

Luc and I rock the transmission back and Grandpa slides out from under it.

I leave Luc holding the transmission and kneel next to Grandpa. "There's blood on your pants, Grandpa. You're hurt."

"It's nothin'," he says, trying to pull himself off the ground, but I yank his pant leg up to reveal a large bleeding gash across his shin.

"Stay here," I say to him. Then I glare up at Luc, who's standing over us. "Don't let him move."

I run into the house and rummage through the drawers in the bathroom till I have everything I need. When I slam back through the door, I find that Luc has followed instructions—for once. He has his hand on Grandpa's shoulder, keeping him down.

"Hold still, Grandpa," I say, and lay the bandaging stuff on the cleanest spot of floor I can find. "This is gonna hurt." I squirt Betadine into the cut and wipe it out with a clean face-cloth. Grandpa behaves and holds still while I bandage him up with gauze and tape.

Luc and I help him to his feet. "I told you that you were gonna kill yourself out here," I say.

"The bolt broke, Frannie. That's got nothin' to do with me bein' old."

We work our way into the house and I can see him trying not to limp. Finally, I wrap my arm around his waist to help him. At first he holds me at arm's length, but then he gives in and leans onto my shoulder.

I lower him into a chair at the kitchen table. "We need to take you to the hospital. That could be broken."

"It ain't broke."

Luc crouches next to him and lifts Grandpa's leg. He manipulates his ankle and squeezes his lower leg, watching Grandpa's face. When Grandpa doesn't wince, Luc releases it and looks up at me. "I think it's fine, Frannie."

I look hard at Grandpa. "You got lucky this time, but I don't want you out there without me."

Grandpa chuckles. "Yes, boss."

"So, what's for dinner?" Luc says, opening the fridge and peering in. He comes out with a carton of eggs. "Omelets?"

"If you're cookin'," Grandpa says.

Luc smiles and starts digging through cupboards for a bowl and a pan.

When we're done eating, Grandpa stares at me where I sit across the table, scowling. "Ya can't still be mad at him after a meal like that." His gaze shifts to Luc. "Where'd ya learn to do that?" he says, waving his fork over his empty plate.

"I pick things up here and there," Luc says.

I blow out a frustrated sigh. Luc's hand slides across and squeezes my knee, and this time I don't slap it away. "Why won't either of you ever listen to me?" I say, exasperated.

They share a glance and both burst out laughing.

And as much as I want to smack them both, I find my mouth pulling into a smile at the sound of their laughter. I bite my lips till they hurt to stop myself from laughing and arrange my face back into a scowl. Luc drapes his arm over my shoulder and kisses my forehead. I shove him away, and when I look back at Grandpa, his expression is pensive.

"So, how's this all gonna work?" he says to Luc.

"What?"

"I'm still not really gettin' my head around your deal."

"As far as I can tell, I'm as human as anyone," Luc says.

Grandpa's brow furrows. "And she made you that way?" he says, inclining his head toward me.

"Her love for me," Luc replies with a nod, his eyes shifting to mine.

"So, I may be jumpin' the gun, but you could stay together . . . get married and have kids and all that?"

My heart ticks up a notch. I've never really thought about the long term. With everything that's happened, thinking ahead to the next day has been a challenge. And Gabe seems to think Heaven has plans for me. Could Luc and I get married someday? Is that in my future—a normal life with a real family?

A gnawing sensation in my gut tells me the answer to that is no. Based on the last few months, I'm pretty sure nothing about my life is going to be normal.

Still, the glimmer of hope in Luc's eyes tells a different story. "Maybe," he answers. "As far as I know, this is unprecedented. I know of no other demon-turned-humans, so I don't really have anything to go by."

Grandpa nods appraisingly. "But you're goin' to L.A. with her."

Luc's eyes lock on Grandpa's and he pulls me tighter to his shoulder. "I am."

Grandpa nods and starts to clear his plate. I pull it out of his hand and carry the dishes to the sink. He settles back into his chair, and when Luc and I are done cleaning the kitchen, I turn and find Grandpa watching us with a wistful smile.

I smile back. "What?"

His smile remains, but his eyes drop. "Ya just remind me of somebody."

I remember what Grandpa told me about him and Grandma getting engaged the summer after high school. They were our age.

I walk around the table and hug his shoulders from behind. "I miss her too," I whisper in his ear.

He reaches up and squeezes my hand.

After we get the engine back on the stand, secured with new bolts, I watch Grandpa to make sure he's getting around okay and change the bandages now that the bleeding has stopped. Once he's promised to stay out of the garage, we head to Luc's.

"So, we're going to the Cove tonight with Taylor and this new dream guy she's seeing."

He cracks a smile. "Where'd she find him?"

"He's in Reefer's band. Got Taylor all hot."

His smile spreads. "Isn't Taylor always all hot?"

I laugh, remembering how she drooled over Luc when he first turned up at Haden High. "Well, we get to meet him tonight, so we'll see."

MATT

As much as I would never admit it to his face, I think my sister's slimy demon is right. I've lost my focus. It's better if I just stay invisible. Frannie's shadow.

I've silently followed her around the last three days, since my screwup at the party. The dutiful guardian angel.

But I never dreamed being a guardian would be this hard. Gabriel told me there'd be temptations. He told me it would be challenging. But he also told me it's what I was meant for— why I was born. And I believed him.

But this is beyond challenging. It's torture.

There's the whole thing about being forced to watch as my sister ruins her life by hooking up with a demon. But that's not the worst of it.

The worst of it is how much I realize I'm missing.

Watching Frannie live her life . . . a life that could have been mine if things had worked out differently . . . I can't help wanting that: the pat on the back from Grandpa; a best friend to give me a hard time; my first kiss from my first girlfriend. But all those possibilities vanished that day ten years ago.

So, now this is my reality: sitting in the hall, trying to figure out what I'm going to say to Frannie when she asks me about going to that party with Lili and Taylor.

How did I think Frannie wasn't going to find out? But then I remember that throb in my groin and realize I was pretty much thinking with the wrong head—which I'm not about to explain to my sister.

As I wait in the hall for Frannie and Luc to finish whatever they're doing in Luc's apartment, Lili comes up the stairs. And she's crying.

My insides turn to cold stone as I watch her turn her key in the locks, and I know I just resolved to stick to the job, but I'm suddenly desperate to help her. I phase to the doorway from the stairs and fade in, visible, as I walk briskly up the hall, reaching Luc's door just as she's slipping inside her apartment.

"Lili? Are you okay?"

She looks up at me with big wounded eyes, and before I even know I've done it, I'm standing in her door with my arms wrapped around her.

"What happened?" I say into her hair.

She stiffens in my arms and pulls away, staring at the floor. "Nothing."

I lift my hand and wipe the tears from her cheek. "This isn't 'nothing,'" I say softly, holding my damp fingers up. Despite my rage at whoever has hurt her, sitting like a boulder on my chest, I feel myself being drawn into her eyes. I'm ultra-aware of her body against mine, and warmth spreads through me until it feels like we're melting into each other. Without really realizing I'm doing it, I lean down and nearly kiss her, but she pulls away.

"It's just . . . forget it."

She starts to back into her apartment and close the door, but I stick my foot in the doorjamb. "Talk to me, Lili."

She looks up at me again, her eyes welling. "It's nothing. I'm just being stupid."

"Tell me."

Her eyes drop to the floor. "It was just this guy. He was following me and I got scared."

My insides twist into a painful knot. "What did he do?"

She just shakes her head, and the tears start to roll down her cheeks again.

"Did he hurt you?"

She shakes her head harder. "No . . . but . . ."

I pull her back into a hug and she doesn't resist this time. "You're okay now. I've got you." What feels like electric sparks crackle between us as I hold her. "Who was it? Did you recognize him?"

"No," she says into my shoulder. Then she lifts her head and looks at me, tears streaking her cheeks. "Wait . . . maybe. He might have been at that party."

I hold her against me a moment longer. I can feel her heart thrum against my chest and I'm sure that, if I had one, mine would be doing the same. Finally, I peel myself away from her. I know what I need to do. "Stay here and lock up."

Her eyes widen. "What are you going to do?"

"Just stay inside." I cradle her face in my palms and wipe her tears away with my thumbs. She looks up at me, and when our eyes connect, something clicks into place inside me. A piece of my existence that had been missing somehow, like a key piece of a jigsaw puzzle.

Lili and I are meant to be together.

I don't feel scared or anxious at the revelation. It just feels right. And she knows it too. I see it clearly in her eyes. "I'll take care of it."

She wraps her arms around me and pulls me close, and I hear myself moan.

"Be careful," she says into my shoulder.

I gaze into her depths a moment more, then step back and pull the door closed, banging on it with my palm. "Lock up."

The deadbolts click into place one by one. But just as I start

183

to phase, Frannie and Luc come walking out of Luc's apartment.

And I'm completely torn between going back to that house to hunt down the bastard who's stalking Lili, or following Frannie.

Do your job, Matt.

I really don't have a choice. I glance back at Lili's door as I follow Frannie and Luc down the stairs and into his Shelby, where I climb into the backseat.

15

✝

Deadly Sins

LUC

Unholy Hell.

Marchosias.

Where did Taylor find Marchosias?

Frannie and I push open the doors into the arcade and see them draped all over each other between the change machine and the air hockey tables. Music pounds from the overhead speakers, and lights flash. The crowd jostles and twists through the room in an unchoreographed dance, shouting over the whistles and bleeps from the arcade machines and the blaring music. But Taylor and Marchosias don't seem to be distracted by any of it.

Frannie shoots me a grin and starts elbowing her way through the crowd. I grab her arm and pull her back. Should I tell her? Either way, it's not safe for Frannie to be here. Because Marchosias can be here for only one reason.

She spins on me, irritation pinching her brow and pulling her lips into a hard line. "What?"

"I know him."

Her eyes widen. "From . . . ?"

"Hell, yes. He's a tender of the Pit and a . . . friend, I suppose. Marchosias."

She glances back over her shoulder as Taylor loops her arms around Marchosias's neck and nearly climbs right into him. "You can't be serious." Her ears flush red as fear and anger do battle on her face. She turns and storms toward them, but I grasp her arm tighter. "Let go of me!" she spits.

"Frannie, stop. He's not here on vacation. He's trying to get to you through Taylor."

She rips her arm away from me. "Well, it's working." She continues across the arcade toward the couple, who haven't once come up for air.

I catch her halfway across the room and spin her to face me, grasping both her upper arms. "This isn't the best strategy, Frannie. Taylor can't know. It would be even more dangerous for her."

She closes her eyes and draws a deep breath, working to calm herself. "So, what are we gonna do?"

"You stay here." I look around, hoping Matt is in the general vicinity. As if he read my mind, I feel a flick on the back of my head. I roll my eyes and rub my head. "I'll go talk to them."

"No. I'm coming. She's my friend, Luc." Her eyes are hard, determined.

"Fine," I capitulate when it's clear that she's not going to be deterred. "Stay behind me."

We weave through the mob and finally reach the spot where Marchosias has Taylor pinned against the wall with his body. Before I know she's done it, Frannie steps around me and tugs Taylor's shirt. "Tay."

Taylor peels herself away from Marchosias, her eyes cloudy and her breathing short. She takes a minute to get her bearings, and her eyes slowly clear. "Oh, hey, Fee. You guys made it." She looks less than thrilled.

But Marchosias looks plenty thrilled. He hooks an arm around Taylor's shoulders and leers at Frannie. "You were at that party. Frannie, right?" he says, reaching out a hand to her.

"And I'm Luc," I say, grasping his hand before Frannie can. There's no way in Hell I'm letting Marchosias touch her.

His smile pulls into a voracious grin. "Marc." He squeezes my hand hard—a challenge—but his eyes stay locked on Frannie.

I drop his hand and we all stand here in awkward silence for a long second.

"So, is anyone hungry?" Frannie finally says. "We could get a pizza next door."

Taylor looks hungry, but not for pizza. "Um . . . yeah, sure."

Marchosias guides Taylor through the mass of humanity toward the door. Just as we reach it, it swings open and Angelique steps through on the arm of a muscle-bound guy about my height, with short blond hair and an unsettling look in his deep-set brown eyes—something twisted and violent. I don't need to be a demon to see this guy is bad news, and most likely already tagged for Hell. Taylor pulls up short, eyes wide, and Frannie grabs her hand.

Taylor doesn't even seem to notice Angelique. Her eyes are locked on the guy. And I remember where I've seen him. The quarry.

"Hey, Brendan," Taylor says, looking a little shell-shocked.

When Marchosias tucks a hand into Taylor's back pocket and squeezes, her eyes cloud as his power washes over her. She leans into him and seems to forget about Brendan altogether.

Angelique's eyes slide over Marchosias and finally come to rest on Taylor. "Taylor," she says with a self-satisfied smirk, trailing a finger along Brendan's abs. She thrusts out her substantial chest and leers at me, as if hanging on the arm of a brute that'd just as soon swing at her as sleep with her is going to make me reconsider her numerous offers. "Hey, Luc."

Brendan's eyes pull away from Taylor and fall hard on me. It's a look meant to intimidate, no doubt. I stifle a chuckle at the memory of him screaming like a girl. That scream will go over big with the tenders when he's spending eternity burning in the Inferno. They live for mortals like him—the ultimate in entertainment.

I rest a hand on Taylor's shoulder and look between Brendan and Marchosias. Taylor's somehow managed to go from bad to worse.

"Angelique," I answer after a minute, nodding in her direction. I can't constrain the scowl as I regard her date. "Who's your friend?"

Brendan glares harder. "Brendan," he says, shoving Angelique off and stepping forward.

I smile and hold out my hand. "Luc."

He looks at it for a moment then grasps it and squeezes. I squeeze back in warning, wishing I could do more.

Brendan turns to Taylor. "And who's *your* friend?" he sneers.

Marchosias's eyes glow red as he extends an arm toward Brendan with an impish smirk. "Marc," he says.

Brendan takes his hand and smirks back as he gives Marchosias the same squeeze he gave me. But I see his eyes widen as his hand is crushed by Marchosias's. He tries to pull his hand free, but a malefic smile curls the corners of Marchosias's lips as a crackle of red lightning shoots over the surface of his hand.

"Ahh!" Brendan yells, his face twisting into a grimace. He drops to his knees as Marchosias's power surges through him. He gives a desperate tug at his arm and Marchosias finally lets go.

Jealously slices through me as I yearn for my old power, wishing I could have been the one to bring this asshole to his knees. I shake my head, pushing the thought back, and loop my arm around Frannie's shoulders as we push past Brendan and Angelique, through the door, and onto the sidewalk.

FRANNIE

"I can't believe what a girl Brendan is," Taylor says with a laugh. She wraps her arms around Marchosias's neck. "All you did was shake his hand, and he's totally bawling on the floor like a baby. That was sweet."

We push through the door into Ricco's and I keep my head down, hoping Ricco won't notice me. But, of course, he does. He holds up his hand to Luc. *"Un toro!"* he says with a wide grin.

Luc nods at him. "Ricco."

Then Ricco's eyes slide to me and narrow to slits. "No discount," he says.

"Whatever." I push past him and sit in Luc's regular booth in the back. Luc slides in next to me as Marc sits across from us and pulls Taylor down into his lap. But his eyes never leave me, even when Taylor buries her face in his.

I look expectantly at Luc. He's supposed to have a plan. One that doesn't involve sitting here watching my best friend suck face with a demon.

"Hey, guys!" I look up at the source of the voice. Delanie slides four scratched plastic plates and a stack of soda cups on the end of our table. She pulls a pad and pen from her short black apron. "I'm training and Dana said I can take your table."

I look over at Dana, who's leaning against the counter, watching Delanie. I wave and she smiles back. "Hey, Delanie. Just bring us a pitcher of Coke and . . ." I look at Taylor for input.

She pulls her face out of Marc's long enough to say, "No onions . . . or garlic." She grins at Marc. When I look at him, he raises an eyebrow and slides Taylor off his lap and onto the seat.

"Just a large cheese," I say, looking back at Delanie.

Delanie repeats the order out loud as she jots it on the pad. "Coming right up," she says, then grins. "I've been dying to say that." She turns and her long black ponytail swings side to side as she struts away toward the kitchen, where she clips our order up in the kitchen window. She spins and grins at me again, clearly proud of herself. Dana gives her a pat on the back.

When I look back across the table, Marc's expression sends a shiver down my spine. "So, Taylor says you've known each other for a long time."

I nod.

He paws at Taylor, but his eyes are still locked on me. My frustration builds, and I find my anger directed at Luc. He should be doing something. Then I feel his hand on my knee, squeezing. His eyes slide to the back of the restaurant and I follow his gaze. The restrooms. I push Luc and he stands, letting me out of the booth.

"Hey, Tay. I need to use the bathroom. Come with me?"

Taylor hesitates and glances at Marc before saying, "Yeah, whatever," and sliding out of the booth.

I grab Taylor by the arm and move through the restaurant to the dim corridor in back that leads to the restrooms. Once out of sight of the table, I pull Taylor up short. I stare hard at her. "Tay, this guy's trouble."

Taylor tears her arm away from me. "Oh, this is rich," she sneers. "You're jealous!"

"Be serious. I am so *not* jealous. I just think he's dangerous."

Taylor's eyes spark and a smile spreads across her face. "And what's wrong with dangerous?"

"No, Tay. I mean *seriously* dangerous. I have a really bad feeling about him."

Taylor's smile doesn't falter. "I've felt most of him, and believe me, there's nothing 'bad.' And you saw what he did to Brendan. He was protecting me."

"Taylor, be serious!"

Her grin twists into a scowl. "You know what, Fee? Just get out of my face. You have Luc, so it's stupid of you to be jealous."

"I'm not jealous," I growl. She's missing the whole goddamn point.

"Whatever." She rolls her eyes. "So do you have to go or what?" she says, throwing an arm up the corridor to the bathrooms. "'Cause I'm going back to the table if you don't."

I just stare at her, trying to figure out what to say so she gets it.

She glares, then wheels and struts back toward the restaurant.

"Tay, wait up." I catch her by the arm just before she turns the corner into the room. "Luc knows him—from where he lived before. He says this guy has done some really bad stuff."

"Well, he's doing some really *good* stuff to me, so you'll just have to get over yourself."

He's bad for you. You don't want him.

I cringe internally as I push the thought with my mind, hating myself for doing this to Taylor.

She just stares at me.

I push again. *He'll hurt you like Brendan.*

Taylor slumps back into the wall and lowers her eyes. "You think he'll hurt me?"

Her voice is suddenly unsure, and this time I cringe outwardly. But she needs to stay away from him. I'm doing the right thing. "I do."

She shakes her head, as if trying to clear it, then lifts her eyes to mine. "But . . ."

"He's bad news, Taylor."

She nods slowly. "Bad news."

Acid builds in my stomach and I feel suddenly sick. I can't shake the feeling that what I'm doing is wrong, even if it is to help Taylor. "So, you'll come with me and Luc?"

She nods again.

I let go of her arm and we head back to the table.

LUC

"So, did Hell run out of real demons? Just wondering why they sent a rank amateur."

Marchosias glares death at me from across the table. "You're one to talk." Red lightning crackles over the surface of his hand where it rests on the table, fist pointed in my direction. "Show me what you've got, Lucifer."

"Seriously, why would they send a tender of the Pit after Frannie?"

His eyes flare red heat. "Your . . . defection left an opening in Acquisitions, which I was more than happy to fill. It's the department with the most potential for upward mobility, what with Beherit burning in the Pit and all." A malevolent grin stretches his face. "He was my last official assignment before making the transition."

Delanie sweeps by the end of our table, sliding the pizza onto it. She sets the pitcher of soda down and scans the table. "Did I forget anything?"

I smile up at her, but it feels strained. I don't like the way Marchosias is looking at her. "Thanks, Delanie. I think we're good."

"'Kay, Luc. Let me know if you need anything else." Her eyes shift to Marchosias. "See you at the studio tomorrow?"

A purely wicked grin blooms on his face. "Wouldn't miss it."

Her eyes light up. "I can't believe you got us set up with this demo. It's gonna be great!"

His eyes devour her as he nods.

"Okay. Let me know if you need anything else." She moves to the table behind me as Marchosias leers after her.

I slide back in the booth and swing a leg up onto the seat. "So, Frannie must not be a priority anymore if they're sending the trainee."

He leans onto his elbows and fingers a slice of pizza. "You forget, Lucifer. I know you better than most."

"You need to back off, Marchosias."

"Why the Hell would I do that? I'm making such beautiful progress. Look at me, sitting here at a table with you and my target." His eyes flick to the hallway in the back and his mouth stretches into a slow grin. "And Taylor . . . let's just say she's the icing on the cake. A tasty bonus. I'm thinking of keeping her."

I feel my blood boil, and it's everything I can do not to jump over the table and strangle him.

"This is between us, Marchosias. Leave Taylor out of it."

His grin stretches wider and his eyes spark. "Sorry . . . too late. She's already *very* into . . . it. You've heard that saying about having your cake and eating it too? Well, I've *had* my cake, if you know what I mean."

There's no stopping it. I shove the table into him and grab his shirt as pizza and soda fly, throwing him out of his seat and onto the ground. "You'll stay away from her."

The surprise clears from his face, and an amused grin replaces it. He picks himself up off the floor.

"And from the looks of it, an added bonus might be reversing *your* tag. All three of you in one fell swoop. That might be an Acquisitions record."

I shake my head. "Not even close."

Taylor and Frannie round the corner from the bathrooms and make their way over to us. When they reach the table, Frannie glances to the mess on the floor. Her eyes find mine. "What's going on?"

"Just a minor disagreement. Marc was just leaving," I answer, glaring at Marchosias.

Delanie steps up behind Frannie. "You need help, Fee?" Her eyes slide between Marchosias and me, then to Frannie.

"No, we're okay," Frannie says, stooping to pick up the empty pitcher on the floor. "Sorry about the mess."

Delanie throws a towel on top of the puddle on the carpet and scoops the strewn pizza onto the dented aluminum tray, then looks hard at Frannie. "You're sure." She shoots a glance at Marchosias.

"Yeah. Thanks, Delanie." Frannie hands her the pitcher.

They stand and Delanie hurries back toward the counter, throwing one last concerned glance over her shoulder.

I throw a bill on the table then grasp Frannie's hand and squeeze. "We're leaving."

"C'mon, Taylor," Frannie says, turning back to her friend, and I see her face fall when she finds Taylor staring into Marchosias's eyes. He draws a finger slowly across her forehead and Taylor sinks into him.

Frannie looks desperately between me and Taylor. "Tay," she says, reaching for her friend's elbow. "You said you'd come with me and Luc."

Taylor pulls her eyes away from Marchosias's and her signature lascivious grin is back. "Change of plans."

Marchosias raises an eyebrow at me, with a slow smile.

Frannie's eyes flick to me, pleading, then back to Taylor. "Tay, come back to Luc's with us . . . please?"

Taylor smirks at her. "And do what, Fee? Watch each other make out? I don't think so."

"I brought some entertainment," Marchosias says, pulling a rolled Baggie from his pocket. An assortment of pills rests in the bottom of it.

Taylor's eyes dart to Ricco, gawking at us from behind the counter, and to the smattering of customers. She grins as she elbows him. "Put that away," she mutters.

Frannie grabs Taylor's hand. "Please, Tay. Come with us."

Taylor looks at her, an irritated scowl pulling at her features. "Um . . . no." She slides out of Frannie's grasp and tucks into Marchosias's side. He drapes his arm over her shoulders and they turn and saunter out the door.

My gaze falls to Frannie, and if looks could kill . . .

MATT

I hover next to Frannie as she storms out the door after Taylor, and I'm furious at Luc for getting Frannie into this. He should never have let her in such close proximity to a demon.

She starts down the sidewalk after Taylor and Marchosias, and spins on Luc when he grabs her arm from behind. "Why did you let them leave?" she yells. She starts up the sidewalk after Taylor's retreating back. "Taylor!" she shouts, with no response.

Luc catches her by the arm and she tears herself away from him. She crouches down on the sidewalk with her hands over her head, and a wounded gut-wrenching growl rolls up from somewhere deep inside her. When she looks up, her damp face glistens in the neon lights flashing from the windows of the Cove.

"My Sway is so useless."

Something stirs in the shadows between the arcade and Ricco's, and I have only a second to react, wrapping Frannie in a field before a mountainous demon is standing on the sidewalk.

"Rhen," Luc groans. His eyes shift to Marchosias's retreating form. "Great. An unholy family reunion."

Before either of us can stop her, Frannie's on her feet, charging Rhenorian. She shoves him, but he hardly moves. "Will you all just leave us alone?"

Luc grabs her wrist and pulls her away as I step in front of her.

But the rumble of Rhenorian's laughter catches us all by surprise. His eyes slide from Frannie to Luc. "I like her. She's a little spitfire."

Frannie twists out of Luc's grasp and steps up into Rhenorian's face again. "You can't take either of us."

"Yet," he responds with a sharp glint in his eye. "But I'm working on a plan." His glare shifts to where I'm standing, invisible. "A good one." Then he's gone.

"What was that?" Luc's voice is sharp, angry, and I turn to see him grasping Frannie's shoulders, looking her over. "He could have killed you."

Frannie looks totally defeated. "He's not gonna kill me. I'm tagged for Heaven."

He releases her. "I wouldn't be so sure."

"Whatever. We need to help Taylor."

He hooks his thumbs in his front pockets and starts after her as she heads up the sidewalk toward his car. "Frannie, I'm not trading your safety for Taylor's. I'll do what I can for her, but you're the priority."

For once, I agree with the demon, but that doesn't mean I'm going to let him off the hook. They slide into the Shelby and I phase into the backseat. "Yeah, good strategy—protect Frannie by going out for pizza with a demon."

Luc's jaw clenches and he shoots me a glare in the rearview mirror. "If I could trust you to do your job rather than dreaming up creative ways to lose your wings . . . ," he growls.

Frannie splits a glare between us, her eyes a storm of fury. "You know what? Both of you can go to hell! I can take care of myself."

I slouch back into the seat. "Frannie, I know you can kick some serious demon ass, but you need to be reasonable. You should never have gone anywhere near Marchosias—or Rhenorian. What were you thinking?"

Her eyes cloud and a shadow passes over her face. "I have to help Taylor." She lowers her gaze and chews her bottom lip. "It's my fault. He's using her to get to me." She shoots a glare back at Luc. "I used my Sway on her. She was gonna come with us. Then he did that thing with her forehead and she changed her mind. What was that?"

"He used a mind sweep on her. It's one of the more powerful techniques we have for getting into someone's head. But remember, Frannie. Even with a mind sweep, he couldn't make her do anything she didn't want to."

She groans and drops her face into her hands, and everyone is quiet for the rest of the ride, absorbed in our own thoughts. Frannie's are on Taylor, I'm sure, and Luc's are probably on Frannie. Mine are still at the apartment. Every second is torture, because I can't get Lili's tearstained face out of my head. Someone is stalking her. And if he was at the party, he's probably a demon. I have to figure out how to protect her.

What would a demon want with Lili?

Her soul is tagged for Hell. I've known that since the minute I first saw her. Probably something happened that was out of her control. But being tagged for Hell doesn't usually warrant demons stalking you. Most mortals tagged for Hell live their whole lives without ever knowing it.

My throat chokes off as I think about the only logical reason for a demon to be stalking a tagged soul.

They want her now. This guy's been sent to collect her.

He can't have her.

I won't let him take her. She doesn't belong in Hell.

How am I going to protect both Frannie *and* Lili? Even I can't be in two places at once.

Luc pulls into the driveway and parks the car. "Do you want me to come up?" he asks.

"No," Frannie answers, but she doesn't reach for the door

handle. She looks at him, and a tear courses down her cheek. He pulls her to his shoulder, and as he tips her face up and kisses her, suddenly I don't want to be here anymore. I phase onto the front porch and wait for them to finish their good-byes.

When Frannie finally steps out of the car and walks past me to the door, her eyes are red rimmed. She pushes her way into the house as Luc backs out of the driveway.

I hover, invisible on the front porch, fighting with myself. I need to stay—but I need to go. I float off the porch and look up at the house as the light in Frannie's room flicks on. She's safe behind Dad's field. No one should be able to get to her.

I ignore the wave of guilt that washes over me as I phase into the hallway in front of Lili's door and knock. I hear someone moving behind the door, but it doesn't open.

"Lili? It's me, Matt," I say through the door.

After a pause that feels like eternity, the deadbolts start to slide and then the door cracks open. Lili stares out at me but doesn't say anything. The door swings wider, and without a word, she takes my hand and pulls me through. When it's closed and the deadbolts are back in place, she tows me to the couch. I sit and she curls into my side. I nestle my face into her hair and hold her until she falls asleep.

16

Damnation

FRANNIE

"I'm not gonna sit around and let some demon do God knows what to Taylor." I bang my forehead on Luc's table.

"She's got choices, Frannie," Luc says.

"But he's after her because of me!"

I've been fighting this crushing guilt since Taylor left Ricco's on Sunday night. I can't sleep and I have the constant sense I'm gonna throw up. But I also haven't been able to eat all week, so there's nothing *to* throw up. I've got to help her, but she won't even talk to me. She doesn't answer my calls and she's never home when I knock on her door.

And this stupid Sway thing . . . I've tried everything I could think of: telling her to stay away from Marc; telling her she doesn't want him; telling her to call me.

It's been almost a week, and the phone hasn't rung once.

Maybe I have Sway, but I don't have any control over it—which makes it pretty much useless.

Luc slides into the chair across the table from me and leans forward, grasping my hand between his. "Why would Taylor and Lili be reading up on demons?"

"What?"

"They were at the library Sunday. They had books on demon lore and black magic and they were copying down conjuring symbols."

My stomach clamps harder. "I don't know." I breathe a frustrated sigh. "So what's Marc trying to do? How does he think he can get to me through her?"

"I'd guess his plan involves trying to get close to you—reverse your tag, but I'd say Taylor's strategy of avoiding you is shooting his well-laid plans straight to Hell." What he doesn't say, but I hear anyway is, *and putting her in danger.*

"Could she know? Is that why they were looking up demon stuff?"

Concern creases Luc's brow. "I hope not."

"Why?"

"You know why, Frannie. If she knows what he is, and she's . . . *with* him—"

"Oh God! Is he trying to tag her?" All the blood suddenly leaves my face, and my vision goes gray around the edges.

Luc stares past me with troubled eyes and shakes his head. "It's possible."

"Maybe we should do what you said. If we just leave, hide somewhere, would he leave her alone?"

His eyes slide to mine, then away. "Maybe."

I jump when my cell phone rings, and when I check it, Taylor's face smirks at me from the screen. I snap it open. "Tay!"

"Marc thinks I'm not being fair."

Just hearing her voice, I can hear the relief in mine. "What do you mean?"

"He says I shouldn't be mad at you. So what were you saying about him being such an asshole?" she sneers.

"Sorry."

"Yeah, whatever. Anyway, he invited you guys to a party at his place. Tonight. Ten."

I look at the clock. It's 9:15. "Great. Where?"

I write down the address as she says it.

"So, see you there," Taylor says, and the line goes dead.

I'm wound way too tight, 'cause when Matt appears next to me, I jump again. "Door? Knock? Sound familiar?"

He points to the paper on the table, his eyes wide. "That's where the party was. That place was full of demons. It's a trap, Frannie. You can't go there."

I glare at him. "The hell I'm not going!"

LUC

Matt's right. Frannie can't go, but I can. "Matt and I will go," I say. "We'll have better luck getting in and out of there in one piece."

"You know, I'm getting seriously sick of all this macho 'I have to protect you' crap. You just got done telling Grandpa you're as human as me, and you know I could take you down in my sleep. Why are you so sure you'll be safe? Maybe *I* should go to protect *you*."

She has a point, but . . . "I'm not their target. And you most definitely are."

"Fine. So I'm their target. What are they gonna do? I'm tagged for Heaven and I don't think that's likely to change in the five minutes it'll take us to go in and bring Taylor out."

I regard Frannie with a wary eye and think about the library—Taylor and Lili with their heads together, thick as thieves. "Maybe we should bring Lili. Between the two of you, maybe you could persuade Taylor to leave without Marc."

"No!" Matt shouts, and we both turn to look at him. His eyes drop to the floor and watch his shuffling feet. "Some demon is stalking her. She's pretty upset. It wouldn't be safe for her to go back there."

"Go back where?" Lili is standing in the door. She takes in our surprised faces. "Sorry, the door was open. . . ."

Except I'm sure it wasn't. I closed it myself. I look her over with a wary eye. She's dressed in her baggy sweats again.

Matt's face softens. He walks over, takes her hand in his, and stares into her eyes for a long minute before turning to glare at me. "Nowhere. It's nothing."

If I needed any more proof that Matt is distracted, he just gave it to me. There's no mistaking the look in his eye. Lili is his priority. He's lost his focus.

Frannie clears her throat. "Taylor's in trouble. We're going to a party she's at. It's at this guy's house. . . ." Her face changes, the concerned creases between her brow giving way to wrinkles across her forehead as her eyebrows shoot up. "Where you guys went to that party the other night," she says, her gaze shifting between Lili and Matt.

The guilt in Matt's face is unmistakable. It's worse than I thought.

I fix him in a glare. "Well, this is just perfect."

The concern is clear on Lili's face as well. "Taylor went back there? We have to go get her." She wheels and heads out the door.

Frannie, Matt, and I follow her down the hall. I have to know more about what we're getting into. "What do you know about those guys? The ones who threw the party?" I ask.

"Not much," she says, trotting down the stairs. "Taylor said this guy she liked told her about the party. Said there was gonna be a band. I invited Matt and we went, but it was a little creepy and then Matt had to go, so I grabbed Taylor and we left."

I glower at Matt again as we reach Lili's truck. He climbs in and makes a big production of fastening his seat belt so he doesn't have to look at me.

"Follow me," Lili says, and starts the ignition.

I glance at Frannie as we follow Lili out of the parking lot. "Do you believe me now?"

She looks at me. "About?"

"Matt and Lili. There's something going on between them."

She gets that defensive scrunch to her face. "They're friends. So what?"

I shake my head. "It's more than that."

Her gaze shifts out the windshield, to the beat-up hunter orange truck ahead of us. "You think?" She doesn't seem as upset about it as she should be. She looks almost hopeful.

We pull up to the curb in a pretty tough section of the city and get out. Lili and Matt meet us at our car. Seconds later, I see Rhenorian pull into a spot on the corner. I hope he's not going to pick tonight to come after us again.

"Ready?" Lili says.

I glance over the hood at Frannie, imploring her with my eyes to wait in the car with Matt.

"Not gonna happen," she says, and takes off up the street toward the blaring music.

We walk into the dark room, and even with the pounding rhythm of the music, a perceptible hush falls over the space. About half the heads swing to watch our entrance.

I don't recognize most of the demons in the room, but their eyes give them away. A few, I do recognize.

Andrus is here. Interesting. He's about as old as they come and head of Public Relations. I'm not surprised he's on the mortal coil. His crew lives on the coil to buffer all the Fire and Brimstone crap that the churches spew. It wouldn't do to have mortals *too* afraid of us.

The undulating bodies part as he starts toward us, and he makes a point of letting his true form shimmer through his human shell, just at the edge of perception.

"Lucifer. What a pleasant surprise." An amused smile pulls

at his lips as his eyes slide past me. "And you brought entertainment."

Matt inches closer to Lili.

"Marchosias sent a personal invitation. How could we refuse?" I say.

Others start to crowd around us, forming a claustrophobic circle, and Frannie instinctively brings her hands up, ready to fight. I touch her arm. "It's okay."

"And this is your friend." His hand starts to reach out toward Frannie's face.

"Where's Marchosias?" I say, stepping in front of her.

His smile pulls into a depraved grin as his hand drops to his side. "Occupied at the moment. Sorry, you're stuck with me."

A snicker rumbles through the gathered crowd. I grab Frannie's hand and push past Andrus and his minions. We scan the room for Taylor and Marchosias. The band is playing, but he's not on the stage. Matt taps my shoulder and points across the room to the kitchen door. We weave our way around undulating bodies and step through.

Frannie gasps and freezes beside me.

The single working fluorescent flickers, strobelike, in the overhead fixture, but even in the wavering light, the scene is clear as day. All the counters and cabinets have been unceremoniously removed, leaving ruined linoleum floors, gaping holes in the walls, and exposed pipes. The only furniture is a nicked and worn wooden table in the middle of the room. The table is strewn with lighters, syringes, empty beer bottles, and a nearly empty bottle of Jack Daniel's, uncapped and on its side.

Also perched on the edge of the table is Taylor, leaning back on splayed hands, head rolled back and eyes closed, her skirt around her waist.

And her legs wrapped around Marchosias.

In a flash, Lili is there, pushing Marchosias off Taylor.

"What the fuck?" he shouts, zipping his jeans.

Taylor looks really out of it—face slack, eyelids drooping over eyes that are forever away. She looks around without really seeing anything and tugs down her skirt. Matt's next to her when Lili wraps her arm around Taylor and helps her off the table.

"Oh, God!" Frannie says, and runs across the room to Taylor before I can stop her.

Taylor doesn't even acknowledge her as Frannie loops an arm around her back and guides her toward me.

When Marchosias looks up and sees me in the doorway, a grin spreads across his face. "Leave it to you to kill the party. You used to be so much fun, Lucifer. What the hell happened to you?"

I'm completely repulsed by the thought of what I used to be. Rage at Marchosias—at myself—swirls my insides into a churning pool of hot acid. In four long strides, I'm on him. I grab him by the shirt and slam his back up against the wall. "You *will* leave Taylor alone."

His eyebrow shoots up. "You can't keep all the mortals for yourself, Lucifer."

I glance back at Lili, hoping she's too involved with Taylor to have picked up what Marchosias just said. She and Frannie are helping Taylor out into the dark of the party. I push Marchosias hard into the wall. "Don't touch her again."

"You're too late. I showed her." His human shell shimmers as the demon he is flashes through—burning red eyes set in smooth crimson skin, angular features, a satyr's body, complete with hooves, and the requisite short black horns. "I showed her and she still begged for it."

I throw him into the wall one last time, shaking with frustration that there's nothing I can do to really hurt him, then let go of him and back out of the kitchen, catching Frannie and the others on their way out the door. Frannie and Lili are on either side of Taylor, mostly dragging her, and Matt brings up the rear with an eye on several demons who have gathered to watch our exit.

"Is she okay?" I ask, knowing the truth. She's not okay. She's tagged for Hell.

Frannie's trying to hide the tears streaming down her face. She can't answer.

"They were doing devil's breath. She's pretty messed up," Lili says.

When I look up, I see why we've drawn attention.

Andrus.

He's leaning against the doorframe, blocking our exit.

"You're not *leaving*?" he says, his eyebrows raised in mock astonishment.

We keep moving toward him, but when we reach the door, he pushes away from the frame, standing square in the middle of it. I look over his shoulder, and Chax is backing him up, outside on the sidewalk.

"Lucifer, you and your . . . bright friend," his mouth twitches as his eyes flick to Matt, "are free to leave anytime you want.

But the ladies—" A feral grin stretches his face into something hideous. "—will be staying." And as he says it, his eyes lock on Frannie.

"Think again," Matt says, stepping in front of Lili. The air charges with static electricity. I can almost see it dance across the surface of Matt's skin.

Andrus's face pulls into a deep frown, and he glares at Matt. "Such a public display? Really? You're sure you want to go there?"

In a flash, Matt has Andrus up against the wall, his forearm across Andrus's throat. The smell of ozone is sharp in the heavy night air, and all the hair on Andrus's arms stands on end.

"Yes," Matt says, his eyes slits and his face an inch from Andrus's.

Chax charges Matt, his fist glowing red, but I lunge forward and grab his arm as he raises it. I twist him into an armlock and throw him, facefirst, onto the floor.

"Go, Frannie!" I bark.

She and Lili skirt past Chax and out onto the sidewalk, dragging Taylor. And that's when I notice Rhenorian, standing under a burnt-out streetlight across the street.

"Damn," I say under my breath.

Frannie glances back at me once they're outside. "Luc . . . ?"

"Go!" I yell.

She hesitates just a second, but Lili keeps moving, so she follows.

I plant my knee in Chax's back, feeling his energy surge under me.

Andrus stares Matt down, his demon form flickering

through his human shell. "I'm finding the company you're keeping these days to be distasteful, Lucifer."

"Yeah, me too. But he comes in handy on occasion."

I peer out the door. Frannie and the girls are nearly to the Shelby. I nod to Matt and we let the demons go, dropping back onto the sidewalk. Matt turns up the glow—a warning that I hope is too subtle for the mortals here to notice. Of course, if he actually starts throwing lightning bolts, that's going to be hard to miss. We back toward the car and I toss Frannie the keys.

Frannie and Lili load Taylor into the back of the Shelby; then Lili jogs with Matt to her truck across the street. I look back at the brownstone and see Rhenorian standing on the walk with Andrus and Chax, and I can hardly wait to find out what fresh Hell the three of them will dream up in retaliation.

Frannie and I dive into the car and close the doors. I hit the gas and we squeal away from the curb.

I glance at Frannie as she drops her face into her hands and sobs.

My heart is in my throat, because I know she blames herself. She doesn't even know the worst of it.

And I'm not about to tell her.

MATT

We get Taylor up to Luc's and he pulls me aside. "She can't know about Taylor," he says to me with a warning glare, then glances at Frannie as she guides Taylor into the bathroom.

"She has to know. If she insists on trying to save her, she's only going to put herself in danger."

"And you don't think she's going to try to 'save' her if she knows Taylor's tagged? It'll be worse. She'll blame herself."

"You have to tell her," I say as Taylor retches over the toilet.

"Not yet."

"Soon," I say.

Lili comes up behind Luc. "Frannie's got Taylor." She waves her hand in the direction of the bathroom, and her face scrunches. "And I don't do puke, so I'm outta here."

"I'll walk you back," I say.

She looks at me. "It's, like, thirty feet. I think I can make it."

"I'm coming with you," I insist as she turns for the door.

Luc scowls after me and heads for the bathroom.

I walk up the hall with Lili. "Did you see the guy? Was he there?"

She shakes her head as she turns her keys in the locks. "I wasn't really looking."

"I want you to stay away from those guys. Give me your cell number."

She looks down at her foot and scuffs her toe at a piece of gum stuck to linoleum. "Can't afford one."

Tendrils of panic snake through me. They're not going to be happy about what happened tonight, and they're already stalking Lili. She's the weak link in the raiding party. A mortal already tagged for Hell. They'll come after her. "I want to know if they come anywhere near you—at work—anywhere."

She glances down the hall before pushing through the door.

I follow. "This isn't the safest place you could live, you know."

She spins around and looks at me. "It's all I can afford."

"No one's helping you out?"

"I've been on my own for a while. And I've got to swing this college thing on my own. I've got some scholarships and financial aid to pay tuition, but my job at the KwikMart doesn't pay much, and that goes for rent and everything."

I watch as she carefully twists all the deadbolts back into place and heads for the kitchen. She reaches into the fridge and comes out with two Cokes. I pop the top and settle into the couch. "What about your family?" I say.

She slides onto the couch and I feel hot electricity course through me when she curls in next to me. "There's no one I care about. I never knew my mom, and my father . . ." Her whole body clenches into a hard ball.

There's a tug at my core, like my insides are being ripped out. I want so much to help her, but I don't know what to do. I drape my arm around her shoulders and pull her tight to my side, stroking her hair.

When her tears start, I find myself wanting to kiss them away. But I don't. She buries her face in my shoulder and I let her cry. When her tears slow, I ask, "Would it help to talk about it?"

She pulls her head from my shoulder. "I don't think I could."

"Well, if you want to—now or later—I have big ears and a small mouth."

Her lips pull into an almost smile. "Your ears *are* a little big, but your mouth looks pretty perfect to me." And when she leans in and her lips meet mine, I'd swear I was just hit with a blast of Hellfire. Heat rips through my human form.

I don't know what to do. God knows I've wanted this. I'm completely torn between pulling her closer and pushing her away. But I can't push her away. I can't make myself do it. So I kiss her back. I'm feeling just short of terrified, but as I melt into her, the fire spreading under my skin settles into a warm glow. I deepen our kiss, needing to feel closer, wanting this—my first kiss with my first girlfriend—to last forever.

When she pulls back, I wait for a second, expecting avengers to appear and strip my wings. When they don't, I breathe a sigh of relief and realize Lili is staring at me, her eyes looking as scared as I feel.

"Sorry," she says. "I thought—"

I stop her with a finger on her warm, moist lips. "You thought right," I whisper and lean in again.

A thrill races through me at her touch. All my desires flare—everything I want but can't have.

Could I? With Lili? If it's love and not lust, would I lose my wings? Because I *do* love her. I've loved her from the second I first saw her.

I cup her cheek in my hand and bring her face to mine again. Now that the fear is lessening, I can focus on her and how it feels to touch her like this. And as we kiss, what I feel . . . it's unlike anything I've ever experienced. I feel emotions swell inside me, and before I even realize I've opened my mouth, I hear myself say, "I love you, Lili."

She leaps off the couch, her eyes wide. "What?"

My heart, if I had one, would be in my throat. "I'm sorry. I didn't mean . . ."

"You didn't mean it. I know," she says, lowering her lashes.

I pull myself slowly from the cushions and stand here, not sure what the right reply is. But I can't lie. "I *did* mean it. I'm just sorry if I shouldn't have *said* it."

She looks even more stunned and backs away a few steps. We stand here, staring at each other for what feels like an eternity, before she turns and runs for the bathroom.

Needing to do something to help her, I follow, but as she reaches the door, she holds up her hand, warning me off. "Just give me a sec, okay?"

I settle back into the couch as she closes the door. I come so close to passing through that wall, invisible, to check on her, but she asked for privacy, so I glue myself to the cushions.

When she comes back from the bathroom, she curls up next to me on the couch. A tear courses a crooked path down her cheek. I wipe it away and kiss her again. "Are you okay?"

"I've just never been with someone who . . . No one's ever loved me before."

"I love you," I repeat, and pull her closer.

She settles into my side and I hold her. And I know this is where I'm supposed to be.

17

✝

Original Sin

FRANNIE

Taylor's in the shower, and I have to keep poking my head in the door to make sure she's upright. I brought her to my house last night when she was with it enough to call her mom, and she stayed over. I helped her to the bathroom twice in the middle of the night so she could heave into the toilet, and spent the rest of the night curled around her in the bed while she shook.

I towel off my wet hair and toss the damp towel at Matt, where he lounges across my bed. I pull my robe tighter. "You think Taylor's gonna be okay?"

I'd almost swear anger flashes in his eyes before they turn sad. "I don't know."

"She's just so . . . messed up. I think that demon did something to her—I mean other than . . . you know." My stomach twists into a hard ball as the image from the party surfaces.

"You'll have to ask your boyfriend about that," he says, his voice suddenly acid.

My eyes shoot to him. "What would Luc know about it?"

"Everything. He's one of them."

"Stop it, Matt," I snap.

His eyes narrow and his voice becomes a growl. "He lies to you, Frannie."

"He doesn't! But, speaking of lying, he thinks there's something going on with you and Lili."

Matt doesn't answer. He just lies there, staring.

"So . . . is there?"

He doesn't look at me. I can see him struggling to get the word *no* out of his mouth, but he can't lie.

I feel myself soften as a flicker of hope tickles my brain. "So, how would that work, exactly? Could you . . . I don't know . . ."

He lifts his head and looks dead at me with a rueful half smile. "No."

"Why not? Luc is with me." I hear the hope in my voice and I know it's selfish. Is it wrong to hope he can have a life?

"It doesn't work that way. Even if I wanted it—"

"Why not? It's not fair."

He jumps off the bed, and his glare burns through me. The hair on my arms stands on end as his power surges, and ozone fills the room. His voice is a low growl. "Don't talk to me about fair. That demon gets everything and I get nothing."

His eyes spread wide and his face pulls into a mask of shock as my stomach drops to my knees. I can't believe Matt just said that. Not only *what* he said, but how he said it. And, from the look on his face, neither can he.

"I . . . ," he starts, but trails off, shocked speechless. He drops his forehead into his hand and rubs.

"Matt . . . I'm . . ." What? Sorry? I lower my lashes and inspect my hands. "It shouldn't have been this way."

He sits back on the bed. "Well, it is," he says, sounding really tired.

I ease into my desk chair and look up at him cautiously. "And you're wrong about Luc," I say, knowing this might not be the right time, but feeling like I need to say it anyway. "He's mortal now. Just like me."

He heaves a huge sigh, but his eyes stay trained on the carpet. "He'll never be like you."

"You're wrong. Luc loves me. He's human. He'd never do anything to hurt me."

"Maybe," Matt concedes. The corner of his mouth lifts in a weary half smile. "But he can't protect you either."

"Well . . . maybe. But you'll lighten up? Cut him some slack?"

He blows out another sigh and looks me in the eye. "As he earns it. I just hope I don't regret it."

I roll my eyes at him. "If you're gonna be any good at this guardian angel thing, you're gonna need to get a grasp on who the real enemy is. It's not Luc."

"According to *you*. You're forgetting that I'm the professional. I think I have a little more insight into people's character than you do."

I roll my eyes again, but I can't stop the smile. "Am I allowed to reassign you?"

Something flashes in his eyes, and for just a second he looks like he might say yes. He pulls himself off the bed. "No."

"'Cause I really think Taylor needs you more than I do."

Matt's eyes drop from mine, and he turns toward the window. "I need you to do something for me." He turns back from the window, and there's something desperate and a little wild in his expression.

"Yeah?" I say cautiously.

He looks up sharply and disappears just before the door cracks open and Taylor drags herself through, wrapped in my bathrobe, her hair twisted into a towel. She still looks like death: tired and too thin, with big purple circles under her dull gray eyes, and skin the color of ash.

"You gonna make it?" I ask her, standing.

"Maybe." Her voice is sour. She doesn't look at me.

I walk over and hug her, even though that's not really our thing. "I'm not gonna let him hurt you again."

She pulls away and glares at me, then grabs her clothes off the floor. "Yeah, whatever."

"You good to go home? You can spend the day here if you want."

"I'm good." She yanks her shirt over her head.

I'm not sure what the right thing to say is. I can tell she's not really "good," but I don't know what to do to change that.

"You're sure you're okay?"

She spins on me and spits, "Just get out of my face, Frannie!" Her face is etched with hatred.

I just stand here staring at her, stunned.

"I'm so sick of you playing holier-than-thou, like you're so seriously perfect or something."

"Tay, I just want to help."

"Well, you can help by leaving me the hell alone." She tugs on her skirt, nearly falling over. She jerks away from me as I try to steady her. "I'm outta here."

"Tay . . ."

She turns and glares murder at me on her way out my door. "Get out of my face!"

And all of a sudden, I'm furious. "You have no idea what Luc and I risked getting you out of there."

"I didn't ask you to. I didn't *want* you to."

"You don't see what he is, Tay."

Her eyes darken as her face pulls taut. "I see him just fine. Leave us alone."

"No. I won't."

She spins and moves as quickly as she can on shaky legs toward the stairs. "Just fuck off!" she says without turning.

"Fine! You know what? Go to hell!" I yell down the stairs after her.

My words trail into deafening silence as she slams her way out the front door. Mom appears at the bottom of the stairs, looking up at me with a question in her concerned eyes. I just shake my head and turn for my room, where I flop back on my bed and stare at the ceiling. Tears roll down my temples as I realize what an idiot I am. Taylor's not thinking straight. She needs my help.

God, I wish Gabe were here. He'd know what to do. And

just as I think it, I smell summer snow and feel something feather soft brush against my cheek. There's an instant of shock and my heart feels like it stalls, but then it picks up double-time as I start to breathe again. I sit up slowly and look around.

"Gabe," I whisper to the empty room, my eyes wide and heart pounding. But the sensation is gone as quickly as it came, and I'm left feeling more alone than ever.

I lie here forever, wishing for Gabe and trying to decide what to do. Finally, I drag myself off the bed and throw on my old jeans and a T-shirt.

"Mom, I'm going to Taylor's!" I yell on my way through the family room, and don't wait for a response.

I jog to Taylor's, but when I get there and knock on the door, it's Trevor who answers.

"Hey, Trev. Can I talk to Tay?"

"She's not here."

My stomach drops. "She didn't come home?"

"She was here for like five minutes. Went right to her room. But then that guy with the hearse pulled up. She bolted out to his car and they took off."

I pull out my phone and dial her number, but it goes to voice mail without ringing. "Shit."

"What?"

"That guy is seriously bad news, Trev." I feel bile rise in my throat as I think about what he did to her.

"I've never even seen him. He just pulls up and Taylor runs."

I back down the stairs. "I've gotta find her. Call me if she comes home," I yell over my shoulder as I turn and jog toward the sidewalk.

When I get back to the house, I jump in my car and head to Luc's.

MATT

Until yesterday, I hadn't really thought about it since Frannie brought it up a few weeks back. But after what happened with Lili, it's been playing in the back of my mind all day: Frannie's Sway is the only way. If she could use it, maybe I could have Lili—have *everything*.

She changed the demon. Why not me?

I can already feel myself changing. I feel things I didn't even know were possible when I'm with Lili.

I glance at Frannie as she drives. She's scowling straight out the windshield, lost in her own thoughts.

I clear my throat, slump deeper into my seat, and start the script I've practiced. "Do you remember when you told me you wanted to make me mortal?"

She glances at me, and her scowl disappears, replaced by caution. "Yeah."

"I want you to."

Her eyes widen, but then her face crumbles as tears threaten. "Oh, Matt . . . you know I want to, but I don't think I can."

"Why not?" I hear the edge in my voice and hope Frannie doesn't.

"My Sway isn't anything. I thought it was, but . . ." She shakes her head and looks haunted. "It . . . I can't do it."

It's out of pure desperation that I can't let it drop, even

222

though I know I should. "You said you wanted to help me . . . to make up for what you did. This is your chance." I feel my face lock in a grimace as sick disgust buries me. I can't look at her. I never intended to say that—play that card. I don't even know where that came from.

When I do look, she glances sideways at me, a tear trailing down her cheek. She scrubs it away with the back of her wrist. "What would I have to do?"

"Just want it, I guess. You know how it works better than me."

A wounded sob escapes her throat. "But I've always wanted that, even before any of this . . ." She waves her hand at me. "I've always wanted you back."

"Maybe that's why I ended up your guardian, but I think you have to want me more than 'back.' I think you have to want me mortal—human."

She shoots me an uncertain glance. "I . . ."

"Just think about it," I say.

She'll do it. I know she will. I can feel her guilt, heavy and thick, like a blanket over her soul. And as sick as I feel inside, the throbbing ache isn't totally from disgust. Because I ache for Lili, and this is the only way I can have her. Frannie wants it this way. She was the one who brought it up in the first place. The knot in my core loosens as I realize I didn't do anything wrong, really—just encouraged her to do what she already wanted to do.

We pull into Luc's parking lot. She cuts the engine and sits for a long minute before turning to look at me. "I'll try," she says.

I push out the door before she can see the elation on my face. I'm pretty sure I'm glowing.

She climbs out of the car, and I realize I'm shaking. I can't stop. I want this so much. I can see the picture clearly in my head: Lili in my arms, so soft and warm . . . touching me, kissing me . . .

A shudder rolls through me. We could leave Haden. Go someplace where no one knows us. Be together—*really* together. Everything in me explodes into a shower of sparks. Maybe I should cut the demon some slack. If this is how Frannie makes him feel . . .

I follow her up the stairs and she twists her key in Luc's lock. My soaring heart soars higher when I pass through the door and see Lili, sitting at the table in her gray sweats. Her hair is pulled off her face in a ponytail and she looks . . . beautiful. Like she's almost shining. Amazingly alive.

But then I see Luc sitting across from her, empty dishes on the table between them. They seem to be engrossed in some intense conversation, and any charity I was feeling toward him instantly vanishes.

I stride over and stand next to Lili. "What are you guys talking about?"

Luc takes a second to respond. His eyes shift from Lili to Frannie and back, and they narrow almost imperceptibly. "Nothing."

He pulls himself out of the chair and wraps Frannie in a hug. "Lili and I made omelets. Want one?"

My hands grasp the back of Lili's chair so hard, I'm vaguely surprised the wood doesn't splinter. I bite my lips together and swallow the fury that's dying to spew from my mouth. How can Frannie be so blind? How can she not see that he's all over Lili?

I'm choking.

Can angels choke? I have to get out of here.

Lili stands. Her eyes shoot to me then away. "I've gotta get ready for work," she says. "See you guys later."

She rinses her dish in the sink and I walk with her to the door, fighting to keep my hands off her.

"I'm heading out too," I say, waving over my shoulder. "I'll be back."

Luc eyes me, but he doesn't say anything.

Once Lili and I are in the hall, I don't even pretend. I lace my fingers in hers and walk with her to her door. "Do you really have to work?"

"Not for a few hours." Her eyes drop and she blushes. "But I was hoping if I left, you might come over."

I smile as all my senses flare. "I'm over. So are you going to invite me in?"

She turns her key in the lock and pushes the door open. We step through, but before she can close it, her face is in my hands and my lips are moving with hers.

I pull back and gaze down into her amazing green eyes. "Sorry. I had to do that."

She smiles up at me and closes the door. Then she takes my hand and leads me to the couch. I look for a spot to sit, but she doesn't seem to care that there are clothes all over it. She pushes me down and slides in next to me, pressing herself into me and kissing me again.

And I feel caught in a riptide. I'm getting pulled deeper and deeper. But I want it. I want it to take me all the way under and never let me up.

Her hands explore and I pull her tighter, feeling things stir deep inside me. Something primal, but undeniable. Lust.

No. *Love.* I love her. Is it wrong to want to be close to someone you love?

I'm drowning in her as my hands move over her back, her waist, and slide under her shirt.

She pulls back. "Stop!"

I take my hands off her and hold them up, hating myself for going too fast. *What's wrong with me?* "I'm sorry. I lost control. It won't happen again."

She buries her face in her hands. "It's not that. I want to be with you, but . . ."

I gather her back into my arms, the tension in my chest easing. "What is it, then?"

She lifts her head and looks at me, unsure and scared. I go suddenly cold inside, convinced she's changed her mind about me.

Her lashes lower. "If I tell you, you'll leave."

"If I promise not to . . . ?"

"It won't matter."

"Try me."

Her eyes lift to mine, and she stares for a moment longer before pushing off the couch and walking to the window, where she stands staring out into the parking lot for a long time. When her voice comes, it's heavy with the weight of the world. "I'm no angel, Matt."

I start. *How can she know?* Luc?

She turns back to me, and the dim lights reflect off the damp sheen of her cheeks. "I've been with guys . . . lots of guys."

My insides unclench as a long, relieved sigh escapes my chest. She doesn't know. And she'll be safe now. I'll make sure of it. No one will ever get near enough to hurt her again. Not without coming through me first.

I stand and move slowly to the window. "Who you've loved in the past—"

Her face twists and her eyes turn to stone. "I didn't *love* them!" she spits.

I feel my eyes widen as everything goes cold. "Oh."

The pain in her voice nearly kills me. I step toward her to comfort her, but she holds up a hand and backs off a step. "I do what I have to do to survive." She turns back to the window as her voice breaks and she tries, unsuccessfully, to stifle a sob.

"I'm so sorry, Lili." I slide closer and lay my hand on her shoulder. I feel so helpless.

She flinches away from my touch and strides into the kitchen, plucking a paring knife off the counter. She rolls the handle in her fingers, scaring me with thoughts of what she might do, before grasping the handle and plunging the tip into the linoleum countertop.

"What can I do?" The crushing pressure in my chest is almost unbearable.

She turns to me, eyes hard even through the tears. "Just go."

"I'm not leaving you. Not like this." I take a step toward her and hold out my hand, but her eyes flash fury as she backs away.

"I don't want you feeling sorry for me. Just get the hell out."

But I don't stop. I step slowly toward her, needing to do something. "No."

"What, you won't leave until you get some?" she says, her face twisting in angry sarcasm. "You're just like all the others." She turns back to the counter and looks as though she's going to pull the knife from the countertop.

My insides contract into a hard ball. She needs to know I'm different, but how? I focus on her—how I feel about her—and radiate it out, trying to make her understand.

"No," I say softly as I approach. "I won't go until you know I was serious when I said I loved you."

She turns, her eyes wide. "You can't love me. I'm unlovable."

I reach her and carefully slide my arms around her waist. "But I do."

Her eyes drop to the floor. "Well, I hate you."

"If that's what you need . . ."

She leans into me, her hands flat on my chest, and I pull her close. "I hate you," she says again.

I kiss the top of her head and bury my face in her hair. "I love you."

She presses into me and I'm on fire. And when she kisses me, it's like lighting a fuse. The slow burn consumes me.

I know I need to back off, for a lot of reasons. She's vulnerable right now, and I mustn't take advantage of her. And there's also the wings thing. I'm pretty sure this is a line I can't cross and still keep them. But it's almost impossible. I need her so much, it's almost as if she were the heart I don't have. A vital piece of me that's missing.

I find the strength to pull away from her. "Lili . . . I can't right now."

She pushes me, hard. "Because I'm too disgusting."

"No. Absolutely *no*. It's nothing like that." I place my hand on her chest, over her heart, and feel it thump under my fingers. She *is* my heart.

She slides out from between me and the counter. "Yeah, right. Just get out." She storms to the door and opens it.

I stand here, feeling the empty black hole that is my insides collapsing down on itself. I need to leave before things get out of control. But not like this.

"Lili . . ."

"Just go."

I walk over to her, but hesitate at the door. I want to show her I'm serious, that I don't just want sex. I stop in front of her and kiss her forehead. My lips move to her ear. "We're going to do this right, Lili. I just need a little time."

How long did it take Frannie to turn Luc?

A few weeks? A month?

For Lili, I can wait that long. And, in the meantime, there's got to be something I can do to reverse her tag. Hope swells inside me, filling me to bursting. I just have to be strong for a little while.

I can do this.

But when her eyes connect with mine, I feel a white-hot surge of desire so powerful that I can't think of anything but the feel of her against me. Fire rips through me, burning away any doubt I had. I've never felt need like this before—totally raw and all-consuming. She closes the door and reaches for my face, bringing it to hers again.

Everything from there happens in a blur—kissing, fumbling with clothes. And then we're on the floor, her body against mine. I work so hard to stop, to make myself think. But when she pulls me closer and whispers in my ear, "I love you," there's nothing I can do. Everything I am becomes part of her.

18

✝

The Demon's Lair

MATT

Lili pulls her face out of my shoulder. "I really *do* need to go to work. Plus my hip is killing me." She shifts on the floor, rubbing her hip, and gives me a shaky smile. "The couch would have been much more comfortable."

I grab her sweatshirt from the floor next to us, wrap it around her, and hold on tight. There's not a word to describe what I'm feeling. Bliss doesn't even begin to cover it. I lift my face from her hair and look into her eyes. She's smiling at me. Which means she must be okay with what we did.

And, apparently, so am I.

At first, as much as I wanted her, I wasn't really 100 percent focused on Lili, because I was sure this was it. I kept waiting for the avengers. But as it went on—*and on,* I think with a smile—I was able to *really* be with her, to lose myself completely. And the sensation was more than I expected or ever could have hoped. Maybe I was right. If it's love . . . maybe I'm allowed to have it.

She untangles herself from me and pulls up off the floor. I prop up onto my elbow and watch her walk to the bathroom, then get up and tug on my clothes, feeling a little awkward. What's supposed to happen now? Do I stay? Do I leave? What's protocol?

I opt for a seat on the couch and admire her from afar as she gets ready for work. When she steps to the door, dressed in a tank top and faded jeans, I pull myself up and follow her. I wrap an arm around her waist, sweep her hair off her face, and kiss her. Her hands are on my face, and when she tips her head and pulls me deeper into the kiss, an electric jolt shoots through me and I catch myself glowing a little. I rein back my power when I feel her jump at the shock.

She pulls back, smiling. "Wow."

"Yeah . . . wow." I smile back and work hard not to glow.

Her smile turns shy and her eyes drop from mine. "So, if you want to hang here, you can. I'll be back around eight." Her expression is hopeful as her eyes flick back to mine. She slides her hand into her pocket and hands me a key. "I have an extra."

"Don't you think you're trusting me a little too easily?"

She arches an eyebrow. "Are you saying I shouldn't?"

The key vanishes into my fist. "No. I just hope you aren't handing out keys to every guy you meet."

It's not even out of my mouth before I wish I could suck it back in.

Her face darkens and she grabs at my hand. "Give it back."

I hold my hand back, and when she lunges for it, I grab her

around the waist and pull her tight to me. "I didn't mean that the way it sounded. I just worry about you."

She pushes away and looks at me, her eyes wary.

"And I'll be here when you get home," I add. I pull her closer and whisper in her ear. "I love you."

Her eyes clear but she doesn't kiss me good-bye. I watch her walk down the hall, hoping I haven't completely screwed everything up, then phase into Luc's apartment.

Frannie scowls into the depths of a mug of forgotten coffee and picks at a cold omelet with her fork. Her forehead is in her other palm, her fingers tangled in her hair, and her elbow on the table. Luc swirls the coffee in his mug and stares at her from across the table.

Trouble in paradise?

Is it wrong that this makes me happy? This was already the best day of my existence. Could it be about to get better?

I pull myself up and sit on the counter, unable to stop the grin. "What's up?"

Frannie pulls her head from her hand. "Shut up. I'm trying to focus."

My brows raise quizzically at Luc.

"She's trying to use her Sway on Taylor," he explains.

"To—?" I ask.

"Get her to stay away from Marchosias."

Frannie stands and walks to the bed, where she flops onto her back with a forearm over her eyes.

I look over at her. "So you're just going to lie there all day and tell Taylor that Marchosias is a scumbag and she doesn't want him?"

"I have to try something. It's my fault she's with him. I can't just sit around while he tags her soul."

I glare at Luc, who winces.

"Call me, call me, call me . . . ," she mutters.

I walk over and nudge Frannie's knee. "If you need me, I'll be outside."

"'Kay," she says from under her arm.

I phase, but it's not into the hall. I go back to Lili's. A shuddering thrill works through me. *She gave me a key.* I'm welcome here . . . invited. I don't have to hover in the hall anymore.

I can't wipe the smile off my face as I wander through the apartment. In the bathroom, I find a bottle of her perfume on the sink. I bring it to my nose, but it's disappointing. It's not the same before it's touched her skin.

I guess the same could be said for me. I'm not the same angel I was before this morning. Being with Lili has changed everything.

Staring at myself in the mirror over the sink, one thing becomes glaringly apparent, even in the dim light of the flickering fluorescents. I can't focus on Frannie when all I care about is Lili. I need to find a way to reverse her tag. That's my new mission. I'll have to talk to Gabriel.

FRANNIE

"The Shelby needs new brake pads," Luc says.

I know what he's trying to do, and I love him for it, but as much as getting greasy under the Shelby with Luc might serve as a nice distraction, it isn't gonna help Taylor. "I've got to go to work," I say, pulling myself off the bed.

Luc balances on the back legs of his chair. "Call in sick."

"No. I need to go. Saturday afternoon's when Ricco's is full of birthday parties. He'll fire me if I don't show."

"I'll go with you," he says, lowering the chair to the ground and standing.

"I'm fine, Luc. Stop treating me like a baby."

He looks at me warily. "You're sure you're okay?"

"Fine. Really."

He still looks unsure. "Call me when you get there."

"Sure." I head to the door and Luc follows. He peers past me, out into the hallway.

"Focus, Matt," he says loudly into the empty hall.

When I get to my car, I pull out my cell phone and dial. "Hey, Delanie. Can you tell Ricco I think I've got the flu?" I say in my best weak rasp when she answers the phone at Ricco's.

"Ugh! You're not spewing, are you?" she asks, disgusted.

"All over." I cough for good measure.

"Gross!"

"Very. So will you tell him?"

"Yeah," she says, and hangs up quick, like she might get what I have through the phone line.

I sit in my car and hold my breath for a second, waiting for Matt to appear and ask me what I'm doing. When he doesn't, I blow out a long breath and I pull out of the parking lot. I pass Rhenorian, parked in the back row. When he follows me with his eyes, but not with his car, I know I'm in the clear. I breathe a shaky sigh and head south, toward the city.

When I get to Marc's neighborhood, I start to second-guess myself, and for a second I think about calling for Matt. But I know he'd try to stop me, just like Luc would have, so I suck it up.

I drive down the street past Marc's brownstone. My gut clenches and my face pinches involuntarily as my mind shows me Taylor on the kitchen table. My heart pounds in my chest as I circle the block, looking for a parking spot close enough to watch his front door. On the second loop, I catch someone just pulling out half a block up and across the street from Marc's. I pull into the spot and sit for a long time, whispering my mantra: "Taylor, you don't want Marc. He's bad for you. You don't want Marc."

I don't have any way to know if Taylor's even in there or not, so I wait and watch for her to come or go.

But instead, I see a beat-up hunter orange pickup truck pull into a spot just up the street from me.

Lili?

Oh, God! She's looking for Taylor too.

I jump out of the car to stop her before she walks into the lion's den, but as she turns toward Marc's, I see she's smiling.

Smiling?

I hear myself groan as the pieces fall together. She's not here to find Taylor. She's here to see that Chax guy. In the second it takes me to process that, she disappears into the brownstone. It's nearly impossible not to charge in after her. But I don't. I have to focus on Taylor right now.

I slide back into my car and wait for any sign of her. After an hour, I'm aching all over from clenching every muscle in my body, and I'm sure I'm gonna die. I've called Taylor's cell a hundred times, but as usual, she's not answering.

Finally, I can't stand it anymore. I step out of the Mustang and cross the street toward the brownstone, but before I reach it, Lili emerges onto the sidewalk. My breath catches as Marc follows her out. And his hands are all over her.

I duck behind a parked car and watch as they make their way toward Lili's truck, just two cars up from where I am.

Low behind the car, I peek around the fender. Lili says something I can't hear.

"I'd be jealous," Marc replies, pressing her into the side of the truck with his body, "if I wasn't already sharing you with half of humanity." He crushes her in a violent kiss that hurts my lips just watching it.

She pulls back and looks up at him. "You have your toy," she says. "I'm the one who should be jealous. What if you fall for her?"

"She's nothing," he says as Lili slides into her truck.

"Just have her there when I need her," she says through the open window. "The timing will be crucial." He leans in the window for another kiss, but she pushes him away and pulls out.

Marc stands, watching after her as her truck chugs up the street and disappears around the corner.

I wait behind the car, my pulse pounding in my ears, trying to sort out what all this means. Lili is with Marc? *How?*

But when Marc turns back toward the brownstone, I step out from behind the car. I can barely breathe, and I'm not sure what I mean to do, but I have to know if Taylor's here.

"Marc!"

He turns, and at first, his mouth drops open. He recovers and his obsidian eyes flash as a slow smile quirks his lips. "Well, what do we have here?"

I glare at him. "Where's Taylor?"

"Where's your boy toy?" he asks, glancing down the sidewalk behind me.

"Is she in there?" I growl, my eyes flicking to the brownstone.

He raises an eyebrow at me and extends an arm invitingly. "Why don't you come in and find out?"

I step toward him, my fingernails gouging painfully into my palms. "Is she here or not?"

His face pulls into a leer that sends ice up my spine. "Don't know. Last I saw her, she was with Chax, after Andrus finished with her."

Without even thinking, I lunge at him and throw him to the ground, where I hold him in a necklock.

He grins up at me, not even fighting back. "Impressive. What are you feeling right now, Frannie? Rage? Hate?"

I see what he's trying to do, and it's working. I can't control the rage churning my insides into a raw, bleeding mass. I want him dead.

I breathe deep and force myself to let him go. I pull myself slowly up off the sidewalk. Losing control isn't helping Taylor.

Marc stands in one smooth motion. "Please, come in." He gestures toward the door with a small bow. "I have a set of Ginsu knives." He lays a hand over his heart and taps his fingers on his chest. A sarcastic smile spreads across his face as he adds, "One of those puppies right here will make you feel *so* much better."

"Is she in there?" I say again through clenched teeth.

"Only one way to find out." He turns and walks through the door, leaving me standing on the sidewalk, staring after him.

I have no choice. Breathing deep to clear the panic in my chest, I step through the door and walk the short, dark passage. I enter the darker room in the back, and in the second it takes my eyes to adjust, there are fingers digging into my upper arms, pulling me deeper into the room. I blink and try to pull loose as I struggle to see who has me. When I can finally make out the figures through the gloom, I see the glowing red eyes of Marc and Chax on either side of me. Andrus sits in a throne of sorts on the platform that serves as the band's stage.

I twist hard and bring my knee up into Chax's crotch. He falls away, surprised, then looks up at me with wide eyes and half a smile. "Unholy Hell! Where'd that come from?"

Marc smirks. "Sorry, dude. Should have warned you."

Chax rights himself and flashes me a grin. He steps closer, but instead of grabbing my arm, he winks, then takes a swing at Marc. He catches him square in the jaw and knocks him back a step. Marc's grip loosens and I swing out with my foot, taking his legs out from under him. He hits the floor, swearing.

From the stage, a low chuckle catches everyone's attention. I turn and see Andrus, grinning at me through a mouthful of fangs. "I think I like you. Your training is going to be such a pleasure."

I glare at him. "My training?"

"Yes, once we reverse your tag—which, by the looks of things, is coming along nicely—you'll need to be trained. Who better to do that than the PR guy? It's all about image and placement. We get you in front of the right people, Swaying them to do the right things, and we're golden. There'll be no stopping you."

I've heard enough. I wheel toward the kitchen, closing the distance in a few long strides, and flip on the light. I glance around the room, trying to block out the image in my mind of what Marc was doing to Taylor last time I was here. The flickering fluorescent light reveals an empty room. Taylor's not here.

Chax starts toward me, but Andrus waves him off.

I spin on him. "Where is she?"

Andrus just grins at me.

I cross the room and fling open a door next to the stage. The room is dark and smells of sweat, rot, and something fouler. I flick on the light switch, and on the worn brown carpet, the bare bulb of a toppled desk lamp illuminates in a pile of dirty clothes. I pick it up and step into the room.

There are two large stained mattresses on the floor, taking up most of the room. Six or seven bodies, all female and some naked, are strewn across them. A few of them stir and lift their heads as I shine the light around the room. None have pink hair. No Taylor.

Part of me thanks God while another part growls in frustration.

I move deeper into the room and crouch next to the mattress, setting the lamp down next to me. I shake one of them—a pretty blonde who looks Maggie's age—by the shoulder. She barely stirs.

"Are you okay?" I say, to no response.

I stand and turn for the door to find Andrus standing there, blocking me in, a hint of wild threat in his expression. Before I can react, he's closed the distance between us and stands only a few inches from me. He loops a hot hand behind my neck and tips my face up. "You'd make a lovely addition," he says, motioning to the girls with a tip of his head.

"What did you do to them?" I growl.

His lips pull into a depraved grin. "Stick around and you'll find out."

"You wouldn't want me," I say, pushing the thought with my mind.

For just a second, his face goes flat; then he shakes his head and chuckles. "Mmm . . . that's very good. King Lucifer will be pleased that you've been practicing." He grabs my face in his other hand and crushes his mouth into mine, grinding my lips against his fangs. I'm surprised by his strength.

I gasp and push away, tasting blood, and trip over the lamp and tangle of clothes on the floor behind me, ending up on my butt.

He chuckles again and holds out his hand for me. "I had to get that in before you changed my mind."

I pull myself up and throw a punch at his face, but he catches my wrist and holds it. *"Where is Taylor?"* I say, yanking my arm away.

"I don't know," he says after a long pause.

"She's not here?"

He hesitates, and something feral flashes in his eyes. I drop into fighting stance, thinking he's gonna grab me again. But instead, he smiles down at me almost tenderly. "No, she's not. We have what we needed from her."

I toss one more desperate glance back at the girls and push past Andrus at a run. I head straight for my car, my heart pounding in my throat. When I get to it, I floor the accelerator and tear out of the city, afraid to look back.

On the way back to Haden, I call the police and tell them about the girls. Then I call Taylor every two seconds—still no answer. *Come home, Taylor.* I say it out loud over and over.

And Lili. What was she doing with Marc?

LUC

Lili stands in my door, looking different—more confident, somehow. Her pale skin contrasts sharply with her dark hair, which is pulled back in a tight ponytail. She brushes her bangs out of her face with the back of her wrist, giving me a clear view of those intense green eyes, and smiles up at me. "Hey, Luc. Frannie around?"

I look away and swing the door open. "She's coming by after work. You can wait here if you want. Shouldn't be too long."

She slides by me, brushing against my arm, and I'm startled as some deep need rolls through me. I shake it off as she passes. She wanders to my CD rack, runs a finger along the titles, and pulls one out. "Can I put this in?" she asks.

"Be my guest."

She does, then eases into a kitchen chair, curling one leg under her.

"You want some coffee?" I ask, pouring myself a cup.

"Not much of a coffee drinker, thanks. So, you're sure Frannie's coming over?"

"Yep."

"When?"

"Soon, I think."

I join her at the table, and she looks me in the eye from under her long, dark eyelashes. "So, what's the deal with you and Frannie, anyway?"

Her question takes me by surprise. "In what way?"

"I don't know. How long have you been . . . together?"

"Technically . . . a few months."

"What does that mean—'technically'?"

"Our relationship was a little . . . complicated . . . at first." I feel the smile pull at my lips, and I let it spread into a grin.

She cocks an eyebrow and smiles back. "How so?"

I lean forward, elbows on the table, and wrap my hands around my steaming coffee mug, staring into its depths. "Doesn't matter. Ancient history."

"So, is she your ideal? You know, your perfect girl?"

My eyes flick to her sly little smirk. I draw a long swallow from my mug, feeling the coffee burn on its way down. "Pretty damn close."

"That's not a yes. What would you change about her if you could change one thing?"

"Wow . . ." That's a tough one, because my first reaction is to say I wish she didn't have Sway—Hell wouldn't be after her and she'd be safe. But it's her Sway that made me what I am—who I am—and I wouldn't trade what I have with Frannie for anything. I picture her face, and a shudder works through me. "Nothing. I'm revising my answer to just plain *yes*. She *is* my perfect girl."

She raises her eyebrows and reaches across the table to touch my hand where it rests on my coffee mug. Her voice is soft, hypnotizing. "Really—?"

For a second, the room seems to shimmer in and out of focus, shapes and sounds blurring together. The last thing I see clearly before my head starts to spin is Lili, leaning toward me, with her elbows on the table and her hand on mine, smiling.

I pull my hand off the mug, plant my elbow on the table, and close my eyes, waiting for the vertigo to pass. But it doesn't. If anything, it intensifies. I hear a faint voice as if from a great distance. At first I think it's still Lili, but then I realize it's Frannie. She's calling my name. And then I feel her touch on my face. My head starts to clear and I look up.

Frannie is there, standing next to my chair. I stand, pulling her to me. The world blurs again as her lips touch mine. A light-headed rush sends my senses whirring, and I breathe deep to keep my bearings. Frannie's in my arms, pulling me closer. She crushes me in another kiss, deeper, grinding her teeth into mine in her urgency.

Tiny bits of bliss surge through me as she pushes me backward toward the bed. She looks up at me with wicked ideas dancing in her sparkling sapphire eyes. And when she rips my T-shirt off in one hard yank, leaving it in shreds, primal lust flares in me. My need to be with her is suddenly overwhelming and insatiable. Her own gravitational field pulls me to her and I moan as our bodies collide.

"Frannie," I growl as I twist my fingers into her hair and yank her mouth to mine, crushing her with my kiss.

She bites my lip and I taste blood, heightening my lust—pure animal need. She pushes me hard and I stagger back onto the bed. She climbs on top of me as everything starts to spin into a black fog.

"You're mine," she says before devouring me with a kiss.

19

✣

When Angels Fall

FRANNIE

I call for Matt when I get to the house, and he's there in a heart-beat, appearing near the window in my bedroom.

"We need to find Taylor." I sound out of breath, which I pretty much am, since I haven't been able to breathe since I left Marc's.

"I might be able to help you with that, but there's nothing I can do about her tag."

I couldn't have heard him right. "What?"

His eyes widen then drop to the floor. "I thought Luc told you."

My legs waver and I manage to make it to the bed before they give way. I drop onto the edge of it. "Taylor's . . . tag?"

When he doesn't answer, I look up at him. "What's going on, Matt?"

"Taylor's soul is tagged for Hell, Frannie. She crossed the line with Marc. There's nothing you can do."

A groan rolls up from my chest. "Luc . . . ?" My throat is so tight, I can't find air. Stars spark, bright then dim then bright again, in my eyes. "He knew?"

"I . . ." I hear him hesitate and wonder why he's even considering defending Luc. He hates him. He finally gives up. "Yes."

I stand and storm out of the room, ignoring my mom's calls as I blast through the family room and right out the front door. When I peel out of the driveway, I hear Matt in my ear. "What are you doing, Frannie?"

I just stare straight out the windshield, unable to find words through the cold steel of my rage.

I can't even remember the drive as I twist my key in Luc's lock and fling the door open, ready to lay into him.

From the stereo, the pounding rhythm of Depeche Mode tells me everything is "Wrong."

And as I look around the room, I know they're right.

The first thing I notice is the black lace bra hanging from the headboard, where the red bra I gave Luc as a talisman has always hung.

And two bodies move together under the comforter.

The blood drains from my face, and everything turns cold as I take in the scene: clothes piled on the floor—Luc's, and some definitely more feminine—the wash of long dark hair across the pillow, the subtle hint of sweet vanilla and citrus, mixing with the heavier musk of warm bodies.

And I can't breathe.

The periphery of my vision blurs and I feel light-headed. As if in a trance, I move forward. In four steps, I'm at the bed, and my heart squeezes tight in my chest as I hear Luc's sigh.

I grab the comforter, tear it back, and can't stop the wounded moan that escapes my throat. It's everything I can do not to double over as my gut clenches into a painful knot.

Lili.

"Oh, God." The words catch in my throat.

I stumble back into Matt, who stands transfixed by the scene in the bed. He catches me and his fingers dig into my upper arms, deeper and deeper, till the pain of his grasp snaps me out of my stupor.

Luc seems totally unaware that they have an audience, completely lost in her. But Lili spares me a sidelong glance as the hint of a smile pulls at her lips. Her hands reach for Luc's face and pull it back to hers.

"No!" I scream, only half-aware that I've done it. I turn to Matt as myriad emotions assault me. I plunge my face into his shoulder and find him shaking. When I pull back and look him in the face, I see fury.

He shoves me aside and charges the bed, pulling Luc away from Lili. "Get off her, you bastard!"

Luc blinks and looks like he's having trouble focusing, as if waking from a dream—not quite able to get his bearings. He looks from Lili to Matt.

"Get up, you son of a bitch!" Matt yells.

Luc rolls away from Lili and he blinks again as his brow creases.

Matt tears Luc from the bed by his hair. "Get away from her!"

As my mind processes what's happening, I suddenly realize that Matt is fighting for Lili, not defending me. "Matt?"

His only response is to throw Luc to the ground and jump on top of him, whaling on Luc's face with his fists. Luc barely raises an arm to defend himself, too stunned to fight back.

Finally, Luc seems to get his bearings. He lands a punch that snaps Matt's head back, and takes the opportunity to shove Matt off. He pulls himself to his feet, his lip bleeding and his cheek starting to swell. He stares at me, his mouth open and his eyes wide—a look of utter shock. I'm obviously early. He didn't expect to get caught. Then he looks back at the bed. At Lili.

LUC

I fight for control of my senses as the illusion flickers and fades. Then it's Lili, not Frannie, lying in my bed.

Satan save me.

I'm dizzy and completely disoriented, but through the fog, I realize what I've done. An agonized cry of despair erupts from my core. "No!"

I swing back to Frannie. She stands, still as stone, supporting herself with a hand splayed flat on the kitchen table, her face twisted in pain. A tear trickles slowly down her cheek, and my heart contracts into a hard ball. I tug my jeans on as she shakes her head in disbelief. "How could you?" It's barely a whisper.

I take a step forward and hold out my hand to her. "Frannie . . .

I didn't . . ." But there's nothing I can say to make this right. I rake my hand through my hair and try to think.

How did this happen?

I search my mind, but there's nothing. Everything is a black fog.

I look back at Lili, on the bed, and to the coffee mug next to Frannie on the table. Tiny scraps of memory tease me: Lili asking about Frannie, touching my hand. Then black lust. Animal need. The certainty that if I didn't have Frannie right that instant, I'd die.

Pure, unadulterated lust.

It hits me like a wrecking ball.

I can hardly breathe as I wheel on Lili, sitting on the edge of my bed. "You! What are you?"

She cringes back from me, pulling the sheets tighter around her, and tears well in her stunned eyes. Suddenly, I'm confused. I want to blame this on Lili, but . . .

I spin back to Frannie, who's retreating toward the door. "No. Frannie, please . . ."

She turns and runs just as Matt takes me back down to the ground, yelling like a Banshee. "I knew it! I'm going to kill you!"

He grabs a handful of hair and slams my head into the floor with it, and I feel his power surge. My hair stands on end as static electricity crackles between us. I throw him off and pull myself to my feet, ignoring the throb in my head.

Matt is on his feet, his glow nearly blinding. Through it, I see licks of white lightning dance over the surface of his skin, and the smell of ozone suddenly hangs sharp in the air. I spin and run for the door. When I hear his tortured cry from behind me, I brace myself for the impact of his lightning bolt hitting my back. But it doesn't happen.

White light erupts in the room, and for a moment, I'm blind. I squint against the glare, lifting my arm to shield my eyes. As they adjust, two figures, shadows in the radiance, converge on Matt.

Unholy Hell. Avenging angels.

It's no myth. They *are* beautiful—angelic, with celestial magnificence that makes it impossible to pull my eyes away. But also terrible in the most beautifully horrible sense—their singular purpose is to destroy.

I've seen them before, of course, but I still can't help the terror that springs to life in my core as I realize why they're here.

Their feathered wings spread wide, glorious, they descend quickly on Matt, where he stands near the bed. His face is set in a grimace, his eyes still locked on me. The sudden, overpowering urge to protect him from the avengers makes me take a few steps into the room. But their cold heat burns, forcing me back.

Matt raises his hand, and lightning crackles over the surface of his palm, building to critical mass. "You won't touch Lili again," he growls, his focus still on me.

Just as he unleashes the blast, he turns his gaze to the angel that's descending in front of him, and his eyes pull wide. The blast of lightning from Matt's palm is absorbed into the intense glow of the angel, eaten alive. The next second, Matt screams as he's also absorbed into that glow.

Through Matt's scream, I hear the sickening crunch of snapping bone as his wings are torn from his body, and as much as I want to, I can't turn away. A blast of charged air hits me as if a bomb went off, and I stagger back into the hall. Then, as fast as it came, the light is gone and Matt lies bleeding on the floor.

I turn and run down the hall after Frannie without a backward glance.

MATT

I feel as though I'm waking from a dream, and find Lili kneeling over me, wrapped in a sheet. I moan as her fingers stroke my face, and when she leans in to kiss me, I explode in a burst of bliss. I pull her to me, kissing her deeper, lost in the feel of her next to me.

She showers my face with kisses. "Are you okay?"

I smile up at her and feel the tug of disappointment at my inability to remember what just happened. We were obviously together—she's naked under the sheet, but . . .

And that's when I realize I'm not. I'm in my jeans and T-shirt. I glance at our surroundings and see we're in Luc's apartment, not Lili's.

I squint up at Lili, fighting to remember. "What—?"

Her eyes cloud as she pulls back from my embrace. "I didn't want to."

An image flashes. Lili. In Luc's bed.

Another. My fist connecting with Luc's face.

I pull myself off the floor. As I stand here, my legs shake. I can't quite get my head straight. My senses feel dulled, my vision blurry. And then I feel a hot trickle down my back. And pain—a deep stinging ache. I press my hand to the T-shirt on my back and gasp when it comes away wet—and red.

Blood?

That's impossible. Angels don't bleed.

I look back at Lili. She's still kneeling, chocolate brown hair strewn across her shoulders. Hot rage—but also hot lust—dulls the pain in my back. All I feel is the crushing pain in my heart as the memory, like a flash flood, hits me full force.

"Lili?"

She stands, pulling the sheet with her. "I didn't want him, Matt, but I had no choice. . . ." A tear trails down her cheek as she gazes at me with wounded eyes.

Cold rage cuts through me. I move to where she stands, not sure whether I want to hit her or kiss her, and she throws herself around me.

"Please, Matt. I'm so sorry."

Slowly, I lift my shaking hands and lay them on her hips. I'm acutely aware of her body under the thin sheet—the only thing separating us—as she sobs into my shoulder. She looks up at me with those beautiful green eyes, and desire explodes through me. I hear my own moan, animal in its need, as I crush my lips to hers. But then the image of her in bed with Luc assaults my mind again, and I push her away.

"You slept with him."

"I didn't want to. You have to believe me. He made me." Her face is all pain and desperation, and my need to protect her is suddenly overwhelming.

I pull her back to me, crushing her into the curve of my body. "Lili," I whisper into her hair.

She nuzzles into my neck. "I don't want to be like this." She pulls back, but her eyes hold me mesmerized. "Promise you'll stay with me."

"I'll stay with you," I say, unable to say anything else.

"Forever," she whispers into my lips.

"Forever," I repeat, pressing my lips back to hers.

I feel the sting where her hand touches my back, and in my mind, something screams in warning. But I can't focus on that with Lili so close. Her lips trace a soft, warm path to my ear, where she whispers, "It's going to be so much better now. You're my angel." She kisses me, slow, soft, then releases me. "It's time to go."

Images dance in the periphery of my consciousness. They're fuzzy, and I'm having trouble making sense of them, but suddenly I'm sure they're important.

"Where?" I ask, trying to get a grip on the reason for the panic that's rising from my core. I close my eyes, trying harder to remember, and feel her press into me again. When I open my eyes, her face is an inch from mine.

"You promised you'd stay with me."

Alarms are ringing louder in my head. "Where are we going?"

Every part of me screams as she pulls herself away from me and sighs. "You have two choices now, Matt. You can walk powerless among them—" She waves an arm vaguely at the world. "—or you can stay with me. Pledge your fealty to King Lucifer, and we can have everything. Your power will grow to be stronger, unhindered by those quaint celestial notions of right and wrong. You'll be free to exact revenge on anyone you choose. Anyone who has wronged you."

The image of Luc—what he did to Lili—solidifies in my head, and I know that's what I want. Vengeance. But . . . "Angels don't pledge fealty to anyone but the Almighty."

She reaches around and presses her hand into my back. She brings it to my face, dripping blood. "You can't go back. No wings."

And then the rest of the image comes clear—white light, burning me with cold heat. The wet crunch of breaking bone, and searing pain shooting through my whole body.

Avengers.

That's when it hits me. When the meaning of her words, the avengers, the blood, and the rage and lust that seem to be consuming me all come together in one coherent thought.

I've fallen.

I stagger back a step as guilt, dread, and terror overwhelm me.

No wings.

I expected it when I first kissed Lili, and again after I slept with her. I knew I was playing with fire, so why am I surprised?

But I'm beyond surprised. My insides collapse as the horror of it dawns.

I can't go back.

Her sheet drops away as she glides back into my arms. "I need you," she whispers, eyes pleading. "Come with me, Matt. Pledge your fealty to my Lord, and we can have it all."

In that instant, sickening despair twists through me as understanding dawns. "When you said *he* made you do it, you didn't mean Luc, did you?"

She stiffens in my arms and shakes her head. "No, not Luc.

You need to understand that I live on lust. I can't survive without it." She peels herself away from me, and I feel my arms clutching tighter, afraid she'll get away. Her green eyes flare as she gazes up into mine and traces my lips with her finger. "But mortal lust can't compare with yours. I could live forever on the lust of my angel."

A singular thought consumes me: *She's mine.* They can't have her. Her lips find mine, setting me on fire. I burn for her, all need and desire. She pulls me deeper into the kiss, and electric bliss surges through me like a bolt of hot lightning. Then my head starts to spin as the material world, including Lili, falls away. I screw my eyes shut against the sickening rush and feel as though I'm being ripped through time.

When the sensation finally stops and I open my eyes, I'm unsure where I am. It's no place I've ever been before. Flickering indigo light filters through what looks like the opening of a cave, but this cave, the one I'm in, is like nothing I've ever seen. The walls sparkle, sort of, but it's like a reverse sparkle. Instead of reflecting back little bits of light, they seem to devour it just as it tries to escape. The floor is glossy black, but feels soft under my feet, like if I move too quickly, I would sink into it. I turn slowly, looking for any clue to where I am.

And then I smell the sulfur—brimstone.

20

☩

Angel's Breath

FRANNIE

I nearly hit three parked cars on my way out of Luc's parking lot when I saw him running after me. I raced out of there as fast as the Mustang would take me. Ignoring my parents, I bolted through the family room and locked my bedroom door behind me when I got home. They've been knocking off and on for the last half hour, twice to tell me Luc was here, but I can't deal with them—or him—right now. I have to think.

I put on my headphones, click on my iPod to block them out, and curl up on my bed, trying to make sense of any of this. The image of Luc with Lili plays on a loop in my head. I see it over and over, and each time, it feels like a little more of me dies.

He cheated on me. I thought that couldn't happen. As long as I wanted him, he was supposed to want me back. That was what this stupid Sway thing was all about. It basically made me irresistible.

But my Sway is nothing. I know that now.

I close my eyes and press my face into the pillow. When I feel a hand in my hair, I'm not surprised. I knew it would only be a matter of time before Kate or someone picked my lock. But when I smell cool winter sunshine, my breath catches.

I sit up and fling myself into Gabe's arms.

"I'm sorry, Frannie. I should have been here."

His breath in my hair, the feel of his arms . . . *God, I've missed him.*

"You should have," I say, and pull him tighter.

"This is my fault."

I push back and look into those incredible, sad eyes. And despite his summer snow and the calm it brings, anger flares in me. "Unless I'm mistaken and you were the one in bed with Lili, I can't see how this is your fault."

"As much as I hate to say it, this isn't on Luc. He didn't know what he was doing."

The hard ball of anger and betrayal in my chest threatens to dissolve into tears, but I won't let myself cry. "Don't defend him. He doesn't deserve it."

"You're right, he doesn't, and I'd love not to. But the sad truth is—this time, anyway—it really wasn't his fault. He was tricked."

I push him back hard. "I saw him, Gabe! She wasn't *making* him do anything." A whimper leaves my chest as the picture materializes in my head again. His betrayal sits like a hot stone in my gut, burning a hole in me. I gave Luc everything—my heart, my soul, my body. I loved him more than anything. If he loved me the way he should have, then whatever Lili did wouldn't have mattered. The certainty that he had to want her, at least a little, cuts like a razor.

But I knew it all along, didn't I? I knew true love didn't exist. Like an idiot, I let myself believe, and this is what I get. A broken heart. Exactly what I deserve for being so stupid.

Gabe shakes his head, his eyes a storm of conflict. "I'm so sorry." He pulls me back to his shoulder and buries me in summer snow. "I've missed you so much," he says into my hair.

I push back and smooth a hand over his face. I can't believe he's really here. He closes his eyes and I feel his moan reverberate in his chest as I press my hand to it. It's a sound of pleasure, but also of pain.

"This is why I couldn't stay."

"You're not leaving again." I'm a little embarrassed by how desperate it sounds, but that's pretty much how I feel.

His smile is shaky. "No. I let you down once. I won't do it again. I promised that I'd always be here for you, and I will."

His words are enough to unclench the knot in my stomach some. He strokes my hair as, little by little, I let myself relax.

I gaze into those eyes, so deep and full of promises, and they take my breath away. *God, he's beautiful.* I realize that I've moved closer, that our faces are just inches apart.

He cradles my cheek in his hand and traces the lines of my lips with his thumb. Then he closes his eyes. "Ah . . . If there was ever a mortal I'd give up my wings for . . ."

I try to ignore the wave of guilt, but I can't. My Sway is completely useless for anything but messing with people. I pull a deep breath and shake my head. "You don't really want me. It's just my stupid Sway. It's not your fault."

He smiles, because there's no lying to an angel. "But it *is* my fault. I can't be trusted around you."

He leans in and kisses my forehead. His cool winter sunshine envelops me, and my wounded heart pounds in my chest. I wrap my hands in his soft platinum waves and start to bring his face to mine, but just before our lips touch, I stop.

Guilt squeezes my heart into a painful knot when I realize what I'm doing. I want to lose myself in him—to make this all go away. Not 'cause I want Gabe, but because I still want Luc. The bleeding hole in my chest is killing me—pain so intense, it's physical. I want it to stop. Gabe can do that for me. But it's not fair—or right.

We both jump at the knock on the door. I untangle myself from Gabe and straighten my wild hair with my fingers. Gabe stands and moves to the window, staring out at the swirling dusk.

"Frannie?" Dad calls through the door. "Can I come in?"

I feel my cheeks flush, and I glance at Gabe. "Um . . . maybe later, Dad."

Gabe turns from the window. "Let him in, Frannie."

"No!" I whisper.

He fixes me in a hard gaze. "You need to let him in."

"Uh . . . just a second. Hold on," I amend, questioning Gabe with my eyes. Then I move to the door and unlock it.

The door swings open, and Dad stands there, angry creases between his brows. He looks first at me, then at Gabe.

I expect him to go all crazy and ask how Gabe got in, but instead, he just says, "What's going on?"

My mouth reacts before my brain, and I start babbling. "Nothing, Dad. We were just—"

"It's happening again," Gabe says, his voice soft.

That stops me cold.

Dad's face pales. "Matt . . . ?"

Gabe's eyes are tortured as he regards my father. "He's fallen, Daniel."

In that instant, I realize Dad wasn't talking to me. His eyes are fixed on Gabe. And, where I thought anger was pinching his face, I see now that it's really worry.

My head spins as I try to keep up. Why is Gabe telling Dad about Matt? And since when is Gabe on a first-name basis with my father? How do they know each other so well? Gabe's met Dad only once, a few months ago. It feels like I've missed something important.

Dad braces himself on the doorframe. Gabe walks over and pulls him through the door with a hand on his shoulder, closing it behind him. "Just tell her. She needs to know."

They share a concerned glance, and Dad looks back at me, his expression grave. "There's something I need to show you," he says, and starts unbuttoning his blue button-down shirt. He pulls it off, exposing a white V-neck undershirt.

Still in shock, I turn away as he starts to lift it over his head. "Dad. What are you doing?" My dad is very modest. I've never seen him without at least a T-shirt on. Even at the beach.

"I need you to see this, Frannie . . . to understand."

I turn back to him and lift my eyes. His back is to me, and I can't hold back my gasp when I catch sight of it. It's everything I can do not to raise my hand and touch the gnarled, white scars covering each shoulder blade.

"Oh my god! What happened?"

He glances over his shoulder, so I follow his gaze. Gabe is near the window, but he's not standing; he's hovering. His shirt is gone, and a pair of immense white wings have sprouted out of his back. He's never shown me his wings before, and now I know why. They're unbelievable. They're feathered, but nothing like I would have pictured—nothing like those stupid paintings you see in churches and stuff. The feathers seem to be made of pure energy—white light.

In a trance, I walk over to Gabe. I reach up to touch the edge of his wing, but he grasps my wrist and holds it. I see the struggle behind his eyes, but finally, he brings my hand to his face and kisses my palm. Then he lets go of me and nods. As my fingers brush over the feathers, I feel electricity sizzle over the surface of my skin. Instantly, all his knowledge, everything he's seen, floods through me and everything goes black.

When I wake, I'm lying on my bed. Gabe sits next to me, holding my hand. He's in his old blue T-shirt again. My father paces behind him, shirt back on. I close my eyes and try to remember what happened just before I blacked out. Dad . . . scars. Gabe . . . wings.

My eyes spring wide and shoot to Dad as I sit up. "No!"

He looks a little sad. "Sorry, but yes."

"You're an angel?"

"No. But I once was."

I glare at him. "What does that even mean—you once were?"

"I fell, Frannie. A long time ago."

I bury my face in my hands. "Oh my god." Then something occurs to me and I look back at him. "Are you really my father?"

He smiles reassuringly. "Yes, I'm your father."

I sit for a second, staring at nothing, and try to wrap my mind around that. The edges of my vision go fuzzy, then dark. When I realize I'm breathing too fast and my fingertips feel a little numb, I pull a deep breath, afraid I'll pass out again. "So, what does that make me . . . ? All of us?" It's hard to get any air behind the words.

"Nephilim," Gabe interjects. "You and all your sisters."

My eyes shift to him. "I don't get it."

Gabe squeezes my hand. "You're only half human, Frannie. All of you."

"I still don't get what that means." I lean toward the edge of the bed, suddenly sure I'm going to be sick.

Gabe's hand glides over my back. "Nephilim are the children of fallen angels and their mortal partners. Your mother is mortal; your father, angel. Most Nephil are mortal, but they may inherit special gifts from their immortal parent—things like exceptional strength, clairvoyance, or other more esoteric skills."

"Like Sway." It's not a question.

Gabe nods slowly, his eyes watching me cautiously.

"What about my sisters?"

Gabe laces his fingers into mine. "They're all special in their own way."

I think about Grace, the way she seems to see through me. "So, do they have guardian angels too?"

Dad shakes his head. "They're not in need of them at the moment."

I swing my legs around and sit on the edge of the bed, feeling cold dread creeping through my gut. "I don't have one anymore either, do I?"

Gabe gazes down at me, but doesn't answer.

Tears sting my eyes. "It's my fault. I wanted Matt to have a life."

"It's not your fault, Frannie." Gabe's eyes shift to Dad. "Matt is not the first angel to lose his wings to Lilith," he says, his voice heavy.

"Lilith? You mean *Lili*?"

I look up at Dad and find a tear coursing down his cheek. "Dad?"

"I was like Matt," he says.

"Like Matt," I whisper mostly to myself. "You mean a guardian angel?"

He nods.

"What happened?"

"I let myself become . . . distracted."

"By Lili," I say, putting the pieces together. "What is she?"

Dad pulls my desk chair to the bed and sits in front of me,

elbows on his knees. He hangs his head, as if it's too heavy to hold up. "She's the first woman—Adam's first wife."

"*The* Adam?"

He lifts his eyes to mine and nods. "Things didn't go well with them, and she was banished from Eden."

"You're joking."

"I wish," Gabe says.

"So, she's a *demon*?"

I keep thinking this has to be a joke, but Gabe's face is dead serious. "She's a demon, but not."

I just stare at him and shake my head, frustration boiling over, as I try to sort all this out.

"Technically, she's still human," he says, "but she's descended to demon status."

Dad takes my hand and blows out a sigh. "It's a really long story, but suffice it to say that Eve wasn't the only one whom Satan got to. Lilith is, in essence, His queen—His Earthly consort. Basically, she's the original succubus."

When I speak, the frustration is clear in my words. "Then how come Matt didn't know she was a demon? Angels are supposed to know that."

"Her soul is human. She doesn't appear any different to us than a mortal tagged for Hell would." Dad shakes his head and drops his eyes. "When you brought her here . . . I just wasn't thinking. I should have known."

This still isn't making sense. She was banished from Eden. . . . "But that was, like . . . forever ago. If she's not really a demon, how is she still alive?"

Dad lifts his eyes to mine again. "Lucifer untethered her soul. She's unbound—free to move between mortal hosts. She can possess anyone already tagged for Hell. She only needs to touch them to transfer."

I press my face into my hand because I can't look at Gabe when I ask. "What does she want with Luc?"

I hear Gabe's sigh, but I don't look up. "I'm sure her goal is you. If she can strip away your support system, you're vulnerable—an easier target."

The vision of Luc's face . . . and Matt's . . .

They would have killed each other.

"What's going to happen to Matt?"

Gabe sits on the bed next to me, and the pain in his voice is unmistakable. "He's fallen. He no longer has a place in Heaven." He stiffens slightly and adds, "It's my fault. I put him in a position he wasn't ready for. I guess I thought . . . I don't know . . ." He leans close. "But the wings thing . . . it can happen to any of us." His voice is low—just for me.

I look at Dad. "So, how can you be . . . here, I guess? How can you be my father? Isn't that how Lucifer became the devil? The first fallen angel?"

"It is. But we all have choices."

A flicker of hope lights the dark of my despair. "So Matt could be okay? Get his wings back?"

The sadness in Gabe's eyes as he answers snuffs out that hope. "There's nothing that makes Lucifer happier than to collect fallen angels. He thinks of them as defectors—more valuable than Earthly souls."

"When I fell," Dad picks up, "I had a choice, as do we all, to join the Grigori and stay on Earth amongst mortals, nearly powerless, or to fall all the way to Hell. He lures us by offering us the ability to keep our power, to travel between planes—all of it."

My mind is reeling and I can't get a solid grip on my thoughts. I shake my head and pinch my face, trying to concentrate. "The Grigori?"

Dad blows out a sigh and stares into my eyes. "Not every angel that falls chooses evil. The Grigori are leagues of fallen angels who live on the mortal coil to protect humanity. It's our charge. Our penance and our redemption." He looks away, at Gabe. "And our only hope of earning our wings back."

Something cold and dark snakes through my insides, making me shiver. "What do you think Matt will do?"

Dad shakes his head. "I don't know, Frannie. I suppose it depends on how angry he is. Being stripped of our wings . . . it feels like a betrayal. Most who lose their wings are not thinking clearly, obviously, or we wouldn't be in that situation."

"So he's . . . gone. They did this to get to me." I say, firming my responsibility for this in my own head.

Gabe's expression is wounded as he nods.

There's no escaping it. I'm cursed. Everyone around me—everyone I care about—gets hurt.

And it's never gonna end.

I feel like I'm suffocating. I stand from the bed and so does Gabe. He starts to pull me into his arms, but I push him away. "I really need some time alone to think."

He steps back and gazes down into my eyes. I can tell he's trying to pull thoughts out of my head, and I'm too tired to care.

Finally, he nods. "I'll be outside the door if you need me."

I hug Dad, then walk to the window and stare out at the branches of the oak tree, swaying in the beginnings of a swirling summer rain shower. I hear the door click shut behind me as I stand listening to the gusting wind shake the windowpane. After pushing the window open, I pull the screen out and lean on the sill, feeling the cool rain sting my cheeks. When I can breathe again, I wipe the rain from my face with my hand, pull myself back through the window, and turn, expecting to be alone in my room. But Grandpa leans against the wall near my door, squinting at me through troubled eyes.

I rush across the room.

He wraps me in a hug. "Your mom called me, told me what happened." He shakes his head. "So, he turned out to be the devil after all."

His voice vibrates through me as I melt into his chest, breathing in the sweet smell of pipe smoke that clings to him.

"I shoulda done something," he says, smoothing my damp hair with a gentle hand. "I thought I saw myself in him, but I shoulda known."

The tears start . . . for me, for Matt, for Taylor. I don't want any of them to be for Luc, but they are. The tears stream down my face as the vision of Luc and Lili comes back full force. My chest aches as the memory wraps itself around my heart and squeezes. I breathe against it. "I loved him, Grandpa." It's barely a whisper, like I can't even admit it out loud.

"I know," he says, his voice hitching. He draws me closer and holds me while I cry. When I'm done, I pull back from his shoulder and he wipes away my tears with his thumb, just like he used to do when I was little. "Get some sleep and we'll figure it all out tomorrow."

At the mention of sleep, I realize I'm exhausted. "'Kay."

He looks at me a moment longer and I can see the pain in his eyes. "Gettin' over a broken heart takes some time, but you'll be fine, Frannie. I promise."

I nod as another tear slips over my lashes.

When he steps into the hall and closes the door, I change and get ready for bed. I climb under the sheets and am just dozing off when the first images of the nightmare startle me awake.

Taylor.

In a matter of just a few minutes, I lost both Luc and Matt. I'm *not* gonna lose Taylor.

I reach for my phone and text Trevor. IS TAYLOR HOME?

NO, is his simple reply.

My heavy heart aches. I clutch my phone to my chest and roll on my side.

And stare out the window.

And pray.

Because it's all I can think to do.

21

✝

Hellfire

FRANNIE

I wake up gasping from the nightmare and feel strong arms squeeze me, pulling me tightly into a hard body at my back.

"Luc," I whisper. But before I've finished, I know it's not Luc—'cause of the nightmare . . . And it's not cinnamon that I smell. The scent that surrounds me, like a drifting cloud, is Gabe's summer snow.

Same as every other night for the last three weeks.

"It's okay, Frannie. It's me. I'm here."

As usual, I feel the terror and panic start to evaporate, like fog in a stiff breeze, as I sink into Gabe, but there's nothing he can do about the hollow ache in my chest. "Thanks."

He brushes the hair off my face with a finger and kisses my ear.

I roll onto my back and look up into his blue eyes, bright in the dark bedroom. "Is it ever gonna stop?"

"It'll get easier."

I let myself believe the lie, 'cause it can't get much worse, and Gabe doesn't know he's lying.

"I just feel like everything is going to crap. Taylor's with that demon. She won't even talk to me. Matt's gone. And Luc . . ." I grimace, and a wounded groan erupts from somewhere deep inside me. God, it still hurts that the only thing I see when I think about him is Lili in his bed.

In the pale silver moonlight, I see Gabe's face pull into a frown. "I'm going to find her, Frannie. I won't let her hurt you again."

I know by "her," he means Lilith, and I hate that I hear guilt in his voice. What happened wasn't his fault. But I don't want to think about her right now. I stare up at the ceiling. "What can we do about Taylor's tag?"

"We'll figure something out."

I sink into him and let his peace wash over me, trying to turn off my mind. It's always better in Gabe's arms, and the closer I get to him, the more I feel it—his peace and love. It's like that's what he's made of. My heart rate picks up again as I remember kissing him—the only true peace I've ever known.

He stiffens in my arms and I realize that, once again, my thoughts have given me away.

"Don't worry, you're safe." I spare him a weak smile.

"Frannie, you know I'd do anything for you, but right now that 'anything' means that I need my wings. I'm useless to you without them." He offers a sad smile. "But resisting your Sway is pretty damn hard . . . mostly because I don't really want to."

"So you want me to stop wanting you," I finish for him.

He drops his head onto the pillow. "That would help."

I push away from him. "Then maybe you shouldn't spend so much time in my bed."

He chuckles and the moonlight brushes his features, making him appear to glow. Or maybe he really is glowing. Who knows? "But I like it here."

I can't breathe as a sudden crushing wave of despair hits me at the thought of him leaving. "Good. Stay."

"Always." He places a finger on each of my eyelids and draws them closed. "Sleep," he says. But even in the safety of his arms, it's a long time before I can.

The phone on my nightstand rings, startling me awake. Riley's face smiles at me from the screen.

"I'm picking you up in an hour," she says when I lift the phone to my ear.

"For what?"

"You're coming into the city with me. I have orientation at State. Taylor was supposed to come, but . . ."

"She's blowing off orientation?" My heart sinks. She was so excited about college. If she doesn't even care about *that* anymore . . .

She hesitates and I hear her sigh. "She's blowing off *everything*. So, you'll come?"

"Oh, Ry, I'm really not up for it."

"You need to get out of the house, and I don't want to go alone."

"What about Trevor?"

"They're doing some family thing," she says after a pause.

"Family thing?" I pull myself up in bed and twirl a finger into the sheets. "With Taylor?"

She hesitates again. "*For* Taylor, really. Kind of an intervention. They have that counselor coming who they saw after her dad . . . you know."

That family has been through so much: her father's suicide attempt, and now this. But my mood improves just thinking about Taylor getting help. Maybe if she comes around, she'll stay away from Marc and I can help her.

"Have you seen her?"

"Only a couple of times. She's almost never home."

"How does she look?"

This time I hear a sniffle as she hesitates yet again before saying, "Bad. Really bad." She sniffles once more and clears her throat. "So I'll pick you up in an hour."

LUC

The balding clerk leans back in his office chair, feet up on the cluttered desk behind the counter, face buried in a comic book.

In his other hand, he holds a Big Mac, Special Sauce dripping down the front of his stained button-down shirt. I stand on my side of the counter for a full minute with no acknowledgment before clearing my throat.

He pulls his face out of the book. "Checking out?"

I slap a wad of bills onto the counter. "Room six. Another week."

He stands, and as I turn to walk away, I see him pocket the cash out of the corner of my eye.

Once out on the street, I wander aimlessly, anonymous in the mix of professionals and tourists. It's the first time in the three weeks I've been here that I've felt drawn to venture farther than the convenience store across the street. Mostly, I've just been lying on the rock-hard bed in my stale hotel room, shaking and staring at the ceiling, feeling like an addict going through withdrawal, and fighting the urge to go back to Haden. To Frannie—my fix.

But I can never go back. It was all a lie—a beautiful illusion. As much as I want it, I can't be what she needs.

At least my Shield still seems to be intact. Last I saw Rhenorian, he was sitting outside the library in his Lincoln. That was three weeks ago, just before I handed Mavis my resignation and slipped out the back door. The day after . . .

My gut twists painfully with the memory.

But Gabriel is back. I left as soon as I knew it for sure. Frannie's safe, and as long as she stays with Gabriel and away from me, she'll stay that way. If there's one thing I'm certain of, it's that he'll pay better attention than Matt did.

I walk in a fog, weaving through throngs of pedestrians

crowding the humid summer streets of Boston. I'm not really sure where I'm going and I don't really care. My mind is focused on working out the rest of my plan. I can't go anywhere near Frannie, but I can still help her. With Gabriel watching her, that frees me up to find Lilith—to find a way to stop her. I just have to figure out how.

I stop, finally, for a Polish sausage at a cart near Fenway Park, even though I'm not hungry, and munch it mindlessly as I set off walking again.

Several headlines at a newsstand catch my eye. More violence and casualties in the Middle East; nuclear testing in North Korea. It's escalating faster than we could ever have hoped.

I start at the realization that I just included myself in the collective infernal "we," and I try to pretend that I didn't just feel a thrill course through me at the prospect of impending death and destruction.

I pull my eyes away from the newspaper captions and turn the corner back toward my hotel.

And stumble.

Frannie and Riley are climbing the stairs out of the Kenmore Square T station.

I lean against a nearby brick building, feeling dizzy, and take a second to get my bearings. When I have my head, I focus my eyes back on the subway station.

They're gone.

A moment of panic roots me to the spot, but I force my feet forward. I walk to the end of the block as quickly as my unsteady legs will carry me, and peer around the corner. A relieved sigh heaves my chest when I see them retreating slowly down the street, Riley with her arm around Frannie, almost as if she needs to support her.

This is stupid—and dangerous. There's a reason I haven't let myself return to Haden.

But my body refuses to defer to reason. At a distance, I follow them. There are enough people on the street that I sometimes lose sight of them in the crowd, and when I do, panic pushes me to move faster—to get closer. And the closer I get, the more I feel it—the play of hot electricity under my skin.

Finally, they slow at a Starbucks. They pause at the door and I slide behind a brick column a few feet away, peering cautiously around the corner.

"I'll meet you back here after the orientation meeting," Riley says. Frannie's back is to me, and Riley's holding both Frannie's shoulders, talking right into her face as if she's afraid Frannie might not hear her. "Will you be okay?"

Frannie nods.

Riley squeezes Frannie's hand and heads down the street away from me. Frannie just stands there for a long minute and I fight to keep my legs from carrying me to her. A group of business people push past her on their way into the Starbucks, and Frannie follows them through the open door.

I wait for several minutes, struggling with my last shred of common sense. I should turn and walk away. I know that would be the safe thing to do. The smart thing.

But, Satan save me, I need to see her face. To be sure she's all right.

When the next group passes by on their way in, I follow them.

Frannie sits alone at a table in the back, hands wrapped around a forgotten cup of steaming coffee, and it's clear that she's definitely *not* all right. I breathe against the crushing pressure in my chest as my heart tries to collapse in on itself.

Her sunken eyes are blank, staring off into nothing—no animation on that beautiful, tragic face.

It's been three weeks, and she's still haunted by what I did to her. My betrayal.

I'm transfixed with guilt, just trying to stay upright, when I realize, too late, that Frannie has abandoned her coffee cup on the table, and the pungent scent of tar—her despair—precedes her as she walks straight at me.

Has she seen me?

In a panic, I phase into the corridor behind her. She hesitates for just a second, then walks faster on her way out the door.

And then it hits me: *I phased.*

The weight of my own despair knocks the breath out of me as I realize what that means—*everything* that it means. I slump into the wall to keep from toppling over, and press my forehead into it as I struggle for air that I don't need.

Frannie truly doesn't want me anymore. If she did, I'd still be human. And I'm clearly not. All the signs I've been denying—trying to ignore or explain away—they're real. I'm a demon again.

Three weeks. It took only three weeks.

With that knowledge, there's only one thing I can do. I watch Frannie walk away. I shrug off the wall, but just before I phase back to my hotel room, my sixth sense buzzes and I feel the weight of a hand on my shoulder. Then the buzz stops and Gabriel is gone.

I hang the DO NOT DISTURB sign on the door to my dark, cramped room before throwing the deadbolt. The scent of stale smoke and mildew overlay something ranker, swirling my mood deeper into despair. I crank the cheap radio on the nightstand and leave it on for the noise as I flop onto the rock-hard bed.

I stare at the cottage cheese ceiling for . . . hours? Days? I have no idea. No one has knocked on my door asking for money, so it probably hasn't been more than a week.

I want to die. *Why can't demons die?*

I'm contemplating whether it would be possible to just phase into oblivion—the demon equivalent of committing suicide—when the sharp smell of brimstone assaults my nostrils, bringing me to my feet.

"How long have you been lying here, Lucifer? I've been waiting outside your door for days." Rhenorian's eyes glow red as he leans against the wall in the corner of the dark room, hands in his jeans pockets, ankles crossed.

I flop back on the bed, staring at the ceiling again. "Then I guess the answer would be days. I thought I shook you. How'd you find me?"

"That ridiculous celestial Shield hides only you, stupid. When you used your power, it was out there for any of us to see. I just happened to be closest." His smile is sarcastic. "I've gotten to know your patterns. Figured you'd stay close to your human."

Perfect. I've got almost no power, and the instant I use it, I'm outed. But the sad truth is, I knew he was here. The thread of Rhenorian's thoughts was in my head, just like the good old days. I was hoping it was my imagination, but no. My nefarious connection is back.

He shrugs away from the wall and stands next to the bed. "Not that it matters anymore, but how did she do it?"

I startle at his use of *she*. He knows. "What?"

"You were human. Now you're not. How does she do it?"

"It's not her."

He rips me off the bed by my T-shirt and slams me up against the wall. "Don't lie to me."

"I'm not lying," I lie. I rub the back of my head. "She has nothing to do with it. It was the angel."

His eyes flare red. "He told me it wasn't him."

I feel suddenly cold, despite my demonic heat. Is Matt in Hell? Is he working with them—or, rather, *us* now? If so, Frannie's in even more danger than I thought. I work to keep my voice even. "And you believed him?"

"Angels can't lie."

And then I realize the truth: Matt was colluding with Rhen . . . "Before he fell," I say, more to myself than to him.

He presses me hard into the wall, and a slow smile curves his lips. "Let's just say he was no fan of yours."

The knowledge of how far Matt was willing to go to get rid of me makes me more sad than angry. I slump into the wall.

He glares a moment longer, then releases me. "Well, it doesn't matter. Now there's nothing stopping you from phasing back with me." He shakes his head. "It's bad, Lucifer. You didn't just screw up. This is treason."

"I know." I step forward, hands in the air as if surrendering.

"You're not going to fight?" A disappointed scowl twists his face, which shouldn't surprise me. He *is* a creature of wrath. Fighting's what he does. "What the Hell happened to you?"

Frannie's face floats in front of my eyes. *Everything . . .* "Nothing."

"So, you're going to come with me, just like that?"

As I stare at the wall, Frannie's face evaporates. She doesn't want me. Even though that's what I wanted, the thought is like a knife to my brimstone heart.

I may not be able to commit suicide, but I know the next best thing. "Let's go."

Hell hasn't changed, but I have. I used to laugh when I said you can take the demon out of Hell, but you can't take Hell out of the demon. I was wrong. And it's not at all funny.

Everything I see as I look around the place that was my home for seven thousand years repulses me—makes me hate what I am and yearn for what I was with Frannie. But that's not me. It wasn't real. And I can't ever go back.

Rhenorian has brought me directly to the Fiery Pit. I stand in my human form, back to a charred wooden post, arms chained overhead. As far as I can see, the hungry eyes of the legions of Hell—my infernal brethren—study me. I look around at the sea of faces, many leering, red eyes glowing, faces eager for the impending show.

"Good turnout," I mumble under my breath.

Rhenorian stands at a cautious distance. "It's a *Diktat.*"

My stomach drops. A Diktat. All of Hell is mandated to be here. I'm meant to be a public display. An example will be made of me. Which means this is not going to be a quick sentencing and execution.

But why? Who in Hell would chose my path—even if they could? I glance across the roiling orange and gold surface of the Lake of Fire to Flame Island and the hulking black mass of the castle Pandemonium. Then, as if summoned by my gaze, King Lucifer appears before me, also in His usual human form: glowing green eyes housed in a sharp, angular face, and a tall, powerful build cloaked in long red robes. Very Zeus-like.

Rhenorian backs off and melts into the crowd as Lucifer walks up to within a foot of me, staring into my eyes. I clench my teeth so hard I feel one of them crack, and try not to let the pain show on my face as His power ravages me—searching out the last vestiges of my humanity. When He releases me, I blow out a shaky breath.

A heinous grin slides over His face. "Commendable, Lucifer. That couldn't have been comfortable."

I clench my teeth again and look straight ahead without answering.

He signals to the crowd, and three thuggish demons, two with ranseurs and one with a cat-o'-nine-tails—part of Rhenorian's security crew, no doubt—step out of the drooling masses. Behind them, in the roiling velvet shadows, there is something else—more of a presence than an actual form. Whatever it is seems to exist just at the edge of perception. It shimmers in and out of focus as I try to get a fix on it, until I'm convinced it's nothing but a trick of the light—an illusion. But then the demons part and the thing moves between them. I catch a fleeting glimpse of something impossibly black, as if it were devouring all light from around it.

As the Mage steps up to Lucifer's side, it takes on solid form: dark as a void with the exception of its red eyes. And long, with limbs that seem to serve no purpose protruding from its twisted, sticklike body. Mages exist in the plane between conscious and unconscious and can manifest physically only in the presence of their creator—Lucifer.

The fact that it's here can mean only one thing. I steel my mind and wipe it clean of anything to do with Frannie. I focus on memories from before I even knew she existed and pray it's enough to keep her safe.

A sad smile flits across Lucifer's face. "It didn't need to be this way." His expression becomes pensive and He brings a long finger to His lips, tapping it there. "It still doesn't." He falls back and paces a wide circle around the pole I'm chained to, then steps up to me with His face just inches from mine. "If you tell me what I want to know," He says, His voice a quiet rasp, "I won't have to send anyone in there to get it." He presses a scorching finger to my temple.

I watch as the Mage leers, exposing a mouthful of red fangs set in its sharp, black face.

Lucifer steps back and regards me. "It's now or never. Make your choice."

I grit my teeth and hold His gaze.

Finally, after what feels like an eternity, He sighs and shakes His head. "I'm going to get what I want one way or the other.

I don't understand why you'd want to make this harder on yourself than it needs to be." He waves a hand toward the Mage and paces another circle.

The Mage's leer widens as it holds its hand out toward me, and I groan with the effort of keeping it out. It's no use, though. I feel it in my head, searching through my thoughts and memories, and I know who it's looking for. I fight to think of anything but her, going back to my earliest memories—my days working the Gates with the Hellhound, Barghest. I focus hard on that. But the memory of Barghest brings me back to how he saved Frannie from Beherit. I try harder to block the memory of her, but the harder I try, the more she's there.

That's all it needs. I see the satisfaction in its face as it connects to her. I groan, because I know what that means. It's pulled her out of my head, and now it's gotten into hers. Mages are the demonic embodiment of a nightmare. It'll haunt her dreams, and through them, it'll show her things. Her dreams are also its window into her world. It'll see what she does—*know* what she does. And, worse, while it's in there, Lucifer can follow it into her head.

No!

I fight harder to push it out, but it's still in my head when it raises one clawed hand to rake slowly through the air. I bite my tongue and grimace as four burning gashes appear across my chest, tearing my T-shirt to shreds. I know it's not real—that it's all in my mind—and I keep telling myself that, but it may as well be real for the pain I feel. Its maniacal grin stretches wider as I fight to push it out.

Lucifer finishes His circle and fixes me in His inquisitive

gaze. "You're such a unique case. I can't help but be curious. You understand, I'm sure."

So that's it. I'm to be a lab rat. He'll tear me apart, little by little, mentally and physically, looking for answers, but also showing all of Hell what happens to traitors. Killing two birds with one stone.

Suddenly, He's on me again, and I brace myself against the inevitable pain. But, instead, He presses into me, and all I feel is His scorching breath in my ear. "I know what she is, and I'm going to have her, Lucifer. She was mine in the Beginning and she'll be mine again. There's nothing you can do to stop me."

What does he mean . . . she was His in the Beginning? Cold dread creeps through me, and my brimstone heart crumbles into a thousand grains of sand.

Dark ideas fill His eyes. "Change, Lucifer."

I've never before been able to disobey His direct command, but I find myself resisting. Some deep part of me doesn't want to change, doesn't want to take my demon form. I search that part out, and my legs buckle when I find the root of it. Because it's Frannie that I see: the piece of her I carry in my heart. The piece of her that's also me, and the piece of me that's unwilling to let go of her.

This is who I want to be. Who I was when I was with her. If I shed this shell—the one I wore with her—the one that touched her—what will happen? What if the memory of what it was to be with her is locked in *this* shell? If I slough it off, I may lose that memory forever. It will be gone, and I'm terrified that I'll never be able to get it back. That memory is all that makes my existence tolerable.

"No."

A collective gasp issues from the minions, and His eyes widen in disbelief. The next instant, a thousand bolts of lightning are coursing through me. I cry out and slump against the pole when they finally stop. A low hiss ripples through the gathered crowd.

King Lucifer's demon form rips through His human shell, and He stands in front of me in His full Hellish glory. He pierces me with burning green eyes set in sharp angular features in His beyond-black skin. My brimstone heart pounds as He unfolds His batlike wings and spreads them, surrounding us in a leathery black cocoon, blocking out all sound and light. As those wings wrap around me, evil rolls off Him in waves, drowning me with dark ideas and depraved thoughts.

His voice is a raw hiss. "What did you say?"

I dig deep and find Frannie again—my strength. "No. I said no."

This time, the force of His power is unbearable—unfiltered Hellfire ripping through my body and destroying everything in its path. The last thing I hear before everything fades into agonizing black is my own scream.

22

Unholy Hell

FRANNIE

The sheets are hopelessly tangled around me, and my heart hammers in my chest as my own scream wakes me from my restless sleep. There was lightning in my head, but it was different this time.

It felt good.

My scream wasn't a scream of agony. It was ecstasy.

Luc.

I felt him—his dark, shadowy energy—when I was in Boston last week with Riley. I even thought I saw him, for just an instant, at the Starbucks—and smelled his cinnamon. He's been with me every day since then, a feeling I just can't shake, tugging at that deep place in my heart that can't seem to let him go.

And he was in my dream too. I felt the lightning in my head as I was doing horrible things to Luc, torturing him. Snakes.

Claws. Fire. And he was screaming, every scream sending another bolt of excruciating pleasure through my brain.

Oh, God—I liked it.

What the hell is wrong with me?

But as my head spins, making me feel sick, I realize that it wasn't really me. The person torturing Luc in my dream was someone else. Someone shadowy—without form or face. I was watching through their eyes as Luc screamed—feeling their bloodlust—and I reveled in it.

A shiver rushes through me and I roll for the trash can next to the bed, afraid I'm gonna throw up. But I don't. I groan and fall back into my pillows as the door cracks open.

Dad pokes his head in. "Frannie, honey? Are you okay?" When he sees me, hair stuck to my sweaty face, shaking, he comes in and kneels by the bed.

I try to breathe my pulse down, but it doesn't work. I look behind me, expecting to find Gabe in the bed, but he's not here. *I need him.* I look up at Dad. "Yeah, sorry. Just a dream." My voice breaks and he doesn't buy it.

His expression is heartbroken as he squeezes my shoulder. "I know it's been a rough few weeks. . . ."

"I'm really okay, Dad." I prop up onto my elbow. "Or at least I will be."

"Do you want me to stay?"

"No. I'm good. Thanks." I drop back onto my pillow and try to smile. I'm sure I don't fool him, but he sighs and turns for the door.

"Call if you need me."

"Sure, Dad."

The door clicks shut behind him and I let loose the tears I'd been holding back. I roll and bury my face in the pillow to muffle the sobs. Then a hand rubs my back and I'm flooded in cool winter sunshine. I sit up on the bed and look at Gabe, where he sits on the edge.

"Where were you?"

"There was something I needed to take care of."

"Luc . . . I dreamed—"

"I know."

The ache in my core forces me to ask. I have to know. "What was that? What I saw?"

The midnight shadows don't hide the concern lining his face, but he doesn't answer.

My heart thrums against the weight pressing down on my chest, and I can't draw a breath. "Gabe—?"

"I'm working on it, Frannie," he snaps.

He's never talked to me like that before. Something's seriously wrong. I feel terror rip through every cell of my body. "Working on what? Where's Luc?"

He hesitates. "In Hell."

The room swims. I can't breathe. The lightning in my head— it was real. I look him in the eye. "He's . . . dead?"

"Not technically."

"Oh, God! Just tell me what's going on!"

He breathes a heavy sigh. "He's a demon, Frannie."

It's like a punch to the gut, knocking all the wind out of me. "A demon . . . in Hell." I look up at him. "He went back?"

Gabe's eyes are sad as he nods.

"Why would he go back?"

He smooths a hand over my cheek. "Guess he didn't think he had much reason to stay here anymore."

I press into him and let him work my heart rate back down to something resembling normal. "So he's gone . . . for real."

"I'm working on some things to bring him back."

I settle deeper into him and breathe against the hole in my chest, trying to fill it. And I do feel it fill—with rage. It bubbles up inside me until I feel myself shaking with it. I've just started to get to the point where the thought of Luc doesn't crush my heart. It's been so hard, but I knew I needed to get over him.

But he went back. Without a second thought.

I push away from Gabe. "Don't bring him back here for me."

Those blue eyes pierce mine to my soul as he reaches up and strokes my cheek with his thumb. His eyes storm, swirling darker, but somehow still bright. And then his lips are on mine, so gentle, but desperate at the same time.

I taste his cool winter sunshine and it explodes through me, lighting up the darkness in my core. I'm blanketed in summer snow, putting out the fire of my rage. I press harder into him, deepening our kiss, needing more.

He stiffens, which brings me back to my senses.

"I don't want you," I whisper into his lips, trying to mean it.

He presses his forehead into mine. "I know." I feel him shudder as he pulls away. "This is so hard."

"I'm sorry. I'm trying not to . . ." What? I'm trying not to want him, I guess. But he makes it impossible not to love him.

He pulls me to his shoulder, and he's shaking. "I'm bringing him back for both of us," he says. "I love you. . . ."

The butterflies that had been tickling my stomach explode

in a flurry. I breathe them back, then pull out of his arms and look into his beautiful blue eyes. "I love you too."

His smile is sad. ". . . but I can't have you. You belong with Luc." He stands and walks to the door. I'll be right here," he says, opening it. "Call me if you need me." He vanishes as he passes through into the hall.

"I need you," I whisper after him.

I drop back into the pillows, determined not to fall asleep again, and lie here watching the moonlit shadows dancing on my ceiling. I trace my burning lips with my finger, trying not to want Gabe . . . or worry about Luc.

LUC

Lucifer continues to pace wide circles around the post I'm still hanging from, scrutinizing me from every angle.

I've lost track of time. It's impossible to tell how long I've been chained here. What I do know is that Lucifer usually likes to drag things out, and in this case, no doubt He'll leave me hanging here for months. Maybe years.

He steps up to me, His leathery face in mine, and I steel myself for another round. "Change!" He roars.

I hang my head in exhaustion and glance at the red gashes across my chest. Gashes that would be bleeding if I were still human, but burn like acid nonetheless. They're everywhere—on my legs, my back. The Hound circles the post a safe distance behind Lucifer, snapping and snarling. He brought the Hounds in when He decided I needed to be a more "visual" example for the masses.

But the Mage still stands, grinning. Waiting.

I wince against the inevitable pain my response will invoke. "No."

Lucifer sighs and snaps His fingers. The Hound's teeth are in my shoulder, tearing at my flesh, the venom sending searing pain down my spine. I wish for each slash to kill me, but I know it's not going to be that merciful.

I feel my resolve slip as pain shoots through every cell of my body. "Okay," I growl through clenched teeth. I try to lift my head, but it weighs a thousand pounds.

Lucifer whistles and the Hound backs off. I sink against the post, twisting in the hand shackles and pressing my forehead into the charred wood. He stares at me, waving His hand impatiently in my direction with a raised eyebrow.

I screw my eyes shut, as if not seeing myself change will make a difference, and focus on holding on to that piece of Frannie in my heart. But just as I'm about to push off my human form, the acrid air swirls and bright white light cuts through the rolling indigo shadows.

The last thing I hear as I'm yanked through time and space in a dizzying rush is Lucifer's roar.

I come to in a soft bed covered in white sheets. In a white room. With white furniture.

Gabriel's. It's got to be.

I pull the sheet aside and examine myself. The wounds in my chest and arms are severe, but healing—one upside of being a demon. But the memory of the burn is still there—a deep, uncomfortable tingle.

I swing around and sit on the edge of the bed, and my head swims.

But then it really hits me. I'm at Gabriel's. Someone had enough pull—*Sway*—to drag me out of Hell. Right out from under King Lucifer.

I feel unsteady again. "Frannie," I whisper.

I know I shouldn't hope for it, but I can't help myself. I spring off the bed and stagger, then catch my balance and reach for the clothes in the white armchair near the bed. I pull on the jeans and T-shirt Gabriel left for me and bolt out the door and down the stairs on unsteady legs.

Gabriel is sprawled on the couch in the living room, one leg propped on the armrest, squinting at a copy of Stephen King's *The Stand*.

"You should really look into reading glasses." I glance eagerly around the room for Frannie, but it's just the two of us. Gabriel rests the open book across his knee and watches me in silence as I stumble over my feet on the way to the chair under the window and drop into it. "So, what happened?"

He cocks half a smile. "It's a very long story."

I lean forward, elbows on knees. "Seeing as I seem to be immortal again, I've got all the time you need."

"We found a loophole."

I glare at him. "As far as long stories go, that one seems a bit lacking."

He shifts uneasily on the couch. "That small portion of your essence that's still a human soul belongs to us, so we exercised our claim to it. Of course, there are always politics involved. It took me a while to convince Him to intervene—Michael was no help on that front—because we had to step on a lot of toes getting you out of there."

My heart sinks and I sag back into the chair, dropping my gaze to the carpet, because I thought . . .

"It wasn't Frannie." I say it out loud to make it real—to confirm it to myself. I was wrong to hope she'd changed her mind and used her Sway to save me.

He confirms what I already know when he hesitates before answering. "No, it wasn't."

So that's it. Frannie is done with me for good.

Acid rises in my throat and I swallow it back, but I hear it in my voice nonetheless. "So, you saved my sorry ass once again."

"Not keeping score, dude."

I sigh. "Why'd you bother?"

"I needed your help." He puts the book down and smirks at me. "Imagine my surprise when I came looking for you and found you in *Hell*."

"You should have left me there."

He sinks back into the cushions and blows out a long sigh. "Frannie needs you."

"She does. She needs me *gone*, and the Fiery Pit is about as gone as I can get."

He pulls himself out of the couch and walks to the window. "It looked like Lucifer had bigger and better things in mind for you," he says, staring out at nothing.

"Doesn't matter. It wasn't anything I didn't deserve."

"You're as bad as Frannie, wanting to take the blame for everything that happens."

"The difference is that most of it *is* my fault." I screw my eyes shut against the image of Frannie's haunted face and haul myself out of the chair. "You should have left me," I say, heading for the door.

"Couldn't. I'm serious about needing your help. Frannie's in trouble, Luc." A guilty shadow darkens his features as his eyes drop to his fidgeting hands. "She's a mess, and I'm not sure I'm not making it worse."

I turn and look at him, into his tortured eyes. He's about to cave. Even though he'd never admit it to me, he's in love with her. And he didn't stop loving her when he was gone and she was with me, which means it has nothing to do with her Sway. But now that Frannie wants him . . .

I bark out a humorless laugh. This is rich. "You pulled me out of Hell to run interference?"

"She belongs with you," he says, his voice laced with pain. "You're the only one who understands what's at stake. She needs your support."

"She has you," I smirk, "an honest-to-God angel. What could she possibly want with me?"

"I can't . . ." He trails off. "I didn't think this could happen.

That I could . . ." He stares hard at me. "I'm a Dominion. You know what happens if I lose my wings."

I can't have this conversation. "You should have thought of that before you fell in love with her." I try to phase back to my apartment, but I should have known that wasn't going to happen from inside Gabriel's living room, what with his Hell-forsaken celestial field. I yank the front door open and storm out onto the porch, needing to get the Hell out of here.

But it's too much to hope that Gabriel will leave me alone. He follows me onto the porch and stares me down. "It was a good act. I really thought you cared about her."

It's all I can do not to send a blast of Hellfire at him, but I'm not going to let on how deep his words cut. "Just doing what comes naturally. I *am* a demon, after all."

"And a Class A asshole."

I start to phase back to my apartment, but I glance up and notice Gabriel's neighbor, standing on his lawn in a bathrobe, staring at us.

"What'd you expect?" I say, bounding off the porch and heading around back.

He follows. "Why won't you help her?"

"I told you. The best way for me to help her is to leave her the Hell alone."

He shakes his head and grumbles under his breath.

I glare at him. "Go find Lilith. She won't quit."

He glares back and starts to shoot off some reply, but his face turns to a mask of shock—then horror. His eyes fly wide. "Your apartment. Now!" he barks. Then he's gone.

23

✢

My Soul to Keep

FRANNIE

Luc's in Hell. That's all I know. Is he safe? Dead?

I can't believe he's changed back—that he's not human any-more. That he's not mine. I don't know what I expected, but I shouldn't be surprised, because *I* did it. I didn't want him. I hated him.

But I always loved him.

I still do.

But that doesn't change what he did. There's nothing he could ever say to make me trust him again.

And Gabe shouldn't trust *me*. I spent the rest of last night after he left trying to convince myself I don't want him. But it's bullshit. I do.

He told me to stay home, behind Dad's field. So, why I'm driving to Luc's apartment, I don't know. I guess I need to be sure he's really gone before I can let go, move on. Seeing is be-lieving, as they say.

I nearly drive away when I pull into his parking lot and see the Shelby. But I don't. I park near his building and sit here forever, fighting the panic that's vying for control. I catch my-self rubbing the rabbit's foot and fingering the sharp edges of the shiny silver key dangling from the key chain in the igni-tion. Finally, I pull the keys, step out of the car, and walk to his building. I feel weak and sick, and I have a hard time keeping my legs moving. Memories flash: meeting Lili that first day right here at the door, hauling the dresser up these stairs, Matt's fall. I almost turn around as the weight of my heavy heart crushes my courage. Pushing myself, I start up the hall.

Cautiously, I stick my key in his lock, trying not to remem-ber what I found inside the last time I did that, and jump when I hear the soft voice from just up the hall.

"Frannie?"

I feel shaky and light-headed as I turn toward Lili, where she stands in her door.

She steps cautiously toward me. "I really need to talk to you, Fee." Her voice is soft, scared.

I blink, trying to clear my mind—to make myself see her as I know she is: a succubus and King Lucifer's consort. But she's just shy, frightened Lili.

Lili, who was in bed with Luc last time I saw her.

My pulse pounds in my ears as I swallow back the bitter bile rising in my throat. "What do you want?"

Her eyes fall to her shoes. "He's not in there," she says.

I pull my key from the last of the deadbolts and push the

door open. She's right. The apartment is empty. I turn back to her. "What do you want?" I repeat, fighting to keep my voice even.

She moves guardedly toward me. "I just . . ." She trails off as she reaches me. "Can we talk?"

I push the door wider and she slouches through. I follow and close it behind us. My eyes scan the apartment again, and when they fall on the bed, I can't help the ache in my heart or the tears that well in my eyes. The memory of me and Luc—our first time and everything I thought that meant—is overshadowed by the image of him in that same bed with Lili. I spin on her. "Just say whatever you have to say and leave me alone."

She lifts her eyes to mine and takes a tentative step toward me. "I didn't want him," she says.

I see them together as clearly as if it were happening right now, right in front of me. "You could have fooled me," I spit.

Her eyes lock on mine and I'm surprised by the sudden strength I see in them. And something else. Something hot and interminable—and ancient. "I want you."

Suddenly, I'm paralyzed by crippling desire. She slides across the floor toward me, where I'm backed against the door, and presses her body into mine. My eyes close as a burst of ecstasy shoots through every cell of my body. I feel her hot breath on my cheek and I moan as I push back into the door. But then her hand is on my face, caressing. Her finger traces the lines of my cheekbone, down my nose to my lips. I open my eyes, and instantly, I'm mesmerized. My pulse races, but it's only partially from fear.

I suck in a ragged breath as the room starts to spin; then

everything blurs as her lips lock on mine. An electric tingle rips through me, and when she tries to pull back, I don't let her. I feel her smile into my lips when my arms, which had been pushing her away, start pulling her in.

"That's it. Just go with it," she whispers.

And at her words, my mind flashes to Luc—how lost he was in her. I feel something—black, ugly, old—swirl inside me, trying to take control.

I pull back and shake my head as alarm bells start ringing in my mind. Instinctively, I grab her arm and twist her into a necklock.

But just as quickly, she spins out of my grasp and backs away from me. "It doesn't have to be like this, Fee. You don't know who I am—what I can do for you."

"Don't you dare call me that," I growl. I feel new strength rise in me as I stare down the real object of all my anger. "And actually, I do, *Lilith*."

She looks stricken. Her face falls and her eyes glisten with tears. "Was it Gabriel? What did he tell you?"

"It wasn't Gabe," I say, thinking of my father's face when he told me about Lilith. How he lost his wings to her.

She lowers her lashes. "Daniel," she whispers, as if reading my mind. She looks back into my eyes, hers deep and full of pain. "He was special to me. My first angel."

I look away before her eyes can mesmerize me again, and I feel rage build inside me. But then I remember the sadness on her face when she met Dad that day in the garage and almost believe her. I'm flooded with random emotions—sorrow, pity, shame, lust—till my thoughts are a tangled mess.

"Special?" I spit. "What about Matt? Luc? Were they special too?"

Something dark creeps across her face. "Their lust keeps me alive. Without them, I'd die. So, I guess they're all special in their own way."

I spin for the door and reach for the handle when she adds, "But not as special as you."

I press my hands into the door and struggle against the wave of desire that threatens to take me under.

When I turn back to the room, she's there, just inches from me. The urge to reach out and pull her to me is almost irresistible. My body aches, my need for her totally raw on every nerve ending.

I can't breathe as I close the short distance between us and press my lips to hers. A moan that's almost a growl rolls up from her depths as she presses closer, pushing me back into the door.

After a minute, my already racing heart races faster when I try to catch a breath and can't. Lili is literally smothering me with her kiss. There's something thrilling about the thought of dying in Lili's arms. I shudder and crush myself into her, my lungs screaming for air. It's almost as if she's sucking the life out of me—and I want her to.

The kiss of death.

Terror prickles my senses, mingling with the intensity of my lust for Lili. I've never experienced anything like this— emotions totally raw and out of control. I tug at her clothes, needing to be closer, and feel her fingers press into my throat, cutting off my minuscule air supply. Stars flash in my eyes as tiny bits of bliss surge through me.

Her lips slide from mine and trace a burning path across my cheek to my ear. "You're mine," she whispers as her grip tightens on my throat.

Over her shoulder, through waning tunnel vision, I see Luc's bed. The bed where I gave myself to him. The bed where he betrayed me.

With Lili.

At the thought of what Luc and I had—what we lost—grief fills me. The hot tear coursing down my cheek snaps me from my trance. Something in my heart tightens as the warning in my head grows louder. And then it's Gabe's voice that I hear.

She's a demon, but not.

I keep my eyes focused on the bed—on my grief—as I push away from Lili, knowing that I couldn't find the strength if I was looking into her eyes. With great effort, I manage to create some space between us. It hurts more than I would have thought to push myself away from her, an aching need that pulls to my bones. Her hand on my throat doesn't loosen, and it's almost a comfort to still be connected.

But as she squeezes tighter, trying to keep her grasp on me, my lungs feel as though they're gonna explode. Stars flicker brighter in my eyes, and panic sends a surge of adrenaline through me. I tug her hand from my throat and twist her into an armlock, spinning and throwing her facefirst into the door. Blood rushes into my head so fast, it makes me dizzy. I feel warm and cold all at the same time as my body tingles back to life.

"What do you want with me?" It's almost a sob as it escapes my raw throat.

She turns her head to the side and looks over her twisted shoulder at me. "Everything. You belong with us—with me."

Even though I don't look in her eyes, I feel her draw on me intensify with her words. Suddenly, I know she's right. I know without a doubt that she and I are supposed to be together. I want her more than I've ever wanted anything in my life.

But as I hold her pinned here, I remember Luc holding me in this same spot not that long ago. I can almost feel him pressed against me, his breath in my ear as he whispers, *I love you with everything that I am.*

Fresh tears spill onto my cheeks as I remember, knowing now that he didn't really mean it. But the memory helps keep my head clear, and I push away from Lilith, backing into the middle of the room.

"I'm leaving."

"Sorry, Fee. No can do." She looks almost sad as she says it, but something in her deep green eyes tells me she means it.

"Move," I say with as much bravado as I can muster.

She continues to stand with her back against the door and shakes her head.

I reach to shove her out of my way, but she lunges for my arm, pulling me into a choke hold.

"Don't make me do this, Fee."

Before she can cut off my airway again, I swing my leg out and catch her in the knee, forcing her to loosen her grasp. I twist out of her arms and back a few steps toward the bed. "Let me go."

"I have orders. My king wants you. I can't let you go."

"I'm tagged for Heaven. You can't take me."

She looks pensive for a moment. "A technicality. But with Luc and Matthew . . . gone—" The smallest smile curves her lips. "—things aren't looking so etched in stone."

I skirt past the table, inching closer to the door. She turns and follows my movement but doesn't counter. I slide past her and reach for the door handle, but just as my fingers brush the cool metal—my freedom—she knocks my hand away.

Her face darkens. "This is for real, Fee. I get what I want, in case you haven't noticed, and right now I want you."

I breathe against the electric tingle that ripples over my skin, and reach for the door handle again. She lunges at me but I block her, grabbing her arm and planting a kick into her knee, buckling it. She drops onto the other knee, and as I punch my hand into her face, she comes up under me and takes my legs out. I fall back, hitting my head hard on the door, and feel a trickle of blood through my hair as I pull myself back up.

"Just come with me, Fee. Please. This can be nice. Easy. I can make you feel things you can't even imagine."

"I'm never coming with you."

A shadow passes over her features, and suddenly she looks frightened. "You have no idea what He'll do to me. . . ."

"I have a pretty good idea," I say, and can't help the sarcastic edge to my voice. "The Fiery Pit?"

She shakes her head as her face pales. "That's for His minions. For me . . ." She shudders and trails off, hollow eyes in a haunted face, as she clutches herself around the waist.

I almost feel sorry for her, but I know now that that's her

ploy. I fell for the helpless act before and let her tear my world apart. I'm not falling for it again.

I use her distraction to make a move for the door again, but her foot swings out, connecting with my hip and knocking me back a few steps. We move through the apartment, exchanging blows, and Lilith manages to always keep herself between me and the door. She looks as bloody as I'm sure I do, but I hold my own.

Panic surges through me with the vague thought that I've never been in a true fight for my life before. Nobody in the studio can beat me. But they're not Lilith. And they're not actually trying to *kill* me. Then I remember myself. If I'm gonna have a chance, I can't panic.

Breathe. Balance.

Sway . . .

Luc would tell me to use my Sway.

She launches a kick at me. I block it and spin out of the way, trying to decide what I'm supposed to convince her of.

I'm tagged for Heaven. You can't take me.

She doesn't even hesitate before lashing out with another kick that connects with my chest, pushing me back into the wall. I shrug off the wall as she charges me.

You don't want me.

This time she *does* hesitate, just for a split second, but it's enough time for my hand to connect with her right eye. She wheels back into the table and it nearly topples.

"You're good," she says, a thread of admiration in her voice. She wipes a trickle of blood from the corner of her eyebrow and leans back into the table as if she's giving up.

I drop my arms and take a step toward the door. When she makes no move to stop me, I breathe a sigh of relief and glance in that direction.

That's all she needs.

Her foot comes at my stomach, fast as lightning, knocking me onto my back on the bed as all the air explodes from my lungs in a painful *whoosh*. In a flash, she's on top of me. I wrap my legs around her and try to twist her into a leglock, but she doesn't budge, and neither does the pillow she's holding over my face.

My air is gone and I can't get it back. The pillow keeps me from getting a full breath. I gasp for air and claw for the crucifix around my neck. Tugging the chain from my neck, I slash at her with it.

"I like jewelry as much as the next girl, but I'm not a demon, Fee," she says, pulling it from my hand. "So, unless you're trying to give it to me, there's really no point."

My strength starts to drain as stars flash in my eyes. My lungs burn. The more I kick and claw, the brighter the stars get, till my limbs feel so heavy that I can't move them. And just before the world goes black, I feel a sickening tug at my insides, like someone is pulling my guts out through my belly button.

When I open my eyes, the world looks different. I feel unsettled. Everything is fuzzy and distorted, like looking in a funhouse mirror. Part of it is blurriness because of my swollen right eye. But that's not all of it. I shift my gaze from the ceiling to scan the room—the toppled chair, the bloody streak on the door. A ripple of panic tears through me as I remember Lilith. I jump from the bed and look around, nearly falling over as a wave of dizziness overtakes me. My body doesn't move how I expect it to and I stagger as I gain my feet. I feel off. Completely foreign in my own body. I spin and take in my surroundings, looking for Lilith. But what catches my eye is me.

My body is laid out on the bed, pale and unmoving.

Me? Am I *dead?*

How can that be me? I nudge my motionless body. Nothing. I feel for a pulse at my neck. It's there, but barely. Dread creeps into my consciousness, and a vague sense of terror tickles my mind, but never fully develops.

With cold objectivity, I look at the bloody hand on my lifeless neck. A human hand with painted blue nails.

I spin for the mirror on the back of the bathroom door, and there Lilith stands, bloody but intact, staring back at me from the glassy surface. I raise my arm—and so does she.

"Welcome to my humble abode." Lilith's voice isn't the sound my vibrating eardrums would create if she were talking. It's an echo inside my head.

No!

Lilith smiles at me from the mirror.

I look back at myself on the bed and am vaguely aware that I should have seen this coming. I have Sight. The last time I almost died, I saw myself dead before it happened. I should have gotten some warning. *Does that mean I'm not really dead?*

"Technically, you're not," comes Lilith's echo in my head.

She senses my confusion and, with triumph in her voice, continues. "I took you to the edge of death—close enough to free your soul. If I actually killed you, the celestials would have stolen it, and that would have been totally unacceptable. You belong with me."

I look back at my body. "I'm not dead?" I say out loud. But it's not my voice I hear say it. It's Lilith's.

"Yet," she answers in my head. "Without a soul, your body won't last long."

Dancing in the periphery of my awareness, several truths tease me. The first is that I could will my soul back into my body. I could use my Sway to convince Lilith to let me go.

The second truth is that I should feel afraid, terrified . . . something. Anything. But I don't feel any of that, because my thoughts are turning to darker things. Things like revenge, and how much I hate . . . everyone. How good it would feel to kill someone. The fleeting notion that that "someone" should be Lilith is replaced by one overpowering thought.

Luc.

Everything that's happened to me, to Taylor, to Matt—it's his fault. Suddenly, I want him dead for what he did, for his betrayal.

I let cold rage have me. It feels so good to let it take control, not to have to hold back. A rush of adrenaline makes me shudder as I walk to the bookshelves, pull one of Luc's ancient volumes of Dante from the middle one, and rip a chunk of pages out of the middle of it. I throw them in the air like confetti. I'm not 100 percent sure that the dry laughter I feel more than hear is mine, but it spurs me on. My arm sweeps the books from the middle two shelves into a pile on the floor before I move on to his CD racks, where I pull handfuls from the shelves and throw them out the still closed window into the parking lot below. The chime of shattering glass feeds and blends with my laughter. I pick up a shard and run it across my palm, drawing a thin crimson line in blood across it. When I lick it off, I savor the metallic salt taste of it as it rolls over my tongue. My moan is a sound of desire . . . longing. Then I hear my voice—but not my voice.

"I want . . ."

Lilith's voice is a whisper in my head, enticing in its promise of forbidden pleasures. "What, Fee? What do you want? If you could have anything, do anything, what would it be?"

I picture Luc, his body moving under mine, vulnerable. I shudder in anticipation as I imagine pulling the shard of glass slowly across his chest, his neck, his face. The blood from my hand mingles with his blood—a blood promise.

That's what I want: to watch Luc die in the throes of lust. To drag his soul to Hell and to watch it burn in the Inferno. The image of the Inferno is clear in my head. As clear as if I'd seen it a thousand times.

"Very nice." Lilith's voice is seductive, encouraging. "We'll make a great team, Fee. I can teach you so many things. And when you're ready, my king will find you a suitable body."

A thread of fear twists through me at the mention of King Lucifer, but almost before I sense it, it's replaced with lust. Lust for Him and for His power. An overwhelming wave of desire crashes over me. I need Him. I need to be in His presence.

"That can be arranged," Lilith says, and I feel her own shudder of anticipation blend with mine.

Suddenly, the air is charged with static electricity. I feel all the hair on our body stand on end as the charge works through me, waking every cell. I tingle all over with need. I breathe deep against the light-headedness and my racing heart as I wait for Him.

Then a wet ripping sound fills the air, and in a flash of red fire, He's here.

He's immense and powerful. I gasp at His beauty and shudder again as He starts to glide toward me, silent and eager. His black, leathery skin seems to absorb all the light around Him and radiate it back out His sharp, angular face through His glowing green cat's eyes. His twisted bloodred horns are encircled within a spiked golden coronet: a reminder of His unending power. And as much as I want Him—need Him—I'm rooted to the floor. I can only watch in awe as He stalks slowly toward me, His lips pulling into a leer.

"Frannie," He rumbles. "Finally, you're mine again. It's been so long."

As He reaches me and sinks the claws of His hand into my shoulder, pain and indescribable pleasure swirl through me.

"Remember," He rasps, low in my ear.

He wraps me in His wings, and I have the sudden sense of familiarity, comfort—the fleeting image of a beautiful angel with deep green eyes. I feel His lips burning into my forehead, and His power course through my body, like being plugged into the universe—fire—burning alive—agonizing bliss. In that eternity, no longer than the blink of an eye, a part of me dies, a little at a time, till the world is a dark swirling pit, full of depraved thoughts, degenerate ideas, and destructive feelings.

The world is Hell.

I'm lost in the dark.

Then . . . there's nothing.

LUC

When I phase into my apartment, what I see nearly kills me. I feel my mostly brimstone heart being crushed by the weight of what I've let happen. In an instant, I'm across the room and on the bed, pulling Frannie's lifeless body to me.

I look to Gabriel, who hovers off the floor near the door in full angelic form, enormous double wings spread wide. He turns on the glow and glides toward us as I turn back to Frannie. But just as I lean down to check if she's breathing, I feel searing heat as a red blast of Hellfire lights up the room, followed instantly by a bolt of white lightning. Ozone overpowers the brimstone and nearly chokes me. My fingers contact Frannie's neck and I find that she barely has a pulse.

I expect Gabriel to help Frannie, but when he glides past us, my eyes snap to the dark image enveloped in his white light: Lilith standing near the bookshelves, wrapped in King Lucifer's leathery bat wings. An apparition. It must be, because it's been eons since the king of Hell has ventured to Earth.

Lucifer leers at Gabriel. He pulls Lilith tighter to His steaming form, as though she's His most prized possession.

"You know she belongs to me, Gabriel," He rasps.

"Let her go," Gabriel responds, edging closer.

I pull Frannie tight to me, confused. That's when I realize that, even though she's alive, I don't sense her essence. No currant and clove. Her soul is gone from her body.

I'm too late.

Despair chokes me as I scoop Frannie into my arms, willing her to live. Another blast of Hellfire takes out half the kitchen, but I barely notice except to shield Frannie's body from the flying debris.

Gabriel sends a bolt of white lightning sailing at Lucifer, where He's backing toward the window with Lilith tucked behind Him. Gabriel's bolt finds its mark, and Lucifer rears up and roars, the sound shaking the windows. He picks Lilith up, tucks her under an immense arm like a rag doll, and with one flap of His wings, He's on the windowsill, shattering the remains of the already broken glass and splintering the wood with the talons of His webbed feet. He spreads His wings, ready to leap, and in a flash of white, Gabriel is across the room. He dodges Lucifer's blast of Hellfire and grabs Him by a wing, swinging Him back into the room.

As Lucifer crashes into the wall near the bed, cracking the plaster and crumbling a section of the mural, I hear it.

Lilith's voice starts low and strangled, as if she's fighting to keep the words from coming out. "You don't want me. Go back to Hell."

When I see Lucifer pause, midstride, on His way to the door, I understand.

Frannie.

I go suddenly cold with the realization. Frannie's essence is in Lilith's host body. I don't know how it's possible, but the terror in my core as I watch Lucifer skirt toward the door with Lilith tucked under His arm tells me it's true.

I lower Frannie's body gently to the bed and stand as Gabriel lunges, knocking Lilith out of Lucifer's arms. Gabriel drags Lilith behind him, where she falls to the floor in a heap. I focus all the infernal power I can muster and send a blast of Hellfire at Lucifer. At the same instant, Gabriel unleashes a blinding bolt of lightning. Both hit Lucifer square in the chest in a crimson and white explosion, knocking Him through the wall into Lili's apartment with a thundering crash.

Lucifer pulls Himself off the floor, and with an agonized roar and the sickening stench of brimstone, He vanishes in a puff of steam.

"Coward," Gabriel mutters under his breath, turning down the glow, but there's a shake in his voice. He turns toward Lilith and shifts back into human form as she pulls herself off the floor. When she speaks, it's clear that Lilith is the one talking again.

"That celestial voodoo works only on demons, Gabriel. I'm no demon. Try it, and everyone—and I do mean *everyone* . . . ," she says with a meaningful glance at Frannie's body, "dies."

Gabriel backs off a step. "Let her go."

She turns to me, but then she pauses as her face contorts. "Leave him alone," escapes from her mouth, sounding weak and choked.

I take a cautious step toward her, panic pushing my heart

into my throat. "No, Frannie. Don't use your Sway for me. Make her let you go."

"You can do this, Frannie," Gabriel says, moving closer to Lilith, hope clear on his still glowing face.

But the confusion on Lilith's face clears and she turns back to me. "She's mine now."

I'm on top of Lilith before I even realize I've moved.

"Let her go!" I roar as my hand wraps around her throat. I throw her into the wall, pushing my glowing fist into her face.

"I can't," she croaks. "You know what He'll do to me if I don't bring her back."

And I do. Lilith is His queen, but that doesn't mean He spares her His wrath. I've heard the rumors—and once, the screams. I glance to the hole in the wall and suddenly understand why He gave up so easily. He knows Lilith won't dare give up His prize, and He's left her to do His bidding.

Gabriel pulls me off her. "Stop, Luc. You can't kill her."

I realize my grasp on her throat has tightened. I drop my hand and step back, unsure what to do. He's right. I can't kill her without killing the host and Frannie too.

Just as I'm thinking it, the girl in front of me shimmers into Frannie. She steps forward, reaching out to me.

A surge of debilitating desire rolls through my body like a tidal wave, knocking me back a step.

"Leave him alone, my ass. If I want him, he's mine," she says, and everything flickers out of focus as she reaches up and touches my cheek.

I hear Gabriel's voice somewhere off in the distance, but I

ignore it, because all that matters is Frannie. I press into her, feel her body against mine, and explode in a burst of searing heat.

"That's right," she says, reaching up for my face and pulling me into a kiss.

Her draw is voracious. I'm desperate to be closer. I gather my essence and seep through her open lips. But as my essence enters her, I'm shocked out of my lust-induced trance by Frannie's voice crying, "No!"

"It's getting a little crowded in here, don't you think?" Lilith's voice interrupts. "Hot and sweaty. And you know how I like hot and sweaty, Luc."

I cringe, knowing that Frannie is listening in on our internal conversation, but Lilith is right. I've never felt so claustrophobic in someone else's body.

Lilith's essence swirls, huge but shadowy and impossible to contain. I can feel the host body's soul, dark and thick, cowering in the corners. A soul clearly already tagged for Hell, which is why Lilith was able to inhabit her body in the first place.

Then I feel Frannie, her white opalescence swirling weakly around my glossy black. And aside from the obvious, there's something terribly wrong. There's no spark to her soul, as if she's too exhausted to continue—spent. Panic chokes my thoughts. I only know I need to get her out of here.

"I could leave and take a few of these souls with me."

"Not going to happen. My king wants you back. Of course, judging from the last time we were together, I'm thinking you won't *want* to leave for long."

Another wave of desire almost takes me under, but I channel it and turn it back on her. As my thoughts clear, it occurs to me that Lilith and I aren't really that different. She's a pawn in His game, just as I was. If I could make her see a way out . . .

"You don't have to do this, Lilith."

Her essence swirls thick around Frannie and me, smoke streaked with crimson. "You know I do."

"He's just using you—all of us—in His twisted game. If He gets Frannie, there'll be no stopping Him."

"There's already no stopping Him. And besides, maybe I don't want to stop Him. When He is the Almighty, things will be different."

"Some things won't change. The torture . . . what He does to you—"

"I *need* what He does to me. There's nothing like His lust in the mortal world. I was hoping Matt's would be enough, but . . ." She trails off. Even though her words are sharp, they're driven by an undercurrent of fear that she can't hide. And, in that statement, I see the difference between Lilith and me. I was born of sin. Lilith chose it. She literally made a deal with the devil all those millennia ago. Where I traded my immortality for love, she traded her mortality for lust.

"I can't live without His lust," she adds, sounding broken. "Frannie felt it. She knows."

Everything spins. Is that what happened to her, why there's nothing left? *What did He do to her?* Guilt rips a hole right through me, leaving me cold and empty.

I let this happen.

I think of Frannie's sparkling sapphire eyes, how alive they were, and I want to die, knowing this is my fault. I wasn't strong enough to deserve her—to protect her.

I call out to her with my mind and move slowly, encircling Frannie's shimmering essence with my own. I work to hide my doubt and insecurity, instead playing on Lilith's. "With Frannie by His side, do you really think He'll still want you?"

"He has *always* wanted me, and He *will* always want me." I feel her fury and fear swirl through us, the red streaks of her essence becoming thicker, more solid.

And then I do it. I blend my essence with Frannie's.

Please, Frannie. Please come back to me.

"Isn't that sweet," Lilith says, all bitterness and hate. "But it's too late. She would have willingly given herself to our king if you hadn't so rudely interrupted."

Frannie's essence burns and swirls, stronger every second. I bask in it, feeling my own essence swell as hers becomes more vivacious. Her anger surges, black pepper in my nose, and then I hear her voice, faint at first but becoming stronger as her raison d'être grows. It sounds like a chant, and as it grows louder, I'm able to decipher the words in the rhythm. It becomes strong enough that Lilith's lips start to move and she says it out loud.

"Let me go. You don't want me. Let me go. You don't want me."

Hope washes through me. I keep my essence blended with Frannie's and send her all my strength. Lilith groans and I use the little bit of control I have to force her host body to stay still when she tries to run. Lilith struggles to hold on to Frannie, and I feel Frannie's resolve falter as Lilith floods us with dark ideas—blood, lust, death.

"No, Frannie, don't listen," I say, and start chanting with her. "Let me go. You don't want me. Let me go."

I feel a different sort of surge in Frannie, and her essence flows stronger. I draw on her strength and send it back, swirling the cyclone inside.

"Luc?" It comes from somewhere deep inside her, accompanied by a burst of warm chocolate.

"Focus," I say, struggling to do the same. "Let me go. You don't want me."

She picks it back up, stronger.

I feel Lilith waver. Her smoky essence ebbs for just an instant, but it's enough. Relief washes over me as I feel Frannie's soul swirl—taste her currant and clove. And then she's gone.

I gather my essence and start to seep out of this body, between Lilith's lips, but a Banshee cry rips through her. I feel a sick tug and realize I'm tethered here by some force.

"No! I can't go back without at least one of you," Lilith cries.

Lilith spins on Frannie, where Gabriel is perched over her body on the bed. He's got one hand on her chest and another on her head. He glances up, the panic in his eyes triggering crushing dread in my heart. "You're on your own, dude," he says, and presses his lips to Frannie's, breathing for her. "Come on, Frannie," he says.

I'm nearly helpless in Lilith's body as she charges at Frannie, determined to get her back. But just before we reach her, Gabriel raises his hand, and white lightning shoots from his palm, coursing through us.

Lilith screams and drops to the floor, and it's everything I can do to stifle my own scream. But as painful as that was, I know Gabriel was holding back or Lilith's host body would be dead. She's not, but the blast is enough to break Lilith's focus.

I think of Frannie, of the person she made me, of all the good she brings out in me, and I feel my strength swell. I push with everything I have. Lilith groans as she fights through the pain to hold me. But she can't, and my essence shoots from her body like a stone from a slingshot.

The force with which I enter my human shell almost knocks me unconscious. I struggle to get my head straight and pull myself off the floor.

Lilith picks herself up, and with one glance back at Gabriel, she staggers for the door. She opens it and runs square into Taylor, standing in the hall. Taylor's eyes bulge at the sight of Lili emerging, bloody, from my apartment.

"Hey, girl," Lilith says.

And then everything happens in a blur.

She drapes herself over Taylor. The next instant, Lilith's body goes limp and hits the floor in a heap, and Taylor is running full speed down the hall.

A strangled, choking wheeze sounds behind me, and I wheel around to find Frannie cradled in Gabriel's arms, clawing at her throat and gasping for air.

Gabriel looks up at me. "Taylor," he barks with a jerk of his head toward the door.

I pause for one more second, fighting my need to run to Frannie, to touch her and make sure she's okay, before stepping over the unconscious brunette who used to be Lilith on my way to the stairs. As I slam through the door to the parking lot, an engine roars and I hear a car bottom out on the curb. I run to the street and catch a glimpse of the taillights of an old black hearse turning the corner.

Marchosias. Damn!

I wait at the curb a moment longer, then sprint back up the stairs to Frannie.

24

✞

The Devil in Me

FRANNIE

My throat is still on fire and my vision is blurry when Luc walks back into the apartment. My stomach turns at the sight of him carrying Lilith's unconscious body.

Gabe rocks me in his arms. His summer snow dulls the pain in my body and my burning lungs, making me forget everything. I sink deeper into him, hoping he'll bury me altogether, and lay my pounding head in the crook of his neck as he gathers me tighter against him.

I recoil farther into Gabe as Luc lays Lilith next to me on the bed. His eyes flick to me momentarily as he covers her with a blanket, making sure that she's comfortable. Then he turns concerned eyes on Gabe. "Will she be okay?"

Gabe smooths a hand over my hair. "I don't know."

Luc stares down at Lilith, his face unreadable. He reaches down and brushes her hair out of her face.

And watching him touch her like that cuts me like a knife. I turn my face away and try to block out the image of the last time I saw them together.

"I need to go." My voice is a hoarse croak as I try to force air through my throbbing vocal cords.

"Sure, Frannie."

I wince and cry out when Gabe hikes me into his arms as he stands.

"Gabriel—?" I'm surprised by the tinge of panic in Luc's voice.

I pull my face out of Gabe's shoulder and look at Luc, but when our eyes connect, he looks away.

I'm so confused. I remember how Lilith made me feel—how much I wanted her—so I kinda get that what happened that night might not have been all Luc's fault. My head is telling me that. But my broken heart still can't get past what he did.

"You know what? Put me down. I'm fine," I say, pushing away from Gabe. The truth is I hurt all over, but they don't need to know that. "Nothing's broken."

Gabe looks at me with troubled eyes. He doesn't argue with me, even though he knows I'm lying. But he doesn't put me down either. His gaze slides to Luc. "Taylor?"

"What's wrong with Taylor?" I shift in Gabe's arms, and the sharp pain shooting through my ribs makes me gasp. I glance at Luc for the answer, but he just shakes his head.

"Nothing for you to worry about," Gabe says, and I feel him pulling that snow crap on me again.

I fight the peaceful calm that settles over me. "That's not an answer."

"I'll find her. Don't worry."

I hear the frustration in his voice, and panic cuts through me. I struggle to get free of his arms, but every movement causes a sharp jab of pain in one place or another. "You'll find her? What the hell does that mean? *Was she here?*" I kick my legs, because they seem to hurt the least. "Put me down!"

He lowers my feet gently to the floor and supports me there. He inclines his head toward Luc, gesturing for him to speak, but with a warning in his eye.

I grab Gabe's shirt and yank. "No! *You* answer me." Gabe can't lie, and that's all Luc does. I want the truth.

"Later, Frannie," he says.

"Tell me now!" The words feel like fire ripping out of my throat.

"She needs to know, Gabriel," Luc says. He steps around the bed, and there's pain in his eyes. "Lilith has her." But then his face pinches as he grimaces and his eyes drop from mine.

Panic tangles with confusion as I look at the girl on the bed. "Lilith is right there."

"That's not Lilith. It's her host," Gabe answers.

I shake my head as frustration rears up, making me want to slap Gabe—to make him stop talking in riddles. *"What the hell is going on?"*

He holds my eyes with his, concern etching his brow. "Lilith has shifted. She's taken Taylor."

"She shifted . . . into Taylor . . . ?" Understanding dawns in some corner of my mind and I go rigid. Taylor is tagged for Hell.

"We'll get her back." Luc won't meet my eyes, but even through the shake in his voice, he sounds determined. He squats down, fingering the loose pages of his original-run *Purgatorio* that litter the floor.

I turn back to Gabe, wincing. "What are we gonna do?"

"You need to go home, Frannie—get some rest. Luc and I are better equipped to track Taylor down and deal with Lilith."

"I want to—"

Gabe cuts me off with a finger to my swollen lips. "You could pull your Sway on me and make me let you do this, but you know as well as I do that you'd only slow us down and get in the way. Is that what you want? Us protecting you? Or do you want Taylor back safely?"

I glare, trying to convince myself he's wrong. "But maybe my Sway can help."

"How?"

"Maybe I could . . . I don't know . . . maybe she'd leave Taylor alone."

"I don't think this is going to be that simple. You're the one she wants, Frannie. It'd be safer for you not to get anywhere near her."

I remember what Lilith did to me, how she made me feel, and in the end, I get that he's right. "Fine."

Luc's voice comes from near the broken window. "I'll drive her home." I turn and his obsidian eyes lock on mine. I feel a pang in my heart as I remember that those eyes aren't human anymore.

"I can drive," I say, furious at the shake in my voice.

"No, you can't," Gabe says. "And I need to deal with this." He waves a hand at the girl on the bed.

I look at Luc, who won't meet my gaze, and spin for the door. "Let's go."

Gabe catches Luc's arm on the way by and fixes him in a hard gaze. "Stay with her until I can get there." His voice is low, and I don't think he means for me to hear, but I turn and glare at him so he knows I did.

In the first few steps, I find that my legs still function, but my left knee is puffy and a little numb. It falters on the first stair and Luc grabs my elbow to steady me as I claw for the handrail. I'm completely unprepared for my body's reaction to his touch. I groan as his demonic heat courses through me, making my already wavering legs refuse to hold me. Luc catches me before I hit the ground, sweeping me up into his arms.

I can't look him in the eye. "Put me down."

He ignores me and carries me down the stairs.

"Put me down," I repeat when we get to the bottom, and he does.

I hobble to the car, and Luc holds out his hand for the key. I hand him the rabbit's foot key chain with the old, worn key to the Mustang, and the shiny, new key to his apartment.

Wordlessly, he takes it from my hand and we climb in, him in the driver's seat.

"I really can drive." I start to cross my arms and slump into the seat before my ribs remind me that isn't gonna work.

In response, he turns the key in the ignition and backs out of the parking spot. For a second, his eyes flick to mine and I see it. Guilt.

Rage rips out of my emotional black pit. "You knew." It's less a question and more an accusation.

He shoots another glance in my direction, but he doesn't answer.

"How much did you know? Did you know what she was? Lili?"

His jaw clenches and he draws a deep breath, but he just stares out the windshield.

"Did you know she and Matt were, like . . . together?"

"I told you that," he says, his voice totally flat.

He *did* tell me that. And I stupidly hoped he was right. My stomach clamps into a hard knot.

"You knew Taylor was tagged for Hell." It's not a question.

His eyes flick to mine again, and there's the guilt.

"How could you not tell me?"

He shakes his head but says nothing.

My mind reels with other questions and things I want to say to him—most of them along the lines of, How could you turn out to be such a lying, cheating bastard? But I know what his answer to that would be: He's a demon—what did I expect? So I seethe internally and force myself not to look at him. And try to ignore the aching hole deep inside me. I close my eyes, press back into the seat, and turn my head toward the window so he won't see the tears leaking down my cheeks.

I remember the reasons I came over to Luc's in the first place—what I saw in the dream. I needed to see for myself that he was gone. But he's here. So close, I could touch him. And I want to. I want to feel his arms around me, his lips on mine.

God, I've missed him.

What's wrong with me? How can I love him and hate him all at the same time?

I brush the tears from my face and cast him an assessing, sidelong glance. His head is propped back on the headrest at a little bit of an angle away from me, one wrist draped over the steering wheel and the other hand on the gearshift. His eyes glow red through his silky black mop, and the occasional working streetlight glints off his eyebrow piercings.

God, I don't know what to think. He looks healthy enough, so apparently his trip to Hell was voluntary. Was I stupid for worrying?

I turn toward him and almost reach for him. But I stop myself. He continues to stare out the windshield intently. He's made no move to say anything. His expression is hard, his face drawn. If he still cared about me, wouldn't he tell me?

Tears threaten again and I choke them off. I think back on Lilith—how she made me feel when she kissed me—and I know what I need to say.

"I know it wasn't your fault—with Lilith."

He stiffens and I can tell he's not breathing as he stares out the windshield. When I'm sure that's all the answer I'm gonna get, I turn back to the window.

"I'm sorry," he says, his voice low, and I hope he doesn't hear the shudder in my breathing as I sob into the window.

I fight to get myself together as he pulls into my driveway and steps out of the car, tossing me the keys. He just stands there, staring at me with hard, obsidian eyes that reflect back any attempt to see deeper. More than anything, I want Gabe's ability to read minds right now.

I realize he's waiting for me to go inside, so I slide out of my seat and start to head for the house, trying not to limp. Halfway up the walk, I turn back to him, trying to read him again. In that instant, before he realizes I've turned, I catch something in his expression. Pain.

I almost run back to him. But the next instant, as his eyes lock on mine, his expression turns hard and stone cold again. And as I step toward him, I realize I'm not gonna be running anywhere for a while. But I have to know.

"Was it all just an act? Did you ever care about me at all?"

His expression shifts through about ten different things so quickly, I can't get a read on any of them, before finally settling back to blank. He stares at me for a long, awkward minute, then slowly shakes his head.

If there was ever any question, at least now I know for sure. This is how he wants it. It's what I needed to know to let go— move on. My chest feels ready to cave in as I turn back toward the house and push through the door. Once inside and out of Luc's sight, I lean my forehead on the door and let the ache in my chest dissolve into tears. But Mom's voice from the kitchen turns my thoughts to how I'm gonna get cleaned up without anyone seeing me. The torn clothes, bruises, and blood would be a little tricky to explain to my parents. *Yeah, remember that girl that Luc slept with? Well, we beat the shit out of each other.*

After listening for a second to Mom's voice, I realize what I'm hearing is her half of a telephone conversation rolling out of the kitchen. The Red Sox game blasts from the TV in the family room. There's a fifty–fifty chance that Dad is asleep in his chair in front of the game. My sisters hate baseball, so I'm sure he's alone.

I listen through the din of the TV, and sure enough, Dad's

snore is just audible over the blare of the commentators. I wipe the tears from my face and smooth my hair with my damp hands before slinking through the family room and up the stairs as quickly and quietly as possible. My intention is to head directly to the bathroom, but before I reach the top of the stairs, I hear the shower running. Someone's beat me to it.

I hurry into my room and close the door. At the window, I glance up at the brewing storm clouds, wondering how it is that the weather seems to match my frame of mind so perfectly. I drop my eyes to the Mustang, thinking idly that I should have put the top up.

And my heart skips.

Luc is still standing at my car, hands propped on the driver door, head hanging between his shoulders. As I watch, he pushes sharply back from the car and paces the sidewalk, then glances up at my window. I duck and cry out as my ribs bump the desk on my way to the floor.

Why is he still here?

But then I remember Gabe telling him to stay.

I skitter along the floor on my hands and knees and cross the room to my mirror, where I use the dresser to help pull myself back to a stand. Looking at my face, it's not as bad as I expected. But then my hand gravitates to the tender knot on the back of my head and I wince. My phone rings and I jump, pressing harder into the knot and wincing again.

I look at the caller ID, hoping for Taylor. It's Riley.

"Have you heard from Tay?"

What does she know?

"Um . . . no. You know she's not speaking to me. What's up?"

"Trev says she just blasted in there, grabbed some stuff, and took off without a word. He's worried."

"I don't know, Ry. That Marc guy she's with is seriously scary. Trev should be worried." I know I am. My stomach is a hard ball of worry.

She's quiet for a minute. "Should we go look for her?"

"Maybe," I say, hoping Gabe already is. I hear the door to the bathroom click open. "Listen, I gotta go. Call me if you hear anything, 'kay?"

"'Kay."

I speed-dial Gabe. "Taylor was at her house just now," I say when he picks up.

"I'll check it out. Are you home?"

"Yeah."

"Sleep. I'll be there when I can." His voice is soft, reassuring.

I feel my chest loosen a little just at the thought of him here. "'Kay. I'll try."

I flip the phone shut and wait till the hall is quiet, then hurry to the bathroom with my towel and bathrobe.

The water feels good on my hot skin. I stand with my hands braced against the wall and let it wash over me, rinsing me clean—on the outside, at least. But I can't shake the agitated twitchiness on the inside: a combination of the memory of being inside Lilith and the unease of the eerie comfort I felt in King Lucifer's arms. I shudder with the memory of the angelic face.

Why was it that face I saw when He held me? Whose face was it?

Finally, I groan in frustration and force my thoughts to Taylor. I have to help her.

I hurry through the rest of my shower routine, and when I finish, I twist my hair into the towel and inspect my face in the mirror again as I brush my teeth. One cut at my hairline above my right eye that you'd have to move my hair to see, a reddish swollen spot on my right cheek, and a puffy lower lip. Easy enough to explain away. The worst of it is under my clothes. I slide my robe gingerly over my bruised body and make my way back to my room. Maggie comes out of the room she shares with Grace as I pass by.

"Why is Luc in our driveway? I thought you guys broke up."

Despite my best attempt not to let him affect me, my heart sputters. "Um . . . we did. I don't know why he's here."

She grins at me, hope sparkling in her sapphire blue eyes. She's always had a crush on Luc. "Maybe he wants you back."

"Not likely," I say, but my heart goes from sputtering to skipping.

She shrugs, disappointed, and heads into the bathroom while I slide through my door. I press the Play button on my iPod just as the phone starts ringing. I run to the desk, pick it up, and look at the caller ID. Taylor! It's her home line.

I bring the phone to my ear. "Taylor. Are you okay?"

"Frannie?" At the sound of Taylor's mom's voice, my heart sinks. "I was hoping Taylor was there."

"No, Mrs. Stevens."

There's a pause. "It's getting late. She's been doing good with her curfew lately. Did she tell you where she was going?"

I can't do this. I fight tears and work to keep my voice steady. "No."

"Well, if you hear from her, tell her to get her butt home, okay?"

"Sure."

I stare at the phone in my hand. Taylor. She's out there and I'm helpless.

Or am I?

"Leave Taylor alone. You don't want her," I say out loud. Then I repeat it over and over in my head, faster and faster. Still repeating the mantra, I pull the towel from my hair, toss it over my desk chair, and turn out my light.

And then my gut clenches as I remember Luc.

In the dark, I stand a cautious distance from the open window and look down into the driveway. When I don't see him, I tug my bathrobe so tightly around me that it makes my ribs throb, and move closer. It's not till I'm at the window, face pressed against the screen, that I notice the glowing red eyes staring at me from the oak branches just outside.

I start to scream and stumble back from the window when Luc pushes through the screen, leaving it in tatters. And before I can check the scream, he does it for me. His lips are hot on mine, and my scream morphs into a moan as his arms pull me to his burning body. He mistakes my moan for pain and lightens his grip.

He pulls away and looks down at me, his expression full of pain and his eyes full of doubt. "Frannie—"

I don't want to hear the rest of that thought, because I don't want to think about any of it. He's here and I love him. That's all that matters. I let go of the robe, lift my hand, and place my index finger softly over his lips. I force my mind to focus on now—here—Luc, and block out the rest. I pull him back to me, silencing him with another kiss, and sway with the music, deeper into Luc with every beat.

He kisses me back. Hard. Deep. Desperate. His lips burn a track across my shoulder, my neck, working their way up to my ear, where he whispers, "I'm so sorry."

The despair in his words crushes my heart. I press my face into his shirt. "It wasn't your fault. I know that now."

I look up at him and he kisses a tear from my lashes. I bring his mouth back to mine and push him toward my bed, sliding my hands under his shirt as we go. But as I smooth my hands over his flawless skin, I gasp and pull away. His skin isn't flawless anymore. Far from it. I lift his shirt and gape at the deep red gashes and puncture wounds covering his chest, back, and shoulders. I shudder as I remember the dream—the torture.

"What happened?" I whisper, afraid of the answer.

A small, sad smile curls the corners of his mouth. "It's nothing. They'll be gone in a few days." He gestures to his cheek, and I notice for the first time that the jagged red scar Beherit left as a souvenir is gone. "Nothing like these." His hand hesitates, then glides along my ribs, where my bathrobe has fallen open. I start to pull it closed, but his hand on my skin feels electric, yet so gentle, caressing my wounds. I feel the ache ease just from his touch.

My body responds to him: a warm glow starting low in my belly and spreading through me till I'm on fire. I press into him again, letting my robe slide off my shoulders and fall to the floor, and I pull his shirt over his head. Then I pull him onto the bed, under the sheets—where he can take my pain away.

As Luc kisses me deeper, I lose myself in him. I need him closer, next to my heart. I want to feel his essence swirling inside me again. I reach out with my mind—not with words, but with the sensation of what I need. And when I feel his essence slip through my lips, like silk, I'm flooded with him. Drowning in him. Goose bumps pebble my tingling skin and I moan and pull him closer.

His essence fills me, a burst of bliss, caressing every part of me and making me shudder. Nothing in the physical world feels like this. I feel him in every part of my body.

It feels like coming home.

LUC

This is so wrong. And so selfish.

It would be too easy to forget everything right now, just pretend that the last weeks never happened, and sink into Frannie, into the moment. And I want that more than anything. I've never been so torn in my existence. I need her. She's my life.

But I can't forget.

No matter how many millennia I live, I'll never forget the pain in Frannie's eyes when she pulled back the sheets and found me with Lilith. I'll never forget the sickening despair that almost destroyed me when I understood what had happened.

And I'll never forget that it was all my fault. Being human was no excuse. Lilith told me what she was that day in the library. I should have known.

And that's just one example of all the ways I could destroy Frannie if we stay together.

Frannie's touch is tentative, trembling, as she pulls me closer. Fire dances over my skin at her every touch, like tiny pyrotechnics. My brimstone heart pounds in my chest. And the feeling of my essence swirling with hers is beyond compare—the sheer bliss of being part of her, blending with the shimmering opalescent white of her soul. I've never seen anything nearly as beautiful, and the rush of sensations takes my breath away.

Being with her like this makes me realize that, in my few short months of humanity, I'd begun to take those sensations for granted—the vastness of her compassion and capacity for love. And the scale of emotions that she brings out in me.

My need to blend not only our souls, but also our bodies, nearly carries me away. I'm lost in the clove and currant of her soul, smothered in the warm chocolate of her love. For just a moment, I believe we can be together—in every way.

Chocolate. She loves me.

The realization makes me want her more, and it's nearly impossible to stop. But what I did is unforgivable. She deserves so much better than this.

And sleeping with me now would reverse her tag.

I draw back my essence and pull away from her lips—her shaking hands—while I still can. "Frannie, we can't. I'm a demon now. Your tag . . ."

Her tag.

It hits me like a lightning bolt. How could I have done that? We can't possess people who are tagged for Heaven. I reach out with my sixth sense to check. She still feels as though she's tagged for Heaven. So, how—?

Her body tenses as she presses her forehead into my shoulder, but she doesn't respond.

I can't keep the concern out of my voice. "I only stayed to . . . watch. To be sure you were safe. I never meant for us to end up . . ."

She releases me and rolls onto her side, away from me. "So, you don't want—"

I cut her off, because I *do* want this. But she shouldn't. "What I want is irrelevant. I don't know what Lilith's next move will be. I only meant to stay here to be sure she couldn't get to you."

At Lilith's name, she stiffens again and pulls the sheets tight around her.

She doesn't look at me, and her voice is a raw wound. "I need to know. When you were with her—"

"Stop, Frannie," I interrupt, because the thought of what I did—what she saw—is unbearable. "Please."

Every cell of my being protests as I roll out of the bed. It's physically painful to pull myself away from her. I retrieve her robe from the floor with a shaking hand, laying it on the pillow next to her, then tug my T-shirt over my head and move to the window. "I need to leave."

But I'm not sure I can.

I stand, staring, for several heartbeats, then take a step back toward the bed.

Stop!

I groan and rip my eyes away from the form of her body under the thin sheet. I clear my throat against the hot lump forming there. "I'll be right outside. I don't think she can get to you here—she'd have to come through a door or window," I say, fingering the tattered screen.

Her eyes don't move from the wall. "Go find Taylor."

"I'm sorry." My voice breaks. I push through the window and climb back into the tree.

It takes longer than I'd hoped to compose myself, sitting on a branch outside. But I don't fight the urge to phase back into her room, because I need to know if Mr. Cavanaugh's field is still intact. I close my eyes and focus on Frannie's bed. When I phase, I feel myself slam into the barrier, and I'm back on the tree limb. *Good.*

I settle into a fork in the branches and wait for Gabriel. And because I'm not hurting anyone but myself by doing it—and I deserve to hurt—I let my mind wander back into Frannie's bed.

25

✝

A Living Hell

FRANNIE

I haven't moved from the spot where Luc left me, and I'm wide awake when the phone rings again at midnight.

Taylor's mom.

Dread pulls at my insides and I think about letting it ring, afraid of what I might say if I answer. When I pick up, her voice is desperate—on the edge of hysterical. "When did you last talk to Taylor, Frannie?"

"Taylor hasn't spoken to me in weeks." I breathe deep and try to keep it together.

"What?" Her tone is sheer disbelief. Apparently, Taylor didn't fill her in.

"I didn't like Marc." I nearly gag on the name. "She was pissed."

I hear her choke back a moan. "The police won't do anything.

They say she's probably out with some boy or something. If you can think of anywhere to look . . ."

My mind is racing—and getting nowhere. "I don't know. She was at Lili's earlier . . . maybe . . . I don't know."

There's a long pause. "Well, if you think of anything . . . or if you hear from her, call me."

"Okay," I say, but she's already gone. Probably dialing Riley.

I sit up, pull on the T-shirt from under my pillow, and hug the sheets to my chest. Where would Lilith go? If she goes back to the apartment, Gabe will find her. But if not . . . is she on the run, or is she still after me? If she's given up, she could be anywhere, but what are the chances of that? So, maybe if I put myself out there, like bait, she'll come to me.

I start to work out my plan: Shake the bodyguards and get somewhere she'll find me. But where? I play out scenarios in my head . . . all the ways this could go. In only a few of them do Taylor and I both come out alive.

The lightning in my head sears through my already throbbing brain, shocking me out of my restless non-sleep. I try to push everything from my mind, suddenly terrified of what this means—who I'll see if I let the image form. But there's no stopping it. I already know who it is.

Taylor.

My stomach lurches as I try to block out the vision of Taylor covered in blood, lying in the woods. I roll to the edge of the bed and miss the trash can when I puke, but there isn't much in my stomach, seeing as I've had no appetite for a while.

And that's when I realize I'm alone. No Gabe. He was here during the night. I felt his summer snow and his cool breath in my hair. It was the only reason I was able to sleep at all. But he's gone now.

I pick up my phone and hit Taylor's speed dial. If Lilith picks up . . . But when it goes to voice mail, I release the breath I didn't know I'd been holding, hang up, and speed-dial *3*.

Riley picks up on the first ring. "Did she call you?"

"No. I was hoping, maybe, that you've heard something."

"Not really. Trev's here. Says his parents are freaking out. The police say she's eighteen and they think she's just a runaway, so they're not doing anything." Her voice lowers and I can tell she's cupping the phone. "Do you think she could have? Could she have taken off with that Marc guy?"

As bad as that would be, I close my eyes and wish it were that simple. Behind my eyelids floats the vision of Taylor bleeding in the woods.

I gasp and jump from the bed as I recognize her surroundings.

"I gotta go, Ry. Call me later." I snap the phone shut without waiting for her reply.

Gallaghers'.

I was so quick to block the image out that I didn't notice details at first, but the grayed shingles of the Gallaghers' shed are there, at the periphery of the image. The ground around the shed is sprinkled with beer cans, cigarette butts, and a used condom. As I replay the image in my head, looking for more detail, I notice that this vision has sound. I can distinctly hear The Fray sing "How to Save a Life." My stomach lurches again when I smell the salty, metallic copper of her blood in the heavy dusk air.

Dusk.

Taylor will be dying behind the Gallaghers' shed at dusk.

I throw on my clothes, gasping for air, and it's not till I raise my arms overhead to slide my shirt on that I feel the stabbing pain in my ribs. I lied to Gabe. At least one of them is broken for sure. But that's the least of my worries.

Mom tackles me with pancakes and sausage when I hit the bottom of the stairs. "You're the only one who's going to get a warm breakfast. Everyone else is still in bed."

My stomach rolls at the prospect of food. "I'm really not hungry, Mom. I'm going over to Riley's," I lie.

At first she scowls, but then her face softens. "You've got to eat, Frannie. I know this breakup has been hard on you, but you can't lose any more weight. It's not healthy."

I'm wasting time. I need to get out of here and talk to Gabe—figure out what to do. I lash out in frustration. "It isn't the breakup, Mom. I'm just not hungry." I turn and bound out the door before she has a chance to respond.

I race down the street, but halfway to Gabe's, it hits me that this may not be the best strategy. What if Gabe scares Lilith off?

I might only have one shot. This might be my only chance to get Taylor back.

Think.

My mind returns to my original plan, before I knew where Taylor was. I can use myself as bait—lure her out. With no Gabe or Luc to scare Lilith off, it could work.

She needs someone tagged for Hell to shift into. What if I can use my Sway to convince her *I'm* tagged for Hell? She'd try to shift from Taylor into me—I'm the one she wants, after all. But I'm tagged for Heaven, so she wouldn't be able to enter my body. The bodies she's shifting between need to be touching— that's what Dad said. So if I push Taylor away during the shift, Lilith would be left without a body. Can she survive that way? Gabe said her soul is human, so I'm pretty sure that'd be a no. My heart races as the plan, along with the danger involved, comes clear in my mind.

All I need to do is get Lilith out of Taylor, and then get Taylor away from Lilith.

Without Gabe or Luc screwing it up.

My Shield is useless against Luc, and Gabe can read my mind unless I'm really careful—so I need to avoid them both.

I flip open my phone and call Riley. I hate using her this way, but it's for Taylor. If I could explain it to her, I'm sure she'd go along. This should work on two fronts. I need to keep Riley safe, but I also need an alibi.

"Riley, can you and Trev come over?"

"Did Taylor call?"

"No, but I have an idea," I say, turning for home.

I'll eat some pancakes—make Mom happy. And if my Sway's worth anything, no one will notice me leave when the time comes.

341

LUC

What I did last night was inexcusable. And if I stay, I'll do it again. I've replayed every caress, every kiss, over and over in my mind. The only way she'll ever be safe is with Gabriel. He should have left me to Lucifer.

That's what I need to do—go back to Hell and face the music. Otherwise, I'm not sure how I'll manage to stay away from her.

But then I remember the Mage. If I go back, I'm certain they'll use me to find Frannie. "I need to go."

"Where?" Gabriel is sprawled on his couch, picking absently at a piece of lint on the cushion.

"Anywhere but here."

"So, after everything, you're still going to run." He smirks. "Coward."

My eyes snap up and I lurch off the chair, my fist hot and red. But as I level it at him, I catch the white lightning dancing across the surface of his skin, and smell the ozone, suddenly thick in the air. He's goading me. I sink back into the chair. "I'm not in the mood for your games."

His face becomes serious and the static charge in the air makes the hair on my neck stand on end. "This is no game."

"There's nothing I can do. She'll be better off with me gone."

He blows out a sigh, and his face tightens. "I wish that were true, but as much as it pains me to say it, she's still in love with you."

"Was. She *was* in love with me, and then I slept with Lilith and fixed that. She wants you now," I say, wanting it to be true.

I shiver at the memory of her warm chocolate. She shouldn't love me. She'll be better off with Gabriel, wings or no.

"No. She still needs you, Luc." He nearly chokes on the words, and his head drops onto the back of the couch.

My face pulls into a pained grimace. As I screw my eyes shut, I see her robe sliding off her shoulders, feel my hands on her skin, and the memory tears a hole in my heart. I prop my heavy head in my hand. "She's tough. She'll get past it." But I won't.

"I'm not convinced." Gabriel's brow creases and he rubs it as though he has a headache.

I look him hard in the eye. "Is she still tagged for Heaven?"

He shifts in his seat, pulling himself straighter. "You should know that without having to ask."

"She seems to be, but . . ."

"But what?"

"How could I possess her if she's still tagged for Heaven?"

He lifts his eyebrows and leans forward, elbows on his knees. "What did you do?"

My eyes drop to the carpet. "I stopped before we . . . did anything we couldn't take back, but my essence was inside her. I felt a pull and I let it go."

A rueful, lopsided smile curves his mouth. "Apparently even the laws of the universe bend to her Sway."

"You think her Sway did that?"

"If she wanted it . . ." He shrugs. "Which is why I need you to stay." He holds my gaze for a moment, then drops his. "I can't trust myself around her."

"So, what's new?" I say, trying and failing to hide the pang of jealousy.

"When you're gone, her pull on me is . . ." His eyes are tortured. "I'm going to lose my wings, and then I'll be useless to her."

My voice is acid. "So you need me to stay here and save you from your sorry self."

He props his head on the back of the couch again and stares at the ceiling. "That pretty much sums it up."

"What if I end up . . ." I trail off and shudder, thinking of last night. "You seem to forget her pull on me is no different."

"Stronger. I'm betting she'll turn you mortal again," he says without lifting his head. The pain in his voice is deep and raw.

I pull myself from the chair. "I need to leave—for a lot of reasons. It's obvious that if I stay, I'll end up doing something I shouldn't, and besides, this is the first place Hell will look for me. Lucifer's not going to be happy about all of Hell witnessing His little example go awry."

He weighs that for a long moment. "For now, anyway," he finally says. "We'll figure out a way to hide you away. Your Shield will help."

"Unless I use my magic. It's sort of a catch twenty-two. I'm pretty sure I can't evade them without it, but the minute I use it, they'll find me."

"Maybe I can help get you a head start."

"That'd be greatly appreciated. But first we need to find Lilith." I feel every muscle in my body tighten as the face of the girl who was Lilith floats in front of my eyes. "Who was she?"

"Who?"

"The girl I . . ." My self-disgust causes my stomach to lurch and I swallow back sour bile at the thought of what I did to her. "The girl who was Lilith's host." Lilith's victim.

Gabriel leans onto the arm of the chair, looking exhausted. "Her name is Robin. I got her settled at the hospital last night. I'll check on her later." Then he looks up into my eyes. "Sleeping with her wasn't your fault, Luc. You know what Lilith is."

I stand and turn for the door, feeling the need to run, and when I open it, Riley and Trevor are standing there. Riley's obviously been crying and Trevor looks pale—in shock.

Surprise widens Riley's eyes. "Luc."

I breathe deep and try to clear my head. "Riley. Any word from Taylor?"

"No. We've been over at Frannie's. She's got a phone list for our class. We're texting everyone to see if anyone's seen her."

Gabriel steps up beside me in the door. "Good. Make sure Frannie doesn't leave her house."

"Why?"

"I just want to know where to find her."

Riley nods. "She wanted me to give you this," she says, holding out a folded sheet of yellow paper. "She said it was easer to write it down than to call you," she adds as Gabriel plucks the paper from her fingers and unfolds it. "She thought maybe you could check these out."

On the paper is a time line of sorts. There are notations of time in the margin—Taylor sightings starting from yesterday afternoon. There are three dark asterisks next to the time stamp "8:30" and a notation next to it: "Luc's apartment."

After that, there are only two additional notations, each

with a large question mark next to them. One says "?10:15ish—Cassidy thinks they were parking at quarry." Then, underlined next to it, is another note. "I don't think so." Obviously Frannie's personal observation. The next line reads, "?11:00—Aaron thinks he saw her at the KwikMart." Frannie's note here says, "Maybe." And the final line on the paper is Marchosias's address. It's been traced over several times and underlined repeatedly. Next to it, Frannie's note simply says, "Here."

"Thanks, Riley," Gabriel says, and she and Trevor head for her car.

I watch them pull out then I turn to Gabriel. "I'm going out to see if I can pick up on Lilith. The Shield doesn't seem to work both ways. They're in my head again. You should check Marchosias's apartment."

"Call if you find anything."

"Got it."

I can't help driving by Frannie's on my way out of the neighborhood. She's standing at the open door, letting Riley and Trevor in as I pass. Her eyes connect with mine and I slow to nearly a stop, savoring the crackle of hot electricity that plays along my skin when I'm anywhere near her. Her Shield is supposed to hide her from Infernals, but it's never worked with me. That's why I found her in the first place when others from the Abyss couldn't. If she's within a city block, I know it.

And now that I have my demon's sixth sense back, her pull on me is stronger than it ever was before. I breathe deep, pushing the images of things that were—but can never be again—

out of my head, and step on the accelerator. My job now is to keep her safe. Period. And with Lilith gone, she'll be that much safer.

A half hour later, I'm cruising near the quarry, frustration doing battle with dread in my black core. I gun the engine and crank the wheel. The car spins a 180 on the narrow dirt road as rocks pepper the wheel wells. I'm fishtailing away from the quarry, on my way to the KwikMart, when the phone rings.

"We've got Taylor," Gabriel says. "She's at the Cove with Marchosias."

FRANNIE

I left Riley and Trevor in my room a half hour ago. They think I'm in the bathroom. If my Sway is worth crap, they'll keep thinking it. Where I really am is parked on the side of the road behind the Gallaghers' house, waiting. It's nearly dusk when I speed-dial Gabe and raise the phone to my ear with a shaking hand.

"Frannie? Is everything okay?"

"I just talked to Valerie Blake. She said Taylor is over at the Cove. I think Marc's with her." About as far from the Gallagher house as you can get before you're in the Atlantic Ocean. And crowded on a Saturday evening in August. "I'm gonna send Trevor over to check it out," I say, hoping he thinks my shaking voice is my worry for Taylor. I hold my breath and wait for the answer I need.

"No. Tell Trevor to stay with you. I'll go for her. If she's there and Trevor approaches her . . . she's a succubus, Frannie. Even though she's Trevor's sister, it'd be dangerous for him."

That's only half the answer I need. "Will you be able to handle Lilith and Marc by yourself?"

"I'll get Luc over there too."

There's the other half. A shaky sigh escapes my chest. "Fine, but hurry."

"On my way," he says, and clicks off.

I sit, gripping the steering wheel with white knuckles. It worked. I'm on my own.

I can't do this. What was I thinking?

I shake my head and push back the doubt.

No. This is right—the only way to get close to Lilith. Gabe and Luc would scare her off, or if they didn't, they'd never let me close enough to her to help Taylor. It's gonna work.

It has to.

I breathe deep, repeating the mantra in my head. I worked it out so that there shouldn't be any loopholes. I step out of the car and into the woods, moving as quickly as I can, but from where I am, there's no real path, so my progress is slow. I start to panic, sure I'll be too late. But the faster I try to go, the more I seem to trip. Adrenaline starts my heart pounding and I try to run, but my flip-flop catches in a tangle of vines and I go down hard.

Just when I'm sure that I must have taken a wrong turn, I make out the shed through the trees, a gray slab framed by green foliage. I claw my way through the bramble to the small clearing, out of breath and bleeding from a zillion scratches and scrapes, and pull up short.

Crap, I'm not alone.

The shed is about fifteen or twenty yards into the woods behind the Gallaghers' house, so I can't see the yard or house from here. Which is exactly why this is the spot couples disappear to when they want some privacy during parties. Taylor's spent plenty of time here, and I caught Riley and Trevor on their way out of the woods during the graduation party.

And now Angelique and Brendan are here. He has her pinned up against the side of the shed, jeans around his knees.

I duck behind a tree in the shadows at the edge of the clearing and try to slow my rasping breath.

What now?

I stand absolutely still, swallow back the panic rising in me, and try to think. But then the noise from the couple stops and everything goes still. I wait a second longer and then peek cautiously around the tree in time to see Brendan chuck the condom onto the ground and zip his jeans. He walks off toward the Gallaghers' backyard without a glance at Angelique, who's tugging her skirt back into place.

She runs after him. "Wait up!"

But he doesn't.

And then I'm alone. I step slowly into the clearing and exhale a shaky breath.

The woods are deceptively calm. The low din of chatter from the crowd gathering in the Gallaghers' backyard filters through the trees to where I am, muffled by the soft hush under the thick canopy of summer leaves. But, as I take in my surroundings, I feel my skin start to crawl. It's the exact image from my head—except without Taylor's bloody body.

I look around wildly for any sign of her and almost have a heart attack when a squirrel bounds out from behind the shed. I brace my hands on my knees and breathe deep to settle my nerves—and nearly jump out of my skin when music starts. But it's not Jackson's car stereo. It's Roadkill. They must be set up at the party.

Suddenly, I'm confused. The music in my image wasn't live. *Oh, God. Did I get this wrong?*

Frustration rips from my chest in a growl.

Between my yell and the music, I don't hear anything else, so I cry out in surprise when I turn back to the shed and find Taylor standing there.

LUC

I'm halfway to the Cove when I feel it. Frannie isn't at her house. I pull my phone and dial her. No answer. I call Riley.

"Hey, Luc," she says in answer.

"Riley! Where is Frannie?"

"In the bathroom."

"The truth, Riley. It's really important."

"I'm telling you the truth. She's in the bathroom. Promise."

"How long has she been in there?"

There's a pause. "Just a few minutes . . . I think."

"Go check on her."

I hear the door click open and a knock. "Frannie," comes Riley's muffled voice. Another knock.

"Um, I think she's in there. . . ."

"Open the door, Riley."

"It's locked."

I swallow my panic. "You're sure she didn't go out?"

She sounds anything but sure. "I don't think so. . . ."

I disconnect and try to focus. She's not very close, that much I know. My demon's sixth sense isn't strong enough yet to get a solid feel for where she is. But the fact that I can feel her at all means she's not all the way across town at her house. Wherever it is, I have to gamble that she'll have her car so I can get her the Hell out if I need to.

I pull to the side of the road and phase behind the Cove. I look in the window of Ricco's, but I already know she's not here. I've lost the buzz.

I try the quarry again. The buzz is stronger, but only a little.

But when I hit the road in front of the Gallaghers', I know she's here, and I catch the thread of Lilith's thoughts. Frannie's car is among the multitude of others parked at the edge of the woods.

Unholy Hell.

I take a sweep of the Gallaghers' backyard, but she's not here. I turn to head into the woods when Chase and Kate see me.

"Hey!" Chase says as they approach. "Flying solo tonight?"

"I was looking for Frannie. Seen her?"

Kate shakes her head. "Not here. She was at home when I left a while ago."

"Thanks," I say, already jogging for the road.

Once I'm out of sight of the partygoers, I cut into the woods and try to home in on Frannie. The trees are dense, and I can't see very far into them, but she's in there. I can feel it. I could phase blindly around the woods searching for her, but with the gathering crowd, I run the risk of someone seeing me. And I might never find her. I'm better off zeroing in on Lilith's thoughts and Frannie's energy.

The golden shadows of dusk make picking a path through the trees and low shrubs a slower process. I trip several times as I weave through the trees at a jog, because I'm focusing on Lilith—targeting her. My foot catches on a tree root and I skid to the forest floor.

And I don't get up.

Because, in the next heartbeat, Rhenorian is on top of me.

"Hey, loverboy," his voice rasps in my ear.

I try to shake him off. "Rhen, this really isn't a good time."

He backs off and rolls me to my back, his knee buried in my chest. "He wants you dead. He doesn't even care that whatever soul you still have is tagged for Heaven."

"Then stop wasting my time and kill me. Either that or get off."

"How'd you pull it off?"

My brimstone heart pounds in my chest. "What?"

"Defying King Lucifer. Slipping out from under His nose?"

"I really don't have time for this." I kick up and wrap my leg around his neck, twisting him into a necklock and slamming him to the ground. "Can we talk about it later?"

He raises his glowing fist and points it at my chest. "Now."

I shove my own glowing fist into his face. "Why all this interest?"

He hesitates. "You've got some of us thinking."

"Thinking? Aren't you afraid you'll sprain something, Rhen?"

He looks nervous, but doesn't back down. "We want to know how you did it."

I roll my eyes. "So, are you going to kill me or what?"

"Probably not."

"That's an act of treason."

"I know."

I let him loose and pull myself out of the dirt.

And hear Frannie scream.

I take off, running deeper into the woods, heedless of Rhenorian.

26

✣

Highway to Hell

FRANNIE

I stare Taylor in the eye, unable to breathe.

She leans against Marc, who's propped against the shed. Her lips pull into a lopsided smile. "Hey, Fee. Fancy meeting you here."

I don't know what to call her. Taylor? Lilith?

"Hey." I can barely get the word out.

"Glad you could make it."

I almost forget what I'm here for when I look into her eyes. They're Taylor's, but not Taylor's. As I stare into them, tendrils of some dark force start to creep through me, making me wish for the vision from my head to come true.

She smiles. "You feel me, don't you?"

Behind her, Marc feels her too. His eyes are hungry, preda-tory, as he yanks her into a kiss, but she shoves him away. He lets out a moan, somewhere between pain and pleasure, when she leaves him standing there and glides across the clearing to me.

"I feel you too. Are you ready, Fee?"

Marc leans back into the shed and just stands there, arms folded across his chest, anticipation in his eyes.

Run!

But I can't make myself do it. In some little corner of my mind, I remember I had a plan.

What was it?

I just stand here, rooted to the ground, unable to move, as Taylor glides closer, slow and smooth as a rattlesnake. She stops just a few inches from me, and I can feel heat radiate off her along with other, darker things. Her smile's gone as she glides her fingers down my cheek. I press into her, unable to stop myself.

"You want me as much as I want you. I can feel it," she purrs.

And she's right. I'm overwhelmed by the thought of being with her.

She continues to hypnotize me with her deep green eyes as she traces a finger slowly along the lines of my lips. When I don't pull away, she trails her finger down my neck to my chest. At her touch, the tingling ache low in my belly explodes out into every part of me, making me gasp.

And that's when she pulls the carving knife from the back pocket of her jeans.

The sight of it snaps me out of my trance. This was the plan. I need to be touching her when I convince Lilith to leave Taylor and enter me. I breathe deep and start the mantra slowly in my head; then I say it out loud. "My soul is tagged for Hell. You don't want Taylor. You want me."

Her body goes rigid and she starts to back away, but I grab her hand and pull her back to me.

"You're not—" she starts.

"I am. I'm tagged for Hell." I wrap her in an embrace, feeling the cold steel blade between our bodies.

She presses into me again and I have to fight to keep my senses. "You're tagged for Hell," she repeats.

"I'm tagged for Hell," I confirm.

Then everything happens all at once.

Taylor pulls me into a kiss just as Angelique steps out from behind the shed. She looks up and sees us, locked in our embrace. Her jaw drops and her eyes pull wide before her face settles into an incredulous smirk. "You've got to be shitting me." She steps toward us. "You two are bi! Unbelievable."

Marc clears his throat, and Angelique's head snaps around. He leans against the shed and raises an eyebrow with a suggestive half smile. "Care to join us?"

Angelique's jaw drops and her eyes dart from Marc to us then back. "Oh my god! Are you guys—? Is this, like, a threesome? Holy shit!"

I keep my grip on Taylor. I can't risk letting her get away. My pulse pounds in my ears, so loud I can barely hear my own voice. "Go away, Angelique."

"Don't get your panties in a bunch, Cavanaugh. I just lost my necklace." She bends down and picks a thin gold chain out of the bracken near the shed, barely taking her wide eyes off us. "Brendan is gonna love this!" she says, leering at Taylor. And then Taylor locks Angelique in her gaze.

"Go away!" I say again.

But it's too late.

Before I can stop her, Angelique is closing the distance between us. She pauses midstride when she sees the knife in Taylor's hand, but then her face changes, the smirk gone. In her face I see her need—raw lust—and she can't get to Taylor fast enough. She stumbles as she reaches us. I put my arm out to hold Angelique back just as Taylor pushes me with her free hand. She grabs Angelique and, at the same instant, plunges the carving knife into her own stomach.

I stand, stunned, for just a second as Taylor's body falls to the ground at my feet.

I hear myself scream, and then I'm on the ground over Taylor, pressing my hands over the bleeding wound in her stomach.

My mind, struggling to preserve my sanity, keeps trying to check out. But I fight to stay focused on Taylor. She looks up at me, confused, and a wet moan leaves her throat as her eyes flutter shut. I look around in panic, hoping for help, and instead find Angelique standing near the shed, wrapped in Marc's arms, with the bloody knife in her hand.

"Go get help!" I scream at her.

She shakes her head. "This was the only way, Fee. You didn't leave me a choice."

I'm hyperventilating as I struggle to keep pressure on Taylor's wound. But she needs more than pressure. I look down at the blood starting to pool on the ground at her side. "Oh, God." Tears stream hot down my cheeks and onto Taylor's pale face. She coughs and blood spews from her mouth.

I fumble my phone out of my pocket with a bloody hand. It

slips from my grasp and onto the dirt twice before I manage to hit 911 with shaking fingers.

"My friend has been stabbed," I sob into the phone when they answer.

They want more information, but I never get a chance to give it to them, 'cause the phone is pulled from my hand.

When I look up, Marc is standing over me. He smiles and shrugs at me, then turns my phone off and throws it into the woods.

"Oh, God," I say again. "Taylor, you're not gonna die," I whisper through my tight throat. "Help!" I yell with the most strength I can muster. But it's like that nightmare where, no matter how hard you try, you can't find your voice. My scream sounds strangled and dry.

"They're not going to hear you. Not with that music," Angelique says.

And that's when the song catches my attention. The Fray, "How to Save a Life," plays from a stereo.

I can't stop the whimper that escapes my throat. It sounds so pathetic and weak—like some kind of useless, feeble, wounded animal.

I'm so weak. And so *stupid*, to think my Sway was anything. It's nothing.

"Oh, God," I whimper, watching my tears mingle with the blood on Taylor's shirt.

And that's when I realize her wet, sputtering breathing has stopped.

"No! You're not gonna die." I repeat it over and over as I press on her chest, and then breathe for her, tasting her hot, metallic blood. Each time I raise my head, I scream for help.

"Yes, she is." Angelique sounds almost sad as she gazes down at Taylor, looking more human than she ever did before Lilith possessed her. She takes a step forward. "I feel your rage. You want me dead, don't you?"

And suddenly I do. Rage tears through me and a primal scream rips from my throat as I launch myself at her and flatten her to the ground.

She squirms under me, but her soft body is no match for eight years of judo training. I don't even have to work to keep her in the necklock.

The knife.

A hand holding a knife hovers over Angelique's chest.

Mine?

Is that my hand? I can't tell. The images are fleeting and my mind can't process them.

But then I hear Angelique's voice whisper, "Do it, Fee. Just do it."

I shake my head to try to clear it, then look down at Angelique. She's not squirming anymore. She's smiling up at me, her hand over mine on the hilt of the blade. I untwist my legs from around her neck and shift my weight onto them, watching as the blade breaks the skin. The bead of blood at the tip of the knife grows, then rolls down her chest in a crimson rivulet. Her hand grasps tighter around mine on the knife and I feel a thrill race through me as I imagine thrusting it into her.

With her other hand, she reaches up and grabs a fistful of my hair. I start to pull away, but then I realize she's not fighting me.

She pulls me closer and I think she's trying to say something, but when my face gets close to hers, she lifts her head and kisses me. An electric burn fills me. My lust for her is sudden and overpowering. I shift my weight onto the blade, feeling the tip slide off bone and into the softer tissue between her ribs. Her hands are pulling—on my neck, deepening our kiss, and on the knife, deepening the wound.

When I pull away, my lust for her blood overwhelms me. I straddle her hips and grip the knife in both hands high above her heart.

She moans, but it's not in agony or fear. Her eyes flash as her hands reach for me. "Do it," she cries.

A jolt of indescribable pleasure crackles through my body. I close my eyes and swing the knife down in a long arc. But before it finds its mark, I'm knocked to the ground from the side. The knife flies out of my grasp and skitters across the bracken into a stand of low shrubs near the shed.

"No!" I scream. And I hear Angelique's cry echo my own over the pounding rhythm of the music.

Luc's voice, soft in my ear, breaks through the haze. I slowly become aware of my surroundings. The earth's chill soaks into my body from below as Luc's heat burns through my clothes from above, his weight on top of me, pinning me to the ground, pressing my face into the dirt.

"Get off!" I scream. My bare toes dig into the damp, earthy bracken as I struggle to get out from under him. But even with the strong must and rot of the forest an inch from my nose, the salty copper of Taylor's blood cuts through, making my stomach lurch, and I swallow back bile.

An animal groan works its way up from my core. "Get the hell off me!" I scream, bucking against him.

"Frannie, stop! It's what Lilith wants." His hand sweeps my wild hair out of my face, and his cheek is next to mine. "She wants you to kill Angelique. She's trying to reverse your tag."

"No!" I push harder, struggling out from under him. When he doesn't let go, I twist and lock my legs around him, rolling and snapping him to the ground.

He looks up at me where I perch over him, his eyes soft. "Listen to my words, Frannie. I need you to hear me."

The world seems to spin back into focus. My breath rasps, but I'm unable to find air.

He continues to stare up at me, as if nothing else matters. "If you do this, she wins. If you kill Angelique, your soul will be tagged for Hell, and Lilith will be free to enter your body. You'll be hers."

It's the scent of Luc's cinnamon that finally pulls me out of the haze. I blink and look around. Two demons stand on either side of the shed, their glowing red fists targeting each other. Marc and Rhen. I can't make sense of the scene, but it doesn't matter. Taylor lies on the ground, her shirt soaked in crimson blood, the smell of it heavy in the dusk air.

I let go of Luc and roll over to sit next to him. My stomach lurches again and I vomit into the bracken between my feet.

"I couldn't save her. . . ." My voice is a shaky whisper, barely audible.

"There was nothing you could do, Frannie."

"My Sway. I should have been able to bring her back."

"Not from Hell. Not yet, anyway. Maybe eventually your Sway will be strong enough. . . ."

I stagger to my feet as I think about the last thing I said to Taylor, and then fall back into Luc, who holds me around the waist. *Go to hell*, I'd said. I told her to go to Hell.

I bend over and vomit again.

Then I hear rustling in the leaves and turn to see Angelique sitting, back against the shed, shirt drenched in blood, staring at me with a tortured smile. "He doesn't understand, Fee. He doesn't get that we need each other." She crawls a few feet into the shrubs and comes out with the knife. "We belong together. You're one of us, Fee." She slowly pulls herself to her feet and holds the knife by the blade, hilt out to me.

Luc's arms tighten around me. "No, Frannie."

But her draw on me is voracious. I step toward her.

"Frannie." Luc turns me in his arms and locks my gaze with his. "Just look at me." I start to crane over my shoulder for Angelique, but Luc's fingers on my chin pull me back. "Right here, Frannie," he says, the index and middle fingers of his free hand pointing to his eyes.

I lose myself in his deep black eyes as he starts leading me back toward the music in the Gallaghers' yard, away from Taylor. In my peripheral vision, I see Rhen, glowing fist in the air, covering our retreat, and I'm confused. *Why is he helping us?*

Angelique calls from behind us. "Frannie, don't let him take you from me. We belong together."

I moan and fold in on myself, my legs refusing to carry me. Luc sweeps me into his arms and he walks out of the woods into the backyard. I drop my head onto his shoulder and try to tap into his strength.

Someone screams. Kate? But I just keep breathing in Luc's cinnamon, blocking everything else out.

I hear Luc tell someone to call the police. People are all around us. I'm jostled in Luc's arms. Someone tugs on my arm, trying to pull me away from him. I grip him with the little bit of strength I can find.

"Oh my god! *What did you do to her?* Give her to me!"

That voice—Reefer. Reefer is yelling at Luc. I try to lift my head to tell him to stop, but it's too heavy—too hard to move.

Leave him alone, I think. *Please.*

And then I'm curled in Luc's arms, sitting on the stairs of the porch. Luc is so hot, and I try to draw on that, but I'm so cold that I can't stop shivering. I'm finally able to force my eyes open. And that's when I notice the blood—Taylor's blood—all over me. My hands. My clothes.

Oh, God—Taylor.

A Banshee scream erupts from my chest. I think Luc rocks me—maybe—but I can't stop screaming. People are yelling, screaming—no . . . wait, that's still me. And then everything fades into oblivion.

I wake up in my bed, a warm morning breeze blowing the curtains back and the scent of cool winter sun all around me. As my eyes focus, I find Gabe sitting in my desk chair at the foot of the bed. He smiles and squeezes my foot through the covers. "Hey."

And as everything comes flooding back, the crushing weight of what I did threatens to take me under again.

I close my eyes. "Taylor?" My voice comes out as a croak. And as I say it, cold dread blankets my heart.

"I'm so sorry, Frannie. I should have been there." The pain in his voice . . .

What he doesn't say is that he wasn't there because of me. I can't stop the strangled whimper from rising in my throat just before the tears spill over. Then Gabe's holding me in his arms, calming me. There's nothing else to say, so I bury my face in Gabe's neck and cry.

By the time Mom comes in, the tears are slowing, but anger still burns like acid deep in my core, directed mostly at myself. Gabe rubs the tears off my cheek with his thumb and shifts back into the chair. Dad stands in the door as Mom slides onto the edge of the bed and grips my hand. "How are you, sweetie?"

What a stupid question. "Shitty."

She wants to reprimand me for my language, I can see it, which really is why I said it—to piss her off. Because I *do* feel shitty and I want everyone else to too.

She pulls a deep breath. "Is there anything you need?"

I shrug deeper into the pillows, trying to vanish into them. "Taylor."

"Oh, baby . . ."

I roll on my side, toward the wall.

"Frannie," she says, then hesitates. "I'm so sorry."

If one more person says that, I'm gonna start screaming again.

The bed quakes as she stands, and I hear the door click closed.

I barely feel Gabe slide onto the bed, but I know he's there, 'cause I start to feel the anger fade away. "I know this is rough, but taking it out on your mother isn't going to help."

I don't want the anger to fade away. I need it to hate myself. "Just shut up! Get out!"

Instead he swings his legs onto the bed and leans against the headboard.

I stare at the wall, unable to block the images from the woods that play out in my head like a horrible movie. "Oh, God." It's more of a sob than anything. "I killed her."

He knows I'm right. I can feel it in the way he shifts behind me. "Frannie, none of this is your fault."

My voice is as bitter as my heart. "I thought you couldn't lie."

"So, you should believe me."

He's really turning on the peace thing. I'm buried in summer snow. My breathing slows and I seem to soften from the inside out. But I can't shake the visions in my head. Taylor. Angelique. Luc . . .

I lift my head out of the pillow and look at him. "Where's Luc?"

"He thought it best if he . . . left."

My heart collapses on itself. "What about Angelique?" I ask, afraid of the answer.

"Lilith has her. She's gone."

A slow groan rolls up from my core. One more life I've ruined. My feelings about her are a jumble. Hate. Guilt. Lust. "I wanted her—needed her. But I'm not . . . I don't . . . with girls."

"Lilith is a succubus. Gender is irrelevant. She can manipulate your darkest thoughts and desires—the baser emotions. Make you see things, want things. She needs her fix and she'll do anything to get it."

"Her fix?"

"She survives on lust. Without it, she'll die."

I shut my eyes, pressing the lids tight against the images trying to form in my mind. I would have done anything on her whim, including kill Angelique. My mind briefly flits to the memory of Lili in Luc's bed, his stunned expression. "Luc didn't know what he was doing . . . ," I say to myself, really understanding it for the first time.

"No, I'm sure he didn't."

My head sinks back into the pillow, too heavy to hold up any longer. My mind shuts down and I welcome the emptiness, like a vacuum. When I realize it's Gabe doing this to me, for a heartbeat I want to be angry, but then I just go with it, letting myself go numb. And I think of nothing.

27

†

Tears from Heaven

FRANNIE

I spend the next five days numb. People come and go, I think. There are blurred images of Riley and Trevor. In them, Trevor looks almost as numb as I feel. A piece of me wants to reach out to him—that piece of me that remembers losing Matt.

But I don't.

Mom brings food, but I can't eat. The more she pushes it, the deeper into myself I withdraw. I hear mumbling in the hall—Mom? Gabe? Dad?—I'm not really sure, and I think Mom might be yelling, but I don't care enough to try to listen. There might be police . . . maybe.

The days go by in a blur of images, just out of focus, and at the end of them, I'm dressed in black, sitting in a church pew. There are people, some of them crying, and Luc. I feel him more than see him. Gabe is with me, always at my side. Which, I think, is the only reason I'm numb. Otherwise, I'm pretty sure the scream that's nestled in my throat would make its appearance.

Grandpa has my hand. I feel his rough, warm skin, and smell his sweet pipe smoke as I lean into his shoulder. The only person I need. The only one I can tolerate.

Other people keep coming up to us, and Grandpa somehow keeps them away. Which is good. Because if I open my mouth to talk, that scream . . .

Then the people are leaving us alone, and everything goes quiet. Father O'Donnell starts talking. I'm vaguely aware of Taylor's parents and Trevor walking up the aisle ahead of a wooden box.

A box.

Taylor.

It starts as a low moan in my chest. And then there's not anything even Gabe can do about the scream.

LUC

She doesn't say anything at all on the way home. She just slumps in the seat and stares blindly at the dashboard.

I sink into the backseat as Gabriel drives, wishing it were me in that coffin. *How could I have let this happen?*

Every once in a while, a soft, agonized moan escapes Frannie's chest, crushing my heart. If I could take away her pain . . . I'd do anything.

Gabriel pulls his Charger into her driveway behind her family in the van. Frannie just sits for a long time, then sort of drifts out of the car and starts wandering across the yard. Her parents watch from the porch, and her father starts to follow, but Gabriel places a hand on his shoulder and nods at me. I follow her across the lawn and onto the sidewalk as she starts up the street in the direction of Taylor's house.

I keep pace beside her. "Frannie?"

She just shuffles up the sidewalk, oblivious of everything. I start to reach for her, but stop. I'm not sure I can touch her without . . .

I step in front of her and walk backward, crouching to her eye level.

"Frannie . . . can you hear me?"

Nothing.

"I know this is . . ." A hot, wet lump in my throat chokes off my words. What am I going to say? *Hard?* This is more than hard. This is impossible.

I realize I've stopped shuffling backward when I feel Frannie's fingers brush my cheek. I look up and she's staring into my eyes. Her fingertips are damp.

"You're crying," she says.

That's impossible. "I can't. I'm a demon now—mostly."

She rubs her thumb over her fingertips. "You are." She brings her damp fingertips to her lips as tears start to course down her cheeks. She turns and sits on the curb, head in her hands. Her fingers are woven into her hair, veiling her face.

I sit next to her, a safe distance between us. "I'm so sorry, Frannie." It sounds so inadequate.

"I couldn't save her. She's in . . . Hell, Luc." Her voice catches on a sob. "And I couldn't get her back."

"It's not your fault."

She rips her head from her hands and glares at me, strands of hair stuck to her wet face. "Of course it is." Her voice is low but feral, almost a growl.

But then her eyes widen. "You're a demon?"

I nod.

Her features twist into a grimace as she says, "Can you go get her? To Hell, I mean?"

At this minute, looking at the pain etched into Frannie's face, I'd be willing to try, even though there's no way in Hell I could possibly succeed—or survive.

"If that's what you want, Frannie, I'll try."

Her eyes close in a slow blink, and when she opens them, hope shines briefly. But then they go dead again. "You won't be able to save her either, will you?"

I drop my gaze. It kills me to see her like this. "No."

"And they'll kill you too."

"In a manner of speaking."

I pull myself up from the curb, because being this close is too hard, and pace out into the street. I lace my hands over my head and pull a deep breath, trying to think. When I turn back to the curb, Frannie is standing, tears heavy on her cheeks again. I pace back without really looking at her, and when I step up onto the sidewalk, she reaches for my arm.

"Luc, I'm so sorry. I know it wasn't your fault—with Lili."

I stand stiff and stare straight ahead, hands balled at my

sides to keep from pulling her to me. Because I can't do this, as much as I want to. I can't go back.

In all my existence, I've never known pain like that—the pain of having everything and then losing it. But it's no less than I deserve. Because she's wrong. It was my fault. Everything that's happened to Frannie since I set foot in Haden is my fault.

I'll destroy her if I stay.

I shrug away from her grasp. "Frannie—"

She sinks back to the curb. "It's too late, isn't it? I've ruined it." She presses her face into her knees, lacing her fingers behind her head.

"I don't think . . . ," I start before my words are choked off by my heart, throbbing in the back of my throat. I pace the sidewalk until I can speak. "Frannie, I just can't do this again."

She doesn't lift her head, but the sound that she makes—a muffled whimper—causes what blood I have left to run cold.

"This—" I gesture vaguely at the world even though she's not looking. "—is just a disaster, for all of us. You have to know it's best this way. I can't stay here."

Finally, she pulls her face from her knees. But she doesn't look at me. "So, that's it? It's over?" She looks up at me then, her eyes dark, dead. "I guess I can try not to want you . . . if that's what you want."

"It is." It takes everything I have to say it, and every cell inside me screams in protest. I glance back toward Frannie's house to avoid looking at her and see Gabriel watching us from the end of her driveway. I bend down and kiss the top of her head, then nod to Gabriel before crossing the street and climbing into the Shelby.

FRANNIE

He's gone. I can feel it without having to look. My heart clenches into a hard ball as some major part of me—my soul?—curls up and dies, leaving me cold and empty.

Of course he doesn't love me anymore. How could he after everything I've put him through? He'd rather be a demon than be with me, and I don't blame him.

I curl my arms around my knees and pull them tight to my chest, straining to hold myself together.

"Come in the house, Frannie. Please." Gabe's voice is soft and low as he crouches next to me.

I look up at him, lost. He holds out his hand and I take it. He draws me off the curb and back to the house, then takes me up the stairs and tucks me into bed.

"Get some rest. I'll be back a little later."

Panic rips the breath from my lungs and I spring to a sit. "Please don't go."

He glances toward the open door and then pulls my desk chair over and sits next to the bed. "All right," he says, squeezing my hand.

I thrash for hours, scared to close my eyes, because every time I do, images of Taylor, Angelique, Luc, play in my head. Every so often, Mom or Dad walk by my open door. Finally, Dad turns off the light in the hall and the room plunges into darkness. When Gabe stands, I'm embarrassed by the squeaky little whimper that escapes my throat.

"I'm right here, Frannie. I'm not going anywhere." He pulls the T-shirt I sleep in from under my pillow. "I just thought you'd be able to sleep better if you were comfortable. I'll be just outside the door."

He steps into the hall, and my shaking intensifies to the point I can hardly undress myself. Finally, I get my dress off, the T-shirt on, and slide back under the covers.

"Okay," I say, my voice little more than a croak.

Gabe steps back into the room and closes the door behind him. He curls into the bed behind me. "You're going to be okay, Frannie. I won't let anything happen to you."

I shudder as I think about all the things that have already happened to me—and everyone I love—and I know he's lying, even though he doesn't.

I can't stop shaking. Even Gabe's presence doesn't completely stop it. I press my back closer into him. But despite his closeness and the calm that it brings, my heart still hammers in my chest. 'Cause I know if I close my eyes again . . . the nightmares—Taylor—Angelique.

"Please try to sleep, Frannie," he whispers in my ear.

"I can't." I shiver violently and he pulls me tighter to him.

I roll in his arms and burrow into him. His cool breath in my hair just takes the edge off the terror that's taken control of me. I nuzzle my face into the crook of his neck and take in the scent of his winter sunshine, trying to forget everything but that. Even still, the panic is there, right on the edge of bursting through. He kisses the top of my head, and a shiver rips through me. I pull my face out of his neck and stare into his deep blue eyes, shining in the pale moonlight, and I try to lose myself.

The closer I get to him, the more peaceful I feel—I know that from experience. He's the only thing that can block out the pain.

"Frannie . . . ," he says as I trail my fingers across his lips. I feel him shudder.

When I bring his face to mine and my lips touch his, his peace washes over me, drowning me in soft numbness, instantly easing the tight ache in my chest. Suddenly, my empty heart feels full—'cause he loves me. I can feel that too, deep and unconditional.

This is where I want to be. I want to lose myself in his peace and love. I want to be so lost that no one can ever find me.

I just want to forget me.

His kiss becomes less tentative, his mouth exploring. His lips devour me, helping me disappear. The further I get into him, the less of me there is. I fumble with the buttons of his shirt. He tugs my T-shirt over my head and his hands and mouth continue their soft, cool exploration, every caress taking me further away from myself.

My heart is still pounding, but now it's not from panic. And my ragged breathing isn't from fear. With every step toward the inevitable, I'm one step further from the pain.

When he rolls on top of me, I slide his shirt off his shoulders and feel his skin on mine—not cool anymore, but hot. I kiss his shoulder and pull at his pants, wanting everything—all of him.

His lips are hot on my neck as he whispers, "Oh, God . . . Frannie." And then his mouth finds mine again and I feel the slow burn under my skin, my heat matching his.

We move together on the bed and I'm almost gone—just one more step. I wrap my legs around him, giving him permission to take that last step and free me from my misery, telling him with my body that I want him to.

And I feel him respond, pressing harder into me, letting loose that last shred of reserve. I slide my hand around to the front of his pants and feel him shudder. He kisses me deeper and there's something desperate about it, like he's suffocating and I'm the air. He needs me as much as I need him. I can feel it. This is what we both need to save us. Each other.

I'm almost gone.

Just one more step.

As I work the button of his pants, his lips slide off mine, trailing a burning path down my chin, my neck, my shoulder, and back up to my ear. His breathing is as ragged as mine as he whispers, "Please, Frannie. Please stop."

A wave of guilt crashes over me as I realize what I'm doing to him.

He groans as I push him off and rolls to lie on the bed next to me. After a few deep breaths, he opens his eyes. He slides off the bed and stands there, silhouetted against the shifting shadows in the moonlight at my window.

I sink deeper into the pillows and try to disappear.

"I . . ." He doesn't finish. Instead, he grabs his shirt, spins, and walks out into the hall, closing the door behind him. Then nothing.

It's quiet, like, forever, and I lie here trying to decide what to do. When it becomes clear that Gabe isn't coming back, I close my eyes and pray sincerely to God to just kill me now.

I sit up when the door cracks open again and pull the sheets around me, suddenly embarrassed, as Gabe steps through.

He turns his back to me. "I think I can control myself now, but it'd make it easer if you had some clothes on."

I roll and grab my T-shirt from the floor. "You don't have to stay," I say as I slide it on, trying to keep my voice even. Truth is, I'm desperate for him to stay, but mortified too. "If I'm making it too hard for you . . ."

He turns and comes to the edge of the bed, where he sits. He holds my face in his hands and gazes at me. "I love you, Frannie. But we can't do . . . this." He gestures to the twisted sheets. "I'd willingly give up my wings for you, but not like this."

Despair squeezes the breath from my lungs. "I know."

I touch his face again—I can't help it, he's so beautiful. "You said when Matt lost his wings, he had a choice of . . ." I lower my lashes and trail off as I realize how selfish the rest of that thought is.

But Gabe always knows what I'm thinking.

"I'm not like Matt. I couldn't stay with you."

"Why not?"

"I'm a Dominion. One of the Second Sphere. I'm not an angel."

My eyes snap back to his and I prop up onto my elbow. "I thought all of you were angels."

"No. The term *angel* is specific to mortals who have attained Heavenly status. I was never human."

I try to process that. "So . . . that means . . ."

"If I lose my wings, there'd be no choice. I'm not from the Earth, so I can't return to it. I'd belong to Lucifer."

My heart pounds in my throat. "Unless I wanted you to be human." And I do. Right now there's nothing I want more.

He looks at me from under his white lashes, and thoughts flash through his eyes so fast that I can't get a hold of any of them. Then he leans in and kisses me again. I tug him onto the bed next to me and stare into those amazing eyes. The question is out of my mouth almost before I realize I've said it. "Did you know Lucifer before he fell?"

He stiffens, but his voice is as always, calm, soothing. "Frannie, don't worry about Him right now. You're safe. Go to sleep."

I shift in his arms, suddenly uncomfortable, but something deep inside me won't let it go. "I'm not worried. I just want to know."

He shakes his head slowly. "I was created just after the War. He was gone by then."

"So . . . you never knew Him as an angel?"

Gabe's eyes narrow. "Where are you going with this?"

I shake my head, because I don't really know. It's just a feeling I can't explain. "Nowhere, I guess."

He kisses my forehead and settles back into the pillows. "Sleep, Frannie."

My eyelids feel heavy and I let them close, but images from my nightmare haunt me—Taylor, blood, Lilith. I place my hand on his chest, over where his heart would be, trying hard not to want what he can't give, but needing to be close. "Is this okay?"

He releases a shuddering sigh and strokes my shoulder. "Perfect," he says.

And sometime, hours later, I'm finally able to sleep.

When I wake, pale gray light filters through the tree outside my window. I'm alone in my bed, and everything from the last five days is a little fuzzy, like I'm just coming out the other side of a five-day binge. It's that same hungover feeling as I lie in the bed for a long time trying to put the pieces together— what's real and what's haze. Taylor's murder was real—no dream could produce pain that sharp. Luc leaving—real. Gabe . . . last night? There's a flutter low in my belly as I remember his amazing, soft touch. Did we really almost have sex? Did he say he loved me? I think that was real too. He'd give up his wings for me . . . that's what he said.

But he's gone.

I push off the wash of disappointment and look at the clock, then grab my phone and call in sick to Ricco again. He tells me not to bother coming back.

28

✣

End of Days

LUC

"Are you okay?" The voice and the hand on my arm startle me as I lean against the cold tile wall of the hospital. I've been standing here awhile, trying to work up the courage to knock on the door to room 322.

Her name is Robin.

I pull my forehead off the wall and try to smile at the nurse. "I'm fine."

She spares me one last concerned glance and makes her way up the hall. I breathe deep and lift my hand to knock, but before I can, the door swings open and she steps out into the hall in a fluttering green hospital gown. She nearly bumps into me before I can get myself out of the way.

"Oh. Sorry," she says. Her eyes are the same green, but they seem duller without Lilith to fuel them.

But it's me who's sorry. I drop my eyes and open my dry mouth, but I can't find words, so I close it again. I lift my eyes and they connect with hers. My heart is in my throat.

She looks up at me and her brow creases.

"Sorry," I say. It's the closest thing to an apology I can manage. I spin and jog down the corridor to the stairs, which I take two at a time. When I reach my car, I can't breathe. I lean against the fender, sucking air.

She doesn't remember. It was clear in her eyes. She had no idea who I was. That should be some comfort, but it doesn't change what happened—what I did to her. And all I could manage was "sorry."

I owe her so much more.

I lean on the fender and debate myself—just like I've done every minute since I realized I was mortal again. I should be miles away—*hundreds* of miles away. Out of temptation's reach. But I can't seem to make myself leave.

Because living without Frannie is like trying to live without oxygen.

It was faster this time. The change took only a few weeks. And I felt it. I knew she was changing me. Frannie said she'd try not to want me. Apparently she didn't succeed, because it's hard to argue with my humanity. The knowledge that she wants me sends a thrill through me at the same time as the thought of being with her again terrifies me.

I push off the Shelby and open the door. Then I slam it closed with a growl. Because I want to go over there. And if I get in this car, that's where I'm going to end up. I pace through the parking lot, trying to clear my head and talk some sense into myself. Finally I slide into my car and head to my apartment.

As I pull into a spot near my building, I realize that I don't even remember the drive, because my thoughts are totally absorbed with Frannie. I sit here for ages, pinching my forehead, where the headache starts to rage out of control. And just as I'm about to cave and start my car, Frannie's Mustang squeals to a stop behind me, blocking me in.

She jumps out of the car and storms over to where I'm parked. From the look on her face, maybe I was mistaken about her wanting me.

She rips my door open and hauls me out by my arm. "Where the hell are you going? Running away again?"

I don't shake free of her grasp, because the feel of her hand on my skin . . . "I was—"

"You're such a coward, you know that? I can't figure out how you survived in Hell all this time."

"Frannie—"

She lets go of my arm and shoves me. "I don't even know why I care. Just go, you stupid—"

I grab her arms and spin her against the car, meaning to tell her to get in her car and get the Hell away from me. Meaning to say something so cruel that she'll never want to come back. But instead, I find myself pressing my lips into hers. My head screams at me to stop at the same time my heart screams to never let her go. She pounds her fists into my chest at first, but then she melts into me, kissing me back. Finally, I get myself under control and pull away. She just stares up at me for a long second. A hot lump forms in the back of my throat as a tear courses a crooked path down her cheek. I back away a step, unsure what to say.

That seems to break her trance. She gazes up at me with eyes that look as scared as I feel, then scrubs the tear away with the back of her arm, pulls a deep breath, and turns for her car. But just as she reaches it, I catch a subtle waft of brimstone. I dive for Frannie and push her through the door, slamming it closed. When I turn, Rhenorian is standing there, grinning at me.

"Whoa! What was that all about?"

I blow out a shaky breath. "For the love of all things unholy, Rhenorian. Don't sneak up on me like that."

"Admit it. She's the one who changed you." The grin is gone from his face and he stares past me at Frannie with hungry eyes.

I bang on her door with my palm. "Go, Frannie!"

She hesitates—a second too long.

In a flash, he has me pinned against Frannie's car. "Make her do it to me."

"I don't know what you mean."

Before I can react, his fist smashes into my face and I hear Frannie scream. Then he grins and swipes his finger across the blood seeping from my split lip. "*This*. Make her do *this*," he says, holding up his bloody finger.

"She can't make you mortal, Rhenorian."

He stands back and looks at me, wiping his finger on the front of my shirt, then his gaze shifts to Frannie. "I wanted to apologize for being so rude last time we met. It's my pleasure to see you again." He reaches past me, holding his hand out to her.

I push away from the car and shove him back. "No, Frannie! Go!"

But she's never listened to me before, and she doesn't start now. Instead, she smiles and pulls herself out of the car. "It's okay," she says, reaching for his hand.

And as their hands meet, in one deft motion she twists his arm, putting him facefirst onto the ground, his arm in a lock and her knee in his back.

"I can't make you human," she says to the back of his head.

"You made Lucifer human," he groans into the pavement.

"Not on purpose."

He twists his head to the side. "Fine. Call your Pit Bull off, Lucifer."

Even though this really isn't funny, I can't help the chuckle. "She's never answered to me. You're on your own."

"Son of Satan!" He squirms under her. His fist starts glowing and he grimaces, trying to turn it in the right direction.

I chuckle again. "Yeah, good luck with that." I stoop down next to him. "What's this really about?"

He tugs once more against Frannie's grasp, then slumps into the pavement. "Let me up."

"Not until you tell us what's going on."

"There's an uprising."

At first I can't process what he's said. "An uprising," I repeat.

"What you did . . . at the Diktat. It made some of us think. No one's ever stood up to Him before. It's never been possible."

He's right. Up until I did it, I never would have thought it possible. His command always carried physical weight. My body bent to His will without question. Something programmed into us at the time of our creation.

"We think it's because you were human. Maybe when you turned back, it short-circuited something."

"So you think if you were human, even for a little while . . ."

"We wouldn't have to obey Him," he finishes.

"Frannie can't do that, Rhen. There's nothing we can do to help you." Though, if there were, I'd seriously consider it. An uprising in Hell . . .

Frannie shoots me a look and I nod. She lets go of his arm and pulls her knee out of his back.

But the second he's off the ground, his glowing fist is pointed into Frannie's face. "Do it! Make me human!"

She glares at me, but behind that look, she's already plotting how to take him down again.

"For the sin of Satan, Rhenorian, what are you trying to accomplish?"

Panic flashes in his eyes as they flit to me and back. "Things are out of control, Lucifer. You've been gone. You don't know."

"You're demons. Nothing is below you. How bad can it be?"

He shifts his eyes from Frannie to me. "Bad. There are public quarterings, the Pit is full to overflowing. And He expects my crew to enforce His insanity. He's brought in Mages and Necromancers as reinforcements." He looks exasperated. "*Mages.* It's bad."

I grimace against the memory of my own recent run-in with Lucifer's Mages.

Frannie takes advantage of his distraction, kicking out with her leg, fast as lightning, and breaking his right arm.

He cries out and pulls it to his chest. "Who the Hell *are*

you?" he groans through clenched teeth, glaring at Frannie with glowing eyes.

She glares back, looking, if possible, even more menacing than Rhenorian. "Someone you don't want to mess with."

He turns wide eyes on me. "Unholy Hell, forget turning human. We just need her to kick the shit out of King Lucifer."

Frannie winces. It's obvious the memory of her last encounter with Lucifer still haunts her.

"You have my support, but I don't think there's much I can do. Maybe Gabriel—"

"You've *got* to be joking. You're in with Gabriel? What next—you gonna sprout wings? Are you turning into a featherface?"

"I thought you wanted help. But if you're going to be picky about where it comes from . . ."

"Would he seriously do it?"

"Unrest in the Underworld works to everyone's advantage." I glance at Frannie. Hers, most of all.

He backs off, still holding his arm, though it's already straightening as it heals. "See what you can do." He fades out, leaving Frannie and me standing alone in the parking lot.

The awkwardness between us is instantly back. I look at her, and I can't keep the concern out of my voice. "Are you okay?"

She nods. "Let's go talk to Gabe."

FRANNIE

We ride in silence to Gabe's. I really have no clue what to say. My head was full of stuff when I was driving to Luc's. Mostly ripping into him about . . . everything. But I was also ready to tell him that I need him to come back. And that I love him.

When Gabe told me Luc was back, the wave of emotion nearly drowned me. It was everything all at once. There was plenty of rage. He cheated on me, then left me—twice. But there was also joy and love. The biggest and hardest to accept was hope.

So, when I saw him leaving again . . . I freaked. And all those things I wanted to say flew out the window.

My heart throbs painfully in my chest, and the ache spreads from there through my whole body. I chance a sidelong glance at him as he drives. It's not too late. I could still tell him.

I draw a deep breath and open my mouth, but then close it again. Why can't I find words?

I love you. It's not hard. Why can't I say it?

He kissed me. He loves me too . . . right?

I just don't know. I turn to look at him, trying to read him. He stares straight ahead, his expression cold and hard.

By the time we get to Gabe's, I'm a mess. I slide out of the car and head up the walk without waiting. Gabe opens the front door and I bound up the stairs to stand next to him. He loops an arm over my shoulders without even thinking.

Luc pauses at the porch when he sees us, closing his eyes for a second. But then his face clears and he continues up the stairs. "Gabriel," he says with a nod. He brushes past us into the family room and drops into the chair under the window. Gabe and I follow behind him and sit together on the couch.

Gabe leans into me. "So, what's up?"

Luc's eyes flick to me, and his jaw clenches; then he takes a deep breath. "Something big is going down in Hell. Rhenorian is asking for help."

"And you think I should give it to him."

Luc shrugs. "It couldn't hurt."

"Don't be so sure. You were one of them. You know they can't be trusted."

"I believe he was sincere."

"For the moment, I'm sure he was." Gabe scrutinizes Luc. "But once he has what he wants . . ."

"I still think we should find a way to support him and his group." Luc's eyes lock on me. "An uprising against Lucifer could only work to our advantage."

Gabe shakes his head. "I'll think about it. But, right now, we have other things to deal with. Frannie is leaving tomorrow."

I push away from him. "I'm what? What the hell are you talking about?"

"We need to get you somewhere safe. I was wrong to think Lucifer would stop coming for you after you were tagged. He won't."

"Where am I going?"

"As far as your family knows, you'll be in L.A. You were leaving next week anyway."

I just stare at him, unsure of what to say.

He turns to Luc. "You're going too."

Luc opens his mouth to protest, but I cut him off, suddenly furious that I seem to have no control over my life. "What if I don't want to go?"

Luc's gaze drops to the floor and I feel Gabe's arm pull me closer.

"I know this is hard, Frannie." The compassion in Gabe's voice feeds my barely contained frustration.

I spring off the couch. "I need to think," I say on my way out the door. When I hit the porch, I take off at a run. I run harder when I hear the pounding of footsteps on the sidewalk behind me. I hit the park at the end of Amistad at a sprint and cut through the trees next to the play structure—where I trip on a tree root and skid facefirst into the dirt in a sprawling tumble. My lungs burn and I can't catch my breath. Before I can pull myself up, Luc is standing over me with his hand out.

I ignore his hand. "I don't need you," I say, pulling myself from the dirt and brushing off my pants.

"I know."

Don't look at him, I tell myself. But I can't help it. And when I do, his black eyes seem to go on forever, right to his core, bearing his soul. I feel a tear slip over my eyelashes before I can get myself back under control. "I don't want you."

He only nods.

I turn and walk deeper into the park. He comes up beside me, matching my stride, his hands in his pockets and his eyes on the ground. Neither of us says anything.

The dusk deepens in the shade of the trees, so we don't notice her till we're nearly on top of her. Luc grabs my arm and pulls me behind him.

I jerk my arm away and step out from behind him in time to see her glide out of the stand of trees just a few feet away.

"Angelique," I whisper.

"Fee," she says, her voice hypnotic, and with that one word, I feel overwhelming desire for her.

Luc backs up a few steps, keeping me behind him. "Frannie, just listen to my voice. Don't look at her. Just listen to me."

He says it over and over as we back slowly toward the play structure, but I can't do it. I can't rip my eyes away from her as she keeps pace with us.

But when she pulls out the knife, still covered in Taylor's blood, I snap. I rip my arm away from Luc's grasp and charge at her. Luc lunges after me, but he's not quick enough. Angelique holds the knife out for me.

In that instant, I want her more than I've ever wanted anything, but I also want her dead. The fleeting image of the knife plunging into her chest sends a shuddering thrill through my entire body. I dive for the knife, needing to touch her while I watch the life run out of her onto the ground. But just as I reach her, I'm tackled to the ground at her feet.

Gabe holds me pinned to the dirt. "Frannie, stop!"

Then Luc is there, murder in his eyes. Gabe scoops me into his arms and starts running. The last thing I see as we turn up the street is Luc ripping the knife from Angelique with one hand and wrapping his other arm around her in an embrace.

As my head starts to clear, my heart starts to scream. I lose sight of them as Gabe sprints up the street. "No!" I scream, then press my face into Gabe. "No, Luc. Please," I whisper.

Gabe puts me on my feet at the house and pushes me through the door. "Now!" he says, fixing me in a hard gaze. "You're leaving *now*."

My hands are on my shaky knees as I struggle to get air through my collapsing throat. "Now? What about Luc?" I gasp.

"He's on his own, Frannie. My priority is you."

I drop to the floor, unable to hold myself up. "Oh, God," I whisper into my hands. Why did I have to run? Why couldn't I have just told him I love him? "If he kills her—?"

"She'll take him," Gabe says flatly, standing over me.

"No!" It starts in my chest, an aching need, and spreads till every cell in me vibrates with it. *Come back to me!* my heart screams, over and over.

I spring off the floor and almost make the door before Gabe blocks my exit. He stands between me and the door and reaches his hand out for my shoulder. I yank away from him when I feel his summer snow start to dull my panic.

"Stop it! I have to help him."

His eyes are full of compassion and pain as he simply says, "No."

Behind him, there's a knock—or really more of a pound—on the door. I jump for the handle and Gabe pushes me back, holding a hand to the door. A moment later, he pulls it open. My heart nearly explodes in relief when I see Luc standing on the porch. I lunge for the door again, but Gabe holds me back with an arm as he scrutinizes Luc. Finally, he lets him come through. Luc's holding his left arm across his chest with his right hand, and there's blood on the front of his T-shirt. And I'm not totally sure it's all his.

I stare at him, unable to breathe, as he steps through the door and lowers himself into the chair under the window without a word, but his eyes don't leave me.

I go to him and kneel, trying to figure out where the blood is coming from. He drops his arms, and I gasp at the bleeding gash across the inside of his left forearm.

Pressing Luc's arm back into his chest, I look up at Gabe, who disappears into the bathroom and comes out with a damp cloth and bandaging supplies.

Luc stares at me with empty, unseeing eyes as I clean and bandage his wound. Gabe disappears again, and when he comes back, he tosses Luc a clean T-shirt. They share a glance, and for a second, I'm sure I see suspicion on Gabe's face before Luc pulls his bloody T-shirt over his head and tosses it in Gabe's direction.

I look at Gabe, but I'm afraid to ask either of them what's going on.

Gabe throws Luc's shirt into the trash and stands in the kitchen door. "We need to get you out of here. It's not safe. Lucifer isn't going to stop."

I sink into the couch, and a sense of bitter relief swirls inside me. Because there's one thing that's become clear in the last few weeks. "He won't want me anymore when He figures out that I don't really have Sway. Not Sway that matters, anyway."

Gabe's smile is sad. "If it were only that easy to convince Him. Someday your Sway might be strong enough."

Anger swirls with the relief, and I lash out. "I don't have Sway! I can't change anything!"

He slides onto the couch next to me and leans back, contemplating that. His eyes shift to Luc. "I think the biggest proof of your Sway is sitting right over there. You've turned him mortal—twice."

I glance at Luc, who's sitting still as stone, hands on knees and face flat, staring at me.

I shake my head. "I don't know how he's doing it, but it's not me."

"Frannie—"

"I can't change shit!" I scream in frustration. "Isn't that obvious? Taylor is *dead*!"

Gabe examines his hands, and his voice is low, meant just for me, as he says, "I know you have Sway, Frannie. I've felt it."

And then, on top of everything else, guilt swirls into my emotional jumble when I think of all the times I've used Gabe. I explode off the couch and stand in the window with my aching forehead against the cool glass. I feel Gabe move in behind me.

"When your Sway has worked—on Luc and me—what's been different?" His voice is soft and soothing in my ear.

I sag into the window. "It's not me. Why won't you believe me?"

He turns me gently to face him and his eyes are deep, full of compassion. "What's been different?" he repeats.

I shake my head, but he catches my chin and lifts it. I gaze up into his eyes as I feel his peace and love begin to take hold. I raise my hand and lay it on his chest as if I can feel his heartbeat. And, because I want to, I do—even though he doesn't have a heart.

The realization hits me all at once. "It worked when I wanted something with my heart."

He brushes his fingers across my forehead, sweeping my hair to the side. "So, when you get this out of the way," he leans in and kisses my forehead as his fingers drop to my chest, "and let this do its job, your Sway is more powerful."

I lean my cheek against him, listening to the heart he doesn't have beat in his chest. "It's love," I finally say. "My Sway is love." The thing I never even believed in till Luc and Gabe came along.

"I think it's more than that . . . that *you're* more than that." His voice is soft, but it vibrates through his chest.

I pull away. "What do you mean?"

"I'm not sure yet, but . . . I don't know. It's just a feeling."

"Please don't say that. I'm pretty sure I can't handle anything else." My eyes slide to Luc, who sits with his forehead in his good hand. I walk over and kneel down in front of him again, taking his other hand in mine. He lifts his eyes to mine and locks me in his haunted gaze. I breathe deep, pull all the armor off my heart, and without a word, I let it say what it's been dying to say.

Luc's eyes seem to focus on me then. And I know he hears me, because they well up and he pulls his gaze away from mine, along with his hand.

"Luc . . . ? What happened?"

He stares at the bandage on his arm, picking at the tape, but doesn't answer.

Gabe's hand is on my shoulder. "Frannie, we need to get you out of here."

My heavy heart makes pulling myself to my feet difficult. I try to clear my head, remember the bigger picture. We're not safe here.

Gabe guides me to the door with a hand on my back.

"But, if they know we're going to L.A.?" I say.

"You're not going to L.A." He grabs my hand and spirits me quickly through the door and into his car. I turn to see Luc following close behind, dark eyes darting.

"Then where are we going?" I shudder when I realize that when I said *we*, I meant all of us—Luc too. What if he won't come? He glides into the backseat, still looking haunted as I fight tears.

"I can't tell you yet. No one can know. Your family—everyone—has to truly believe you're in L.A."

Theory of a Deadman plays, filling the room and drowning out my thoughts as I shove clothes into my canvas duffel bag. I pull my iPod off the speakers and shove them both into the bag before zipping it shut.

Gabe's propped on my doorframe, looking anything but calm. "You ready?"

"I guess." I take a last survey of my room, then glance at Luc, standing vigil at my window. He hasn't said a word since Angelique. I have to know what happened, but I can't bring myself to ask again. I hesitate a second longer before asking instead, "You coming?"

My heart pounds, but it holds its breath as he turns from the window and locks me in his dark gaze.

And makes me wait forever for his answer.

29

⸸

No Good Deed Goes Unpunished

MATT

This is Hell. And Frannie and her demon put me here.

No good deed goes unpunished.

A mirthless bark of a laugh escapes my throat.

My only consolation is that they're going to burn in Hell for all eternity too. I'm going to make sure of it. Because if she hadn't been such a total moron, she would never have fallen for a demon in the first place.

A demon. What was she thinking?

She thinks she can hide behind Gabriel's ridiculous Shield, but we're twins—the unbreakable bond. I'm pretty sure I can find her. And it will help my cause that she always thinks everything is her fault. She'll feel guilty about what happened to me . . . and she should.

I can use that memory—and others—to make her pay. Because, with King Lucifer's help, I've found my unique talent. My gift. The one that Gabriel never even mentioned I should be looking for. Which makes me wonder if I've been on the wrong side all along. Either way, there's no going back. I've sworn my fealty to King Lucifer. What choice did I have, really?

At first I wasn't sure it was the right move.

Now I am.

The celestials were all about holding me back. But my new king has shown me things—ways of using my power—that I could never have imagined.

I lie on the floor with my fingers laced behind my head and stare up at the ceiling of the cave, at the light being sucked into the black stone surface like reverse sparkles, and try to figure out how that works. I feel my newfound power pulse inside me, like a wild beast, starving and waiting to be unleashed for the hunt. And then I feel something else—Lili's hands. Stroking. Caressing. Making me hungry in a whole different way. I turn my head, and the expression on her face says everything. She's insatiable.

She had to leave Angelique behind because mortal bodies don't survive the shift between plains. But King Lucifer has what she calls a "vessel" here for her—a body. He can send for her whenever He chooses. He built it to His preferences, so the claws and the horns took a little getting used to, but it's still human in most ways. And pretty damn hot, though a little battered. Apparently our king wasn't happy about her coming back empty-handed.

She won't tell me what happened, but she says she deserved

it. Still, when I saw the bruises, rage ripped through me. I still can't help wanting to protect her. Even from Him. The only good thing to come of it is that He seems to be done with her for a while. He's promised Lilith to me for as long as I want her, which I'm thinking might be forever.

I trace the purple bruise on the inside of her thigh with my finger and raise an eyebrow. "Again?"

She shrugs. "It's what I do."

"But I need to practice."

She rolls her glowing green eyes at me.

"Sorry, but you're the only humanish sort of person down here."

She sits up and pushes back from me. "Fine. But you know our deal. If I let you hurt me, you need to make me feel better after." An innocent little smile curves her lips, completely at odds with the gleam in her greedy eyes.

That look stirs raw lust deep inside me. "You're not going to need to twist my arm." I tingle all over in anticipation.

"But that sounds like fun. What if I want to?" Her lips pull into a pout and I can't help myself. I crush my lips to hers, aroused even more at the taste of her blood on my tongue.

Licking the blood from her split lower lip, I pull back. I guide her hand to the deep claw marks across my hip. "If I didn't know better, I'd say you were trying to dismember me limb by limb."

Her pout pulls into a smile. "Maybe later." She curls her legs under her, hands braced on the ground, accentuating certain curves and making me want her right now. "So, go ahead. Practice."

I think about going with Lili's suggestion and bagging the practice. But if I'm going to be ready to deal with Frannie anytime soon, I have to stay focused.

I close my eyes and clear my head, then slowly scan Lili's mind. I can't read it, but I can pick up on memories and get the flavor of them. I choose one that has a particularly dark, thick feel to it and I focus my power like a laser beam. And then I watch as Lili's face contorts with the pain of the memory. Tears spill over and evaporate off her cheeks in Hell's intense heat. I push harder and her head drops into her hands. She sobs at first, but her moans of grief gradually turn to screams of agony.

An electric thrill sends fire coursing through me, and I crawl to where she sits, still screaming. I pull her hand from her face and feel my excitement build as I stare into her terrified eyes.

Because, let's face it, Lili deserves a little payback too.

I buzz all over as my lips lock on to hers, smothering her scream. The scream becomes a feral moan, and she grabs me and throws me to the ground.

Then I let go of her mind while she takes her turn with my body.

ACKNOWLEDGMENTS

When I think back on the last year, it strikes me how steep my publishing learning curve has been. I've had some excellent (and very patient) guides along the way, to whom I owe a huge debt of gratitude. They include my truly fabulous agent, Suzie Townsend, cheerleader extraordinaire and the hardest worker I know, and Melissa Frain, my seriously cool editor, who has always been right on my page creatively, and wasn't afraid of this book. Thanks also to my Tor Teen crew for their enthusiasm and dedication to getting *Personal Demons* and *Original Sin* out into the world and into so many hands.

Once again, a huge thanks to my family, who have been my greatest source of encouragement and support. My husband, Steven, has supported my insane work schedule, and never called me crazy when I was obsessing over my imaginary friends. (Even though I'm sure he thought it.) My girls, Michelle and Nicole, continue to inspire me. My brother, Russ, has served as my right-hand man, and my mom, Harriet, and sister, Sherri, have helped spread the word.

One of the luckiest things that could have happened to me was stumbling upon my amazing critique partner, Andrea Cremer, at a writing conference when *Personal Demons* was in its infancy. She's helped me to explore possibilities I never would have seen on my own and take this series to a whole new level. Thanks also to Kody Keplinger and Courtney Moulton for inspiring me with their work and being an endless source of encouragement. Additionally, I want to thank everyone in the Elevensies for all the support you have shown me and for taking me in and making me one of your own.

And, because my Muse is still a wannabe rock star, a special thanks to Isaac Slade and The Fray for writing the haunting lyrics to "How to Save a Life," which shaped this novel from Frannie's perspective, and to Adam Gontier and Three Days Grace for the amazing song "World So Cold," which, unfortunately for Luc, is the musical embodiment of this entire novel.

But, most of all, thanks to you, my readers, for giving me a chance to entertain you. There aren't words to truly express my gratitude.